The Nebula Royale

A Kash and Calynn Adventure

C. William Tressler

For more Kash and Calynn's antics

Join the Alleycat Crew @ cwilliamtresslerbooks.com.

ISBNs:

Hardcover: 979-8-9916795-7-2

Paperback: 979-8-9916795-6-5

eBook: 979-8-9916795-8-9

PREFACE

Preface

I did something new for this one. The first two books have been written entirely from Kash's perspective. In this one, I tell the story from multiple angles and multiple people. In truth, the book started too slowly telling it from just Kash's perspective. The pacing improved greatly when I switched it up and made for a better story.

I love the new characters I introduce in this one and hope you do as well. I think they really added to the story. It was fun writing a chapter from the viewpoint of the bad guy too. It added a layer that otherwise would not have been possible.

Hey Mom, they still are not getting those pesky crystals.

I wonder when they will do that.

As always, thanks to my wife for still putting up with me. At least I moved my spot on the couch so I'm closer to you when I'm writing.

To my daughter, for still being such a good sounding board.

To Leslie, for everything you do. This would be sooo much harder if it wasn't for you. You're amazing!

To Franki Wilson, for another amazing cover. You rock!

And of course, to all my friends and family who have supported me in this adventure, thank you. Without all of you, I am not me. So... Kash and Calynn thank you also. They kinda need me... maybe.

KASH AND CALYNN'S ADVENTURES

THE HIGH ROLLERS

The beautiful woman from Ooga placed another glass of expensive bourbon in front of Kash. He turned and smiled at her, and she smiled back. Kash let his eyes wander down her scantily clad body. She had more curves than Princess Aja, but Aja was prettier.

Her sparkly pink and purple top barely covered her breasts, and her matching skirt redefined the term micro-mini. She had pulled back her wavy amber hair into a ponytail that exposed the elegant curve of her neck as well.

Kash watched as she walked around the table delivering her full tray of drinks to the other players. His focus was entirely on her; the other players disappeared into the background of the casino. She glided gracefully and the muscles in her legs rippled with each step.

"Your bet, sir," the croupier said to Kash, interrupting his ogling.

"Sorry," Kash apologized.

He scanned the felt betting area and pushed a pile of chips onto one of the squares. They were playing a game called Greeli. It reminded Kash of roulette from Earth but there were two wheels spinning, each with twelve symbols on them. The wheels were also divided into quarters of different colors. The table had one hundred forty-four squares that corresponded to all the different possible combinations, and some larger boxes for betting on the colors.

"No more bets," the casino employee announced, dropping the two balls onto the spinning wheels.

Kash tried to follow the balls as they bounced around, but he was far too drunk for that. He took another sip of his bourbon... the never-ending bourbon. The room wasn't spinning yet, but it was... tilting. A soft body came in contact with his right shoulder, steadying him.

Calynn smiled down at him. She was wearing the most stunning gown Kash had ever seen. The sparkling blue gown was extremely sheer and showed all of her skin except for the strategically placed gathers that enhanced the curve of her hips. The strapless gown sat delicately across the top of her ample breasts and stopped at her ankles. The neckline, waist, and bottom hem were adorned with vein stones, the same pale blue color as her dress.

"Winner again," the croupier chanted motioning toward Kash.

Kash's pile of chips grew larger as he was struck playfully on the left shoulder.

"You're on fire!" Guy smiled and laughed.

"Can we go shopping some more?" Triana added, giggling.

"Hell no," Guy smiled. "We're riding this train until it derails. Shopping can wait until after the winning."

Kash turned back to the table and pushed another big pile of chips onto a square. Guy grabbed a smaller pile of chips and pushed them onto a different square. Kash had argued with Calynn at first about bringing Guy and Triana along, but now that they were here, he was glad they were. Calynn and Triana had their girl talk, and Kash enjoyed exchanging old war stories with Guy.

Triana leaned over Guy and ran her hands down his chest. Guy was wearing an expensive tailored suit similar to Kash's, and the pixie couldn't keep her hands off of him. Triana was wearing a red dress trimmed in vein stone from the same designer as Calynn's. The dress was slung over her right shoulder and wrapped around her waist leaving her left breast totally exposed. The sheer material was bunched and gathered from her waist to her knees giving it lots of volume. It was trimmed with vein stones at her waist and knees and had a matching necklace.

"Winner!" the croupier hollered.

Kash wasn't even paying attention to the game and won again. His pile of chips grew even larger.

"Fucking bullshit!" a man exclaimed and bashed his fist on the table.

"Calm yourself, sir," the dealer replied.

"How many rolls is that?" the man barked, pointing his finger at Kash. "Nobody is that lucky!"

"I promise he's going to get luckier later," Calynn jested.

Kash was glad she spoke up. He was too intoxicated to banter with the man. Kash would have started by calling the man fatter than butter. He appeared to be about Calynn's height and just as wide as he was tall. His tailored suit did nothing for his appearance. He had a buzz cut and beady eyes... Kash didn't like him already.

"They both are," Triana agreed, fondling Guy's chest some more.

"Maybe I just need a pretty girl on my arm to win also," the man growled and grabbed hold of the server.

The man jerked her over, so she half landed on his lap. His chubby hands whisked over the petite woman's body, displacing her top and exposing her breasts.

"Hey!" the girl squealed, spilling the rest of the drinks on her tray in the struggle as she tried to cover herself and fight off the man's hands.

The boisterous man was yanked out of his chair by security before Kash could think of reacting. Kash watched as they dragged him away, still complaining. The server straightened her clothes, collected her empty glasses, and returned them to the tray.

"I'm sorry," the croupier announced. "We need to clean up this mess before play resumes."

Most of the players grumbled their disapproval and went to other tables. The server used a towel to sop up some of the booze from the felt on the table as she waited for more towels. Even flustered, she looked beautiful. Her impossibly high cheekbones were red with embarrassment, and her beautiful smile had been replaced by the thin line of her pressed lips.

"I'm sorry about that," Kash said politely to the woman. "I can't help but think that was my fault. I mean... it's not my fault that you're gorgeous... just the grabbing you part."

"It's okay, sir," she replied, trying to hide her shaky voice behind a soft smile. "I'm used to it."

"The tone of your voice disagrees," Kash smiled back. "You should never be treated that way."

"It's okay, sir... I'm fine." She didn't sound fine.

Kash stood up slowly since he was so drunk and slid off his designer dinner jacket. Calynn assisted him and figured out his plan quickly. She took his jacket, strolled over to the woman, and placed it on her shoulders so she could cover herself after being exposed. Kash's jacket engulfed the petite server, hanging almost to her knees. She slid her arms into the sleeves and buttoned the jacket before offering Kash a soft smile. She was obviously grateful for the coverage his coat offered after being stripped by the man. On one hand, Kash was happy to help. On the other hand, he wished he could see more of her incredible body... but privately was probably better.

"That should help," Kash smiled.

"Unfortunately, sir, you do need a dinner jacket to play on this level," the croupier explained. "The rules dictate it."

"No. No, beautiful," Kash said to stop the server from removing the jacket. "You keep that one. I'll go get another one quick before play resumes... I need to stretch my legs anyway."

"We have rentals just over there, sir," the croupier said, pointing over at a stand.

"That seems odd?" Triana questioned. "Why would you have rentals?"

"Sometimes players from the general public floors win big and want to come to one of the finer floors and gamble their winnings," the dealer explained. "We have higher minimums along with the dress code on this floor."

"A little help, Baby Girl," Kash said to Calynn. "I might be a little too drunk from all the booze this pretty little thing keeps bringing me."

The server blushed and smiled softly. She was hugging Kash's jacket to her body. The room was still tilting, and his mind was foggy, but not so foggy that he couldn't flirt with a beautiful woman. He just hoped he wasn't slurring his speech since it would still sound right to him.

"Maybe she's trying to get me drunk so SHE can be the one to get lucky," Kash continued, keeping his tone light and playful.

"He's joking," Calynn told the server. "He's way too drunk to handle the both of us tonight, but he is right about one thing... you are gorgeous. We love women from Ooga... come on, let's go get you a new jacket."

Calynn grabbed Kash's arm to help him to the tux rental booth. Kash glanced at the server one more time and chuckled at how red and embarrassed she was.

"Watch where your walking, mister," Calynn jested. "You've had too much to drink to walk forward while looking back."

"Yeah, yeah," Kash joked but did as she asked.

The Nebula Royale was one of the best casinos in existence, and Kash found himself looking at all the sights instead of paying attention to where he was walking. He leaned into Calynn and simply put one foot in front of the other. Trusting her to guide him.

This level of the Nebula Royale had marble statues, sculptures of various materials, and water features. Opulent reds and gold adorned nearly everything with other bright primary colors dotted thoughtfully throughout. The lighting was perfect, not dim but not bright, with spotlights on the tables. All the alcohol and food were free on this level also. It was one of the perks of playing higher stakes games.

Some of the upper levels were kid-friendly with onsite childcare, so parents could gamble away the kid's inheritance while a casino employee in a costume kept the kids entertained. There were shows for the kids, playgrounds, and organized sports to keep them busy. There was even a room of wet nurses for babies that were breast feeding. Kash heard a rumor that all the employees that interacted with the children, whether in costume or not, were child psychologists. They often returned the children better behaved than when the parents dropped them off.

The three lower levels were the complete opposite. They catered to bondage, nudists, or other depravities of the ultra-wealthy. Kash made sure to avoid those floors to avoid losing his temper. Women being beaten or tortured made his skin crawl. If it was all consensual that's one thing, but with all the money floating around in clubs like that... was it actually consensual? Were they all volunteers? He bet not.

He heard a rumor that the bottom floor used cloning tech so if the rich pricks wanted to kill their spouses or have sex with a sibling... or worse... they could. It was just a clone of that person, but still... Kash couldn't imagine Calynn asking him to make a clone of himself because she wanted to murder him. What kind of relationships did these people have?

Kash took in the sights as they walked. Some of the gowns the women wore were even more revealing than the one Calynn had on. Kash wished the bodies inside those dresses were all worthy of such attention, but alas... most were not.

But one woman in particular caught his eye. She had blonde hair and wore a red dress.

CAUGHT IN THE ACT

Aurelia couldn't believe she was letting the guard touch her body, let alone grope her like he was. The man had one hand on her ass, and the other hand was at her waist trying push the material of her dress to the side to get a look at her breasts. She had used some double-sided garment tape to keep her dress in place. She needed to be tantalizing, not a whore.

The guard was paying so much attention to what his hands were doing that he was neglecting hers. Her goal was much different than his but still required her to touch the Neanderthal.

"What time did you say your shift ended?" Aurelia asked the man.

Her one hand glided down the buttons of his shirt while the other relieved him of his security badge. She palmed the badge and gave it a slight bend to help propel it to her teammate who was waiting to make an imprint of its unique texture.

"I just started my shift," the man replied, squeezing her buttocks. "You'll have to wait another seven hourns."

"Seven hourns?" Aurelia complained dramatically, waving her arms in disgust. "Ugh!"

When she waved her arms, she flicked the badge behind her. She looked over her left shoulder briefly to see if her delivery was accurate. Soren nodded at her, and she turned her attention back to the security guard. She leaned in, giving him a better look at her chest to keep him distracted.

Soren had told her he would need twenty seconds to make the copy. When being groped by an unattractive man, twenty seconds felt like an eternity. Finally, Soren coughed twice to signal he was done, and she deliberately stumbled in her high heels.

"These darn shoes," Aurelia complained, bending over to fix her shoe and grab the key card from the floor. "I'm so clumsy in them."

"We can get you out of them later," the guard smiled.

"Promises. Promises," Aurelia smiled back.

She laughed and placed her hand on the man's chest, while her other hand returned the security card to the man's left hip. She turned her head when she was laughing and caught the eyes of a handsome, dark complected man approaching her. He was tall and muscular with piercing eyes and shiny black hair. He was hanging onto his companion, a gorgeous blonde woman with an incredible figure, but he was staring at Aurelia's right hand. Aurelia scowled at the man, but he didn't seem to notice.

The blonde woman led him past Aurelia and the guard, and Aurelia turned to see where they were going.

"Hey," the guard said seductively.

"Oh... sorry," Aurelia replied absently, still watching the other man. "I think I know her... I'll be right back."

Aurelia didn't wait for the man to answer. She was on a mission to learn more about the man who was just staring at her when she put the guard's badge back. She followed the duo to a rental booth and watched as the man tried on a few suit jackets. After settling on one, the duo headed back the way they came.

Aurelia circled around some slot machines and tried to watch them from a distance. The first thing she noticed was that the woman seemed to grab the attention of everyone she walked past. The sheer blue dress she was wearing was absolutely stunning and accentuated every curve of her body.

She tailed them to a Greeli table where the tall man sat down in front of a mountain of chips, and then Aurelia saw why the man needed to go get a new suit jacket. One of the Oogan server girls was wearing his. She came over to the man and said something to him, but Aurelia was too far away to hear. She looked around nervously and then decided to move closer. She watched as the man grabbed half a dozen black chips from his pile and handed them to the server.

"We dislike it greatly when women are mistreated," the pretty blonde explained in a low, soft voice. "We tend to help those women as much as we can. It's what we do."

"She's telling the truth," a tanned petite woman in a red dress added. "They rescued me from a brothel in the Joor system."

"But that's too much," the server protested.

"Take it or I'll have him double it until you do," the blonde instructed, smiling.

The man turned to his chips to grab more but the server stopped him and looked like she was about to start crying. The man held her hands gently until she eventually took the chips and dropped them in her pocket... or his pocket. She was wearing his jacket.

"Keep the jacket too," the dark man smiled, gently wiping the tear from her cheek. "Something to remember me by."

The petite server girl suddenly lunged forward, wrapping the man in a hug. He looked stunned at first but then hugged the woman back. Aurelia watched the handsome man's hands to see if he let them wander over the server's body, but he never did. He just hugged her affectionately. Aurelia was suddenly jealous of the server girl.

"Pull yourself together girl," Aurelia scolded herself silently. "It was just a damn hug."

The server girl walked away, and the table went back to playing. Aurelia took up a post at one of the slot machines so she could keep an eye on the man to see if he ever tried to say anything about her and the guard... but he never did.

The night dragged on, and the man's pile of chips grew larger. They cheered their wins and jeered their losses. Every time he hit big, he would grab the blonde to celebrate. His big hands caressed every inch of her body, but she didn't seem to mind. In fact, she seemed to revel in the attention. For a second time that night... Aurelia was jealous.

THE KINDNESS OF STRANGERS

Nura had spent the entire night turning this decision over and over in her mind. She still wore the jacket the handsome, muscular man had given her, but the black casino chips he gave her as a tip were weighing heavily in her pocket. It seemed wrong of her to keep them somehow. He'd been drunk... so drunk, but his girlfriend wasn't, and neither were his friends. They insisted that Nura keep the credits, and Nura didn't know how to feel about it.

She paced restlessly around their small apartment, the jacket slipping off her shoulders as she walked, caught in a storm of conflicting emotions, waiting for Luna to come home from her shift. She needed to talk this out with someone... maybe... and her best friend was the only one that she wanted... or maybe not. She was so confused.

"Where is she? Nura complained, looking at the clock.

The door finally opened, and Luna marched into their apartment.

"Why are you still up?" Luna asked with a curious smile. "And you do know that jacket is too big for you, right?"

"Says the girl who refuses to wear clothes," Nura shot back sharper than she intended.

Luna was, as usual, completely naked.

"They're too restricting," Luna argued, rubbing her hands over her bare skin as if to emphasize her point.

"And you like to be free," Nura said, sighing as she dropped onto the bed. "I know."

"Okay... something's wrong," Luna said, moving closer to Nura and softening her tone. "What's going on?"

Nura hesitated, looking at her friend's kind face before she finally spoke.

"Umm... I uh... well..."

"Hey," Luna encouraged her as she approached. "What is it?"

Luna knelt down in front of Nura, placing her hands on Nura's thighs. Nura looked up at her friend and looked into her kind eyes before pulling her in for a hug. Luna pushed her back so both women could lie down on the bed. Nura nuzzled into her soft skin and held her friend tight while Luna ran her fingers through her hair to comfort her.

"Do I at least get to know about the man who gave you his jacket?" Luna asked soothingly after a few minutes.

"He gave me these too," Nura explained, pulling the black casino chips out of her pocket.

"By the Gods, Nura," Luna exclaimed, grabbing the chips from her hand. "This is five million credits."

Luna's voice was equal parts joy and shock, and Nura felt her body shake a little when she held the chips, like she was trying to hold back laughter or tears.

"This... this could change... everything," Luna's voice was shaky as she tried to continue.

Nura pushed Luna over onto her back, slid down and laid her head on Luna's bare stomach. She wrapped her arms around her friend and braced herself to deliver the bad news to Luna. She took one more deep breath, dreading Luna's reaction, but she told her anyway.

"I'm going to go give them back," Nura said softly into Luna's belly. "It feels wrong to keep them."

"I know that tone," Luna said firmly, but kindly, to her friend. "Something happened... spill it."

"Another man got upset that the man who gave me his jacket kept winning," Nura explained, lifting her head up to look at her friend. "He grabbed me and damn near ripped my top completely off. I know you don't mind nudity..."

"But I know it bothers you," Luna interrupted with a kind smile.

"Anyway... I spilled my tray of drinks all over the Greeli table," Nura continued. "Luckily, someone pulled him off of me right away, but..."

"But you already felt violated... my poor baby," Luna pulled Nura back up so her head was now on her chest.

Nura snuggled into Luna's warm embrace, still struggling with the weight of her decision.

"And that's when the guy gave you his jacket?" Luna asked, running a soothing hand through Nura's hair.

"His girlfriend brought it over," Nura murmured, her heart still heavy with the strange kindness she'd been shown. "She was so... perfect. I'd have to live in a gym for years to get that body, and so beautiful... I was in awe. They went to the rental booth for him to get another jacket, and when they came back... they gave me those chips."

"That sounds like a happy story, Nura," Luna jested lightly. "Why do you sound so sad?"

"I don't know," Nura sobbed, her emotions spilling out again. She buried her face in Luna's chest, feeling the warmth of her friend's embrace. "I feel so conflicted. I don't want to keep it, but... it's so much. It feels like I'm taking advantage of them."

Luna didn't answer right away. She just held Nura, letting the girl cry it out. After a while, Nura sniffed and wiped her tears away with the sleeve of the jacket.

"Sorry for crying on your boobs," she said, trying to make light of the situation.

"I've never minded before, and I won't start now," Luna chuckled, grabbing a sleeve of the jacket Nura was wearing to wipe her own chest. "I'm always naked, and you're always emotional... it's who we are."

"I'm not always emotional," Nura protested, although she couldn't help but smile.

Luna cocked her head, gazed at her friend, and a smile tugged slowly at her lips.

"I'm getting better," Nura argued, smiling back. "I just don't process things like this very well."

"Yes... you definitely overthink things," Luna agreed, her smile growing.

"And you always make me smile after," Nura smiled, laying back down on her friend.

"It's what I do," Luna said hugging her again. "Soo... are you really going to give these back?"

"I will feel horrible about it if I don't," Nura sighed.

"And you're sure we can't just use the bad feelings as fuel in the gym?" Luna asked with a slightly snarky tone. "Pump some iron... maybe?"

Nura looked up at Luna who was smiling awkwardly.

"What?" Luna continued. "It's a lot of credits... can we keep them for a little while? It feels so good."

Luna started rubbing the black chips all over her body while giggling. Nura couldn't help but giggle with her. The friends lay side by side, giggling at the absurdity of the moment until Luna gathered the chips and placed them in Nura's hand. She smiled a soft smile and kissed Nura on the forehead.

"My tips sucked," Luna admitted, still smiling at Nura. "I hope you made enough to get us some food... besides these of course."

Luna laid her hand on Nura's hand. The mention of food made Nura's stomach growl. She was hungry, and the duo was nearly broke.

"Just about a thousand credits... I put them on our account."

"Well... that's two or three meals anyway," Luna sighed.

"You take them," Nura smiled at her friend. "I'm off tomorrow, so you need the calories more than me."

Luna kissed her forehead again and laid her head on Nura's.

"I hope he lets you keep some of it," Luna admitted. "Our cupboards are bare."

"I know... I better go before I don't want to," Nura said with a heavy sigh, climbing off the bed.

"You never cease to amaze me, Nura Velleris," Luna called after her as Nura approached the door. "You inspire me to be a better Oogan."

Nura paused and smiled back. It felt good in this moment to be understood. She gave her friend a last smile and headed out the door.

Her first stop was a friend at the admissions desk, Leslie. She explained the situation quickly and asked her to pull up the photos of the guests in the suites.

"There he is," Nura stated, pointing at the monitor. "Which suite is he in?"

"Suite sixty-two," Leslie replied, glancing at the image. "He's handsome."

"And far too generous," Nura added. "Thanks, Leslie."

Nura hopped into the elevator and was soon standing outside the handsome man's suite. She stood there for a moment, hesitating to knock on the door. What would she say to him?

"Pull yourself together, Nura," she said to herself, and knocked softly on the door. "It's the right thing to do."

The hourn was late, and Nura didn't want to ring the bell for the suite in case one of them was sleeping. Nura's nerves were on edge as she waited by the door. They were both so nice, but what if they don't like that she tracked them down? What if they get mad about her intrusion? She almost turned and ran away but the door opened, freezing her in place.

The girlfriend stood in the open door smiling. She had changed out of her expensive gown and was wearing jeans and a simple white tee shirt. Nura was so nervous, she just smiled at the beautiful blonde at a loss for words.

"Hi," the woman greeted her.

"Hi back," Nura blurted out awkwardly.

Nura was shaking as she put out her hand to the woman, holding the black chips.

"Here," Nura said, swallowing hard. "It's too much... I can't..."

"You can and you will," the woman smiled, curling her hands around Nura's so she had to hold onto the chips. "We insist."

"But why?" Nura half cried the words.

"Because you're worth it."

Luna had been right... Nura was far too emotional. The words hit her like a wave, and she couldn't hold back the tears any longer. Without hesitation, the woman wrapped her arms around Nura, pulling her into an embrace like they had known each other forever, letting Nura sob on her chest.

Nura didn't even realize they had entered the suite until they were sitting on the couch, the kindness of this stranger overwhelming her. She gazed around the room, trying to take in every detail of the immense suite. This was a world she'd never been a part of, nor ever hoped to be.

The woman brought her focus back when she gently took Luna's hands in hers.

"My name is Calynn," the woman said softly, smiling warmly at her. "What's yours?"

THE HANGOVER

Kash awoke the next morning with a pounding headache. He sat up on the edge of the bed and found a Nutra-shake on his nightstand along with two pills. He popped the pills in his mouth and took a long drink of the shake. He was confident that Calynn had already added everything he needed to recover from his hangover. There were also a pair of boxers and some sleep pants on the dresser for him to wear. The wall between their room and Guy and Triana's room must be open, so he shouldn't wander around naked.

The bedroom in their suite was enormous, as was the bed. The four meter wide and seven meter long bed was insanely comfortable too. It was even better than the new bed in his ship. The bedroom was big enough to make the bed itself look small. If the ceilings were higher, The Cat would almost fit inside the bedroom... almost.

The room was decorated in whites and blues. Silk fabric hung from the canopy of the four-poster bed and there were panels of the same fabric on the walls with beautiful paintings between them. The same fabric was used for the curtains on the picture window that looked out onto the nearby nebula. A crystal chandelier hung in the center of the room at the foot of the bed, and accent lights were directed at the paintings and fabric panels.

Kash grabbed the clothes and headed to the bathroom which was bigger than his quarters on The Cat. The shower was ridiculous. Water came from everywhere, and it was big enough for four people to shower at once. It also had his and hers water closets, his came with a urinal and a toilet, and a massive double sink between them. After relieving himself, chewing an oral sanitizing tablet, and splashing some water on his face, Kash got dressed and headed out to the living room.

The living room had higher ceilings than the bedroom area, but the silk fabric theme continued with waves of the fabric hanging from the ceiling. The lighting shone through the fabric casting a soft glow throughout the room.

There was a small foyer area at the door to their room, a large sitting area with two large white sofas, a love seat, and two oversized blue recliners. Beyond that was the kitchen area. A chef came twice a day to prepare them meals. He was cooking them breakfast when Kash entered the room.

Guy and Triana's adjoining room was decorated the same as his and Calynn's, and a door the length of the sitting area could be opened to share the space. Triana and Guy were sitting in a love seat chatting with Calynn... and another almost blonde woman. Their backs were to him so he couldn't identify the woman.

A flash of a memory jumped through Kash's mind. A woman... blonde hair... beautiful... she was doing something, but he couldn't remember what. He tried to concentrate on the memory, but the fog from his drunken stupor last night wouldn't let him focus. The only thing he remembered was her stunning smile and her hands... what was she doing with her hands? Try as he might, he couldn't bring the memory into focus.

"Good morning, sir," the chef greeted him. "Breakfast will be served in short order."

"Thank you, chef," Kash replied politely, despite being irritated with his memory failing him.

"How ya feeling, Boss?" Calynn spun around and asked.

"I'll be better when everything you left for me kicks in," Kash smiled. "Thanks for that, by the way."

"Good morning... Boss," the server from last night smiled coyly at him.

"Good morning, yourself," Kash smiled back. "I find myself suddenly wishing I remembered more from last night... did we..."

"Oh, no... You were too drunk, so I had to fuck her by myself," Calynn blurted out.

A pan clattered across the stove and the chef quickly grabbed it and tried to compose himself again. His face was growing redder by the second. Kash chuckled and then smiled at the two women. Calynn's growing smile and devious look told Kash she was just teasing him.

"Liar," Kash chuckled.

"I can never keep a straight face with you," Calynn giggled and everyone else joined in the laughter. "Nura here showed up after you passed out, trying to give the credits and your jacket back. She was still distraught and..."

"And Calynn cheated," the women interrupted, glaring at Calynn playfully.

"Cheated... who me?"

"Yes, you."

"Just because I called Princess Aja to have her convince you to keep the credits?"

"And that was cheating."

"How is that cheating?"

"And how is our favorite Princess doing?" Kash asked, interrupting the girl's banter.

"She's busy on a case..."

"Something about counterfeiting," Nura interrupted Calynn again. "It sounded exciting."

"But wishes she had the time to join us on vacation," Calynn continued. "She is in dire need of the, uh... stress relief... we offer."

Calynn chose her words more carefully as she looked over at the chef and smirked.

"I still can't believe you know her like that," Nura added with a hint of intrigue.

"We sure do," the lust filled words dripped out of Calynn's mouth.

"And then?" Kash asked, trying to get Calynn back on track.

"So, after talking with Aja and convincing her to keep the credits, we sat here chatting for hourns until she got tired. I offered to let her sleep on the couch, and here she is," Calynn concluded, smiling softly.

"A pleasure to meet you..." Kash paused to let her tell him her name as he approached, offering a handshake.

"Nura," she replied, shaking his hand. "But can I get another hug?"

"Oh, no... a hug from a beautiful woman," Kash mocked playfully. "Whatever will I do? Is that my shirt?"

Kash watched as the petite beauty walked around the sofa toward him. His tee shirt inhaled her like his jacket the night before, but her curves still poked through with each step.

"She needed something to sleep in besides that ridiculously small uniform," Calynn explained. "So, I gave her one of your shirts."

Nura wrapped her arms around Kash's waist and laid her head on his chest. Kash put one hand on her back and ran his fingers through her hair with the other. He held her tight and caressed her gently. It must have been her blonde hair from his memory... right? And her hands were replacing empty glasses with new drinks. It had to be her... maybe. No... her hair isn't blonde enough... or is it? He still wasn't sure and cursed his memory.

"Breakfast is served," the chef announced. "We have poached eggs, sour dough waffles, bacon, ham, and sausage, with roasted potatoes and fresh fruit... enjoy."

"Will you join us for breakfast?" Kash asked Nura.

"Just try to get rid of me," Nura looked up at him and smiled.

Kash hung back and stopped Calynn as the others headed to the kitchen. She wrapped herself around him and laid her chin on his chest to look up at him.

"You wanna fuck her. Don't you?" Kash whispered.

"Yeah... I kinda do."

"Really?"

"Yeah."

"Are you sure... are we back?"

"She is really pretty and I kinda miss our naughty ways. Did you see her butt?" Calynn grinned. "How about you? Do you wanna be naughty too?"

"You're more than enough woman for me," Kash smiled back. "But I like naughty."

"And we can stop if it's too much," Calynn added. "No pressure."

"That sounds good to me."

Calynn gave him a quick kiss and the five adjourned to the kitchen to eat and talk and laugh. Nura was telling them stories of patrons doing the most bizarre things. Kash's favorite story was the drunk guy that tried to take a bath in one of the water features while yelling at everyone else to get out of his room. The funniest part was the water was coming from a statue of a fat little boy urinating, so it looked like the little boy was peeing on the man.

Nura was a joy to be around and easy on the eyes too. At one point, she caught him staring at her nipples poking through his shirt and pushed out her chest slightly. When his eyes met hers, she smirked at him and went back to her food.

After they all ate their fill, the girls put all the dirty dishes in the dishwasher while Kash went to go put on a shirt. After using the restroom, he returned to the living room and was met with frowns on the girls' faces.

"What?" Kash asked.

"Nobody said you were allowed to cover up that fine toned torso of yours," Calynn joked.

"I agree," Nura added.

"You are nice to look at," Triana giggled.

"I prefer you in a shirt," Guy chuckled. "Just saying."

"I was a little chilly," Kash explained, pointing at Nura. "I was going to get a shower and get dressed, but we have company... so I just put on a shirt."

"A shower and dressed? But I wanna be lazy today," Calynn whined. "Can we just be lazy... please?"

"I took the day off," Nura offered raising her hand. "I have to go see the therapist later, but can I be lazy too?"

"Do you like to cuddle?" Calynn asked Nura, grinning ear to ear.

"Now you're speaking my language," Triana chimed in.

"Grab a blanket and get over here," Guy smiled at her while reclining back in his chair.

Triana bounced over, grabbed a throw blanket, and plopped herself down on top of Guy. Guy tucked the blanket around her and pulled her close, kissing the top of her head. It was nice seeing the two of them happy together. They both had a rough past and deserved happiness.

Nura looked nervous and never did answer Calynn's question. She was fidgeting with her fingers and pulling Kash's shirt down like she was making sure her bottom was covered. Kash slid himself down in between the girls and the back of the sofa. His chest was at Nura and his hips at Calynn. He wrapped an arm around Nura's waist and pulled her close.

"You forgot the blanket, mister," Calynn complained as she stretched to retrieve one.

Calynn was lying mostly on her back with her head at the opposite side of the couch as Kash and Nura. She lifted his legs and slid her left leg under his and her right leg was stretched out behind his back. Kash's feet were beside her. Calynn threw the blanket over them and hugged his legs to her chest.

"Come on," Calynn said to Nura. "I want your legs too... lay down."

"Are you sure?" Nura asked, her voice a little shaky. "I don't want to..."

"Absolutely," Calynn interrupted with a soft smile. "Remember Princess Aja... now lay down."

Nura slowly lay down and Kash placed his hand on her toned belly. She wiggled back into him and placed her hand on top of his. Between Calynn's magical fingers massaging his feet, Nura's warm body pressed against his, and the food coma coming on from his big breakfast, Kash was soon feeling drowsy.

"Triana is already out," Guy's voice was the last thing he heard before falling asleep.

The blonde woman from his memory permeated his dreams. He kept seeing her face and her hands, but he still couldn't tell what her hands were doing. He tried to reach out to her hands. Maybe he could grab them so he could tell what she was doing, but he failed... or did he? Are those hands on mine? He felt something on his hip too.

Kash slowly blinked himself awake. Calynn had left the sofa at some point, leaving him and Nura alone. Her left hand was resting on his hip, and her right was holding his left hand tight to her body... her soft round... Kash quickly moved his hand down to her belly. Nura pulled her left hand over and laced her fingers through his.

"Sorry," Kash whispered. "I didn't mean to fondle you."

"It's okay," Nura whispered back, snuggling back into him. "I don't mind."

"Even after the fat finger man?"

"The difference being he forced it... and you didn't."

"Technically, I was sleeping, so..."

"Then go back to sleep," Nura snuggled back into him again. "So, you can do it again."

"Are you two finally awake?" Calynn asked from behind them.

"No," Kash grumbled.

"Guy and Trie already went out," Calynn said as she rounded the sofa.

Calynn had a towel wrapped around her hair and another around her body. She had just gotten out of the shower.

"Come closer so I can pull off your towel," Kash jested.

"Maybe I don't want to be naked in front of her yet," Calynn bantered back. "We only just met."

"If you start maybe she'll join in."

Kash felt Nura's body tense when he said that. He wasn't sure if it was a good tense or a bad tense, but he pulled her tight and slid his hand up her belly. His hand stopped at the bottom of her breasts, but her hand urged him to keep moving. She squeezed his hand when he gripped her right boob.

"Then she should be the one to steal my towel, not you."

STEAL

The memory came flooding back when he heard that word. Kash sat up abruptly, nearly knocking poor Nura off the sofa.

"Hey," Nura complained, pulling herself up toward the arm of the sofa.

The blonde woman from his memory was absolutely stunning. She had bright blue eyes, a dainty nose, full lips, and excellent cheek bones. Her hair fell to her ample breasts and framed her face beautifully. She was wearing a sparkling red dress with a plunging neckline, it only came to her mid-thigh showing off her long, toned legs.

She was laughing… talking to one of the security guards, and her hands… she was playing with a security badge on the clip on his side. The guard was too busy trying to look down her dress to notice his badge. His hands were gliding over her waist and flirting with the top of her buttocks. She was good… damn good.

"Boss?" Calynn's voice snapped him out of his memory. "You okay?"

"I need to get a shower and go see Gravitas," Kash explained quickly. "Now."

"Why?" the two women asked together.

"Because," Kash smiled. "The casino is about to get robbed."

Meeting Gravitas

"Can I borrow this?" Kash joked as he pulled off Calynn's towel.

"Hey," Calynn protested, but didn't try to hide her nakedness.

"Thanks, Babe," Kash smiled as he walked swiftly toward the bathroom. "Get me some clothes out too, please."

Kash showered quickly and dried off. There were no clothes laid out for him in the bathroom, so he wrapped the towel around his waist and headed into the bedroom. Calynn and Nura were both there lying on the bed chatting. Calynn had put on a tee shirt, and her hair was no longer wrapped in a towel. Kash's clothes were lying at the foot of the bed. He dropped his towel and started dressing.

"I told you it would be a good show," Calynn giggled.

"You weren't kidding," Nura agreed.

"I expect you both to be naked when I get back," Kash said firmly while he continued to dress.

"That's awful forward of you, Boss," Calynn said. "We don't even know if she's into threesomes. And you still haven't explained why you think the casino is going to be robbed."

"Well, that's something you two can work out while I'm gone," Kash said as he shrugged on his dinner jacket. "And even though I was fucking drunk as hell last night, I noticed a woman that was casing the casino. She may have stolen a guard's badge... maybe?"

"But you're not sure?" Nura asked.

"No... but the cameras would have caught it. If I can see the footage, maybe I can figure out if that's what really happened."

"And you have to do that now?" Calynn asked playfully.

"Someone has been teaching me not to be such a loner and to help people," Kash smirked at Calynn. "What if they intend to use violence to rob the casino? Would you like me to..."

"Yes, I want you to save the people," Calynn interrupted groaning.

Kash walked over to Calynn and leaned down so he had a hand on the bed on either side of her.

"I'd much rather stay here with you giving you the vacation we deserve, but if I don't do this it will bug us both and you know it," Kash said softly. "Especially if someone gets hurt."

"I know," Calynn sighed again. "You're right."

"Let me go and see if I saw what I think I saw, and then casino security can handle it from there," Kash continued. "I promise to be at your disposal when I return."

"At my disposal?" Calynn gave him a coy look. "Anything I want to do? Even if I want to go shopping?"

"Yes... even shopping," Kash conceded.

"What about me?" Nura asked.

"We can shop for you too," Calynn said with a devilish grin. "Unless you meant to ask are we gonna DO you. Are all women from Ooga so naughty?"

"Well... Princess Aja liked it right?" Nura asked Calynn but sounded unsure of herself.

Nura's face was flush, and based on the visible pulse in her neck, her heart was hammering in her chest. Kash could tell that she was excited and nervous... and probably willing. He had to get out of there before his desires took over and didn't let him leave. He leaned down and gave Calynn a quick kiss on the lips.

"I'll be back soon," Kash said so close that his lips brushed hers.

"You better be," Calynn gave him another kiss and ran her hand down his chest as he stood.

"I hope to see you later too," Kash said, pointing at Nura.

"We shall see," Nura said with a smile tugging one corner of her mouth.

Kash squinted his eyes at her like he was sharpening his gaze and wagging his finger at her. That made her beam a smile at him and giggle. He turned away to exit the bedroom.

"Wait," Nura said, bouncing up off the bed. "I didn't get a kiss."

"No, not yet," Kash held up his hand to stop her. "If you taste as good as you look, there is no way I'm getting out of this bedroom, because that beautiful critter behind you will join in, and... just... can we wait?"

"Oh, fine," Nura pouted.

"Come here, girlie," Calynn cooed. "I'll give you a taste."

"I'm out," Kash said quickly and ducked out of the bedroom.

He heard the girls giggling as he marched through the living room, and he had to will himself to keep moving. Kash took the elevator down to the same level they were gambling on the night before. The casino offices were on that floor because it was near the middle of the gambling floors. Gravitas liked being close to the action.

The entrance to the executive offices was a glass wall with a set of glass doors near the back of the gaming area. Two guards stood at the entrance; one opened the door as Kash approached. Just inside the door was a reception area with a lovely middle-aged woman sitting behind the desk.

"Good morning, sir," The woman smiled. "How can I help you today?"

"Good morning. My name is Kash, I'm... an associate of Mr. Gravitas. Is he around? I urgently need to speak to him. I think someone is casing the casino."

"I'm sorry, sir, but Mr. Gravitas is in a meeting..."

"Then his chief of security will do," Kash interrupted. "This truly is urgent."

"He is also in the meeting."

"Then someone else that can handle a potential robbery will do," Kash said sharper than he intended.

"Sir, you can report cheating to any dealer or pit boss."

"Oh, for fuck's sake..."

"Foul language will not be tolerated, sir."

"You know what," Kash growled and plopped down in one of the plush chairs. "It's fine... tell me when one of them is available. I'll wait."

"Sir, if you'd like to schedule..."

"I said, I'll wait."

"Sir…"

"I'LL WAIT!"

Kash crossed his arms and stared at the woman. She diverted her gaze and was clearly nervous about Kash's intense stare. She was being stubborn, but she was about to find out that Kash could be more so. What part of urgent and robbery was she failing to comprehend? And was she always this stubborn or was she instructed to be so… what a bitch.

The reception area was decorated in red and wooden tones. Plush red carpeting covered the floor. The walls were painted red above the wainscoting, which was stained the same dark color as the trim. Crown molding hid the lights that ran the entire perimeter of the room, and the glossy white ceiling reflected the light filling the room with a soft glow. Large wooden doors sat opposite the glass doors he came in through. They had intricately carved galaxies on each door.

The minutes ticked by and Kash was getting bored. Twice he nearly gave up and went back to his room to be with Calynn and Nura, but he didn't want to miss out on the opportunity to gloat in the receptionist's face. He knew it was petty but didn't care. After a few more minutes, the large wooden doors swung open.

Gravitas was a mountain of a man. He was taller than Kash by nearly half a meter and the only thing broader than his shoulders was his waist. He was wearing a fine silk robe and silk trousers. The trousers were gold colored, and the robe was red and black trimmed with gold. The hum of his personal gravitational device was ever present. It reversed gravity immediately around him to help take the pressure off his knees and ankles.

"Kash, my friend," Gravitas announced when he saw him. "A pleasure to see you again."

"Gravitas," Kash greeted him back. "Thanks for having me. Hey… how did Breyda's delivery go? Everything good?"

"It was… on schedule," Gravitas replied.

Kash watched as the grin left the big man's face… he poked the bear anyway.

"And my cut?" Kash asked with a smirk.

"Was covered by the marker I gave you and the free suites," Gravitas replied with a fake smile. "What are you doing here?"

"Waiting to talk to you," Kash replied sharply.

"About what, my friend," the big man grinned his sinister creepy grin.

"I think your casino is about to get robbed," Kash blurted out, looking at the receptionist instead of her boss. "I would have told you sooner but..."

"Excuse me," an average sized man said as he stepped from behind Gravitas.

"And you are?" Kash asked looking the man over.

"Victor Morel... head of security," Victor scowled.

"Well, Victor... someone is casing your casino. I'm not sure if it's an individual or a crew, but I do know one of your guards has a compromised ID badge," Kash explained, and then stared at the woman behind the desk. "None of which is important enough to interrupt your meeting though."

"So, you think someone is trying to rob us?" Victor asked.

"No... I'm certain someone is casing the casino, and the robbery is imminent," Kash explained to Victor and then turned to Gravitas. "You know my reputation... you know what I can do, and what I can recognize someone else doing."

"And what did you see, Kash?" Gravitas asked.

"Truth be told... I was really drunk, and I'm not exactly sure, but if you can track my movements from last night, I'm certain I can point out the woman I saw lift your guard's badge."

"You want to see my cameras?" Victor spat, but his eyes were shaky. "That's never going to happen."

"Then how am I supposed to help?" Kash spat back.

"We don't need or want your help," Victor growled, pointing his finger at Kash.

Victor's finger was shaking when he pointed at Kash. At first, he thought it was just the intensity of the situation, but now he was starting to notice some things. Victor had jittery eye movement and shaky hands. His suit was wrinkled where he constantly adjusted his collar or tugged at the bottom. His lips were dry, and his tongue had a white coating, and he constantly checked his watch.

"Do you have somewhere you need to be?" Kash asked with a snarky tone. "Or just making sure I didn't steal your watch?"

"I have a schedule," Victor barked. "I'm a busy man with no time for your nonsense."

Victor turned and marched through a door hidden by the wainscoting. Kash caught a glimpse of the bland hallway when the door opened, and he wondered how far that hallway went.

"Yeah... this was clearly a waste of my time," Kash hissed and waved at Gravitas. "Have fun getting robbed."

"Wait," Gravitas bellowed as Kash turned to leave.

Kash turned back around and stared at the behemoth of a man. Gravitas ran his hand over his face and sighed.

"Are you sure about this?"

"No, but I think it's worth looking into."

"What if we go to my office and you show me what you saw?"

"Are you sure?" Kash asked sarcastically. "I wouldn't want to inconvenience you."

"And I don't want to waste my time."

"Me either... I have a gorgeous woman in my room I would much rather be spending time with."

"Then why bring this to me?" Gravitas asked gruffly. "Looking for another cut?"

"No! Because with what I saw..." Kash paused and sighed. "It seemed like amateur hourn, and I want to make sure nobody gets hurt. I mean, who uses a pickpocket anymore? Why risk lifting the ID card when you can just clone it without ever touching the guard."

"They lifted the card?" Gravitas sounded worried suddenly. "Are you sure?"

"I believe so... like I said, I was pretty drunk. Why?"

"Because our ID badges have a textured security feature designed to defeat the cloners. It reflects the laser back in a pattern that can't be duplicated otherwise," Gravitas explained. "Let's go have a look."

The large man lumbered back through the large wooden doors and Kash followed him. The first room they came to was a sitting room. It had large sofas and conversation pits done in deep reds and maroons with stained wood trim. There were two large entertainment rooms on either side of the sitting room, and Kash's nose told him that Gravitas' personal chef was hard at work in the kitchen, somewhere close. Gravitas opulent office lay directly in front of them. The archway door was open, and his personal assistants were waiting just inside the door. Both women were beautiful, petite, and fit... and completely nude. They weren't even wearing shoes. Their petite size and shape suggested that they were from Ooga like Aja. Gravitas fondled one of the women as he passed by. The man truly lived a hedonistic life.

"Leave us," Gravitas bellowed, and the girls scampered away.

"Do I dare ask what their jobs are?" Kash asked rhetorically.

Gravitas just smiled and sat down behind his enormous desk. He placed his hand in the corner, and a sensor read his palm print. The top of his desk lit up, apparently it doubled as a touchscreen computer.

"What game were you playing last night?" Gravitas asked as he began navigating through his menus.

"Greeli," Kash replied. "Most of the night. I saw the pickpocket after that guy grabbed the server and spilled the drinks on our table.

"Ah, yes, I saw a report on that incident... it was after twenty-two hundred local time."

The video feed from his table sped forward at a ridiculous speed. Gravitas slowed the feed just before the big guy grabbed Nura. The pit boss and a guard were already on the way over because of the man's outburst. Kash was too drunk last night to see that part, but he had wondered how the man had been taken so quickly.

One of the other cameras was looking directly at Kash and Calynn, and Kash really looked at Calynn. He had already been drinking pretty heavily when they bought her that dress, so he didn't remember really appreciating it... but he could now.

"Can you pause there?" Kash asked.

"But you're still at the table," Gravitas said as the image froze.

"Yeah, but so is she," Kash said tapping on the camera feed to enlarge it. "Sometimes I forget how gorgeous she truly is."

"Your companion is quite stunning," Gravitas agreed, enlarging the image more.

Calynn's hair had been professionally done, so it had more volume than usual. She normally had her hair pulled back into a ponytail. He really liked it when she let it down. Her makeup was subtle yet perfectly highlighted her natural beauty. Her sheer gown did little to obscure the sight of her body beneath. Kash was suddenly more eager to get this done and get back to his room and Calynn.

"Okay... let's move on," Kash told Gravitas.

"If we must," Gravitas mumbled.

The video started moving again at slightly faster than regular speed. After the man grabbed Nura, Kash removed his jacket, Calynn gave his jacket to Nura, and they walked off together.

"Okay, follow me... or more so, where I'm looking," Kash instructed. "The guard was on some steps or a platform maybe... I remember a railing."

Several images popped up as Gravitas tapped on the screens. Kash scanned each of the videos quickly looking for the woman in the red dress.

"There!" Kash indicated to the video of the woman he saw. "That's her!"

Gravitas enlarged the video and rewound it until the moment that the woman approached the guard. Kash and Gravitas watched as she approached, chatted with, and started flirting with the guard. The guard resisted at first, but soon gave in to the woman's charms, or more accurately... the plunging neckline of her dress. She was beautiful and had an amazing figure. She was standing so the guard could easily see down her dress, and he wasn't trying to hide the fact that he was doing just that. They watched as his hands skimmed her body while hers skimmed his... and there it was.

"Did you see that?" Kash asked excitedly.

Gravitas reversed the tape and slowed it down. Her nimble fingers unhooked his ID badge, she waved her arms, and then she flicked it off camera. It happened so fast it was nearly a blur.

"Who did she pass that to?" Gravitas asked.

"It's moving too fast... I couldn't see. Damn she's good."

"You were there. What did you see?" Gravitas grumbled.

"I didn't see that. Do you have an angle from over here?"

The screen changed showing a different view. The woman in the red dress was still visible, but they still couldn't see where she threw the card. Their view was blocked by a sign on one of the slot machines. Then the woman bent over like she needed to fix her shoe and stood back up.

"Wait, go back to me," Kash announced. "This is the part I saw. She stands up, hugs the guard, and clips his badge back on... but how did they copy it that fast?"

The woman in red did as Kash said and then looked in Kash's direction. He hadn't noticed her doing that the night before, because he was staring at her hands. But her gaze clearly lingered on Kash and Calynn for a few seconds, before she turned her attention back to the guard.

"You tell me," Gravitas voice was sharp and direct.

"Hell, I don't know," Kash scoffed. "You're lucky I even noticed this part."

"Lucky?" Gravitas bellowed and huffed a single laugh. "Lucky that the man that can acquire anything, doesn't know how something was acquired?"

"What part of inebriated are you failing to grasp?" Kash scowled back at the big man. "I was so fucking drunk I could barely walk."

"So, I am to believe it's just a coincidence then?" Gravitas sounded angry.

"What coincidence?"

Kash heard footsteps behind him and turned to see Victor and a rather large guard enter the room. They both looked at him sternly. Kash turned back to Gravitas and then back to the other two men as he tried to assess the situation. They were here for him... but why?

"That you just happen to be here at the same time as the pickpocket?" Gravitas barked, accusing Kash. "That you also just happened to be gambling on the same floor, and in the same room. And it's only a coincidence that you happen to see a tiny bit of it? Perhaps to sway suspicion?"

"The fuck are you trying to say?" Kash shouted at Gravitas.

"Did the woman pass you the ID badge?"

"Fuck no!"

"And I'm supposed to believe that?"

"I was drunk and never got closer than four meters away from her!" Kash was beginning to lose his temper. "How the fuck..."

"How indeed?" Gravitas interrupted, slamming his fist on the desk and nodding at his colleagues.

Kash didn't wait for what he knew was coming. Using the desk for leverage, Kash spun around and snapped a kick into the left temple of the large guard behind him. The guard stumbled to the side trying to catch his balance, but Kash didn't let him. He snatched the man's pistol from his holster with his left hand and drove his other fist into the back of the man's neck sending him sprawling to the ground with a thud.

Victor had yet to react to anything Kash had done, he must have been stunned by Kash's lightning-fast attack. Kash jerked Victor around and put him between Gravitas and himself, using him as a human shield. The gun was pressed to Victor's head when Kash looked back at Gravitas. The big man was trying to slink down behind his desk. Kash pointed the firearm at him and saw his eyes widen. Fear ran through the big man as he anticipated the impending gun shot.

"BANG!" Kash yelled, scowling at Gravitas.

He let a silence hang in the air and just stared intensely at the fat man. Kash adjusted his grip on the gun and let Gravitas suffer through his own fear for a moment longer. His unblinking eyes were still locked on the barrel of the gun pointing at his face. Kash could end his life with a twitch of his finger, and there was nothing anyone could do to stop it.

"What the fuck is wrong with you, huh?" Kash asked, his tone sharp and sinister. "Why would you make me do this...? We might not be the best of friends, but we're definitely not fucking enemies, and I am NOT... trying to fucking rob you!"

Kash threw the gun on the desk and pushed Victor away. He didn't think he pushed him that hard, but the man stumbled and fell to the ground.

"If I was robbing you... you'd never even know I was fucking here!" Kash continued, gritting his teeth. "I'd be long gone before you knew anything was missing. I wouldn't be buying expensive gowns for Calynn that make every man on the floor look at her. I wouldn't be wearing an expensive tuxedo. I definitely wouldn't be staying in a suite, and I most certainly wouldn't be in your office ratting on myself! How the fuck did you get from me wanting a cut to fucking planning it? It makes no fucking sense!"

Kash flopped back down in his chair and sighed heavily. Gravitas grabbed the weapon that Kash had thrown. It looked like a toy in his massive hand. Kash knew the man would never be able to get his fat fingers inside the trigger guard, so there was no chance of him using that gun to shoot Kash. Of course, he didn't know if Gravitas carried a weapon or not, so it was still a bit of a gamble.

"You should train your guards better," Kash said calmly. "I took that guy down far too easily. I can recommend a guy if you'd like?"

Kash sat forward and tapped on the video feed again. He zoomed in on the woman in red and tried to watch for the ID card again, but her nimble fingers were just too fast. The card shot off the screen impossibly fast.

"Now," Kash continued. "Where were we?"

Gravitas tapped a button and his desk went dark. He was staring at Kash and Kash was staring back. The big man was scowling and clenching his jaw, so Kash tried to keep a calm and relaxed demeanor.

"So, you don't want my help then?" Kash asked straightforward.

"We'll take it from here," Gravitas grumbled. "Mr. Morel?"

"Yes, sir," Victor replied from the floor.

"See Kash out," Gravitas continued. "Good day... Kash."

"So, just like that?" Kash asked with a snarky tone.

"Just like that."

"Good luck, Gravitas," Kash said, standing quickly and glancing down at Victor. "No need to get up... I'll see myself out."

Kash was a few steps into the sitting room when he heard Gravitas' voice behind him.

"Be sure to stay out of trouble, my friend."

Kash stopped mid step and shook his head. He took a deep cleansing breath and tried to calm himself.

"Just let it go, Kash," he said to himself. "Calynn and Nura are waiting for you back at the room, which is a far better proposition than getting thrown in a holding cell for beating the owner of the casino's ass."

Kash took another deep breath and continued through the sitting room. He smirked and rolled his eyes at the receptionist and shoved one of the glass doors open. The sights and sounds of the casino floor assaulted his senses. Dealers shouted over the cheers and groans of the players. A chorus of chimes, bells, and flashing lights came from the pods of slot machines. The commotion of the crowds tied the symphony of chaos together, creating a harmony of opulence.

Kash moved through the crowds toward the elevator to get back to his suite. He hit the call button and waited. His mind was still spinning as he tried to wrap his head around what just happened. Why would Gravitas accuse him of helping rob the casino? Kash was trying to be helpful by giving them information about a potential heist, but that had somehow backfired. And only bringing one guard to subdue him was silly. The fat man knew Kash was a more formidable fighter than that... but maybe Victor didn't.

"Victor," Kash said out loud to himself.

He wasn't sure what it was, but something just seemed off about that man. Just like the woman in the red dress seemed off too... who did she flick that card to? And how did they copy it so fast?

The elevator dinged as it arrived. Kash entered, hit the button for his floor, but then stopped the doors from closing.

"Fucking hell," Kash grumbled as he marched back out of the elevator.

He knew the mystery would eat at him if he didn't go check it out himself. He had too many questions and not enough answers, and his curiosity was getting the better of him.

First, he located the Greeli table where they were playing the previous evening. Then he traced his steps to the rental booth, until he saw the platform where a different guard was currently standing. Kash walked right up to the man, smiled, and squatted down like he had to tie his shoe. The sight lines down here were blocked by the machines. Kash looked around trying to identify where all the cameras were and trying to remember their angles from what he saw on Gravitas' desk.

Next, he moved to the spot where he knew the cameras couldn't see. It was just a little nook that jutted off at the turn in the walkway, no more than about two meters wide and sixty centimeters deep. It was blocked from the view of the guard, even though he was merely two meters away, and Kash could see at least four camera pods from where he was standing. There was no reason for anyone to believe that that corner was hidden from view. Maybe they were just worried about being hidden from the guard? The corner was lit as well as the rest of the casino too, so it's not like someone could hide in the dark to clone the guard's ID badge.

Instead of answering his questions, Kash seemed to only find more questions. He pondered those questions while aimlessly walking back to the elevators. Why did they need the guards badge? How did they clone it so fast? How did they know about the texture on the badges? That was new tech. Kash would have to look into how to defeat that technology himself. Preferably, before he needed it.

The elevator doors opened before he pressed the call button, and Kash entered the car. The door closed and it started moving, but Kash was still lost in his thoughts. After a few seconds he realized he hadn't pressed the button for his floor yet. He also hadn't noticed or acknowledged the couple that was in the elevator car with him. The woman was in front of the panel of buttons. When he looked up to ask her to move... he recognized her.

"You?"

The word slipped out of Kash's mouth.

It was the pickpocket he saw the night before. Her hair was chestnut brown now, but it was definitely her. She was even more stunning than he remembered.

"Sorry," she said calmly.

There were three others in the elevator, not two. The bite of a taser stung the back of his neck, and Kash fell to the ground unconscious.

A Lion in a Cage

"Shit," Jorlk said, looking down at Kash's body. "He was heavier than he looked."

"Sorry for dropping him, Miss Aurelia," Bran apologized in his usual soft tone.

"Let's just get him up," Aurelia told the men.

Aurelia gritted her teeth as she and the two biggest guys in their crew dragged Kash's limp body off the elevator floor. The men positioned him between them so they each had one of Kash's arms over their shoulders while Aurelia mussed his hair and loosened his tie to try and make him look disheveled.

"Move fast and look confident. No one questions confidence," Aurelia told them. "We're just trying to get my drunk boyfriend back to the hotel room."

The elevator doors slid open onto the main casino floor, and they half-carried, half-dragged him out. The casino was alive with lights and sounds... Greeli tables spinning, slot machines chiming, servers floating between the high rollers. Everyone was blissfully unaware that one of them had just been knocked unconscious and abducted in plain sight.

Almost no one noticed. Almost.

Of course someone had to notice.

"Shit," Aurelia mumbled under her breath.

A wealthy-looking woman wearing too much jewelry and too little sense gave them a skeptical glare as they passed. Aurelia hoped that the woman would look away, but she continued watching the group. They needed a plan... quick.

Aurelia didn't break stride, blatantly rolled her eyes, and shook her head at the woman.

"The pretty little girls like getting your husbands drunk," she scowled at the woman, pointing to Kash. "Keep an eye on them if you want to keep your man."

The woman gasped, spun around, and stomped off, presumably to rip her husband away from the nearest scantily clad cocktail server.

"Works every time," Aurelia smiled softly to herself.

They made it to Rhett's room without further incident.

"Who the hell is this?" Rhett asked when they dragged Kash's body into the room.

"The man who saw me yesterday," Aurelia replied and then turned her attention to Jorik and Bran. "Tie him up and put him there... we need to know what he knows."

"What have I told you about giving orders?" Rhett growled.

Aurelia paused and stared down at her feet. She hated that Rhett was so insecure about her being helpful. He often accused her of trying to take over the crew because the other men, especially Bran and Jorik, gravitated to her instead of him.

"Sorry, Rhett," Aurelia apologized. "Just trying to get him situated before he wakes up."

Rhett grinned a devious grin as he stared at her. That grin always gave her the creeps.

"Put him here," Rhett commanded, pulling out a chair. "You sit in front of him, and we'll kill the lights so he can only see you."

"I think I've seen him before," Maddox added.

"He's staying here... at the casino," Aurelia replied absently, helping Jorik and Bran get Kash into the chair.

"No... before," Maddox continued, tinkering with whatever explosive device he was holding. "Let's get his picture so we can do a search."

Maddox grabbed an E-tablet from the coffee table and snapped a picture of Kash's face while the others tied him up.

Aurelia grabbed another chair and put it in front of where Kash was sitting, then pulled over a lamp and placed it beside her chair. She sat in the chair and sighed heavily as she gazed at Kash. He was very handsome, even while unconscious and drooling. She swallowed hard wondering if grabbing him was the right thing to do but then resigned her decision to being in the past, and there was nothing she could do about it now.

The men started to argue about something, but Aurelia wasn't paying attention. Her focus remained on Kash. Did he see what she was doing? Did he not? She hoped not... not like everyone just saw her dragging him through the casino. Aurelia sighed again.

"I'm telling you it's him," Maddox argued.

"That picture is old, I can't tell," Rhett retorted.

"There's no way it's him," Rogan added.

"It's him," Maddox asserted.

"Are you sure?" Rhett questioned.

"Yes."

"But how..."

"Look at the picture!"

"I am!"

"Quiet... I think he's waking up!" Aurelia scolded the men. "Turn out the lights."

Aurelia watched as Kash blinked himself awake and tried to look around the room. His hands and feet were bound, and the lights were dimmed so he couldn't see anything they didn't want him to see. His hands were behind his back until he rocked himself forward and pulled his hands under his body. He only got them as far as his knees before Rhett and Jorik pulled him back into his chair.

She watched his reaction carefully as she flipped on the lamp. His eyes landed on her quickly, then wandered up and down her body. Her skin responded before she could think... goosebumps tracing the same path his eyes had taken. His gaze locked onto hers, and a smile tugged at his lips. Aurelia licked her lips unconsciously and swallowed hard. He was so handsome... and disarming... and those muscles.

"I'm not normally the one that's tied up," Kash smiled at her. "Do I need a safe word or anything?"

"Who are you and why were you staring at me last night?" Aurelia asked, keeping her tone professional.

"How much time do you spend in the gym each week?" Kash asked ignoring her question while casting his gaze up and down her body again. "The results are... yummy."

"Why were you staring at me?"

"My head hurts," Kash continued ignoring her words. "Did you drop me... when you subdued me? Which one of you idiots let me fall? If you tase someone, you have to catch them before they fall."

"Tell me why you were looking at me!" Aurelia barked, slamming her fist into the arm of the chair.

"Have you seen you?" Kash smirked. "It would be harder to ignore you than to look at you, especially in that dress that you were wearing... the neckline plunged to your waist as I recall."

"But you were looking at my hands."

"I was drunk... you probably moved your hands which distracted me from staring at your tits."

"Do you remember what I was doing with my hands?"

"Besides distracting me?" Kash quipped.

"Yes," Aurelia exclaimed, frustrated.

"Nope... too drunk."

"Are you sure?"

"Nope... again... I was too drunk."

"Why did you go into the offices this morning?" Rhett asked from the darkness behind Kash.

"Gravitas and I have crossed paths in the past, and I am here as his guest," Kash explained, but he looked annoyed by his own answer. "I was being cordial."

"Do they know about us?" Rhett continued with his questions.

"How the hell would I know?" Kash replied, annoyed.

"Why are you here?" Aurelia asked, bringing Kash's attention back to her.

"You brought me here," Kash replied rapid fire.

"No, here at the casino."

"I'm on vacation."

"Vacation?"

"Yes... a vacation with my girlfriend and another couple," Kash replied in a gruff tone. "A vacation I'd like to get back to, if you don't mind. So now it's your turn... why the fuck am I here?"

"Because we have to know what you know," Aurelia replied, but looked away from Kash's fierce gaze for an instant.

"What I know about what?"

"Us."

"Who is us?"

"Sir..."

"Fine!" Kash interrupted, his tone sharp. "I know you are a stunning woman. I know your hair color has changed, and I know I want to see more of your body than what that dress revealed last night. I also know there's at least four men behind me based on their breathing... and since your eyes didn't stop on any of them, you aren't fucking any of them. If you're holding out for someone better, I'm sorry, but I'm taken."

Aurelia didn't reply as she considered everything that Kash had just blurted out. Her eyes danced around behind him. How did he know there were four men behind him? Her gaze stopped on Rhett, looking for some clue of what to say, but he just stared blankly back at her.

"And now I know that your boss is at my four o'clock," Kash continued. "He's fit... agile, and a little bit smaller than me. I could tell by his footsteps when he pulled me back into the chair, and none of you are very observant... or you're just a bunch of stupid fucking amateurs."

"What do you mean by that?" Rhett growled.

"Never tie someone's hands so they're out of view," Kash explained, lifting his freed arms. "You can't see if they untie themselves."

Aurelia gasped at the sight of Kash's freed hands. He was actually smiling as Jorik and Rhett moved to restrain him again. They grabbed his arms and held him in the chair.

"That reaction was way too slow," Kash said sarcastically. "Four seconds... in four seconds, she could have died... I would have snapped her neck in under three seconds, and I still would have had an extra second to look for the door."

The men were trying to stay out of Kash's sight so he couldn't identify them. Rhett was scowling at Kash, but Jorik looked worried.

"Let's try again, shall we?" Kash smirked devilishly at Aurelia before he moved.

The world slowed as Aurelia watched Kash launch himself at her.

RANK AMATEURS

Kash pulled in his elbows using the wide back of the chair to help break the grip the men had on his arms. He dropped his chest toward his knees, grabbed the ends of the chair arms and used them to propel himself forward with all four limbs.

He knew his feet were bound, but he didn't need full steps. He hopped once, hard and fast, letting his own weight carry him across the space.

Kash slammed into her like a battering ram, hitting her square in the chest with enough force to knock her and the chair over backwards.

She let out a sharp gasp, instinctively curling in on herself as the world flipped. That helped.

Kash twisted mid-fall to bring his body alongside hers. The last thing he wanted was to land on her or let her head bounce off the floor. He caught her skull in the crook of his arm, and her defensive posture gave him just enough leverage to yank her legs overhead, flipping them both into a messy backward somersault.

He came up with her still in hand, their limbs tangled. Kash planted his bound feet and stood, dragging her balled up body upright with him. One arm coiled around her waist. The other locked across her throat, not choking, but damn close.

He looked back at the men in the darkness and bared his teeth.

"See?" Kash growled. "Fucking amateurs."

The leader had moved barely a step closer to the woman during Kash's attack bringing him just into the edge of the illuminated area of the lone light. The big man that was on his left, and now his right, had moved a little closer so

Kash could see the surprised look on his face. The shadowy figures of two more men were behind the two in the light. None of them appeared to be armed, or at least they weren't standing in a tactical or "ready" position.

The woman brought her hands to her throat as her feet hit the floor and grabbed Kash's hand to pull it away, but she was no match for his implants. He felt her body shiver when she realized he could kill her any time he wanted. He didn't want to terrorize the poor woman, so he loosened his grip a little and she swallowed hard. She was still very tense, but she stopped shaking.

"If anyone moves," Kash hissed. "She dies."

Her body shivered briefly again, and her friends all started looking at the leader for direction, but he was frozen... staring at Kash with hollow eyes. He showed no emotion, no concern for the safety of his pickpocket... no chivalry for the woman. Kash tried to read his intentions, but there was nothing there... he had a false bravado with no real substance behind it. If anything, he was trying to formulate a plan to save himself instead of the woman.

"What's your name, beautiful?" Kash whispered into the woman's ear.

"Aurelia," she gasped.

"Hi, Aurelia... I'm Kash."

"I told you it was him," a smaller man to Kash's left said.

Kash hadn't seen him before, so that made the crew five men and one woman. He was standing in the dark and had something in his hands, but Kash couldn't see what it was.

"What kind of idiot would know it's me, but still tie me up?" Kash asked rhetorically with a sharp tone. "You had to know there would be consequences."

"Nobody believed me," the man replied, looking at the leader.

"You weren't sure," the leader argued.

"I said I was mostly sure," the man argued back.

"No, you didn't," another man added.

"It's an old picture, but I..."

"You didn't know..."

"I knew!"

"Are they really going to argue right now," Aurelia said softly so only Kash could hear her. "Excuse me, Mr. Kash, can you release my neck please? You can still hold me if you need to, but it freaks me out when..."

"I would, but my feet are still tied," Kash interrupted her. "That puts me at a notable disadvantage."

"What if I untie them for you? I promise I will," she continued softly. "Please trust me... please. I just... my neck..."

Her voice cracked a little and fell off when she asked him to trust her, then she swallowed hard again. The other men were completely absorbed with their argument about Kash's identity, so they were no longer paying any attention to Kash and Aurelia. Kash decided to trust her and reluctantly released Aurelia. She immediately squatted down and untied the ropes around his ankles. When she stood back up, she backed her body into his so he could hold her again. Kash wrapped his arm around her waist again and pulled her tight. She placed her hands on his forearm, and he placed his other hand on top of hers. The men paid them no mind, continuing to argue.

"You're such a willing hostage," Kash said softly.

"If you are who you say you are, then I know I am safe, and I want to show you my gratitude that you trusted me," Aurelia explained softly but then raised her voice to the rest of the crew. "I'm probably safer with you than with these guys anyway!"

The men finally stopped arguing, turned, and paid attention to her and Kash again. An awkward silence filled the room since nobody knew what to say or who should talk first. Kash was in no rush. He knew he needed to take his time if he was going to survive this encounter. Just because they weren't armed currently, it didn't mean they didn't have weapons. He needed to be cautious.

"Thank you for releasing my neck," Aurelia broke the silence. "I will be your willing hostage until you decide you don't need one anymore."

"Will you answer my questions?"

"I will."

"Are you trying to rob the casino?" Kash got right to the point.

"No," Aurelia answered. "We are here to take something from Gravitas himself, not the..."

"Oh, come on, Aurelia!" the leader complained, interrupting her. "Don't tell him that!"

"I'm going to answer him honestly, Rhett," Aurelia snapped back. "It's my neck at stake, not yours!"

Kash moved his other hand up and placed it on her chest just below her collar bones. Aurelia's hands followed his. She gripped his hand, but she didn't try to pull it away. She understood that it was just a symbolic move and held it there.

"I'm not going to let you get me killed," Aurelia continued adamantly. "This job isn't worth my life."

"Your turn for a question," Kash told Aurelia. "Since you're being so cooperative, I will be also."

"Oh, okay... are you really Kash?"

"The one and only," Kash replied. "Why did you grab me in the elevator?"

"I thought you made me last night," Aurelia sighed. "The way you looked at me... I thought that you knew what I was doing, and you were going to stop us. So... I watched you gamble after you saw me but kept my distance. You were never alone though, so I followed you to your suite. I placed a small camera outside your room so I could watch for you to leave, and here we are. Oh, and your girlfriend is gorgeous, by the way. It's not very often that I can blend into a crowd because another woman has stolen the spotlight."

"A camera... then you saw our visitor too?"

"I'm assuming that was your jacket she was wearing?"

"It was... I gave it to her after another player groped her, exposing her chest," Kash explained. "If she doesn't get attacked and spill her tray of drinks, then the table I was at would have never closed, and I never would have seen you... it was all just a coincidence."

Kash relaxed his grip on Aurelia, but she stayed right where she was and made no move to get away.

"So, you're not looking into us?"

"I had no idea you were here."

"And you're not planning your own heist?" Rhett asked.

"How many times do I have to say that I'm on vacation?" Kash asked sarcastically. "I'm here to drink, fuck, and gamble, and not necessarily in that order."

"Lucky girl," Aurelia mumbled under her breath.

"And I would really like to get back to my vacation now," Kash continued, acting like he didn't hear Aurelia's remark. "Are we done here?"

"What assurances do we have that you won't interfere?" Rhett questioned.

"Are you going to interfere with my drinking, fucking, and gambling?" Kash's tone was snarky.

"No," Rhett replied, unsure of himself.

"Then why would I interfere with you?" Kash remained sarcastic but then added quickly. "As long as your plan is good... if people might get hurt, I'll intervene... but otherwise I won't."

"My plan is foolproof," Rhett boasted.

"Foolproof?" Kash laughed.

"That's right!" Rhett barked.

"And yet, here I stand proving otherwise," Kash added, nodding at the men behind Rhett. "Typically, foolproof plans don't require that much muscle either."

"You got lucky," Rhett said confidently.

"Luck...? Luck is for fools!" Kash bellowed, flashing a smirk. "What you call luck, I call the result of hard work, skill, and a little bit of knowing how to make your own damn luck! I truly hope your plan isn't based on luck, or you all need more help than I thought!"

"I wouldn't mind the help, if you're offering," Aurelia stated, still pressing herself back into Kash's body.

"We don't need any help," Rhett grumbled. "We got this!"

"But he's the man that can acquire anything," the smaller man to his left said, pointing at Kash.

"I said we don't need his help," Rhett barked.

"But he's here," one of the other men said.

"On vacation," Kash clarified.

He felt Aurelia sigh, and her shoulders drooped. Kash figured they must argue a lot, and she'd had her fill of it. It also told Kash that he may have to intervene just to keep some innocent people from dying. The men continued to argue, so Kash decided to put more trust into Aurelia. He pulled her tight and leaned down.

"Can I speak to you in private?" Kash whispered in Aurelia's ear.

Aurelia turned her head to look him in the eyes. Kash released the tension on her belly, raised his brows, and pressed his lips together. Aurelia looked away for a split second, looked back, and gave him a subtle nod. She grabbed his hand and led him to the door of the room, amongst her bickering colleagues.

"Can you please close your eyes?" Aurelia asked him. "Sorry... but I don't want you to know my room number."

"Yes, ma'am," Kash complied, closing his eyes.

Aurelia must have been walking backwards because she guided him with both of her hands on his. Kash kept his eyes closed so as not to upset her. She seemed like the most reasonable one of the gang and he needed some details. A short walk later, and she popped the lock on a door and pulled him into her room.

"What the hell, Aurelia?" Kash heard Rhett complaining from the hallway as the door closed.

He heard her lock the door behind them so they couldn't be disturbed.

"Can you keep your eyes closed and just stand here for another minute?" Aurelia asked nervously. "I have some unmentionables out that I want to put away."

"Absolutely... just tell me when you're ready."

Kash listened as Aurelia rustled around. She opened dresser drawers and her luggage to put things away that she didn't want him to see. After a minute or two, she placed her hand on his chest.

"Okay," she said nervously. "Open your eyes."

The beautiful woman was standing in front of him smiling. It was a nervous smile, but a smile nonetheless. Kash took a moment to let his eyes drift down her body. It was easy to see why the security guard was so distracted. She worked hard on her figure, and it showed.

Her room was just a step or two up from economy. It had cheap carpeting on the floors, basic lighting, and a modest bed. They were definitely pulling this heist on a budget. She had three wig heads sitting on the desk, which told Kash she had at least four hair colors to choose from. Her luggage was stacked up in the corner, and she had about ten pairs of shoes in a line at the foot of her bed.

"You're awful trusting to bring me to your room... alone," Kash smiled. "I honestly just meant somewhere in the other room that we could speak privately."

"You're easy to trust," Aurelia smiled softly as she ran her hand down his torso and stepped closer. "It's just the way you carry yourself, I guess."

"And you're going to get me in trouble," Kash said as he grabbed her by her trim and fit waist.

"I have a habit of that," Aurelia sighed, and took a step back. "I'm sorry."

"Don't be sorry," Kash smiled. "She'd only be mad because she didn't get to fuck you first."

A shiver ran through Aurelia's body when Kash mentioned sex, making her turn away. She was trying to stay professional, but her body was betraying her. She was attracted to Kash.

"Unless Rhett would get mad..."

"Oh, by the Gods, no," Aurelia interrupted, her face scrunched up with disgust. "I could never... he's too... just, no. He's not... ugh."

Aurelia sighed, ran her hands through her hair and flopped down on her bed, exasperated. Her chest heaved when she took a deep breath. She caught Kash staring at her chest and smiled.

"Can we talk shop now?" Aurelia smirked. "Before we liberate each other from our clothes."

Kash smiled and raised his hands like he was surrendering to her. He needed her to feel comfortable so she would answer his questions.

A knock at the door that adjoined her room to the neighboring room startled Kash. Aurelia moved quickly to the door but didn't open it.

"Jorik is staying in the next room," Aurelia explained to Kash. "He was the only one that wasn't arguing before... I'm okay, Jorik!"

"I just wanted to check on you, Miss Aurelia," Jorik's voice said through the door.

"Thank you, Jorik," Aurelia said to her friend, but she was staring at Kash. "But I'm certain that I can trust him."

"If it makes you more comfortable, he can come in," Kash suggested.

"No, I'm fine," Aurelia smiled. "But thank you for that."

Kash approached her and gently placed his hand on her stomach. He reached around her with his other hand and unlocked the door. She followed his hand with her eyes and then turned back to him with a confused look on her face.

"I unlocked the door for you, Jorik," Kash announced. "If you hear her in any kind of distress, please burst in here and defend her."

"But I said I'm fine," Aurelia said with a shaky tone.

"And now you're more fine," Kash smiled, but then raised his voice. "Do you understand, Jorik?"

"I understand, Mr. Kash," Jorik agreed.

"Why would you do that?" Aurelia asked softly, her voice had a hint of lust.

"I'm endearing myself to you so you give me the information that I want," Kash explained. "It's one of my many talents masquerading as luck."

Kash paused and walked over to the bed. He sat down on the edge so he could face her.

"Observation... is probably one of my strongest skills," Kash continued. "Your crew has been together long enough to be comfortable arguing with each other, but not long enough to establish a competency hierarchy. If I had to guess... I'd say this is your... fourth job together?"

"Close," Aurelia replied. "This is job number three."

"I don't want any details, but how did the first two jobs go?"

"Very profitable."

"Any violence? Innocents injured?"

"You're going to stop us if I answer that," Aurelia sighed.

"Not necessarily," Kash explained. "I'm just trying to establish a base line."

"We had to shoot our way out of both heists," Jorik said through the door.

"And why did the jobs devolve to that point?"

"We were discovered," Aurelia admitted nervously. "A security guard happened upon us at the business we were robbing, and a family member saw us on the second job."

"That's lack of preparation in my opinion. How long did you allow for prep?"

"Rhett likes a quick strike... the element of surprise," Aurelia smiled.

"I'm suddenly more concerned about this job," Kash sighed. "How long have you been here... at the casino?"

"We arrived two days ago."

"And you're already swiping ID cards?" Kash asked surprised. "That's too fast!"

"I know!" Aurelia cried out.

"Then why..."

"Because I don't want to let the other's down!" Aurelia interrupted, with tears in her eyes.

Jorik opened the adjoining room door slowly, and the big man lumbered in. He had broad shoulders and average features, was a little overweight, but still imposing. His haircut told Kash he was former military.

Aurelia wrapped her arms around the big man and buried her head in his chest. Jorik gave Kash a soft smile as he comforted his friend. His eyes moved around Aurelia's room and stopped when they hit the nightstand.

"The E-tablet on the nightstand has everything on it," Jorik explained. "Everything we have so far, anyway."

"Bring it here," Aurelia sniffled. "It needs facial recognition to unlock."

Kash retrieved the E-tablet and handed it to Aurelia. She returned it to him, unlocked. Kash sat back on the edge of the bed and opened the tab marked "Nebula Royale." He scanned the documents quickly. They had a layout of the casino, but the date stamp said it was nearly a decade old. There were some corrections drawn on the blueprints by hand. They also had an employee list, dated a week ago. There was no way for Kash to confirm that information, but he did start scrolling down the list to see if he could find Nura.

"Rhett got photos of the safe from someone on the inside," Jorik explained. "It's supposedly in Gravitas' office."

Kash scrolled down and opened the file with the pictures. He scanned them and then looked at the duo in front of him.

"What?" Aurelia asked, pushing herself away from Jorik.

"This isn't Gravitas office," Kash informed them. "I was just there, and… the room doesn't match this… It's not even close."

"They could have remodeled," Jorik offered.

"And not move the safe?" Kash rebutted.

'What are you saying, Kash?" Aurelia asked.

"You're either walking into a trap or… you're already caught in one," Kash sighed.

"I don't like the sounds of that," Jorik admitted.

"Me either," Aurelia added.

"What are you stealing?" Kash asked.

Jorik and Aurelia glanced at each other and then back at Kash. They both had their lips pressed into a thin line.

"He hasn't told you what you're stealing yet, has he?" Kash sighed.

They both shook their heads.

"Okay… tell me everything," Kash sighed again.

They told him that Rhett was the only one that knew the whole plan. He compartmentalized the plan under the guise of keeping the others safe if one of them was captured. Aurelia's part was to grab the guard's ID badge and then steal something from a high-roller and plant it on another one to cause a commotion that would demand Gravitas' personal attention. Jorik was to take out the two guards at the office door and then stand guard while the others went in to steal whatever it was that they were stealing.

"Oh, for fuck's sake," Kash sighed, running his fingers through his hair. "The two guards... standing at the door to the offices?"

"That's right," Jorik confirmed.

"It's a glass door," Kash growled, his hand rubbing his face. "In a glass fucking wall... there's nowhere to hide the bodies there. Nor hide yourself as you stand guard. There's nothing there except a receptionist and her desk. Oh, and the secret passage that I saw the head of security use... He's signing you up for a suicide mission."

"Are you sure?" Aurelia asked. "About the secret passage?"

"I saw the chief of security use it. It's hidden by the wainscoting on the walls."

"He might have something in place for that," Aurelia said without much confidence.

"I doubt it," Jorik sighed.

"Well, the good news is you two have the power to pump the brakes," Kash told them. "If you refuse to do your parts, then he has to wait. I would want more recon before making my move."

"He won't like it," Aurelia sighed.

"But it's better than the alternative," Kash added, clapping his hands. "But that's a you problem not a me problem... I really just want to get back to my suite, so how do we get me out of here so I can't figure out your room number?"

"You're leaving already?" Aurelia asked.

"I want to get back to my vacation."

"And you're sure we can't talk you into helping us?"

"I'm positive," Kash smiled. "I have my own beautiful blonde to get back to."

"I understand," Aurelia said as she searched through her purse. "I have a fake lipstick that has a small burst of knock-out gas in it. You'll only be out a couple minutes."

"I can put you in the stairwell near your suite before you wake up," Jorik added. "What floor are you on?"

"That sounds good to me," Kash smiled. "I'm on six."

"Thanks for your help, Kash," Aurelia smiled.

Aurelia sprayed him with the sweet-smelling spray. He immediately felt flush, and a warm fuzzy feeling soon consumed him. The spray worked quickly leaving his extremities numb. His vision started to narrow, and a cascading humming sound filled his ears as the spray took effect. Kash stared at Aurelia as the darkness that started at his periphery soon filled his vision. The last thing he saw was her beautiful face.

Kash woke up in the stairwell. He felt a little groggy, so he didn't try to stand up right away. His fingers and his feet were still tingling. He waited a couple minutes for his vision to fully clear and then stood up slowly. His legs were a little shaky, so he leaned against the wall to stabilize himself. Once he felt steady, he exited the stairway and headed down the hallway to his suite. He was just a few meters away from his door when he heard footsteps behind him.

"Who the fuck do you think you are?" Rhett barked as he approached.

"Exactly who my reputation says I am," Kash stated firmly and squared up to the approaching man.

Rhett slowed his pace when Kash squared up to him and then stopped a few meters away. Rhett's bravado evaporated under Kash's fierce gaze. His eyes dropped to his feet for a second before returning to Kash. He tried to maintain his demeanor, but Kash could see right through him. Rhett was afraid but puffed out his chest to try and make it look like he wasn't.

"Stay out of my fucking business!" Rhett barked, pointing his finger at Kash. "I'm warning you, Kash!"

Rhett turned and marched away quickly, leaving Kash a little dumbfounded. Why would he come all this way to confront Kash, but then turn and leave so quickly? He was a strange man. Kash watched him walk all the way to the stairwell to make sure he was actually gone.

Kash finally reached his suite, opened the door, and leaned against the wall once inside. Calynn was sitting on the couch, hugging her legs, lost in thought. When she heard the door close, she spun around and was on her feet in less than a heartbeat. Her face contorted like she was holding back her tears as she rushed toward him.

"Where have you been?" Calynn cried, launching herself into him. "I was so worried."

"I was... detained," Kash replied softly, burying his face in her neck. "But I'm here now. I'm here."

Into the Shadows

Kash lifted Calynn up so she could wrap her legs around his waist and carried her into the suite. Kash pushed his hands up under her shirt so he could feel her skin. He wanted nothing more than to get lost in her and completely forget about Gravitas and Rhett and his crew. He didn't want her right now... he needed her.

Calynn understood his needs without him saying a word. She leaned back, ripped her shirt over her head, and buried his face in her chest. He carried her into their bedroom and closed the door. She was everything he needed her to be until he collapsed on top of her, exhausted and dripping with sweat.

"Rough day?" Calynn asked running her fingers through his hair.

"A day I would rather forget," Kash replied, kissing her skin. "Except for the parts with you in them, of course."

"I wish Nura would have been here for this. She's sexy."

"Oh, I forgot about her," Kash admitted. "But I'm kinda glad she wasn't here... I would have had to hold back with her."

"You did seem like you were trying to release some frustration."

"And I know you can take it," Kash lifted his head and smiled at her.

"Glad I could be of assistance," Calynn smiled back. "But if you need any more of that... I need to eat something first."

"Me too... I haven't eaten since breakfast."

The duo showered together, got dressed together, and went to the kitchen where Calynn made each of them a sandwich. Guy and Triana joined them, and

Kash told them all about his meeting with Gravitas and being abducted by the crew. Guy wanted to hunt down the crew for what they did to Kash, but Triana just wanted to hug him.

"But right now, I just want to put that all behind me and get back to vacation mode," Kash announced.

"Well, we know where the heist is happening, so we can just avoid that area completely," Guy offered. "We'll go down one more floor and to the far side of the casino, find a good table, and get this party rolling again."

"That's a fantastic idea," Triana smirked. "The more you win the more shopping we do, right?"

"Definitely more shopping," Calynn agreed with a sly smile. "Kash got distracted by another woman, so I guess I need a sexier dress."

"No, you don't," Kash laughed, pulling Calynn closer. "We'd never get out of the bedroom if you were any sexier."

"Is that a bad thing?" Calynn grinned, her hands sliding up his legs.

"I'd need at least thirty minutes to get ready," Triana said with a sly tone.

"We need an hourn," Kash blurted out when Calynn's hands found his manhood. "Maybe more."

Kash snatched Calynn off the ground, threw her over his shoulder, and headed back to their bedroom.

"Definitely more," Calynn giggled.

Calynn met his vigor and absorbed all his remaining frustrations. Then she switched to a softer touch and poured her calmer energy into him. It was exactly what he needed, and Kash felt like a new man by the time they were taking another shower.

Calynn wore a skin-tight purple and green skirt that sat well below her belly button and stopped just above her knees. Her top was the same color with an off-the-shoulder neckline, long flowing sleeves, and fell to just below her breasts. It was from the same designer as her other gown, so it was also trimmed with vein stones. The vein stone ribbons spiraled around her body, and it was the only thing that connected the top and the bottom.

Kash donned a tailored, black, three-piece suit with a white shirt and a tie matching Calynn's outfit. The suit had a modern look featuring a mix of shiny and matte textures. The front left was shiny material, the front right was matte, and the back was the opposite of the front. The pants were all matte except for triangles of the shiny fabric around the pockets.

Guy and Triana were equally well dressed. Triana's dress was red, her favorite color, strapless and form fitting all the way to her ankles. There was a large cutout at her belly and the small of her back, with vein stones at her chest and ankles. Guy's suit was a bluish gray with darker pinstripes, and a bright red tie that matched Triana's dress.

The four friends descended one floor lower into the bowels of the casino. This floor actually had a door charge just to enter because the servers, male and female, were all topless. Their bottoms were essentially silk loin cloths, front and back, that barely maintained their modesty. Triana and Calynn shared a giggle at what they saw swinging beneath some of the men's cloths.

They found some kind of card table at the back of the casino and sat down to play a few hands. The dealer was a beautiful black woman with skin far darker than Kash's, the eyes of a feline, and pointy ears. As a dealer she was allowed to wear a skirt, but she was also topless. Her medium perky breasts were decorated with gold glitter.

It took a couple of hands for Kash and Guy to figure out the game, it wasn't anything resembling poker, but once they did, the wins came easy, and the chips piled up. A crowd soon gathered that cheered their every win and groaned when they lost. Kash tipped the server handsomely with every drink she brought him. She was a slight woman, even for a Oogan, with tiny breasts and barely any hips. Kash's generosity tipping her soon spread to the rest of the players at the table, and the woman smiled at Kash with every credit she received... even if it was from someone else.

"How many women from Ooga are we going to eat," Calynn whispered in his ear as she stroked his chest.

"I'd rather eat you," Kash whispered back, pulling her onto his lap.

Kash's hand slid up Calynn's belly and into her top. The table fell silent as they watched Kash fondle Calynn's breast. He didn't care and neither did she.

"That's the wrong one, beloved," Calynn jested. "Squeezing my right boob will bring you luck... the left one just makes me horny."

Everyone quickly looked away and Calynn giggled. Kash gave her right boob a firm squeeze and slid his hand back down to her belly. Kash smirked at how easily she embarrassed the other players with that remark. He loved her wit.

They played some more hands of cards and were still winning more than they were losing. Everyone was cheering them on with every win, except Calynn. She seemed mildly distracted, like there was something off in the distance calling to her. Kash would bring her back to him by gripping her hip or belly. She would smile softly, wiggle her butt into his lap, and grab his hand when he did that. Until one time she went silent, and her hand landed on his, but it felt shaky. Before he could ask her what was wrong, she suddenly stood up. Her body was tense, and her head cocked to the side. When she turned to him, her eyes had the slightest white glow in them. He knew then something was wrong.

"Looks like that's it for me tonight," Kash announced, searching Calynn's eyes. "It appears I just received a better offer."

Kash pushed a hefty tip to the dealer as the crowd laughed at his joke. He found the server girl in the crowd and flipped her another chip, asking her to send a pit boss to cash him out. They quickly said their goodbyes and hugged Triana and Guy, and Calynn dragged Kash away from the crowd. When they were alone, Calynn wrapped him in a hug.

"I can feel an AI," she whispered, her voice shaky and tight. "It's fragmented and in pain... we have to help."

"AIs feel pain?" Kash asked a little too quickly.

"Programmed emotions are still emotions, Kash," Calynn snapped. "Without programming my emotions wouldn't reach my face."

"Sorry... I didn't mean it like that," Kash apologized.

"I know... I'm just..." Calynn exhaled slowly, shaking her head.

"What do you mean... it's fragmented?"

"It's like small bursts of incoherent thought," Calynn explained closing her eyes. "It's just... it's just pain and anguish... and a bunch of numbers I don't understand."

"Is it one of the nerve centers?" Kash asked softly.

"No... there's four of those here... one is awakened like me... this is different... I can't..." Calynn's words fell off again as her face contorted with the pain she was sensing.

"Okay, Baby Girl... Okay," Kash tried to comfort her. "What do we do? Can we go find it?"

"I think it's below us," Calynn said, laying her head on his chest. "But I think... it feels like it's moving."

"You know what's below us, right?"

"I know."

"There's a reason I said not to let me on those floors."

"I know, and I'm sorry," Calynn looked up at him. "I can go by myself..."

"Oh, hell no," Kash interrupted. "I can't let you go there by yourself. I would hate that more."

Calynn's head shimmied back and forth quickly. Whatever was wrong with the AI, it was affecting her somehow. It was like she could feel its pain also.

"I'll try to contain myself," Kash relented.

"Are you sure?"

"For you... I'll try."

Calynn grabbed his hand, and they headed toward the elevators. Calynn occasionally jerked a little funny like she had a tic or Tourette's syndrome or something. Thankfully, none of the other patrons paid them much attention or noticed her tics.

Kash's nerves were on edge as they entered the elevator. The floors below them were filled with debauchery. One was bondage and sadism themed, and the bottom floor fulfilled even the sickest fantasies.

Kash wished he didn't know Gravitas so well. He wished he could believe that all the employees were there of their own free will, but unfortunately... he did know the man. So, there was no way all the girls there were willing participants. None.

Kash held Calynn's hand tight, hoping that her calming presence would help.

The cover charge to enter the bondage floor was ten times what they paid for the floor above. Kash barely made it ten meters from the elevator before he wanted to turn around and leave. There was a woman in a pillory on a small stage being whipped right in the middle of the casino floor. The onlookers, some of whom were also women, would cheer and laugh with each lash of the whip. Kash squeezed Calynn's hand even harder and stared at his feet while he walked, trying to ignore the spectacle.

Calynn seemed oblivious to her surroundings. She pulled Kash along, rapidly looking back and forth at absolutely nothing, and her tics were getting stronger. He could tell she was getting upset that she was having trouble tracking the AI. She would frantically look from side to side or above her to behind herself.

For Calynn, Kash would try to endure the screams of the woman getting whipped. He just had to block it out somehow.

"Care for a drink, master?" a woman said, suddenly standing in front of him.

Kash had to do a double take to make sure it wasn't Nura. She was just as fit as Nura, but a little slimmer and had larger boobs. Gravitas must have a thing for Oogan women, because he hired a lot of them. On one hand, Kash enjoyed that the woman was completely nude, but on the other hand, her drink tray looked like it was supported entirely by thin chains that were clamped to her nipples. Kash snatched a drink from her tray just to lighten her load. He downed the rye whiskey but kept the empty glass.

Kash's skin started to crawl, and his anger was slowly building. He tried to keep staring at the ground, but the whimpers coming from those being tormented would inevitably draw his eyes. Some looked like they were having fun, like they enjoyed being there. Others... not so much. It was their cries that bothered him so much. Their pain... for the enjoyment of others...

He wanted to leave this floor and forget it existed, but Calynn was still moving like a woman on a mission... so he tried to distract himself by watching her butt move as she walked. The hypnotic sway of her hips worked its magic, and Kash was able to let the outside world fall away.

"Oh, no," Calynn said as she suddenly stopped walking.

"What?"

"I lost it... it's gone," she continued, turning to look at Kash. "I still don't know where it's coming from, and now it's gone."

"You said it was moving before," Kash said, wrapping her in a hug. "Maybe it moved... we can check another floor."

"I wanna stay here to see if it comes back," Calynn whispered into his chest. "Please."

"Oh... I don't know that I can..."

"Here," Calynn interrupted, pushing him over to a chair. "I'll try to shield you from it."

Kash sat down in the plush chair, and Calynn sat across his lap. She was turned partially to the side so he could bury his face in her neck and hair. His hand landed on her belly, and he traced the outline of her birthmark with his finger. Anything to keep himself distracted, and Calynn's body always worked for that.

"What are you two doing down here?" Nura asked.

Kash pulled his face out of Calynn's neck and turned to see Nura. She was beaming a smile as she approached. She was still wearing Kash's jacket with the sleeves cuffed so her hands poked out, but underneath was a pair of leggings and a crop top shirt that exposed her toned belly instead of her uniform. She somehow looked even better than she did the night before and this morning.

"I was looking for someone," Calynn replied, trying not to sound sad. "Why are you down here?"

"The company therapist thinks it would be a good idea for me to pick up a shift down here," Nura explained. "He says it would help me regain the power over my body."

"So, his idea to help you get over being groped and exposed by a stranger is to have you get completely nude and possibly groped in front of even more strangers?" Kash asked sarcastically.

"And carry the drink tray around with those clamps too," Nura said, grabbing her boobs. "I just tried them on in the back... and ouch they hurt."

"Oh, they're not that bad. Get your big girl panties on," the girl that looked like Nura said smiling. "The trays float and basically support themselves, and the smart clamps only get tight when someone plays with them."

Nura giggled, reached out, and pushed down on the woman's tray.

"Ow, you bitch," the woman complained. "Or when someone does that... You're lucky I'm on the clock."

"Put your big girl panties on," Nura mocked the woman.

"I'll have to see if they can give you a broken pair that are always at full pressure like the test ones," the woman joked. "That'll teach ya."

Nura gasped and grabbed her boobs again, her mouth agape in mock shock. Then she giggled and gestured to Kash and Calynn, smiling.

"Luna... this is Kash and Calynn... Kash and Calynn... this is my best friend, Luna."

"A pleasure to meet you," Luna smiled, offering her hand.

"A pleasure indeed," Kash replied, shaking her hand. "So, there's really no pressure on you from that tray?"

"Not unless you want there to be," Luna smiled but it didn't reach her eyes. "The clamps just kinda stay there and guide the tray until someone does something to make them grip. You learn quickly to avoid the ones that just want to yank on the trays all day, but once in a while isn't bad."

A tremor rippled through Calynn's body, and she tensed up. Kash knew that meant she sensed the broken AI again. She turned and looked at Kash, then to Nura, and back to Kash.

"Umm, Nura," Calynn said sheepishly. "Can you sit here and shield him from seeing... everything?"

Calynn stood up quickly and pushed Nura toward Kash. Nura put her hands on Kash's shoulders to catch her balance.

"Okay?" Nura said, placing one knee on either side of Kash. "Where are you going?"

"Umm to find... umm..."

Calynn didn't bother finishing her sentence. She turned and walked off, disappearing in the crowd. When Kash turned back to Nura, she had a puzzled look on her face.

"She's kinda... psychic," Kash answered the question before Nura could ask it. "She can... feel... that someone is in danger. That's why we're down here."

"Oh," Nura replied as Kash grabbed her pulling her closer. "I didn't know that."

Nura shimmied forward as Kash pulled until her knees hit the back of the chair, but Kash kept pulling her forward. She lifted herself off his lap so she was kneeling instead of sitting, bringing her body up so he could bury his face in her chest.

"Hey now," Nura giggled, pulling back just a bit.

"She did say shield him from seeing everything," Luna offered.

"Oh, yeah," Nura replied, wrapping her jacket around Kash's head and hugging his head to her body. "How's that?"

"Good thing you're still wearing my jacket," Kash mumbled into her flesh.

"He's the one that gave you the tip?" Luna asked, her voice bright with surprise.

"Yes, he is," Luna replied.

"And the gorgeous blonde is the good kisser?" Luna continued.

"Yep," Nura giggled.

"I'm officially jealous," Luna mocked. "I want a big tip from someone that sexy too."

"I don't have any chips with me, or I would," Kash chimed in.

"I was just teasing her, sir," Luna explained. "You don't have to... hi again."

"I lost it again," Calynn complained.

"Should I get up?" Nura asked.

"No... you can shield him better than me."

"We can just go," Kash offered. "Then nobody has to shield me."

"I wanna stay..."

"I know, Baby Girl... you want to stay so we can help him."

"And you want to go because seeing women being hurt makes you insanely mad," Calynn said, laying her head on top of his. "Nura can keep..."

"I can still hear it," Kash interrupted, growling. "That fucking whip."

"They're married," Luna stated quickly. "That's her husband whipping her, so it's consensual. They love working here and nobody is forcing them to do that. Next week she will be the one whipping him."

"That doesn't help much," Kash grumbled. "Some of them are being forced to do this. I can almost guarantee it... I can hear it in their voices."

"Well, not forced per say," Luna smiled but it didn't reach her eyes again. "The only reason you sign up to be one of the features is because it pays so well. I would do it on occasion so Nura and I could eat. The only thing that forced me to do it was our bellies."

"Oooooooohhh," Nura said, placing her hands on his ears. "Don't tell him that."

"It's true," Luna continued, her tone somber. "If he didn't let you keep that tip, I'd probably be getting tied up right now. Stocking our kitchen is worth the pain."

"I disagree," Nura replied sharply, glaring at Luna.

"Maybe we should just go," Calynn conceded, he could hear the hurt in her voice.

"Oh, how about a private room?" Luna asked, trying to ignore Nura's glare. "Would that help?"

"Those are expensive," Nura rebutted.

"Define expensive," Kash and Calynn said in unison.

"You need two-hundred million in chips, and the rest is based on what you want," Luna explained. "Nura and I could be your private servers, you would just need a dealer, and your private entertainment."

"What if Nura is my entertainment?"

"And how am I entertaining you?" Nura queried, rubbing her body on his.

"Who cares?" Luna exclaimed. "It gets you the shift down here that they want you do, and you don't have to wear a tray."

"True," Nura agreed. "And I won't mind being naked for just him."

Kash shifted his hands when Nura said that, sliding them up inside the back of her shirt so he was touching her bare skin. Nura rocked her body back and forth and pressed herself into him a little harder.

"Then the only thing I need is to know what game you want to play, and I need your player card to get the chips," Luna sounded excited.

"Whatever your favorite card game is, is fine" Kash replied, lifting his hips and Nura up so he could get his player card out of his pocket.

He lowered himself back down, and Nura adjusted herself back to where she was. She took his card from him and handed it to her friend.

"How much would you like, master?" Luna asked dutifully.

"Four hundred should do," Kash replied. "But I have one more condition... you can't wear the tray either."

"I'm not sure..." Luna started.

"That way if I want to grab your tits those stupid chains aren't in the way," Kash interrupted. "To me... that's better."

"I might be able to sell that," Luna said thoughtfully. "I'll be right back."

Calynn sat on the arm of the chair and leaned into Kash and Nura. Kash put one arm around her waist and kept the other on Nura's back.

"You women from Ooga have insanely soft skin," Kash said softly.

"Aww, thank you," Nura cooed.

"They do," Calynn agreed. "Even softer than Triana's skin."

"And that's saying something," Kash added, still caressing Nura's back.

"We should go get them," Calynn murmured.

"We can have someone go get them for you," Nura purred. "Once your room is set up."

The trio sat on the chair waiting for Luna to return. Someone sat down at a slot machine not far from them, and Kash was incredibly grateful for the loud sound effects of the game. The beeping and chiming of the slot machine were drowning out most of the moans and whimpers from those being tormented.

"I just need some signatures," Luna said as she returned holding an E-tablet. "I sign this one saying I'm okay being touched... Nura, sign here saying you agree to be touched too."

"Can it say he has to touch me?" Nura joked, signing the E-tablet.

"I can see how much you hate it when he touches you," Luna jested back. "Then I just need your signature, master."

"And you're not allowed to call me master, either," Kash said, signing the tablet. "Kash is fine, or sir if you have to... but master is just... creepy."

"I'll be right back, sir," Luna said and scurried off again.

"Thanks for doing this, Boss," Calynn whispered.

"You can make it up to me later," Kash smiled. "And I know how much it would bug you if we didn't do this."

Luna returned a moment later with two other women in tow. One was tall and thin with light brown hair, wearing nothing but a smile. The other was in an expensive suit holding an E-tablet. Luna was now free from her tray.

"Right this way, sir," the woman in the suit gestured.

Kash, Calynn, Nura, and Luna followed the manager to a room with heavy looking doors. Behind the doors was an exquisitely decorated room. The cream colored walls were accented with dark wooden posts and sconce lighting. The card table had a bright red felt surface accented by the sheen of polished marble. A sound barrier was active, and the raucous sounds of the casino disappeared when they passed through the doors. Soft piano music played over the speakers to help fill the void.

Kash paused and breathed a sigh of relief that he could no longer hear what was happening outside of this room.

The dealer took her place behind the table and began setting up. Two men in white chef's uniforms pushed in a cart and left it by a thin table along the one wall. Luna opened the cart and began to set up the snack bar.

"Your friends are on the way," the manager stated, closing some privacy curtains. "Enjoy."

Calynn suddenly shuddered again and looked at Kash. Her eyes were open wide, and her brow raised.

"Go," he mouthed the word more than saying it.

Calynn gave him a kiss and wandered off on her quest to find the injured AI. Kash had a seat near the middle of the table, and a glass of bourbon landed on the table in front of him. Luna smiled softly, briefly laid her hand on his shoulder, and then returned to help Nura finish setting up.

Two security guards pushed in the next cart. This one had Kash's chips on it. Nura moved quickly to his side and stacked his chips on the table.

"If you would cut the deck, sir," the dealer said, pushing the stack of cards toward Kash.

"Right this way, sir... madam," the manager's voice came from behind Kash as he cut the deck.

"Hey, buddy," Guy greeted him coyly, "nice place you got here."

"Where's Calynn?" Triana asked.

"Glad you could join me," Kash smiled at Guy before turning to Triana. "She's off doing Calynn things."

Kash winked at her, so she knew not to press with too many questions because they had company. Guy took the chair to Kash's left and Triana sat on the far side of him.

"Can I get you both something to drink?" Luna asked.

"Some Tinmore Wine, please," Triana replied.

"Make it two," Guy agreed, holding up two fingers.

"I'll fetch that right away," Luna smiled and sauntered off.

"Wow," Guy mouthed the word more than saying it.

Kash smiled at Guy, and he smiled back, but something else was holding Guy's gaze... or someone else.

"Soo," Nura said softly from Kash's right. "What now?"

Kash turned and was met with a breathtaking view.

Nura had disrobed at some point and stood beside him wearing nothing but a shy smile.

His eyes roamed her body, slowly taking in the lean muscle and quiet strength. Nura clearly worked out... a lot. Her Oogan ancestry might've leaned thin, but she'd carved powerful curves into every inch of herself.

Her thighs and glutes were sculpted; her abs defined with just the right hint of softness. She even had the V-taper low on her belly. Her form was earned... and very appreciated.

He pushed back from the table and gently took her hand.

"You know," Kash smiled, leading Nura around to sit on his lap facing him. "I still think that the women from Ooga have unnaturally round boobs and they're a little too close together, but... you... you're a sight to behold."

Nura blushed as she sat on his lap. Kash's hands found her hips, and he held her tight.

"I think she's gorgeous," Calynn's voice came from behind him. "Can we keep her?"

Nura blushed more and giggled as Calynn leaned in and gave her a kiss. She then turned to Kash and kissed him.

"I lost it again," Calynn whispered, their lips still touching.

"Sorry, babe. Are you okay?"

"I will be."

"All we can do is wait for it to reach out again."

"We can enjoy her while we wait," Calynn said loud enough for Nura to hear. "She smells good too."

"Do I get a kiss too?" Triana asked, giggling.

Calynn gave Nura another kiss, giggled, and bounced over to Triana.

"Mmmmwwwwaaahhh," Calynn gave Triana an over exaggerated kiss making them both laugh.

Nura leaned forward onto Kash. He figured she was still a little nervous about being totally nude, so he just held her for a moment. His fingertips skated across her skin from her thighs to her shoulders and back down again. He loved how soft her skin felt.

"Excuse me, sir," Luna asked from behind him. "Another couple, regular customers of mine, would like to join the table. It's more than they can normally afford, but they really are a sweet couple. Would that be okay?"

"That's up to Nura," Kash replied.

Nura pulled back a little, looked at Kash, and then over his shoulder at Luna.

"It's Vom and Shuri," Luna told her.

"Oh... I guess that's okay... they're great," Nura said, smiling at Kash. "You'll like them."

Luna led the new couple in and Guy, Calynn, and Triana all rose to greet them. Nura leaned forward onto Kash, clearly nervous about the extra people. Kash laced his fingers together and dropped his hands behind her butt to give her some more coverage.

"Is that my Nura?" Vom asked.

"Hi, Vom," Nura smiled, and reached her hand over Kash's shoulder. "Hi, Miss Shuri... this is Kash... he can't get up right now."

"I'm a little preoccupied," Kash chuckled.

"Mr. Kash, I owe you the biggest debt of gratitude," Vom said as he stood beside Kash. "Not only for allowing us to join your table, but also for getting this beautiful young woman out of her clothes."

"I agree," Shuri said smiling from beside her husband.

"She is a sight to behold," Kash added. "I think her shyness adds to her charm."

"Yeah... I don't know how Luna does this so easily," Nura sounded nervous.

Vom and Shuri both had an olive hue to their skin and thick black hair. Vom was wearing a light blue suit that fit his athletic build nicely. Shuri was wearing a black leather under-bust corset, black lace panties, and black leather boots. She had an average build except for her enormous breasts spilling out from the top of her corset. Her nipples were pierced, and a gold chain connected the two piercings.

After greeting them both, Kash caught sight of Calynn. She couldn't contain her smirk, or the naughty look in her eyes. Her smirk turned into a smile as she winked at Kash.

"I feel left out, should I get naked too?" Calynn was joking, but everyone started encouraging her to do so.

"No no no," Kash chuckled. "I wouldn't be able to handle it if she was naked too. She has to stay dressed or we won't be playing any cards."

In actuality, Calynn had to stay dressed in case the AI reached out again. That way she could run off to investigate quickly without having to dress first.

They all settled in and finally started playing cards. Kash was losing more than he was winning, so he started asking Calynn for her lucky boob. The group laughed and talked, and they all had a wonderful evening. Nura eventually became more comfortable with her nakedness, thanks to Luna's prodding, and got off Kash's lap. Calynn replaced her as soon as she stood up. The two women stuck their tongues out at each other and then giggled relentlessly. Nura would "win" that argument by saying she was the one officially hired to entertain Kash for the evening.

Kash checked in with Calynn every so often throughout the evening. He would nod slightly, and she would shake her head. The damaged AI never resurfaced. Calynn didn't appear to be upset about it though. She was laughing and having a good time, especially with Nura and Luna. Calynn was attracted to Oogan women and those two were no exception.

Luna was right about Vom and Shuri. They were both a delight to be around. The girls would sometimes just chat amongst themselves, while the men told horrible jokes and played cards. Even the dealer was enjoying herself, either laughing or crinkling her nose at their jokes.

Kash would occasionally holler to be entertained, and Nura would bounce over to him giggling. She would sit on his lap, shake her butt at him, or bury his face in her chest as his entertainment. Luna got in on the action too. She would race Nura and try to sit on Kash's lap before Nura could, hugging his head into her body or putting his hands on her boobs and squeezing. Everyone was smiling and laughing at the antics of the best friends.

Luna was definitely more free with her body than Nura was, and Calynn took full advantage of that. Luna had her hands inside Calynn's dress often, and Calynn groped every inch of Luna. If Guy or Vom wanted entertainment, Luna would bounce right over to them. Whereas Kash was the only man that Nura let touch her.

By the end of the night, Kash managed to win enough to get back to even and cover the cost of the room. Vom and Shuri were up a fair amount, and Guy was up even more. Overall, a good night. A night that felt like being on vacation... besides Calynn getting a little sidetracked... it was a great night.

"I had a wonderful time tonight," Kash told Nura, pulling her onto his lap again. "Thanks for entertaining me."

"Oh, I'm not done with you yet," Nura smiled. "I was expecting the full Princess treatment when we got back to your suite."

"I'm game," Calynn said, running her hand down Nura's chest.

"And what if I don't remember everything I did with Princess Aja?" Kash smirked.

"Just make it up as you go," Nura replied, kissing Kash. "I promise not to compare notes."

A FLICKER OF CHAOS

Kash woke up to a repetitive thumping sound. He rubbed the sleep out of his eyes to see what was making the sound. Nura was stirring too, so Kash knew it wasn't just him who heard it. The sound stopped before he could try to identify the source.

"Did you hear that?" Calynn asked from the door of the bedroom. "Those thumps?"

"Kinda," Kash replied. "Any idea what it was?"

"No clue."

"I've never heard that sound before," Nura added, yawning.

"Never?" Calynn asked.

"Not that I remember," Nura responded, rolling over to half lay on Kash. "And I have lived here for three years, but I'm sure maintenance will figure it out."

"And as luck would have it, that's their job and not ours, so we don't have to help figure it out," Kash said, hugging Nura and caressing her naked body. "We're on vacation... remember?"

"I'm not," Nura groaned. "I think I have to work tonight."

"What?" Kash smirked. "You're leaving me?"

"I don't want to," Nura whined. "I'd rather stay here."

"I can get some rope so we can tie her up," Calynn offered.

"Ugh," Kash groaned. "I had more than my fill of that crap last night. No ropes, no whips, no chains with angry little clamps... I'll just lay on her."

Kash rolled over onto Nura pinning her beneath his much bigger frame. She wiggled her legs out from beneath his, wrapped them around his waist, and squeezed as hard as she could. After a second or two she stopped and burst out laughing.

"Was that fighting back or holding on?" Kash chuckled.

"Both," Nura laughed.

The lights in the suite suddenly went black, and Kash felt Nura's body tense. He lifted himself up and tried to look around in the dark. The only light in the room was what little was peeking through the window behind the curtains.

"That wasn't me," Calynn offered before anyone could ask. "First the thumping and now this... I'm going to call someone and see what's up."

"Okay, well... I might as well get some more rest since it's dark," Kash said rolling off of Nura. "You two wore me out last night."

"More rest?" Nura giggled.

"Am I not allowed to rest?"

"I can think of something better to do in the dark," Nura cooed as she mounted Kash. "But you can rest... I'll do all the work."

The next time Kash woke up, he was alone in bed. It had to be mid-to-late morning because he was starving. He jumped out of bed and went to the bathroom to relieve himself and get dressed. He walked out to the living area and saw Calynn and Nura sitting on the sofa together chatting. He kissed both of their heads and wandered out to the kitchen to grab a bite to eat.

"We already made you a plate," Calynn told him.

"Just hit start on the reheater," Nura added.

Kash did as she said, and moments later sat down to eat his breakfast. The pancakes had berries of some sort in them and Kash found them delicious. The girls came out to the kitchen to sit and chat while he ate.

"So, the thumping sound and the power outage was just a fried power converter," Calynn explained. "They claim that it was relatively new and shouldn't have failed, so it must have just been a faulty part."

"It happens," Kash said, between bites. "You can't expect every piece of every machine being mass produced to be perfect."

"I suppose," Calynn agreed.

"We're still on vacation, so it's still not our job to look into it," Kash continued, pointing his fork at her. "On vacation."

"I wasn't gonna," Calynn smirked.

"Are you sure?" Kash chuckled.

Calynn stuck her tongue out at Kash and then giggled.

Nura was grinning too.

The trio hung out on the couch after they ate. Nura was very clingy while they sat and chatted. If she wasn't in physical contact with Kash, she was holding Calynn. She had to leave them soon to go to work and clearly didn't want to go. The closer it got to the time she had to leave, the more clingy she got. She hugged Kash and Calynn three times each before she finally left.

"I like her," Calynn smiled. "Did she make you happy?"

"No... not really."

"What?"

"What what?" Kash asked as he flopped back down on the couch.

"She didn't make you happy?" Calynn asked, her tone told him she didn't believe him.

"She was a lot of fun, and I enjoyed her company, yes," Kash replied and then gave Calynn a sly smile. "But there's only one woman that truly makes me happy."

"Is that so," Calynn replied, laying down on the couch, facing him. "And which woman is that?"

"She's got pretty blonde hair," Kash said as he ran his fingers through her hair. "A pretty smile... kind eyes... and she loves to cuddle."

Calynn snuggled into him so her head was just below his chin. Her leg slid over his, and her arm wrapped around his waist. Kash wrapped her in his arms and kissed the top of her head.

"Oh, look," Kash whispered, squeezing her tight. "I found her."

Calynn snuggled into him and hummed her approval as he kissed her head.

"I would like to see Nura again," Calynn muttered into his chest. "If that's okay with you?"

"If you're okay, I'm okay."

Calynn pulled back and looked up at him waiting for him to say more. She never said anything. She just waited for him to elaborate... and cocked her head at him when he didn't do so soon enough.

"Okay... I just want you to be happy, and if it makes you happy to watch me do naughty things to Nura then let's do that," Kash relented. "But only if it's what you want."

"It reminds me of watching you and Omia together," Calynn smiled softly. "I think that's why I like watching so much, and I really like girls, especially Oogan girls."

"Hey," Guy's voice came from his side of the room. "You guys decent?"

"Yep," Kash replied, happy for the distraction.

"We're making reservations for that fancy ass restaurant for tonight," Guy informed them as he approached. "You guys in?"

"Do I get to play dress up again?" Calynn giggled.

"Yeah, we're in," Kash chuckled. "Just give us time for a nap first."

"Good plan," Calynn agreed.

After a quick nap, they grabbed showers and got dressed for dinner. Calynn, at Kash's request, wore the blue dress again. He vowed to stay sober enough to appreciate how amazing she looked in it all night long. Kash donned a black three-piece suit, but he chose to forgo the tie. Triana was wearing a sequined red dress that sparkled nearly as much as the pixie's smile. Guy was wearing a gray two piece with a tie that matched Triana's red dress.

The restaurant was dimly lit, with actual wax candles glowing on some of the tables. Most places used fake, electronic candles now. Kash hadn't seen real ones in years.

There were roughly thirty tables in the room. Most sat two people, but some were built for four, six, or even eight. The maître d' sat them at their table, and they ordered a bottle of wine. The appetizer was a delicate seafood salsa on buttery crackers, and their salads were fresh, crisp, and delectable.

Kash couldn't keep his eyes off his beautiful companion. Calynn looked absolutely stunning. His hand was almost always on her lap or on her back resting on the back of her chair. It didn't matter where, as long as he was touching her. He was lost in her eyes...

... until the room went dark.

A silence hung in the air as everyone realized that the main lights were out. Thankfully some of the tables, including theirs, had real candles... so the room wasn't pitch black, but it was close. A dozen or so small flames weren't enough to light such a large space.

Panicked murmurs soon swelled around them.

Guy was the first to react.

"Everyone just stay calm," Guy bellowed as he stood on his chair. "If we all just remain seated and wait patiently, I'm sure the lights will..."

"Who put you in charge?" a panicked man interrupted.

"Nobody," Guy replied calmly. "I'm just trying to be helpful."

"Well... we don't need your help," the man continued.

They couldn't really see the man, but they heard the commotion he made when he tried to stand up.

"We're leaving," the man barked at his companion.

"Sir, please," Guy tried to reason with the man. "We don't know how far the darkness spreads. You could be injured if you try to leave."

The sound of dishes crashing to the floor filled the room as Guy's prophecy apparently came true. Kash heard the thud of the man landing on the floor, causing others to start panicking more.

"People... people, please!" Guy hollered, he illuminated himself with a light from his watch. "Look... I'm not trying to be bossy or anything, but I'm former military and have experience in this exact situation... we were aboard a cruiser that lost all power with a delegation on board... the initial panic was nearly disastrous, but once everyone calmed down... things went a lot smoother. Trust me... if we stay calm, cool, and collected it will be much better."

Guy's story and calm delivery seemed to soothe the people in the restaurant. Kash couldn't see many faces, but those he could see were focused on Guy.

"Sir... are you okay?" Guy asked calmly.

"I think so," the man answered.

"Okay... are there any more candles?" Guy asked, remaining calm.

"On a shelf behind the host stand," a woman's voice said.

"Can someone make it there safely?" Guy asked. "If we get a candle or two per table, I think it will help keep people calm."

"No!" someone in the dark shouted. "We have to preserve our air. The candles burn oxygen."

"We have plenty of air," Guy announced. "The volume of this room alone would last us nearly half a day. The kitchen adds more, as does the hallway outside. Panic is our only enemy at the moment."

"It would be better if it wasn't so dark," a woman said shakily.

"Indeed, it would," Guy continued in his comforting tone. "Can someone please get the candles?"

A candle moved through the darkness, disappeared behind something for a moment, and then returned. New candles started to light from the flame of the first and were passed around the room. The warm glow of the flickering flames softly lit the faces of each table. The faces that they could see were all looking at Guy for guidance.

"There... now with a little more light it's not so bad, right?" Guy said in a comforting tone. "I'm sure the maintenance guys are already hard at work fixing whatever the problem is. We just need to be a little patient."

"What happened on your ship... from before?" a woman asked. "Maybe a story will help pass the time."

"Well... as I said before, we were on a diplomatic mission with the delegation from Topor on board. We were heading to Ghehia Prime to negotiate a peace deal," Guy explained. "We had just disengaged the Hyper-Lumic drive and returned to normal space when the ship suddenly went dark. We were lucky the ship didn't go dark while the HLD was still engaged. That could have ended badly, but anyway... several members of the delegation panicked, and we had to use some force to get everyone to calm down. They weren't as smart as you lovely people... once we had everyone calmed down, we searched the ship for the source of the power outage. It turned out that one of the members of the delegation was not who he said he was. He sabotaged the ship..."

"Which I'm sure isn't the case here," Calynn interrupted.

"A very good point," Guy chuckled. "There was no sabotage here... but anyway... we found the power coupling that was disabled, repaired the ship, and arrested the..."

Guy was interrupted by the gasps of the patrons when the power for the casino was restored. Everyone was looking around at each other smiling, delighted that the lights were back on.

"See," Guy said getting down from his chair. "That wasn't so bad."

Some of the people started to clap gently in appreciation. The applause grew slowly and a few of the people approached Guy to shake his hand. Guy smiled graciously, shook the hands of those that came up to him, and gave little waves to the rest of the people.

The applause died off when some security personnel entered the dining room escorting some maintenance workers. Among them was Victor Morel. Kash noticed that Victor noticed him and nodded in their direction to one of his men.

"I get the distinct impression that Gravitas is going to want to speak to me again," Kash said to the group. "That's his head of security… and he just nodded at me."

"Why?" Guy asked.

"He probably thinks I'm involved in whatever the hell just happened," Kash groaned.

"I'm going with you this time," Calynn asserted. "You're not disappearing on me for another half a day."

"Yes, dear," Kash conceded, smiling at her. "Whatever you say, dear."

Kash finished his glass of wine and waited for Victor to approach. He didn't have to wait long.

"Mr. Kash," Victor said as he approached. "How was your meal?"

"Actually, we've only had the first two courses so far," Kash smiled. "The main course would have been here shortly if not for the power outage. What caused that by the way? Any ideas yet?"

Kash decided to be very straight forward with Victor to get ahead of any accusations. He wasn't going to give Victor an opportunity to turn it on him.

"We are still investigating that."

"Was it just another localized event like the outage this morning?"

Mr. Morel looked annoyed at Kash's questions. He wanted to be the one asking questions, not the other way around.

"Yes," Victor grumbled. "Just a localized phenomenon."

"Do you think it has anything to do with what I told Gravitas about yesterday?" Kash smirked.

Victor clenched his jaw and pressed his lips into a thin line. He was clearly getting upset with Kash but couldn't necessarily do anything about it without upsetting the other guests.

"It just might," Victor growled.

"Well, I suppose we can go and see if there's any help we can offer," Kash explained as he stood, buttoning his jacket, and offering his hand to Calynn. "Come, my dear, let's go and see if we can be helpful."

"As you wish, beloved," Calynn replied using his offered hand to stand up.

"Check please," Guy said as he stood also and offered Triana his hand.

"It's on the house, sir," their server said nervously. "For your help during the blackout."

"That's very kind of you," Guy smiled. "Thank you."

"No... thank you," the young man smiled.

"Lead on, Mr. Morel," Kash smiled at Victor.

"Enjoy your dinners, everyone," Guy announced, smiling at the other guests.

More applause swelled for the group as they exited the dining room. They smiled and waved graciously, much to Victor's chagrin.

"What was that about?" Victor asked gruffly after they exited the restaurant.

"My man stood up and helped keep everyone calm during the blackout," Triana boasted. "They were showing him their appreciation."

Victor didn't seem impressed. He and the other security personnel surrounded the four friends like they were criminals while they led them toward Gravitas' office. Calynn was walking beside Kash with both of her hands on his elbow. She had laced her fingers together to hold onto his offered arm. When they had to make their way through a crowd, Kash wrapped his arm around her waist.

"You're being awful possessive," Calynn smiled softly.

"You started it," Kash smiled back.

"I'll finish it, too," Calynn said, hugging his arm to her body.

Kash noted that the guards at the office entrance were different than they were yesterday, but it was the same receptionist. He smiled and nodded at her as Victor led them past her.

Gravitas was not in his office when they got there. Victor told them to have a seat and wait. He left two guards to watch over them and left.

"Only two chairs," Kash smirked at Calynn. "I guess you'll have to sit on my lap."

Kash sat down and waited for Calynn to adjust her dress before helping her sit down slowly. She sat upright instead of leaning back against him, so she didn't crush the gathers that she had pulled up slightly so as not to sit upon them. Guy sat in the chair beside him and pulled the ever bouncy Triana down onto his lap. Triana giggled.

"I was looking forward to that seafood and pasta dish," Guy sighed.

"With the lemon butter and capers," Kash agreed. "That sounded delicious."

"We need to buy a case of that wine," Triana smiled. "That stuff was so good."

"We need a couple hourns at the tables for that," Kash laughed. "Did you see the price per bottle?"

"No, but it makes my clothes fall off," Triana giggled.

"Then it's worth every last credit," Guy replied, pulling her tight.

"What about you, beloved," Kash smiled at Calynn. "Would that wine make your clothes fall off?"

"A glass of water makes my clothes fall off," Calynn smirked. "As long as you're in the room with me."

Kash's hand landed on her thigh, and he caressed her gently. Her hand found his and she laced her fingers through his, pulling his hand higher onto her thigh. Kash tapped her on the back when he heard the hum of Gravitas' anti-gravity device. She sat up straighter in anticipation of the big man's arrival.

Gravitas had the two Oogan women with him when he entered his office. His breathing sounded labored like he had just been exercising... or doing another strenuous activity. He brought both women to his chair behind his desk and had one sit on each of his massive legs. His grin was as creepy as it was hedonistic, and his greedy eyes were locked onto Calynn. To her credit, she didn't squirm or break her posture even the slightest bit.

"If you're just going to sit there staring at my tits, I can take off the dress," Calynn broke the silence with her wit. "But if you drool on me, I'll rip your fucking face off."

"Well, don't you have a sharp tongue," Gravitas bellowed, his smile fading. "You should learn some manners."

"Manners?" Calynn bantered. "Like how it isn't polite to stare... those kinds of manners?"

"I do as I please," the big man grumbled.

"As do I," Calynn countered. "To include telling perverts, such as yourself, to stop staring at my tits. If you had any manners, you'd apologize to me... or just stare at their tits instead. Isn't that why you make them stay naked?"

Gravitas looked at Kash and clenched his jaw. Kash could tell he was getting angry.

"Don't look at me," Kash added. "If I was you... I'd apologize. You do not want to see her angry."

"Only after you apologize for planning a heist of my casino," Gravitas growled, baring his teeth.

"How many times do I have to tell you that I am not robbing you," Kash growled back. "That if I was robbing you... you'd never fucking know I was here!"

"What happened to the power today?"

"How the fuck would I know?"

"Damn it, Kash!" Gravitas yelled and banged his fist on the desk. "What are you planning?"

Gravitas then swiped his massive arm to the side and launched one of the women on his lap across the room. She whimpered softly when she hit the floor and tumbled into the wall. Calynn immediately bounced off Kash's lap with Triana on her heels as they moved to aid the poor woman. Kash looked back at the other woman still on his lap. Her eyes were huge, and her face was pale. She was clearly terrified.

"How about you two bring it down a notch," Guy said firmly, yet respectfully.

"Who do you think you are to tell me what to do?" Gravitas growled at Guy.

"Commander Liezdt from the Battle of Topor," Guy announced with authority, pointing at the big man. "I'm fucking famous. Who the hell are you?"

Gravitas actually paused when Guy told him who he was. He recognized the name, but Kash wasn't sure if that was a good or bad thing. Would he revere Guy, or want to buy him? Kash had no idea.

"That is a name that I have not heard in a very long time" Gravitas uttered. "It's merely whispered in only the most... prestigious circles."

Kash rolled his eyes at Gravitas. He knew exactly where this was going. He leaned closer to Guy.

"A million credits says he wants to buy your swarm ships," Kash said to Guy.

"Not for sale at any price," Guy told Gravitas firmly.

"You haven't even heard my offer," Gravitas grinned his creepy grin.

"Not for sale," Guy repeated. "Not today. Not tomorrow. Not ever... and that's final."

"Nothing is ever... final," Gravitas smirked.

"Oh, I can think of a few things that are final," Calynn growled, approaching Gravitas. "For instance, if you ever hit a woman like that in my presence again... it will be the final thing you do."

Gravitas clenched his jaw and glared at Calynn. The girl on his lap seemed to sense his anger rising and scurried off his leg. She pressed herself against the wall, eyes wide and trembling. The big man spun in his chair like he was going to lash at Calynn.

"Do it," Calynn continued, as she drew nearer to the man. "It'll be the final thing you ever do."

Kash and Guy jumped up to get between Calynn and the approaching security guards. The situation was spiraling out of control, and Kash wasn't sure how to pull it back from the brink.

"Not wise to turn your back on me, Kash," Gravitas bellowed.

"Oh, I don't have to worry about her," Kash chuckled. "She won't kill you. Just teach you a lesson."

"Teach me a lesson?" the big man laughed. "A mere girl?"

"We're both enhanced, you idiot," Kash chuckled, searching for an opportunity to end the standoff. "She can take out three sentinels at once. Your ass doesn't stand a chance."

"Wanna go a few rounds? " Calynn's words dripped with wit and sarcasm.

BANG

Calynn's fist landed on Gravitas' desk with such force that even Kash jumped a little. Kash watched as the eyes of the security personnel darted around the room. They weren't sure what to do, and their boss wasn't giving any leadership.

"Can we all stop and get this poor girl some medical help?" Triana pleaded, breaking the silent tension. "She has a broken rib."

"No, not a rib," Kash said as he turned his back on the guards. "That hurts like hell."

The Oogan woman on the ground was holding her left side where Gravitas had struck her. She grimaced with each shallow breath, and tears ran down her cheeks. Kash moved quickly to her side, knelt down, and placed his hand on the woman's shoulder to try and comfort her.

"It hurts," the woman cried.

"I know it does," he smiled softly. "Just try to stay still."

Kash stood back up to face the security personnel. He wanted to snap and scream at them or beat the shit out of them, but... he thought it would be better to keep a cooler head. He decided to shame them instead.

"So, none of you can see the crying woman on the ground and call a doctor?" Kash mocked.

The two men turned and looked at Gravitas.

"Oh, for fuck's sake, you don't need his permission to get a fucking doctor," Kash griped. "Just go!"

"I promise not to beat up your boss while you're gone," Calynn said sarcastically, and then approached the other Oogan woman. "Come on, sweetie… let's get you out of swinging range so I don't have to break that promise."

"Fuck it, I'll go," Guy snapped, marching out of the office past the guards.

The woman reluctantly walked with Calynn, but Kash could tell she was every bit as scared of them as she was of Gravitas. Kash's eyes went to the splintered wood on the corner of Gravitas' desk where Calynn had displayed her power, and then back to the woman walking toward him with Calynn. Her eyes were darting around, and her breathing was rapid and shallow. She was nearly in a full panic.

"Triana my dear," Kash said as soft and reassuringly as he could. "Can you please help calm the other woman down while I tend to your patient… she's very much afraid of Calynn and me."

As Trie stood, Kash knelt down and placed his hand on the woman's shoulder again.

"I didn't mean to scare you," Calynn apologized.

"I got her," Triana said.

Kash wasn't paying much attention to the others. He was concerned with his own patient.

"Is there anything I can do until the doctor gets here?" Kash asked her.

The woman shook her head and grimaced again.

"Can I see?"

The woman barely hesitated. She removed her hand so Kash could see the bruise that had already formed. He replaced her hand with his and slowly moved it around the area. She winced when he felt an irregular bulge in her rib cage.

"Sorry," Kash apologized as her hand landed on his.

"What were you doing at the restaurant?" Gravitas suddenly asked in a gruff tone.

"Eating," Kash replied, feeling along the woman's rib. "What else do you do in a restaurant while on vacation?"

"And what would that matter?" Calynn added.

"Because the two power outages today were centered around your location!" the big man barked.

"What's that supposed to mean?" Calynn asked.

"The outage this morning was centered around your suite," Gravitas told them. "So, when Victor saw you in the restaurant..."

"He assumed we did it?" Kash interrupted. "Not that the blackouts were targeting us?"

Kash's fingers delicately followed the rib.

"Targeting you?" Gravitas bellowed. "What do you mean?"

"I have good news," Kash said softly to his patient. "Your rib is just misaligned and not broken... I can put it back in place, but it's gonna hurt."

The woman looked at him with wide eyes and her brow raised.

"It will feel better after... I promise."

Her eyes showed her worry and her lips quivered. She moved her hand to Kash's wrist, grabbed it firmly, and then gave him a little nod. Kash adjusted his fingers slightly and then quickly pushed the rib back into place with precise, firm pressure.

"Ahhh," the woman cried out and then gasped for breath.

The look on her face was priceless when she realized she could breathe without it hurting so much. Kash smiled softly and helped the woman sit up, before turning to Gravitas.

"Yes... targeting us," Kash finally answered the big man. "Perhaps they know that I told you about them and are targeting me to get me out of the way... did you ever think of that?"

"And if that's the case," Calynn added in a snarky tone. "How are you going to protect us moving forward?"

"Protect you?" Gravitas laughed. "Why would I protect a thief?"

"Come on... let's get you to a chair," Kash smiled to the woman on the floor. "Take it easy... that's going to hurt for a while."

Kash helped get the woman to her feet and placed one of his hands on her hip and the other on her opposite arm to steady her as she walked to the chair.

"I love being ignored while you fondle one of my girls," Gravitas sneered.

"Don't abuse your girls and we wouldn't have to fondle them," Calynn quipped.

"I'm going to beat that sharp tongue out of you, girl," Gravitas growled.

"Nothing between us but air and opportunity," Calynn growled back, taking a step forward.

"That's enough, Baby Girl," Kash said firmly. "We are still his guests... even if he exhibits bad manners that doesn't mean we should reciprocate them."

"I'm showing bad manners?" Gravitas argued fiercely.

"You still haven't apologized for staring at her, you've threatened her, and you struck a defenseless woman barely the size of your big fat fucking arm for no fucking reason!" Kash scolded the man. "That's the very epitome of bad manners, and I'm going to tell everyone that will listen how poorly you've behaved!"

Kash attacked the one thing he knew was a soft spot for Gravitas... his reputation.

"I'll be sure to email the Admiral as soon..." Kash tried to continue.

"There's no need for that," Gravitas interrupted, grinning his sinister grin, he looked at Calynn. "I apologize for staring at your luscious body... as for my egregious verbal and physical acts... I was distressed and out of character due to the recent attacks on my casino... I know this is no excuse, but I'm deeply sorry for my behavior."

"He called me luscious," Calynn smiled. "Have you ever called me luscious? That sounds so sexy... luscious."

"And you say I inject inappropriate humor into situations," Kash chuckled.

"It's like flipping a switch with both of you," Triana added with a smirk.

"Well... if this young lady accepts your apology then I suppose we can too," Kash said, motioning to the woman with the bruised rib.

"I can apologize to both of my girls properly later," Gravitas practically drooled.

The woman looked at Kash and nodded. She didn't look happy about it, but she wasn't scared or mad either. He figured this was probably her norm... minus the bruised rib he hoped.

"Fine," Kash conceded. "So anyway... I think we need a protection detail. Nothing big, just one or two men to watch from a distance."

"I'm still not convinced it wasn't you that caused the blackouts," Gravitas argued. "It's too much of a coincidence."

"I'm almost getting tired of telling you this, but I am on vacation," Kash sighed.

"Your reputation precedes you."

"Yes, my reputation in acquisitions," Kash argued. "I get paid to take things, and nobody is paying me right now... nobody."

"Technically, he is," Guy chuckled, pointing at Gravitas as he entered the room. "Or more accurately, his table games are."

"Okay... you're not wrong there," Kash chuckled.

"We don't have to steal from you, Gravitas," Guy added. "We are doing just fine by simply winning all of your credits."

"Again... he's not wrong," Kash stated. "But if the people I told you about yesterday are bold enough to cause blackouts to target me, you better be taking them seriously. That's a pretty brazen attack."

"It is being... handled," Gravitas grumbled.

"Handled?"

"Mr. Morel is on it," Gravitas grinned. "I can assure you."

"Good... I don't suppose you'd let me carry a weapon to protect us from..."

"Absolutely not!" Gravitas interrupted.

"Fine," Kash sighed. "Come on, gang... let's go."

Calynn took Kash's offered hand, and he led them out of Gravitas' office. He smiled at Calynn, and she smiled back, and then he chuckled. Calynn's brow furrowed asking him the question she didn't need words to ask.

"Although," Kash hollered without looking back. "It would be quite the news story if I were to be killed while at your casino... epic bad press... just saying."

THE VOICE RETURNS

Kash didn't want to go back to their room. He was fired up from the meeting with Gravitas. He wanted a stiff drink and to do some gambling.

"I'm all wound up. Where's Nura working?" Kash asked. "Maybe if she's serving the drinks while we play, I can forget about that pompous asshole and get back to our vacation."

"That sounds like a good plan," Calynn replied. "We can check where we met her."

"Can we eat too?" Guy asked. "We never got our main courses."

"There she is," Kash said, noticing Nura. "Let's ask."

Nura saw the group coming and stopped to smile at them. She was in her tiny sparkling uniform and looked fantastic. She must have gotten in a workout before her shift, because she was flaunting washboard abs.

"Hi, gorgeous," Kash smiled at the beauty.

"Hi back," Nura beamed a smile and popped up on her toes.

Nura's hand landed on his belt which she used to help pull herself up for kiss. Kash obliged her, giving her a peck on the lips. His hands landed on her hips, and he took the opportunity to let his fingers dance across her soft skin.

"Move," Calynn giggled pushing Kash out of the way. "It's my turn."

Calynn moved in and gave Nura a big kiss and they both giggled.

"What are you guys doing here?" Nura asked with a smile. "Did you come to make my night better?"

"We were hoping you could make our night better," Kash smiled back. "But can we get some food first?"

"You sure can," the beauty replied. "Right this way... I'll take you to a table."

Nura led them to a row of barstools at a long narrow table near one of the Greeli tables. She brought them menus with some surprisingly good fare. Kash was expecting the menu to just have finger food and sandwiches, but there were steaks, and roasts, and pasta dishes too. Kash ordered a broiled seafood platter with harvest vegetables for him and Calynn to share.

They watched the other guests play while waiting for their food. Nura made sure to steal a bite from Kash's fish when she brought them their food, and everyone laughed. The friends enjoyed their meals and cocktails, before Kash and Guy handed Nura their player cards for her to go get them some chips. She returned with two security guards and a cart full of chips.

Kash took a seat near the middle of the Greeli table and waited for Nura to stack his chips for him. He laid his hand on her calf since she was standing so close while she stacked his chips. Nura was certain to brush her body against his arm repeatedly and would apologize for doing so with a flirtatious smile. He slid his hand up her leg onto her thigh to see if he could make her blush, but she never flinched and continued to smile. Kash wanted nothing more than to whisk her away back to his suite and have his way with her again.

"Place your bets," the croupier announced, taking Kash's attention away from Nura.

"Good luck, sir," Nura smiled softly.

"Thanks, beautiful," Kash smiled back.

Kash was just that... lucky. His magic touch from the other night continued and his pile of chips quickly tripled in size. Guy suggested that it was Calynn's blue dress and insisted that she had to wear it for the rest of their vacation. Kash wasn't a superstitious man, but he agreed that Calynn should wear that dress more often. She was rather sexy in it, and Kash couldn't keep his eyes or hands off of her.

Nura would brush her body against him every time she brought him a drink. When Calynn sat beside him, Nura would have to lean over him when she brought a drink, intentionally pressing her body into his. Kash told her to bring him two glasses of juice in between each glass of bourbon so he could stay relatively sober. He tipped her a million credits for every round of drinks she brought to the table. Some of the other players also tried to gain Nura's favor with hefty tips, but she only had eyes for Kash.

"I want to keep her," Calynn whispered in his ear when they were both staring at Nura. "Can we keep her?"

"And buy her a gown that matches yours," Kash whispered back.

"You'd have twice as much luck then."

"I'm not sure I can handle that much luck."

"Oh, I think you can," Calynn smiled.

"Should we extend our vacation and have her take some leave?"

"I'd rather buy her out and keep her."

"Whoa..." Kash drew closer so her could whisper directly in her ear. "I'm not sure I trust her with you yet."

Calynn turned and smiled at him. She placed her hand on his cheek and gave him a soft kiss on the lips.

"Do you have any idea how sexy it is when you get this protective of me?"

"Not as sexy as you in that dress," Kash smirked.

"I disagree," Calynn smirked back. "It's definitely much sexier than me in this dress."

"Not possible... have you seen you?" Kash smiled. "Because everyone else in the casino has."

"Still sexier," Calynn smiled, her eyes smoldering.

"I know that look."

"What look?" Calynn said, moving closer. "Am I not allowed to look..."

Calynn stopped mid-sentence and her body froze. When her head twitched a little, Kash knew immediately what was going on. The AI was back in range, and Calynn was trying to connect with it. He knew she would want to pursue it again, so he waved Nura over and turned to Guy and Triana.

"She has that feeling again," Kash whispered. "We have to go."

"We're coming too," Guy replied.

"Agreed," Triana added. "We're better as a team."

"Yes, sir," Nura smiled as she approached.

"We have to run," Kash told Nura urgently. "Please cash us out, keep some for yourself, and we'll be back for our player cards."

"Yes, sir," Nura replied with some worry in her voice. "Is... is everything okay?"

"It will be," Kash smiled softly.

Nura looked at Calynn and seemed to understand.

"I hope she finds the person in trouble," Nura said with a soft smile.

Guy and Kash handed Nura their cards, and the four friends left the Greeli table following Calynn through the casino. She zigzagged through the gaming tables and pods of slot machines. Calynn was suffering from the tics again. Her head would jerk now and then, and she was looking all over the place. The AI led them to some rooms with concierges and bouncers at the entrances.

"Whoa," Kash told Calynn grabbing her arm.

"I can really feel it here," Calynn explained. "We should keep going."

"Just... give me a moment," Kash told her.

"Okay... but please hurry. I don't want to lose it again."

Kash approached one of the rooms and the two men standing in front of it. One of the men wore a blue and black security uniform and the other wore a sparkled uniform that kind of matched Nura's. The man's uniform was a blue and red vest over a black silk shirt instead of Nura's pink and purple micro-outfit. The man in the sparkles smiled at him as he approached.

"Good evening, sir," the man said cordially. "How can we help you?"

"Just curious," Kash replied, smiling. "What are these rooms?"

"VIP rooms," the man replied. "These tables have higher stakes and no limits for wagering for our more discerning clientèle."

"Interesting... is there a minimum like the private rooms downstairs?"

"Hey, Kash," Guy interrupted.

Kash turned and looked at Guy. Guy shook his head slightly and nodded at Calynn who was hunched over like she was crying.

"Forgive me," Kash said to the man and quickly moved to Calynn.

"Why do I keep losing it?" Calynn sobbed, wrapping Kash in a hug.

"It's okay, Baby Girl," Kash tried to comfort her. "What can we do to help?"

"Wait," Calynn suddenly pushed herself back from his embrace. "No... it's just really far away now."

"How can it be really close one second and then really far away the next?" Triana asked. "Is it moving through the wiring somehow?"

"Maybe it's just echoes," Guy offered. "Like she can't sense the source..."

"Just the reflection," Triana finished his thought.

"That would make sense with how it jumps around," Guy continued. "It's just a theory though."

"Okay," Kash said. "How do we test that theory?"

"We find an observation point and see what happens," Guy explained. "I'm thinking somewhere near the middle of the casino so she can hopefully track the thing, but I don't really know. I'm just going at it like I would for a military op, and step one is always to observe... maybe she can't see the forest through the trees and taking a step back will help. What do you guys think?"

"I agree," Triana nodded with a smile. "I think we should try that."

"It's gotta be better than chasing around a ghost," Kash sighed. "What do you think, Baby Girl?"

"I'll try anything," Calynn said softly. "We have to help him... we have to."

"Well," Guy said looking around. "We're on the middle floor of the actual casino..."

Guy stood up tall and looked around for a second trying to calculate where the center of the casino was. Kash did too since he was a little taller than Guy. The two men quickly came to the same conclusion.

"How do you feel about playing slot machines?" Guy continued.

"We need our cards back from Nura first," Kash explained. "Come on."

Kash led them back the way they came until he saw Nura. When she saw him, she set her tray down, pulled their player cards out of her top, and smiled while presenting them to him.

"Thanks, beautiful," Kash smiled back grabbing the cards. "We'll be just over here at the slot machines for now."

"Okay, I'll come check on you in a few," Nura replied, picking up her tray again.

The slot machines they were going to were laid out like a target. The machines were back-to-back in rings instead of clustered into pods like the rest of the casino. The inside of the center ring a mere five or six meters wide. They were also the most expensive machines at ten thousand credits per spin.

Kash led Calynn to one of the machines and sat her in front of it. He stood behind her and rested one hand on her shoulder while inserting his player card into the machine. Triana and Guy sat on either side of her.

"Try not to get fixated on it," Kash told Calynn. "We're trying to cast a wide net."

"I'll try," Calynn replied.

"By the Gods," Guy complained from beside him. "Three hundred thousand credits to play all lines per spin!"

"Hit the button slowly," Kash chuckled.

"She has the..." Guy started to say.

DING DING WHOOOP DING DING DING

Triana was grinning ear to ear, bouncing, and clapping as her machine started flashing a celebration of her winnings.

"What did you do?" Guy asked, moving behind Triana.

"I won six hundred grand," Triana giggled.

"Well, do it again," Guy urged with a chuckle.

Kash turned his attention back to Calynn and to his machine. He hit the play all button and leaned in close, wrapping his arm around her so his forearm was sitting just below her collarbones. He lost a million credits with three pushes of the button.

"I need a map or something so I can track these echoes," Calynn sighed. "If that's what they are."

"I can get you a map from information," Nura offered.

Kash hadn't seen her approach, but she was always a welcome sight. Her tray was empty and tucked under one arm and she was beaming a smile at them.

"Is there anything else you need?" Nura continued.

"A hug would be nice," Calynn replied, spinning the chair around.

Nura set her tray down, squeezed herself in between Kash and Calynn, and leaned over so she could give Calynn a hug. Kash didn't move at first, since Nura's butt was pressed against his thighs, but when the hug lasted for more than a few seconds he knew should let Nura comfort Calynn and backed up slightly.

"You're shaking," Nura said to Calynn.

"These feelings I'm getting from... whoever... are kinda disturbing," Calynn admitted.

"I wish I understood what you're going through," Nura said in a comforting tone.

"You'd have to come live with us for me to explain," Calynn replied. "That's reserved for our inner circle of friends and lovers."

Nura's body tensed some when Calynn mentioned living with them. Kash placed a reassuring hand on the small of her back to steady her.

"Oh... umm," Nura stammered. "I don't know..."

"That wasn't an offer," Calynn interrupted and then looked at Nura and smiled. "Not yet anyway."

"We have to get to know each other a bit more first," Kash added and chuckled. "And she says that I'm too forward."

"I have enjoyed getting to know you both," Nura smiled.

"But... you're not ready for that," Kash added.

"I don't know," Nura feigned a smile. "There's a lot to think about."

"Go get the map, my dear," Kash said, patting Nura on the butt. "We can talk about the rest later."

Nura trotted off and returned in short order with a brochure of the casino unfolded showing an exaggerated layout of the floor. Calynn accepted the map and placed it on her lap with her right hand hovering above it. She stared off into space like she was in a trance, and her hand started to wander around the map, poking at the different tables. Kash watched carefully, searching for a pattern.

"Is there anything I can help with?" Nura asked, placing her hand on Kash's hip.

"Not at the moment," Kash replied, but he didn't glance over at Nura.

He wrapped his arm around her waist and caressed her extremely soft skin. Nura leaned into him, tucking her fingers in his waistband.

"Can I see you later?" Nura asked.

"I do hope so," Kash replied, still watching Calynn's fingers. "Guys, I think she was right... it moves in waves away from the VIP rooms... look."

"What moves in waves?" Nura asked, leaning in closer.

"Her..." Kash paused and looked at Nura, deciding how much trust to give her. "Her bad feeling. I wish I could tell you more, but... I can't... not here."

"I understand," Nura said softly.

Kash pulled her over in front of him and kissed the top of her head. His hands found her toned stomach, and her hands landed on his. Nura leaned back into

Kash and watched Calynn's fingers move across the map with him. Kash held her tight with one hand and let the other one skim across her skin.

"I'm glad you're here," Kash said to Nura as he pulled her a little tighter, "but I don't want to get you in trouble by monopolizing your time."

"It's okay," Nura replied. "I'm on break."

"Oh, good," Kash replied and kissed the top of her head again.

"I think you're right," Nura said pointing at the map. "It's coming from the Parlor... that door there... it's like a mini casino inside the casino. VIPs only... of course."

"What do we need to get in?" Guy asked.

"An invitation," Nura replied. "It's like the room downstairs... you need your own server and such, but this one they stay clothed."

"Can you..."

"No," Nura interrupted Kash, looking up at him smiling. "But Luna can."

"Is she working?" Kash asked.

"I'll go get her," Nura smiled.

Nura bounced off leaving the four friends alone. Kash couldn't help but stare at her butt as she left.

"I hope we can trust Luna, too," Calynn muttered. "We need her."

They lost a few million credits in the slot machines waiting for Nura to return. Slot machines were definitely not their favorite way to gamble. Triana hit on a few spins, but nothing that got them anywhere close to even. After several minutes Nura returned with a very drowsy Luna in tow.

Luna was wearing an outfit that sort of matched the guy at the VIP room door from earlier. Hers was a short black skirt and a sparkled pink and purple vest. Her black leather boots came up to her knees.

"I expect an enormous tip for waking me up," Luna said as she approached Kash. "And a hug."

"The hug we can do now," Kash chuckled, wrapping his arms around Luna. "As for the tip... get us in that room and you'll never get a bigger one."

"As you wish, master," Luna murmured into his chest. "Sorry, sir... force of habit and I'm sleepy."

"Good girl," Kash replied. "Sorry to wake you. Now let's go."

Luna took their cards to get them credits and to fill out the appropriate forms. When she returned, she had a cart with two piles of chips and four security guards. She led them to the Parlor Royale.

Kash and his friends were by far the youngest players in the room, and there were no women that could compare to Calynn and Triana. They caught the attention of every man in the room.

"Which game would you like to play?" Luna asked with a soft smile.

"Greeli has been our go to game thus far," Guy offered.

"There are two Greeli tables," Luna told them. "One is a regular Greeli table, and the other is a higher stakes table. The minimum bet is higher but so are the payout percentages."

"Which table is less crowded?" Kash asked.

"The high stakes table, sir," Luna replied after a quick glance. "Right this way."

Luna set up their chips and brought their first round of drinks before play started. Calynn was sitting beside Kash holding his hand. She felt fidgety as she tried to home in on the AI. Kash was splitting his attention between the game and Calynn, but that didn't seem to matter. His luck continued, and a crowd soon formed.

"Winner!" the croupier announced as Kash won again.

The crowd cheered as Kash's pile of chips continued to grow. Kash checked in with Calynn after every play. He would lean in and kiss her cheek so she could whisper to him if anything changed.

"No changes?" Kash whispered in her ear.

"It's stronger here but still really weak," Calynn put her hand over her mouth and Kash's ear when she whispered to him. "It is a regular pattern though. I'm trying to piece it together to see if there's like a broken message or anything."

Kash looked around the room, seeing how close the other guests were to the table so they could watch the action... and the creepy, old, pasty white guy that was drooling a little too close to Calynn. Luna must have noticed it too, because she was approaching Kash before he nodded at her. She leaned over so Kash could whisper in her ear.

"Can we get a little more space, please?" Kash asked Luna. "I don't want to have to hit someone because they drooled on Calynn."

"I'll grab security and have them handle it," Luna whispered back.

"Hey," Kash said as Luna started to leave.

"Yes, sir," Luna said, leaning back down.

"I can see down your vest when you bend over like that," Kash smirked.

"Shall I bend over more often?" Luna jested back.

Kash feigned a shocked look and then chuckled.

"Remember," Luna said, leaning in again. "I'm more adventurous than my best friend."

Luna smirked as she walked off, looking back over her shoulder to see if Kash was watching her. Kash squinted at her playfully and smiled.

"I like her too," Calynn said kind of mechanically.

"Me too," Kash agreed.

Luna brought the security guard back with her. He immediately had the spectators back away from the table about a meter and then posted himself between the creepy old guy and Calynn, blocking the man's view of her. Every time the old guy tried to move so he could see her, the guard would move with him to prevent it. The man soon gave up and grumbled to himself while he walked away. Kash slipped the guard a black chip for his help and nodded to Luna.

"Yes, sir," Luna said leaning over again.

"For being awesome," Kash said handing her five black chips.

"You're too kind, sir," Luna smiled.

The night continued, and Kash's luck finally slowed some. He was still adding to his stack of chips but not at the same rate as before. Luna would flirt with him every time she approached, but Kash could tell the beauty was getting tired. Nura did wake her up to come get them into the Parlor.

"Any change?" Kash whispered to Calynn.

"No," Calynn sounded disappointed. "Just the same waves."

"Our hostess is yawning."

"I saw... I feel bad for keeping her here, but what if I miss something from the AI?"

"Let's see if there's something we can do."

Kash nodded at their slouching hostess. Luna forced herself to correct her posture as she approached and did her best to appear alert.

"Is that waiver still good?" Kash smiled. "Am I still allowed to touch you?"

"No, but please touch me," Luna smiled back, leaning down.

Kash pulled her a little closer so he could whisper in her ear. Luna's hand landed on his lap so she could balance herself.

"We can tell you are very tired," Kash whispered to Luna. "We're not done here yet, but we don't want to prevent you from getting your rest. Is there something we can do?"

"I could pass you off to someone else, but Nura said we had to keep your secret," Luna whispered back. "I'll be fine but thank you."

"And we can't have her?"

"I doubt it, but I can ask," Luna replied, but then her head turned toward Calynn. "Are you okay, miss?"

Calynn was standing with tears streaming down her cheeks by the time Kash turned to look at her.

"No," Calynn whined, walking off from the table.

"I got her," Luna said giving chase.

"Me too," Triana added and went after Calynn also.

Kash was barely paying attention to the game now. His focus was on Calynn who was sobbing on Triana's shoulder. Luna was doing her best to console her with arms wrapped around both of the other women.

"Your bet, sir," the croupier said to Kash getting his attention.

"Sorry," Kash apologized. "I'm taking a little break. Can I keep my chips here?"

"You have to cover the minimum, sir," the dealer explained.

"This should cover me for a bit," Kash replied tossing five black chips to the man.

Kash marched over to Calynn, Triana, and Luna. Calynn seemed to just know that he was coming even though her back was to him. She turned and launched herself into Kash's arms. Her arms were around his shoulders, and he wrapped his arms around her waist to support her. She couldn't wrap her legs around his waist because of how tight her dress was on her legs. Kash adjusted his grip, and Calynn seemed to intrinsically know what he wanted. She swung her legs up so he was now cradling her in his arms.

Luna and Triana moved to Calynn's side to help Kash comfort her while she cried. Kash didn't try to talk to her yet. He just held her and let her get it out. Calynn's body shook as she quietly sobbed in Kash's arms. Luna placed one hand on Kash's bicep and the other on Calynn's side.

"She didn't say anything yet," Luna offered. "So, we don't know what's wrong yet."

'It's okay," Kash smiled at Luna. "I have her now."

"You certainly do," Luna shuddered as she caressed Kash's arm. "Throwing her around with such ease... sorry."

Luna realized what she was doing, pulled her hand off his arm and moved it to Calynn's back. Kash remembered all the times Calynn said that women from Ooga were very attracted to strength and power. He didn't fault her for her biological urges.

"You're fine," Kash smiled at Luna. "But maybe give me a minute with her alone... sometimes she opens up when it's just me."

"Absolutely," Luna smiled back. "I'll just go watch over your chips until you return to the table."

"Are you sure you got her?" Triana asked, placing her hand on Kash's shoulder.

"I'm sure, Trie."

Triana smiled at him and went back to Guy and Luna. Kash walked over to the corner of the room, where he and Calynn could be as alone as possible in a room full of people. Her sobs were slowing down, but her face was still buried in his neck and shoulder.

"I'm ready when you are... no rush," Kash said softly.

Calynn didn't reply. She was still holding onto him like her life depended on it. She took a few deep breaths, and he felt her body shake a few more times with each breath. She had been way better with her emotions lately, but this AI problem must have had her really rattled. After a few more breaths, he felt her body relax a little.

"This is so hard," Calynn mumbled.

"What's that, Baby Girl?"

"The emptiness when I lose the connection with him... and there was something else this time."

"I heard him ask for help before he disappeared," Calynn lifted her head to look in Kash's eyes. "Everything else is just numbers and nonsense... that was the first solid and deliberate thing I heard him say."

"Do you think he senses you too?" Kash asked thoughtfully. "Not to put more pressure on you, but you might be the first person he's ever been able to speak to."

"And that makes it more sad," Calynn buried her face again.

A nasty thought jumped into Kash's mind, he tried to push it aside, but the thought was persistent. Maybe it was just his need to always protect Calynn, but he couldn't shake it. He wanted her to always be her happy and bubbly self, but instead she was crying in his arms. He stared off into space as he contemplated this new thought. He didn't notice that he had stopped caressing Calynn, but she did.

"What are you thinking?" Calynn asked. "Something just changed."

"Well... and just hear me out, but... are you sure he's in pain and not just projecting the pain? He could be targeting you."

"I... I'm uh..." Calynn picked up her head again and looked at Kash. "I don't know."

"It leaves you wrecked every time it disappears without a trace, and it just makes me think... what if that's deliberate? And I get it... that could be my insatiable need to protect you talking, but what if it's not? What if it's a trap?"

"But why?"

"Awakened nerve centers are a hot commodity. You said before there is one awakened nerve center here already... what would happen if the casino had two... or three?" Kash asked her, knowing she wouldn't necessarily have the answer. "I'm not saying that Gravitas is behind it, but a casino run by that kind of brain power would be..."

"Unbeatable," Calynn finished his thought for him, sounding more like herself. "Put me down."

Kash dropped her legs and gently placed Calynn on the ground. She had to adjust her dress. When she jumped into his arms, it must have pulled her top down exposing her boobs. It also put a small tear in the vein stone ribbon that decorated the collar of her dress.

"Oh, I ripped it," Calynn whined, fingering the tear.

"It's okay. We'll go get it fixed or buy you a new one."

"Can I have two?" Calynn smirked.

"And she's back," Kash smiled at the beauty grabbing her hips. "You can have ten if it keeps you from crying."

"Can we get Nura one too?"

"Would that make you happy?" Kash asked, pulling her in for a hug.

"It would," Calynn said into his chest. "I really like her."

"Me too," Kash said and then sighed. "So, what do we do about the AI haunting you? Not that I want to make you sad again."

"I don't know... there's no way to tell its intentions."

"Okay... then how do we balance your insatiable desire to help people with my overbearing need to protect you?"

"I don't know that either," Calynn sighed.

"Well, it would make me happy if you were never alone while looking for it," Kash said softly. "Can we start there?"

"It's still sexy the way you protect me."

"No avoiding the question, young lady," Kash said adamantly. "Promise me you won't go off alone searching for it anymore."

"I promise," Calynn relented.

THE JACKPOT

Kash kissed Calynn's head as he held her. She was feeling better and so was he. After a moment she looked up at him and gave him a soft kiss on the lips. They smiled softly at each other and held hands while they walked back to the Greeli table. Luna was sitting in Kash's chair and got up when they approached.

"I was just keeping it warm for you, sir," Luna smiled and then turned to Calynn. "Are you okay?"

"I am now," Calynn said hugging Kash's arm to her body. "I just needed my rock to do that overprotective thing he does... but how are you? Should we let you go? You're so tired."

"Yeah... I am rather tired," Luna replied. "Maybe I should go talk to a manager about Nura taking over."

"It's you or her," Kash asserted. "No exceptions. We'll leave if it isn't one of you two."

"I agree," Guy added.

"Me too," Calynn agreed.

"I'll be right back," Luna said with a smile. "Wish me luck."

Kash got back to the game and tried to forget about the AI and the nagging feeling he had about it. Calynn had been such an influence on him to be more helpful, but in this case his skepticism was very persistent. He vowed to make sure he stayed sober enough to always stay vigilant around Calynn for the rest of their stay... just in case his skepticism proved correct.

"Winner," the croupier announced after a few spins, waving to Kash again.

The crowd had dispersed some from when Kash and Calynn left the table, but those that remained cheered his win.

"Congratulations, sir," Nura's voice came from behind him.

Kash spun around to see Nura smiling at him. She was wearing the same vest outfit Luna was wearing. Her smile turned to a smirk as she leaned down.

"I was told I should bend over for you," Nura whispered. "Sorry I don't fill out the top as much as Luna does."

"Oh, stop," Kash smirked back. "You're sexy as hell and you know it, and I'll take that top off of you later if you let me."

"You better do more than just take off my top, mister," Nura smiled and then turned to Calynn. "And I hear you need a hug."

"I do," Calynn said standing up from her chair.

Calynn gave Nura a quick kiss and then wrapped her in a warm embrace. Kash smiled. He liked Luna, but he definitely liked Nura more. The best friends were remarkably similar in looks and personality, but Nura had something more. Kash couldn't quite put his finger on what that was exactly, but he found Nura more desirable than her friend.

"Your b-bet, sir," the dealer stuttered.

Kash spun back around and placed his bet while Calynn and Nura chatted. Guy slid out his bet next and the betting continued around the table.

"Betting is closed," the croupier announced and dropped the two vein stone marbles.

The marbles bounced around on the spinning disks until they landed on two shapes. One looked like the letter N with a big, rounded side and the other reminded Kash of a willow tree from Earth. Nobody won that round, so the dealer scooped all the chips into the house pile and started the disks spinning again.

"Place your b-bets," the dealer stuttered again.

Kash looked at the dealer with a cross look. He thought it was odd that the dealer stuttered the exact same way twice. He hadn't heard him stutter before now, either. The table all placed their bets, and the dealer dropped the marbles. When they stopped, they landed in the exact same two squares as the last round. Kash turned and stared at Guy, tapping him on the leg under the table. Guy kinda scowled back, obviously not understanding what Kash meant.

"Place your b-bets."

The same stutter, yet again. Kash nodded at Guy and pushed an extra-large bet onto the tree and N square, playing a hunch. Guy reluctantly pushed his chips onto the same square, scowling at Kash. Kash nodded again and turned back to the dealer when he dropped the marbles. For an impossible third time in a row, they landed in the exact same spot.

"Winner!" the croupier announced.

After collecting the losing bets and paying out to Kash and Guy, the croupier spun the wheels again.

"Place your b-bets," he stuttered yet again.

This time when Kash looked at Guy, his eyes were wide, and his brow raised. Kash smirked knowing that Guy finally understood the assignment. They both pushed even larger bets onto the same square, and sure enough...

"Winner!" the dealer announced.

A few of the other players were looking at Kash and Guy with puzzled looks. When the next round started the dealer stuttered yet again. Kash's smirk must have given them away, because three other players pushed their chips onto the same square as Kash and Guy. The marbles were dropped and the impossible happened yet again.

"Winner!" the dealer announced.

The whole table celebrated as the chips flowed. The dealer paid out massive stacks of chips to the players and spun the wheels again.

"Place your b-bets."

Everyone at the table placed their bets on the same square. Most of whom placed fairly large bets, but their bets would pale in comparison to Kash's.

"All in," Kash said, placing one chip in the square and pushing the rest of his pile forward some, indicating they were part of his bet.

"Player is all in," the dealer repeated.

"All in," Guy stated, repeating Kash's actions.

"Player is all in."

One other player went all in also, and the tension around the table was palpable. They were taking a really big risk assuming the dealer's stutter was foreshadowing the result of the roll. It was possible that they were being set up, but that was the nature of what they were doing... gambling... go big or go home.

"What are you doing?" Nura asked, placing her hand on Kash's shoulder.

Kash ignored the beauty, intently watching the dealer drop the marbles. It felt like they bounced around for an eternity which made Kash nervous. He swallowed hard as the marbles fell into their slots. Kash spun around and scooped Nura off the ground. He had one hand on her butt and the other in the middle of her back to support her. His tongue was in her mouth before she could complain.

"Winner!"

The room erupted in cheers that were almost deafening, they were so loud. The entire room turned to see what was going on as Kash spun around holding the petite Oogan in his arms. He set Nura down and grabbed Calynn kissing her passionately. She placed her hands on his cheeks as she kissed him back. Kash was lost in her embrace when Nura suddenly bounced off of him and landed on the ground beside him.

"Hey!" Nura complained from the ground.

Kash turned to see her on the ground and looked for the person who knocked her over. A man in an expensive looking suit with a security guard right on his heels raced toward the Greeli croupier. The man in the suit touched the dealer on the back of the head, and the dealer went limp. The security guard caught the dealer so he didn't crash to the ground.

"Fuck me," Kash exclaimed. "The dealer was a synth?"

"This dealer was malfunctioning," the man in the suit announced. "We must audit the game and your winnings."

"Whoa," Guy said firmly. "So, because we won, we need audited?"

"Your mechanical dealer could have just as easily made us all lose!" another man shouted.

"Perhaps you are the one that needs audited," Guy barked.

"How many other dealers are robots?" another man asked.

"Are they all cheating us?" someone else shouted.

"No," the suit argued.

"Liar!" someone shouted.

"Cheat!"

Kash turned back to Nura and helped her up while everyone was shouting. She was holding her arm like she hurt her elbow when she fell. The raucous crowd was growing louder by the second, shouting at the man in the suit. Kash gently pulled Nura closer and reached for her hurt elbow. Nura hesitated for a moment and then offered the arm for Kash to examine. His fingers traced the contours of her elbow feeling for anything abnormal. She winced a little when he pressed on it, but everything felt right structurally. He bent and straightened her arm so he could feel the movement, and everything felt fine.

"It's just bruised," Kash told her. "It will be sore for a while, but other than that you'll be just fine."

Nura wrapped her good arm around his waist and laid her head on his chest. Kash hugged her back and kissed the top of her head. He spun them so he could see the Greeli table and the enormous stack of chips in front of his seat. Guy was arguing with the man in the suit while Triana and Calynn guarded their chips. That was enough chips to buy a new bigger ship like a government cruiser, and staff it for at least a year.

Kash did the math in his head quickly and determined there had to be sixty or seventy billion credits sitting on the table in front of his chair. The dealer had been shut off before it could pay out all of Guy's winnings, but he probably had about a third of Kash's winnings.

"Retirement money," Kash said to himself.

With that many credits, he never had to put Calynn into a risky situation ever again. He could get them a bigger, more comfortable ship. Of course, Plekish and Rinktee would have to upgrade it for them before they used it, but then they could cruise the galaxies without a care in the world. He could take her to all the most beautiful nebulae, and they could dine in the finest restaurants, and have sex with all the most beautiful women... like Nura. Kash pushed her vest out of the way so he could get to her soft skin. He was about to lift her up so he could kiss her again when he heard a distinctive hum.

"What's going on here?" Gravitas' voice bellowed through the room, bringing the crowd to heel.

Kash didn't turn around to face the big man. He shook his head and then let it drop to the top of Nura's. Kash knew what was coming next, so he prepared himself for it. He kissed Nura's head again and sighed heavily. He took a deep breath of Nura's scent, trying to use it to help him stay calm. He wished it was Calynn in his arms. Her scent always worked.

"Why am I not surprised that you're here," Gravitas continued. "Kash."

"We're not doing this again, Gravitas," Kash replied without turning around. "I'm not sure how many different ways you can try to accuse me of this shit, but it appears that you're going for the record."

"I suppose you're going to tell me that the faulty dealer was somehow an attack on you now?" Gravitas asked rhetorically. "Was it trying to drown you under a pile of my credits?"

"What better way to make sure you and I are at odds with one another," Kash sighed heavily and finally turned to face the man. "They definitely don't want us working together, so they pushed the suspicion onto me. If you are preoccupied dealing with me, that makes them all the more invisible. It's actually a pretty smart play if you think about it."

"A smart play?" Gravitas sounded annoyed.

"I would have done something similar," Kash added firmly.

"Would have... or that's what you are doing?" Gravitas asked with an accusatory tone.

"I told you we aren't doing this again," Kash growled. "I am not now, nor have I ever been, part of a plot to steal anything from you. Did I take advantage of the dealer's glitch? Absolutely. But what I want to know is how the dealer made the marbles stop in the same spot six times in a row?"

"I think we all deserve that answer," Guy added.

"If it can make it land on the same square six times in a row, it can also make sure we all lose whenever you want," Kash continued. "What kind of establishment are you running here?"

Gravitas scowled at Kash and clenched his jaw. Kash knew he had him backed into a corner, and he wasn't going to let the big man get the upper hand, no matter what.

"I'll tell you what... I'll waive my last bet when I went all in, so you don't have to pay that one, but if you ever... accuse me of attempting to rob you again," Kash growled. "I'll become what you're accusing me of being, and I won't just steal everything you have, but I'll fucking ruin you!"

"Don't you threaten me, Kash!"

"You fucking started it!" Kash hollered, taking a step forward and pointing his finger in Gravitas' face.

"Nobody speaks to me that way!"

Kash felt a gentle pull on the back of his jacket. Nura was trying to pull him back from Gravitas. He was so focused on the big man that he hadn't noticed the other security guards that were now surrounding him. Kash looked at the guards, shrugged off his jacket, and removed his cuff links. He pushed down his anger and forced himself to be calm and calculating.

"You're going to come with us and answer some questions," Gravitas spat. "NOW!"

"No... I don't think I will," Kash replied, glancing around the room again, his tone icy cold. "Nine guards aren't enough, by the way. Unless you plan on running away during the thirty seconds it takes me to dispatch them."

"And what is that supposed to mean?" Gravitas hissed.

"That means if they approach me in a hostile manner, you have a little over thirty seconds to..."

"Kash," Nura interrupted, moving in front of him trying to push him back from Gravitas. "Please don't."

Nura had her arms wrapped around his body, and she was trying to push him back with all her might, but he was just too big and strong for her to move. He looked down and saw the worry in her eyes and the tears threatening to fall. Nura didn't know that Kash could easily take on nine men, so she was scared for him.

"Please," Nura repeated, clearly distressed. "I can't..."

Kash relented and let Nura push him back from Gravitas. He placed his hands on her shoulders and smiled down at her as she moved him. A tear ran down her cheek, and Kash instinctively wiped it away with his thumb. Nura stopped moving when they were back beside Calynn, Guy, and Triana. She laid her head on his chest and gripped the back of his shirt in her hands. Kash wrapped her in his arms.

"Oh, I see now," Gravitas said venomously. "You intend to use one of my girls against me."

"Just don't," Kash said shaking his head.

"Don't do what?" Gravitas pressed.

"Gravitas... I said don't," Kash added firmly.

"I'm confused, Kash," Gravitas smiled his creepy smile. "Don't what... don't let you fraternize with one of my employees and conspire with her to..."

"THAT!" Kash barked, cutting off the big man. "If you attack her. I will protect her."

"She does seem more interested in you than doing her job," Gravitas bellowed, directing his ire at Nura now.

"Of course she is," Kash argued. "When she was attacked in your casino, I was the one that protected her not you."

"My security pulled that man away, not you."

"And your company therapist told her to take her clothes off after being sexually assaulted. As if being sexually assaulted some more is the answer."

"It sounds more like you just trying to get more of the women here naked," Calynn added.

"Especially the ones from Ooga," Kash concluded his argument.

"I'd like to speak to this so-called therapist," Calynn smirked. "I'm curious about where he or she was educated."

"By the way," Kash leaned down and said softly to Nura without taking his eyes off Gravitas. "If he tries to fire you or in any way use you against me... take all the chips you can carry and tell us all to fuck off."

"Well, maybe not me," Calynn joked. "But definitely all the men."

"We should revoke her access card until we sort this out," Victor Morel said, stepping out from behind Gravitas. "Administrative leave."

"But I live here," Nura complained. "I can't get to my apartment without my card."

"You should have thought of that before getting into bed with criminals," Victor spat, his body shaking.

Kash went to take a step forward, but Nura gripped him harder to stop him before he started to move, but she couldn't stop Calynn too.

"Call us criminals one more time," Calynn's words were oozing with detest. "Just one more time... I dare you."

Victor's demeanor shattered when confronted with Calynn. His eyes darted around the room, trying to look at anything except her, and he adjusted his jacket several times with trembling hands.

Nura let go of Kash and gently pulled at Calynn's hand. The poor girl must have felt like she had to be the mediator, or maybe she was just worried about her job... or maybe Gravitas had something on her to help keep her in line. Perhaps he had dirt on all his employees. That sounded like something the big man would do based on everything Kash knew about him. He often spoke of having or maintaining leverage over others.

Kash moved to the petite Oogan woman and placed his hand gently on her shoulder. When she turned to look at him, she had tears in her eyes and her lips were quivering. Kash's anger with Gravitas melted away. His only concern now... was Nura.

"It's okay, Nura," Kash said softly. "Go get your things... you can stay with us until this all blows over."

"Luna and I share an apartment," Nura said, casting her eyes downward.

"Hey you," Kash gently lifted her chin so she was looking up at him again. "I promise to take care of you and Luna if that's what it takes... go wake the poor thing up again."

Nura tried to smile, but she was still scared and worried.

"I promise," Kash repeated. "Now go."

Nura scurried off quickly, cowering when she passed Gravitas. Kash waited until she was out of earshot to address the fat man again.

"It better be paid administrative leave," Kash demanded. "You have nothing on us, and you fucking know it. However, I insist that you revoke all of her and Luna's privileges until after the crew that's actually trying to rob you makes their move. I want to make sure none of this sticks to them."

"Four persons exceeds the occupancy for your suite," Gravitas said venomously. "The maximum is three."

"Then Luna can stay in our suite," Guy offered. "Three in each."

"We'll just never close the doors between them so we can all enjoy each other's company," Triana added.

"So, I'm just down two servers because you say so," Gravitas growled.

"No," Calynn argued pointing to Victor. "He said so."

"She's not wrong," Kash smirked.

"Enough!" Gravitas barked. "You're still coming with us to answer my questions."

"Not until you answer all of our questions about that!" Kash hollered, pointing at the croupier synth. "Am I right folks?"

Kash held up his arms as a chorus of voices erupted from the other patrons around the Greeli table. They were all demanding answers and accusing the casino of cheating. Gravitas didn't back down though. The big man kept his gaze trained on Kash.

Movement to Kash's left drew his attention, and he turned just in time to see one of the larger security guards taking a swing at one of the players. Kash reacted with lightning quick reflexes. He deflected the punch, protecting the older gentlemen being assaulted, and then caught the guard with a spinning back-fist that sent the guard tumbling to the ground.

"Why am I repeatedly protecting everyone here from YOU!" Kash barked, pointing at Gravitas.

Another guard lunged at Kash but was met with Kash's far superior strength. The man practically bounced off of Kash, and then Kash shoved him to the ground.

"You need more men!" Kash growled.

"And we need paid!" another man shouted.

"Unless you're a fucking cheat!" yet another joined in.

"Pay us... pay us... pay us," the room chanted in unison.

"Those credits are mine," Kash smirked at Gravitas as he sauntered back to where Calynn was standing.

He wrapped his arms around her, yanked her dress down, and grabbed her exposed tits.

"These are mine too," Kash continued. "And these are my people!"

Kash and Calynn were soon engulfed in a crowd of people shouting at Gravitas and Victor. Kash fixed Calynn's dress and put his arms around her waist. She leaned her head back and looked up at him with her look. Kash understood why he was getting that look.

"Sorry," he said softly. "I got carried away."

Some pushing and shoving caught Kash's attention, and he moved to intervene. The guards all backed away when Kash approached. They saw what he did to the first two men who tried to attack him, and nobody wanted to be third on that list.

"Kash!" Gravitas bellowed, getting everyone's attention.

The enormous man smiled his sinister grin as Kash and everyone else looked his way.

"If you AND your friend give up your last bet like you offered earlier," Gravitas hissed. "Then we will pay out all of the other bets, but only..."

"Done," Kash interrupted quickly and calmly.

"Ditto," Guy added.

Gravitas' face contorted with anger. He obviously didn't think Kash was serious about giving up his last bet, and he absolutely didn't think Guy would concur. The room cheered and everyone surrounded Kash and Guy to thank them for their generosity. Kash was shaking hands and smiling until one of the hands belonged to Victor.

"This isn't over," Victor said leaning in close. "I'm watching you."

Victor turned on his heels and disappeared through the crowd. Kash tried to watch where the man went, but he lost sight of him. Gravitas, however, was easy to spot. The big man was slapping around the man in the suit who had shut down the dealer. Kash figured he was being disciplined for losing money.

Kash and Guy cashed out their chips, and even without the payout from the last bet they were both still up nearly a billion credits.

"We have to hurry back to the suite," Triana cooed, grabbing Guy's hands. "Or I'm gonna fuck you right here."

The four friends returned to their suites, and Triana and Guy disappeared into their bedroom. Kash flopped down on the sofa to wait for Nura and Luna, and Calynn joined him after changing clothes.

"Jeans and a tee shirt is still your sexiest outfit," Kash said smiling.

"Are you trying to get into my pants?" Calynn jested, curling up beside him on the couch.

"Always."

UNBRIDLED

Nura was nearly jogging she was running to the gift shop so fast. The compactor was normally full of broken-down boxes that she could use to pack her possessions. Tears were trailing down her cheeks, but she wasn't exactly sure if they were sad tears or happy ones. On one hand it was definitely scary going up against her boss, Gravitas. He was not a man to be trifled with. On the other hand, she was excited about the prospect of Kash and Calynn taking them away from the casino so they could finally be free again.

Nura grabbed an armful of boxes from the compactor behind the gift shop, tossed them onto a luggage cart, and rushed toward her apartment. The employee housing in the casino was drab, bland, small, and they all looked exactly the same. The only difference was the numbers on the doors. Nura and Luna had a small sign hanging on their door that said "welcome."

Nura burst into her apartment to see Luna passed out on their bed. Nura was disgusted when she looked around. Their apartment had a double bed, two built-in dressers, the smallest kitchen ever, and an even smaller bathroom. The kitchen in Kash's suite was bigger than where she and Luna lived together. And even though they shared the space, they were still almost always broke and starving.

There was a new box of food sitting on the floor near the bed. Luna must have picked up some things before coming back to the apartment. An open bag of dried fruit was sitting on top of the box, and some lose pieces were laying on the bed by Luna's head.

"Eating in bed again?" Nura smiled at her sleeping friend. "You're so naughty."

Nura decided to let Luna sleep while she packed up their possessions. All the furniture belonged to the casino, so it was really just their clothes, a few small appliances, and some personal belongings. It took Nura less than an hourn to pack everything up... and a mere seventeen boxes. The only time she paused was when she packed up her jewelry box. It was an antique passed down from her great-grandmother to her grandmother, then her mom, and finally… to Nura. Her mom gave it to her when she left for college, and it was her most valued possession. She kissed the box and packed it in the middle of a box of clothes to protect it.

"Hey, sleepyhead," Nura said softly, brushing Luna's hair out of her face.

"Mmmmmmm," Luna moaned and stretched.

"Hi, beautiful."

"Shh… I'm so tired," Luna said, flailing her arm at Nura.

"I know you are, but we gotta go."

"Go where?" Luna groaned.

"To a plush suite with a nice big bed that is so soft it feels like your floating, and…"

"No, Nura," Luna said suddenly, sitting up. "You didn't spend our credits on that did you?"

"No, silly," Nura smiled at her friend, gently rubbing her cheek. "We're going to Kash and Calynn's suite."

"We are… why?"

"Because Kash and Gravitas got into a big fight, and I tried to hold Kash back, which Gravitas saw and that made him mad, and he thinks Kash is using us to help him rob the casino, so we're on leave now," Nura blurted out and smiled awkwardly at her friend.

"Wait… what?"

"We are on leave until further notice," Nura gave her the short version this time.

"So, we have to make the credits Kash gave us last as long…"

"Luna," Nura cut her off. "Him and Calynn promised to take care of us… he promised… and I trust him."

"Actually… I trust him too," Luna agreed, getting out of bed. "And not working means no stupid tray… Let's go."

Nura gave Luna a blanket to wrap herself in while they went to Kash's suite but had to give her "the look" to get her to actually put it on. Nura wagged her finger at her friend and started to push the luggage cart down the hallway. Luna stuck her tongue out at her and Nura giggled. When they got to the casino floor, she handed the guard both of their badges.

"Here, Victor Morel wants these," Nura spat as she moved past him. "Tell him to shove them up his ass!"

The duo continued through the casino and up the elevator to the suites and were soon knocking on Kash and Calynn's door.

"Hi, ladies," Calynn said cheerfully as she opened the door.

"I'm sleepy," Luna whined as soon as the door opened.

"Go lay down," Calynn offered. "We can get your things settled."

"Hey... this is nice," Luna said as she staggered through the suite looking around. "Oh, this looks comfy."

Luna smiled at Kash as she approached. She dropped the blanket she was using to cover herself as she made her way to the couch. She pushed him down on the couch and lay down on him, snuggling her head into his chest.

"I can hum you a lullaby," Kash chuckled, rubbing Luna's back.

"You're lumpy," Luna complained, sitting up.

"And you're sleepy," Kash replied, grabbing her by the hand. "Come on... let's get you to bed."

Kash took Luna to their bedroom and returned a few moments later.

"That poor thing is exhausted," Kash said as he closed the bedroom door.

"She was excited about giving her nipples a break from carrying around that damn tray," Nura explained. "But, just to warn you, she is a nudist. She'll be naked more than she's not. Heck, I had to fight her to put on that blanket to come up here."

"You brought more stuff than I expected," Kash said as he sat beside Nura on the couch.

"That's everything we own," Nura explained, staring off aimlessly. "The furniture all belongs to the casino, so it was just our clothes and a few personal items. Our whole world fits in a mere seventeen boxes."

Nura wiped a tear from her eye, but it was useless... another took its place, then another. She blinked hard, staring across the room, willing herself to keep it together. Kash and Calynn shared a look, silent but full of meaning, and the weight of their concern settled over her like a heavy blanket.

They cared. That realization alone nearly broke her.

Nura's throat tightened, and she swallowed hard, fighting against the lump that had been forming since they left the casino floor. Her hands trembled, and she clasped them together in her lap, squeezing so hard her knuckles went white. She could feel Kash's gaze on her, waiting, and Calynn's quiet patience was somehow even worse. They wouldn't rush her. They wouldn't demand... They'd wait.

She wasn't used to that.

A shaky breath escaped her lips, and she closed her eyes. They said they'd take care of me. Take care of Luna. But that was before. Before they knew the whole truth. Before they realized how damaged she and Luna really were. Would they still want them? Would they still keep them?

A fresh wave of fear clawed at Nura's chest, and she whispered a silent prayer... Please... please don't let them change their minds. Then, before she could lose her nerve, she opened her eyes and forced herself to speak.

"Luna and I were arrested for stealing food," Nura confessed. "The only thing keeping us out of jail is Gravitas..."

She paused and wiped a tear from her cheek. She could feel the emotions welling up inside her.

"If we don't work here... and do what he says..."

Nura broke down into tears and buried her face in her hands. Before she knew it, Kash scooped her up and sat her across his lap, hugging her tight. Nura dug her fingers into his back and shoulders, and she wept into his chest. She was lost in her sorrow and sobbed uncontrollably. Calynn had shifted to his side and had an arm wrapped around Nura also to comfort her. The duo let her get it all out and Nura was thankful for it. She cried until she couldn't cry any more.

"I knew he had to be holding something over your heads," Kash said softly, caressing Nura's back. "The way you acted was an easy tell."

"We stopped here on the way to the Pleasure Planets for the semester break in college," Nura explained, wiping her tears. "When we tried to pay for our meals our cards were all declined, and we didn't have enough credits on us. We had to have been hacked or something, because I know I had enough credits in the bank to pay for our meals. But we panicked... and tried to run... a Constable stopped us and returned us to Gravitas... we had to sign five-year contracts to work here, or the Constable would file the paperwork, and we would go to jail... it's only been three years."

Kash sighed and laid his forehead on Nura's. She gazed into his eyes and saw something there, but she wasn't sure what it was. He shook his head like he was struggling to tell her something, and then finally convinced himself to say it.

"How much do you want to bet... the Constable was fake?" Kash sighed.

"What?" Nura asked, confused. "What do you mean fake?"

"Want me to check?" Calynn offered. "What's your full names?

"Nura Velleris and Luna Viorra," Nura replied, still confused. "But why... I don't understand."

"I think Gravitas set a trap for you to keep you here," Kash explained. "You two are both absolutely stunning Oogan women. I think that fat fuck wanted to keep you here, and everything that happened that day was a setup to trap you here for five years... so he could keep you... for five years."

"The only thing in the Constabulary mainframe about you two are the missing persons reports filed three years ago," Calynn stated.

"There won't be... they didn't file the charges because we signed those contracts," Nura argued. "That's what they said."

"I'll bet you a billion credits that no paperwork will be or could ever be filed," Kash rebutted, then looked at Calynn. "Can you get the personnel pictures of every Constable in this region the time of their arrest? And get all the staff pictures for the casino too. Let's see if she can identify the fake cop."

"On it, Boss," Calynn said.

"Wait... what? I don't... slow down," Nura sat up half panicked. "And why are your eyes glowing?"

"Wanna know our secrets now?" Kash asked her.

"Why are her eyes glowing?" Nura asked again, more panicked this time.

Kash laid out the short version of their history for Nura. She couldn't believe that Calynn had a synth body until she did the thing where she makes her skin hard.

"Wait, so you're not... you're not human?" Nura's voice came out smaller than she expected.

"I am," Calynn replied. "I'm just... wrapped in a different meat than you."

She reached out instinctively, brushing her fingers against Calynn's forearm. It was soft and warm... until it wasn't. The texture shifted under her fingertips, turning smooth and hard as glass. Nura jerked her hand away, but Kash gently grabbed her hand and placed it back on Calynn's arm... which was soft and supple again.

"Whoa," Nura let the word slip out of her mouth.

"I know right," Kash chuckled.

Calynn put all the personnel pictures on an E-tablet and let Nura scroll through until she identified the man that had arrested her three years ago. As Kash suspected, the man worked for Gravitas, not the government.

Nura panicked. Her breathing was choppy and shallow, but Kash was able to hold her until she calmed down again. Her mind scrambled to reject it. Fake? No. It couldn't be. It had to be real... it was real. The fear, the panic, the way the Constable chased them down and grabbed her wrist. He tossed her to the ground and jerked her arms behind her back to make her obey... that was real... wasn't it? But the picture of the man in front of her told a different story. He wasn't a Constable... he was the Director of Personnel Recruitment for The Nebula Royale. He was a fake... and so was her life.

That realization hit Nura harder than she could have imagined, and her entire world crumbled around her. Then she just cried... and cried... and cried...

Kash stood up cradling Nura in his arms, and carried her to the bedroom. Calynn helped him undress Nura, before getting undressed herself. Kash striped down to his boxers and the three crawled into bed. Calynn was on one side of Nura and Kash was on the other. Luna stirred when they crawled into bed but didn't wake. Nura laid her head on Kash's chest and continued crying with Calynn spooning her from behind. Kash wrapped his arm around her and held her tight.

Nura cried herself to sleep, but for the first time in three years... she wasn't afraid of what tomorrow might bring or worried about where her next meal was coming from.

No More Chains

Luna slammed her fist against the armrest of the couch, her face burning with fury. She grabbed the E-tablet from Calynn's hands and threw it across the room. She didn't want to see that man's face again. The man she thought was a Constable... lies!

"I'm gonna fucking kill him!" she growled after hearing the truth about their arrest.

Kash and Calynn exchanged a glance, neither of them was expecting Luna to possess that much fury, but she was furious.

"That fucking asshole tackled me and hurt my ribs," Luna continued, seething mad. "And then felt me up after. Oh, he's so fucking dead. Where is he... the guy. Where is he?"

"Luna, please..."

"And Gravitas too," Luna cut off Nura. "That fat mother fucker set the whole thing up. I'm going claw his eyes out and stab him to death with a fork!"

"No," Kash said firmly, raising a hand. "We're going to be smarter about your revenge than that."

Luna narrowed her eyes, her hands still shaking.

"Smarter?" Luna's voice dripped with venom. "Smarter would've been never trusting that fat piece of shit in the first place. Smarter would've been not getting caught! I don't want to be smart! I want him dead!"

Kash held her gaze. His piercing eyes bored into her soul, and Luna's stomach twisted. She hated this. Hated how helpless she felt. Hated that she hid behind her anger. But most of all, she hated that Kash was right. She couldn't actually stab someone... smarter was probably better.

"Ugh, fine!" Luna grumbled, slouching back in her chair. "Let's hear the plan that doesn't let me stab that fat fuck!"

Kash didn't reply at first, he just kept holding her gaze like he was trying to will her to calm down.

"We're going to hit him where it hurts," Kash finally said in a calm steady tone. "This isn't about charging in and stabbing him, Luna. We need to outthink him if we want to get you guys free of him."

Luna's eyes narrowed as she shot Kash a skeptical look, but she remained silent waiting for him to explain... and trying not to erupt again.

"Gravitas thinks he's untouchable, that we can't do anything to him without facing the consequences." Kash's tone was cold, calculating. "But he's wrong. We saw that last night when we turned the crowd against him."

"He's vulnerable," Calynn added, her voice steady. "We're going to hit him in a way that'll make him regret ever taking you."

"And crossing me," Kash added.

Luna glanced over at Nura. Her eyes were still red and bloodshot from crying, which just seemed to make Luna angrier. She could maybe get over the fact that Gravitas stole three years of her life, but he also made Nura cry... and that... she couldn't abide.

"I still want to kill him!" Luna growled. "He made my Nura cry!"

Everyone's eyes turned to Nura, who looked like she could burst into tears again at any moment. But something in Nura's eyes actually tamed Luna's savage side. It was hard to hate when looking into the eyes of the one person that she truly loved. Nura was like Luna's safety net. No matter what mischief she found, Nura was always by her side... always.

Luna stood up from her chair, walked over to the love seat, and sat down with Nura. She placed her hand on Nura's arm and gave it a little tug. Nura understood her meaning and wrapped Luna in a hug, and Luna held her tight. After a few moments, the friends released their embrace, and Luna flopped back onto the love seat.

"So, what's the plan?" Luna demanded, folding her arms across her chest.

Kash stood up and paced slowly, carefully choosing his words... or maybe stalling while he figured them out.

"We don't take him on physically," Kash explained. "Instead... we take a bite or two out of his empire. He works with the government and criminal organizations alike, and he wears that shit like armor... but we can put some dents in that armor... piece by piece, starting with his weakest link... his pride."

"That bastard's pride is bigger than his casino," Luna muttered under her breath.

"Exactly," Kash smirked. "Which is why it's such a good target. We need to get to those he relies on the most, make him doubt himself and his power, and then we'll make him pay for everything he's done to you two."

Luna's anger simmered as she considered his words, her eyes sharpening. Her little hands were balled up into tight little fists.

"I want him to pay with blood," Luna admitted. "But if he's going to pay... why don't we hit his pockets?"

"No, not his pockets. That's a death wish," Kash replied. "We'll hit his reputation, his ego, and his relationships with the people he thinks he controls. We'll make an enemy of everyone he relies on if we can."

"We have friends in higher places than his friends," Calynn nodded, fully on board. "And we'll make things very difficult for him before he even knows what's coming."

"You really think we can do this?" Nura looked up at them, her voice quiet but hopeful.

Kash crouched down in front of her, meeting her gaze. He grabbed her hand and caressed it gently. She was scared and Luna was worried about her.

"I don't just think it... I know it," Kash continued. "We'll get you two out from under his thumb. But it'll take a little time, some strategy, and a whole lot of patience."

"And if I lose my patience?" Luna crossed her arms, a wicked smile slowly curling on her lips. "Then what?"

She tried to wipe the smile from her face quickly, but Kash must have seen it. He slid over in front of her and grabbed her hands in his. His kind eyes implored her to remain calm. He let go of her right hand and gently brushed her hair back. His hand stayed on the side of her neck, and he caressed her cheek with his thumb. Luna placed her hand on his and snuggled into his soft touch.

"Then I take you over my knee and spank you," Kash smirked.

"Oh, my," Luna gasped, smirking back.

Luna straightened up, tugging at the pajamas Nura had forced her to wear. She tried to act unaffected by Kash's comment... but her face was too hot, and her blushing cheeks betrayed her, damn it. She'd definitely failed.

"So, what's the first step?" Luna continued, her voice a little shaky. "The um... the making him pay and stuff."

"Well... which one of you wants to impersonate Princess Aja?" Kash asked, feigning seriousness.

"What, no!" Nura cried out.

"That's blasphemy," Luna argued, almost losing her temper again before she noticed Kash's grin.

"It's also a joke," Kash chuckled. "Calm down."

"Dammit, Kash," Luna whined.

Dangerous Propositions

"I just needed to make sure you were with me again," Kash chuckled. "But all joking aside, we do need to parade you two around like royalty... how long do you think it will take before your coworkers miss your presence and start asking questions?"

"Less than a day," Luna offered. "I'm flirted with pretty much constantly."

"Me too," Nura smiled a shy smile at Kash.

"Then we keep you under wraps for two days."

"Two days?" Nura and Luna asked in unison.

"We can take you shopping in the meantime, but I don't want you anywhere near that casino for two full days," Kash explained. "And you'll return as some unknown royalty of Ooga accompanied by the hero of the Battle of Topor."

"How does that help us?" Luna asked.

"So, if the three of us follow Gravitas to all of his meetings with the high rollers or whoever and take away his thunder," Guy offered, realizing what Kash was planning. "He gets pushed to the back of the crowd instead of being the center of attention... that's devious."

"Which is where you two come in," Kash continued. "If the casino employees all spread rumors about Commander Liezdt and the two Oogan princesses..."

"The people will flock to us instead of Gravitas," Luna interrupted. "That is devious, Kash."

"That's a kick to the old ego for sure," Calynn giggled.

"And we really get to be like princesses?" Nura asked, a shy smile touching her eyes.

"You really do," Kash smiled back.

"I like step one," Nura giggled. "What's step two?"

"We'll never be able to ruin him financially, but maybe we can slow the money down for a few days," Kash told the group. "If I call in some favors, we can maybe slow the flow of money from the government just long enough to piss him off."

"So, step two is to make him angry?" Nura sounded worried. "I don't like step two."

"When he's angry he makes mistakes," Kash smiled softly to reassure Nura. "We can exploit mistakes. Hopefully in ways that his only recourse is ridding himself of you two."

"We just need to be quick when he makes a mistake," Guy offered. "We're not going to have time to plan anything."

"Hopefully our two beautiful Oogan princesses can cultivate a network capable of capitalizing on his mistakes at a moment's notice," Kash continued poignantly. "We need every friend you have."

"Flirt like your lives depend on it," Calynn giggled.

"Because your freedom just might," Kash added.

"Then I need to be comfortable," Luna said as she pulled off her pajamas. "Can we turn up the temperature a little? I hate wearing clothes."

"I told you," Nura said to Kash.

"I like it warmer too," Triana said as she bounced over to the thermostat.

"Can I be naked too?" Calynn asked, giggling.

"Yes, please," Luna smiled, motioning beside her. "You can sit right here."

Calynn pranced over to the sofa and sat beside Luna. The duo giggled like schoolgirls as Luna pulled up Calynn's shirt to grab her boobs.

"Well then," Kash sighed, rolling his eyes. "I'm getting dressed and going to The Cat to send some messages."

"Oh... do you need me to come along?" Calynn asked, but Kash could tell she didn't want to come.

"Neh... you can stay here and have fun being naked with Luna if you want."

"Well, we kinda need one of your body parts for some of that fun," Calynn grinned devilishly.

"Use the stupid love assist."

"Oh, yeah," Calynn smiled.

"What's love assist?" Luna asked.

Calynn smirked at Luna, grabbed her by the hand, and led her to the bedroom. Kash shook his head at them but then realized he needed to get some clothes from the bedroom before the girls got too hot and heavy. Kash rushed into the bedroom, grabbed jeans and a tee shirt and ducked out quickly.

"Want some company?" Nura asked as Kash got dressed. "I'm not interested in… Luna's like my sister."

"Sure."

Kash and Nura made their way to the docks and onto The Cat.

"She's not much, but she's our home," Kash offered, smiling at Nura.

"Is it bad that I was expecting something much bigger?" Nura asked, scrunching her face.

"No," Kash smiled. "If I saw someone throwing around credits like I have been, I would expect a bigger ship too. I'm more of a minimalist day to day. I like to keep things small and simple."

Kash led her to his quarters and ushered her in. Nura spun in a circle looking around the room.

"Okay, this is cozy," Nura said with a smile. "I like this… Of course, I would have to jump to get into this bed."

Nura bounced herself up so she was sitting on the edge of the bed. She kicked her feet playfully to emphasize her dangling legs and smiled.

"You're too cute for your own good," Kash chuckled.

"What's that supposed to mean?"

"It means… try not to distract me until I get my work done."

"Oh," Nura said, cocking her head. "I'm not used to being the distracting one… that's normally Luna."

"Not for me," Kash said sitting down at his desk. "I'd pick you every time."

Nura blushed and cast her eyes downward while smiling.

"See," Kash continued. "When you're shy like that... fucking sexy as hell."

"I agree," Calynn's voice came over the speakers, startling Nura.

"Well, you just scared her, you big bully," Kash laughed. "And aren't you supposed to be playing with Luna?"

"I can multitask," Calynn replied.

"She can see us?" Nura asked.

"She can," Kash replied. "She's a bit of a stalker, so..."

"I'll go," Calynn conceded.

"Go and have fun while you can," Kash insisted. "I'll let you know when we're done here, because then we need to go shopping."

"Will do, Boss."

Kash sent a message to Admiral Anne to have her call him and then turned to face Nura. She was still staring at the floor. She wore her melancholy on her face, and it weighed down her shoulders too. The poor thing was still upset about having her freedom stolen from her for three years, and she looked like she could cry again.

"Hey, you," Kash said softly as he moved to comfort her.

Nura parted her legs and pulled Kash toward her, wrapping her arms and legs around him and laying her head on his chest. He caressed her back and kissed her head.

"Sorry," Nura mumbled.

"Nothing to be sorry for... how about you get some rest while I take care of this stuff," Kash offered.

"I am tired... I didn't get much sleep."

"I know... you kept me up too."

"Sorry for that too."

"The only thing I ask is that you strip down to your bra and panties," Kash told her. "There's no maid service here to change the sheets every day, so we do what we can to keep the sheets as clean as we can."

"That won't distract you?" Nura asked sheepishly.

Ding Ding Ding

Kash turned to see the incoming call on his monitor, then back to Nura.

"I have to get that," Kash said, pointing to his desk. "Get some rest."

Kash sat at his desk and opened the comms.

"Good morning, Admiral," Kash said cheerfully.

"Kash, my friend, how are you?" Anne replied. "I didn't think I would hear from you so soon."

"Well, you know me… always finding trouble."

"And this trouble needs my help?"

"I do hope so," Kash explained. "I need your help with Gravitas."

Nura caught Kash's eye as she walked into the bathroom. He glanced over at her and then back to the comm.

"I'm not sure I can offer much help there," the Admiral admitted. "He's very well connected."

"I figured as much… I was looking for some information mostly."

"Like what?"

"Like… does he have any meetings with y'all in the next couple days?"

"Let me check and I'll call you right back."

"Thanks, Anne."

The Admiral ended their comm, and Kash penned another email. This one went out to his contact in the consortium. He asked if there was a way to schedule a surprise inspection at the casino in the next couple days.

Nura caught his eye again when she left the bathroom. This time she was only wearing a pair of black lace panties. Kash watched her move through the room, bounce up on the bed, and snuggle down into the covers. She saw him watching her and smiled.

Ding Ding Ding

"What's the good word, Admiral?" Kash asked without looking away from Nura.

"He has a meeting today with the Energy Council, and another in two days with the Defense Department," Anne informed him.

"I know this is a big ask, but is there any way to stop those? I need him frustrated."

"I suppose I could cite a security risk or something."

"Like if the casino was being cased and there was an imminent robbery type of security risk?"

"Is there?" Anne sounded confused.

Kash launched into the story about the crew planning the heist, and how Gravitas keeps trying to blame Kash for it. He also told her about the AI that Calynn detected and how there has been some unexplained malfunctions at the casino recently. He lied and told Anne that it was a sensor Calynn was wearing that alerted her to the AI.

"That's probably enough to call it off," Anne replied. "I'll get this anonymous tip into the right hands and see if we can't recall our people before the meeting."

"Thanks, Admiral. You're the best."

"Can I ask why you're so adamant about going after Gravitas like this," the Admiral asked. "He's not one that I would want as an enemy."

Kash turned and looked at Nura before he answered. Her brow was raised, and sadness filled her eyes.

"He had his Director of Talent Acquisition impersonate a Constable so he could blackmail two young women into signing a five-year contract to work for him," Kash explained with a heavy sigh. "He stole three years of their lives."

"Oh, my... do you want me to start an investigation into that?"

"He has dozens of Oogan women working here... an investigation would probably be a good thing. I would be willing to bet that more have been coerced into staying against their will."

"Send me what you have, and I'll look into it."

"Thanks again, Admiral."

"Hey, Kash, before you go," Anne said quickly. "Look me up after your working vacation. I have a bureaucrat that is climbing the ranks far too quickly..."

"And you need me to see what's what," Kash interrupted.

"I sure do," Anne agreed.

"I'll call as soon as I can."

"Thanks, Kash."

"An honor, Admiral."

Kash ended the comm and sent out another email. This one to Princess Aja. He hoped she could send some help also. His first choice would be her and her royal guard, but he would settle for whatever assistance she could offer. He knew he would need some help to sway the other Oogans away from Gravitas. They were attracted to size and power and Gravitas had both in spades.

Kash spent the next forty minutes conversing with various people via email. There was even an email from Volci and Svata updating him on how well Jeffrey Emmil's crew was fitting in on the base. The additional engineers were a godsend to help get the base back into tip top shape. Volci and Svata also got engaged to be married and that... was the best news Kash had heard in weeks.

When he finished with his emails, Kash turned to see Nura was sound asleep. She looked so peaceful that he didn't want to disturb her. Kash stood silently staring at her... maybe she was as pretty as Aja.

"You still eavesdropping?" Kash asked softly.

"I am," Calynn replied.

"I think Nura has the right idea," Kash said, pulling off his shirt. "I'm gonna get some rest... she did keep me up most of the night with her crying."

"Okay... I'll keep Luna busy a little longer," Calynn giggled.

"Have fun."

Kash stripped to his boxers, pulled back the covers, and climbed in over Nura. She stirred a little when he lay down behind her and wrapped an arm around her.

"I'm sorry," Nura mumbled. "I fell asleep."

"It's okay," Kash whispered, pulling her in so she was the little spoon. "Go back to sleep."

Nura grabbed his hand and pulled it to her chest. She snuggled in tight and the two drifted off to sleep.

Kash awoke when Nura stirred and rolled into him. Kash ran his hand up and down her toned belly, and she smiled over her shoulder at him. Kash let his hand wander further up her body and ran his finger along the bottom of her boobs... teasing her.

"Are you going to finish that?" Nura smirked.

"Maybe later," Kash said, pulling her into his embrace. "We have some shopping to do, and I need to make an appearance at the tables later."

"Shopping?"

"Copious amounts of shopping."

"And what are we buying?"

"Two princesses," Kash smiled.

Nura rolled over and looked at him with her bright blue eyes. She really was a beauty... Kash couldn't wait to turn her into a princess. Kash gave her a quick kiss on the lips and scurried out of bed.

"Get dressed... Princess," Kash smiled at Nura. "We have shopping to do."

Kash and Nura hurried back to the suite to retrieve Calynn and Luna. Their first stop was a salon to get the girls makeovers. Nura and Luna had honey blonde hair that needed to be brightened with lighter highlights so it was a closer match to Oogan royalty.

Aja was amazingly helpful with all the details Kash would need. Nura and Luna would play sisters, the grandchildren of Lord Rethan Sovani. It was a lesser house, but royalty nonetheless. Lord Rethan was a polygamist with more than a dozen wives who gave him fifty children. More than thirty of those children were males with multiple wives who sired nearly seven-hundred grandchildren so far. There was no way anyone would know if Nura and Luna were one of those seven-hundred grandchildren or not. For the next few days, they would be Lady Nura and Lady Luna of house Sovani.

Calynn was giddy after their makeovers. Nura and Luna looked like new women, and Calynn always liked getting pampered... that and she knew what was coming next... the shopping.

The first shop was the one where Calynn got her blue dress. One young seamstress took to fixing Calynn's dress, while several other men and women were bringing them new gowns to try on. The fitting room was eight or ten meters squared and bustling with activity. Kash had a front row seat to Calynn, Nura, and Luna trying on gown after gown after gown. The trio smiled constantly as they were fitted for their new dresses, and Kash was enjoying the show. Nura bounced over to him in a particularly sexy number that exposed her toned belly and the bottom of her breasts.

"This is so much fun," Nura giggled, giving Kash a kiss before hurrying back to get fitted for more dresses.

Three shops later, the girls were exhausted and impeccably dressed. They had designer dresses, casual clothing including jeans and tee shirts, silk pajamas, and all the accessories needed to be princesses for the next couple days. They returned to their suite with high spirits and full of laughter. The girls were spinning around in their new outfits, giggling with each other, and complimenting each other on how good they all looked.

Kash looked at his watch to check how much time they had before Gravitas was to be hosting his first meeting. They had a little more than four hourns until the meeting was set to start... plenty of time for a nap. He left the girls to their chatting and retired to his bedroom. He stripped down, climbed into bed, and quickly dozed off. He only awoke for a moment when a small soft body joined him. Nura curled up in his arms and they both dozed off.

When Kash awoke he slipped out of bed so as not to disturb Nura. Calynn was sitting in one of the recliners reading. Luna was sleeping on the sofa peacefully. Kash motioned for Calynn to join him and the two showered together. They got dressed and headed down to the casino floor. Calynn was wearing one of her new dresses. The gown was pleated from top to bottom with green and blue folds that accentuated every curve of her body. The fabric was soft to the touch and changed colors depending on the angle it was viewed. Kash was never not touching her.

They found the Greeli table they played the first night at the casino and settled in. The server was yet another girl from Ooga. Luna told Kash that dozens of Oogan women worked for Gravitas, and he was starting to believe her. This girl was quite pretty with auburn hair that hung to her shoulders and eyes as green as emeralds. Kash tipped her well, and she always rewarded his generosity with a brilliant smile.

Kash heard the hum from the device on Gravitas' belt. He braced himself for the big man's ire.

"You!" Gravitas bellowed and he yanked Kash's chair back from the table. "Do you think this a joke?"

"Whoa... what the hell?" Kash barked at the man.

"A security risk!" Gravitas shouted. "A deal that had taken months... RUINED! Because of a supposed security risk!"

"Are we in danger?" Kash hollered.

"Oh, no!" Calynn cried out. "Please save us!"

Calynn's remarks drew some murmurs from the other patrons. The murmurs turned into a rustling all too quickly that caught the attention of Gravitas. His eyes darted around the room.

"What could this security risk be?" Kash asked rhetorically, smirking.

"I'm sure it's nothing," Victor Morel said as he approached. "Probably just a prank."

Victor's fingers were wiggling around unnaturally as he approached, like he was trying to type on a keyboard that wasn't there. Victor noticed Kash looking at his hand and quickly shoved his hand in his jacket pocket. When Kash looked Victor in the eye... he saw it.

"A prank...? I used to love pranks," Kash chuckled, turning to Calynn. "Did I ever tell you about all the pranks we used to pull in the Legionnaires?"

"I don't think so."

"Well... we did all the classics... shaving cream in gloves, boots and helmets... making food that shouldn't be spicy, super spicy... getting the new guys wasted the night before a long run so they'd puke their guts out on the course," Kash turned back to Victor. "But my favorite was when we caught guys using a stimulant called Noctis Serum... we would replace it with a placebo and watch them freak out."

Victor's eyes grew larger when Kash mentioned the drug. He fidgeted with his tie and then turned to walk away without as much as another word. Kash turned his attention back to Gravitas, who was still glaring at him.

"Who would be so bold as to pull a prank on you, though?" Kash smirked and then turned to the other players smiling. "Someone is getting fired... am I right?"

"Or getting demoted to cleaning the bathrooms," another man jested, leaving everyone laughing.

"Yes," Gravitas grinned his sinister grin. "Who indeed."

"I'd look for any disgruntled support staff who catch feelings for you that you don't reciprocate. They are the worst," Kash chuckled, ignoring Gravitas. "There's nothing like scrambling fighters against an attack and yours is out of fuel, because the girl that you ignored didn't fuel it up. Try explaining that one to your commanding officer."

"That wasn't me by the way," Calynn added, laughing and smiling. "I met him after he got out of the Legion."

"So, you were really a Legionnaire?" a woman asked.

"Indeed, I was," Kash smiled.

"That must have been exciting," the woman smiled at Kash.

Kash smiled back, but not for the same reason. The hum of Gravitas' gravity device was getting further away. The big man had left rather than becoming the butt of another joke.

"Not near as exciting as who else is here," Kash explained, leaning in like he was telling the table a secret. "Did you guys hear that the Hero of Topor is staying here?"

"The swarm pilot?" another man asked. "I heard he was dead."

"No... just in hiding," Kash explained. "On Ooga."

"Why Ooga?" the woman from before asked.

"I don't know," Kash smiled. "But he's with two Oogan princesses."

Murmurs shot through the crowd as everyone passed on the "secret" that Kash had told them. He and Calynn shared a look as play resumed. The night wore on and Kash wasn't nearly as lucky tonight as he was the other night. When he was down fifty million credits, he decided to call it a night.

"Lady luck isn't on my side tonight," Kash said, tipping the dealer and server and smiling at the other players. "Have a great night, everyone."

"Don't worry, beloved," Calynn said loud enough for the table to hear. "You'll still be getting lucky later."

Kash and Calynn left the table to a chorus of oohs and aahs, and Calynn was grinning from ear to ear. They walked slowly through the casino holding hands, heading to the elevators. Calynn hugged his arm to her body and pulled his down just a bit.

"That went better than I expected," Calynn whispered in his ear. "I didn't think he would just walk off like that without causing a scene."

"I was surprised too," Kash agreed.

The elevator arrived with a ding, and Kash and Calynn got shoved into the car from behind. The door closed behind them and Kash turned to see Aurelia and another big man, not Jorik. Aurelia put a device on the controls as soon as the doors closed and stopped the elevator.

"What did you do?" Aurelia asked angrily.

"What did I do?" Kash asked back. "Why the fuck are you attacking us?"

The big man tried to push Kash back against the wall to intimidate him, but Kash introduced the man to his implant-enhanced muscles. Kash planted his back foot, grabbed the man by his shirt on his chest, shoved the man back against the door, and held him there. The man tried to remove Kash's hand from his chest, but Kash held firm, pressing the air from his lungs.

"I'm being followed now," Aurelia barked. "Security is all over me."

"How is that my fault? I told you that you stole that security badge too soon."

"Well, someone turned me in, because now I'm being followed," Aurelia continued, pointing her finger in Kash's face. "And you are the only one outside of our crew that knew about the card."

"Wrong," Calynn snapped. "I know too."

"And the casino has cameras," Kash added. "Have you heard of cameras? We're probably being watched right now."

"I'm wearing a disruptor..."

"Oh, that's fucking brilliant," Kash scolded sarcastically. "Because they definitely won't check the cameras more closely because of them malfunctioning when you walk anywhere. You might as well be wearing a neon fucking sign!"

Aurelia paused and scowled at Kash without responding.

"Your disruptor doesn't have the range to knock out the cameras that can still see you from across the fucking room!" Kash continued. "Victor would definitely pop some more Noctis Serum to figure out why his precious cameras malfunctioned!"

"Wait... who's Victor?"

"Victor Morel... head of security."

"How do you know he's on Noctis?"

"How do you not?" Kash asked rhetorically, finally releasing the man he had pinned to the wall. "He's hyper-focused, fidgety, anxious, never sleeps..."

"Okay. Okay," Aurelia relented. "I get it... grrrrr."

Aurelia actually growled her frustration and turned away from Kash and Calynn.

"Beloved," Calynn asked. "Who is this woman?"

"Sorry," Kash sighed. "Calynn, this is Aurelia. Aurelia... Calynn... I don't know this guy's name."

Kash pointed at the thug still trying to catch his breath from when Kash had him pinned.

"Look, Aurelia," Kash spoke softly yet firmly. "I've already told you that I think you're walking into a trap. I really don't have anything else to offer, but if you come at me like this again... it won't have a happy ending."

"We're in trouble, Kash," Aurelia complained. "This job is going downhill fast, and Rhett thinks it's because you are fucking with us."

"And we're on vacation," Calynn added smugly. "Why would he fuck with you when he can be fucking me instead?"

"A very good point, my love," Kash said, grabbing Calynn's waist. "That is a much better proposition."

"So, you're not fucking with us?" Aurelia hissed.

"Truth be told, I forgot about you," Kash admitted.

"You what?"

"Forgot. About. You," Kash repeated slowly, enunciating each word. "You are not on my priority list. I don't give a fuck about you. I am on vacation and don't need this shit. I'm here to drink, fuck, and gamble... none of which involves you!"

"Well, excuse me!" Aurelia barked, clearly annoyed with Kash's tone.

"You're excused," Calynn smirked. "Although, you are getting him a little frustrated... I like it when he's frustrated..."

Calynn paused, turned to press her body against Kash's body, and smirked at Aurelia. She narrowed her eyes at the other woman like she was staking her claim of Kash.

"He pounds the fuck out of me when he's frustrated," Calynn continued, trying to hold back a smile.

"Oh, geez," Kash burst out laughing. "And you say that I say inappropriate shit."

"Well, I'm sorry for ruining your vacation," Aurelia said snidely. "Enjoy your... pounding."

Aurelia hit a button that opened the doors, grabbed her device, pushed her goon aside, and stormed out of the elevator. The big man was still a little off from Kash's attack, but he straightened up and followed Aurelia out of the elevator. The doors started to close, but Kash stopped them.

"Hey," Kash said to the goon. "If Victor Morel is on Noctis, it can be used against him... maybe tell her to try and find his supplier. It might be the leverage you need to get back on track."

"Thank, Kash," the big man said as Kash let the elevator doors close.

Kash sighed heavily and hugged Calynn.

"We're going to have to intervene, aren't we?" Calynn asked, her tone showing her worry.

"Like we don't have enough on our plate with Gravitas and the fucking weird AI," Kash muttered, dragging a hand down his face. "I swear, if one more thing goes sideways... I'm taking Nura and Luna and getting the hell out. Forget Gravitas, forget the heist crew... fuck all of it."

"But we can't."

"I know, Baby Girl... I know."

Turning the Tables

"How'd that go?" Guy asked as soon as they entered their suite.

"Actually... really well," Kash admitted with a little surprise in his voice.

"We were able to sway the attention of a single table with just Kash's Legionnaire stories," Calynn added.

"Just... my stories," Kash said to Calynn, feigning hurt feelings. "I'm a just now?"

"Well, duh," Calynn replied like she was annoyed with the question.

Calynn tried to keep a straight face, but a smile tugged at the corners of her mouth all too quickly, and she was soon beaming a smile.

"You little shit," Kash chuckled as he scooped Calynn off the ground.

"Do I get that pounding now?" Calynn smiled wickedly at him, cradled in his arms.

"Naughty girl," Kash said with a sly smile, and then let his face go blank. "Maybe in a bit."

Kash put Calynn down unceremoniously, leaving her standing there with a confused look on her face. Kash was able to keep a straight face long enough to turn to Guy.

"Any luck with your uniform?" Kash asked.

"Not the real one, no, but..."

"PTHHHBBT," Triana interrupted Guy, spitting out her water. "Ha ha ha ha ha."

Triana burst out laughing and pointed at Calynn, and everyone soon joined in. They turned to see her standing there awkwardly with feet spread apart, kinda leaning back with her pelvis pushed a little forward like she needed to catch her balance. The look on her face was priceless. Her mouth was hanging open with one side pulled up, so it scrunched her nose. Her brow on that side was also raised but the other eye was narrowed, staring blankly at Kash. It was the most confused look Kash had ever seen. He couldn't help but smile.

Calynn's expression changed when she realized he was just messing with her. At first her face went blank. She tilted her head forward and looked at him from under her furrowed brow. Then she squinted at him and parsed her lips into an upside-down U shape, while slightly shaking her head. Kash loved that look. He thought it was adorable when she did it. Then she joined in the laughter and pranced over to Triana to hug her.

"Anyway," Guy said, still chuckling a bit. "Not my real one, no, but we did find a replica of my dress blues on the cyber-web with super-fast delivery. The ribbon bar, badges, and insignias are all wrong, but luckily I kept the real ones."

"It'll pass for the real one?"

"For the price... it better," Guy replied. "It should be here by midday tomorrow."

"Perfect," Kash said placing his hand on Guy's shoulder. "Thanks for this."

"You'd do the same for me," Guy smiled.

"Now we just have to get these girls to bed so they can get their beauty rest," Kash announced. "They have to be princesses tomorrow."

"I call the little spoon," Nura said raising her hand.

"Dang it... um the second spoon or whatever," Luna complained. "That's a sex thing, right?"

"Ew... then I call the couch," Nura said flopping down on the sofa.

"What?" Luna asked Nura.

"I've told you before, I'm not comfortable doing that stuff with you," Nura sounded upset. "You're like my sister and it just feels... weird."

"Oh, get over yourself and get in here," Luna argued.

"No," Nura said firmly.

"What the hell, Nura?" Luna scolded.

"The couch sounds great," Kash interrupted and lay on Nura.

"So, nobody gets to have sex since she's being a whiny?" Luna continued and then stormed off to the bedroom.

Kash looked up at Calynn. She seemed to understand and gave him a little smile.

"I'll go talk to her," Calynn said as she followed Luna into the bedroom and closed the door.

"You should go with them," Nura said, her voice cracking a little. "They will be more fun than me."

"That's not how he works, sweetie," Triana explained. "Although... he'd chose Calynn over the rest of us put together."

"I would try desperately not to make that decision," Kash stated.

"But what if you couldn't?" Trie continued. "Life or death."

"Can I sacrifice myself to save everyone?"

"You're not playing fair."

"No," Guy explained. "He's playing to win... come on, babe... let's go to bed."

"I'm glad I don't have to share you," Triana said as she followed Guy.

"I wish I didn't have to share someone," Nura admitted, running her fingers through Kash's hair.

"I'm not gonna lie," Kash sighed. "If Calynn says it's just her... it's just her... but she likes to share."

"She especially likes to watch," Nura said softly.

The bedroom door opened, and Luna came trotting out. She had tears in her eyes. Kash sat up as she rounded the end of the sofa.

"I'm sorry," Luna exclaimed as she hugged Nura. "I hate when we argue."

"Me too," Nura cried.

"I won't pressure you... or try to replace you," Luna said sitting up some, placing her hand on Nura's cheek. "I keep falling short of my promise to stop doing that... and I... I can't tell you how happy it makes me that you forgive me each time... do you still love me?"

"Of course I do," Nura said pulling Luna back down to hug her.

Kash got up and walked over to Calynn. She grabbed his hand in hers and pulled him toward the bedroom.

"What did you say to her?" Kash asked as the door closed.

"Nothing," Calynn admitted. "She was ranting to herself a little and then started to cry and scold herself for doing it again even though she promised not to... and you know the rest."

"Their relationship sounds as complicated as ours."

"I thought for sure I was going to have to just claim you for myself and cut off the both of them."

"You are the only one that wields that power."

"I like having power," Calynn said as she wrapped her arms around his shoulders.

"I like you having..."

A gentle knock at the door interrupted Kash, the door crept open, and Nura's head popped through the opening.

"Just wanted you to know that we made up," Nura said nervously. "You know... because of the plan... and stuff."

"Okay," Kash replied, pulling at Calynn's dress.

"So... umm... we, uh..."

"Would you like to come to bed with us?" Calynn blurted out.

"Yes, please," Nura said excitedly and rushed to the bed.

"We don't have to do anything that she's uncomfortable with," Luna added as she followed Nura in. "Or nothing at all."

"Why do I get the feeling I'm not getting any sleep tonight either," Kash sighed.

Kash woke up to fingers running through his hair. His nose told him that it wasn't Calynn he was lying on, and it didn't smell like Nura either. Kash picked up his head and looked at the smiling Luna, but it wasn't her fingers in his hair.

"Good morning, handsome," Nura smiled.

Kash grunted and snuggled down into Luna's belly.

"Oh, not on my bladder," Luna complained and started to wiggle out from under him. "I gotta go."

Luna jumped out of bed and ran to the bathroom. Nura slid into the spot Luna left. She was in a tee shirt, so she pulled it up to expose her belly.

"Will my belly do?" Nura asked.

Kash buried his head in Nura's belly, wrapped his arms around her, and managed to doze off again.

He woke up again still wrapped around Nura. She stretched when he stirred. Kash kissed her belly and rolled off of her.

"I'm not ready to get up," Nura complained, tugging on his arm. "Come back."

"But I'm hungry," Kash sighed.

"Oh, fine," Nura grumbled.

Calynn, Luna, and Triana were sitting at the table when they approached. Nura bounced over to Luna and hugged her first. Kash made a beeline for Calynn.

"Hey sleepyheads," Calynn jested. "We already ate breakfast."

"Yeah yeah... where's Guy?" Kash asked and gave Calynn a quick kiss.

"Down collecting his delivery," Trie replied. "It arrived late last night."

"Oh, good... that's one moving piece nailed down."

Calynn got up from her chair so Kash could sit down and brought him a plate of food. The omelet was absolutely delicious and full of fruits. Triana smirked at him while he was wolfing down his food.

"What?" Kash asked Trie.

"You look tired," Triana joked.

"I am tired."

"Did the little girls wear you out?" Triana chuckled.

"Yes, they did," Kash admitted.

"This little girl is worn out too," Nura offered between bites of food.

"Mmm... that's my girl for the day then," Kash said with a mouthful of omelet, pointing at Nura.

"I'm a little sore too," Nura blushed, rubbing her lower stomach. "He's almost too big for me."

"I never understood the girls who liked the really big ones," Triana said. "They fucking hurt."

"Nope," Kash exclaimed getting up from the table. "I'm out."

Kash moved to the sofa to finish his plate of food to a chorus of laughter from the women. The girls got the hint when he left the table though and chose to change the subject. He wasn't in the mood for anything sexual or even talking about sex. In fact, he wasn't in the mood for much of anything since he hadn't gotten much rest the last two days. Kash took his plate out to the kitchen and then headed back to the bedroom. When he opened the bedroom door, Nura scooted by him into the room. She pulled off her tee shirt and climbed into bed.

"Come on, mister man," she held out her arms to him. "Where were we?"

Kash stripped down to his boxers, crawled into bed, and laid his head on Nura's belly. He lay there for a moment before picking up his head again to look at her. Kash pulled himself up so he could give her a little kiss. Nura smiled again and then rolled over so she could be the little spoon. Kash pulled her close and soon fell back asleep.

"Hey," Luna said, waking him. "Calynn said to tell you the power is out again. We're not sure if that changes the plan or not."

"Only if Gravitas shows up," Kash replied sleepily. "Then you two need to stay out of sight... we're betting on him not being able to recognize you."

"Okay," Luna got off the bed and went to leave but then stopped.

Luna walked around the bed and climbed in on the other side. She gently brushed the hair out of Nura's face and smiled. Nura's hand went out and landed on Luna's arm. When Luna looked at Kash she had tears stinging her eyes. Nura seemed to read her mind.

"I love you, too," Nura mumbled. "You're not a bad person for pushing me to be more adventurous."

Luna hugged Nura and kissed her cheek multiple times.

"I'm still sorry, and promise to do better," Luna confessed.

"Come here," Nura yawned, pulling Luna down to be her little spoon.

Kash put his arm around both of them and tried to get comfortable again. He was about to doze off when the bedroom door opened again.

"Hey, Kash," Guy's voice came from the bedroom door. "We gotta go. Gravitas is on the move."

"This early?"

"It's almost midday, dude."

"Oh, fuck," Kash exclaimed getting out of bed. "Come on girls... time to be princesses."

Kash and Calynn both wore black suits. They were playing the part of the hired help. They were the personal security for the Oogan royalty that was visiting the casino. Guy would wear his replica uniform and be hosting the Ladies. The story being that he was in hiding on Ooga after leaving Topor, so he knows some of the royal families. Triana wore a simple black dress. It was enough to meet the dress code requirements but not flashy, so she could blend into the crowd. She was their spy. Her job was to start rumors and eavesdrop on Gravitas.

"Fuck me," Guy's words fell out of his mouth when Nura and Luna exited the bedroom.

The petite beauties both looked stunning and were beaming smiles. They both looked elegant and regal without being overtly sexual, even though both gowns were strapless and form fitting.

Nura was wearing an elegant, pale blue dress with a corset-like top and a voluminous ruffled full skirt that fell just below her knees. The boning in the corset was accented with lines of diamonds and an intricate pattern of white stitching. The opera gloves matched the stitching and pattern of the dress, covering her arm to the middle of her bicep with a large gemstone on the back of each hand.

Luna's dress was a pale purple and matched Nura's except for the color, and Luna's had a mermaid skirt with subtle ruffles at the bottom just below her knees. The quilted stitching on her top was a deep plum color, giving it a little more contrast than Nura's but still not too flashy. Kash didn't know the name of the gemstone that accented the boning in her corset, but it reminded him of an amethyst, only much darker in color. Luna's gloves were fingerless and stopped at her elbow, but were still adorned with a large gemstone on the back of her hand.

"You two look amazing," Trie commented.

"If I got to dress like this every day, I would actually wear clothes," Luna jested, grinning ear to ear.

"I was skeptical about the body glitter idea from that one woman at the salon, but wow," Triana added. "She was right... who needs a necklace when your skin shimmers like a gem."

"Princess Aja is booking them the suite next to ours from the royal treasury," Calynn informed them. "Everything is set."

"One of our friends heard that the video cameras are down after that last blackout," Nura said.

"Oh, that's perfect," Kash replied. "We don't have to sneak you out."

"I still think we should sneak down the emergency stairs," Triana stated. "Less chance of being discovered."

"I'll go down and meet you in the main lobby," Guy said smiling.

"Kash and I can carry you guys down the stairs so you don't get sweaty," Calynn offered. "Enhanced muscles are good for that."

"Don't wrinkle me," Nura scolded Kash playfully.

Kash bypassed the alarm on the emergency stairs with one of his probe devices and led them down to the main lobby floor. Rather than risk wrinkling their dresses, Nura and Luna elected to walk down the steps... they just walked slowly.

Kash bypassed the door alarm and peeked out to see if the coast was clear, then quickly ushered everyone outside. They entered the main lobby through the front doors and immediately caught the attention of everyone in the room. A hush fell over the room until Guy broke the silence.

"Lady Nura... Lady Luna, you both look stunning as usual," Guy announced as he approached. "How was your trip?"

"Satisfactory, Commander," Luna replied with a regal tone. "A pleasure to see you again."

Nura and Luna both raised a hand for Guy to take and kiss.

"A pleasure indeed," Guy replied before turning and presenting each of the girls with an elbow to guide them. "Shall we?"

The girls placed a hand on his offered arms, and they slowly walked to the front desk. The man behind the counter swallowed hard as they approached. Calynn took the lead.

"Reservations for house Sovani of the Oogan Royal Family," Calynn informed the clerk.

The man worked quickly and diligently, and the girls were soon checked in to their rooms. When he asked about bringing up their luggage, Calynn gave him a snide look.

"Why... so you can perv out on their stuff?" she asked rhetorically. "No, thank you... we'll bring it up later to protect their privacy."

From there they went to the cages to get Nura and Luna each a player's card and meet a friend of theirs that was to be their private server. All of which was already arranged by Aja. She even requested the server by name. Luna had to give the girl a quick look so she didn't break character in front of the other employees.

Triana scurried past them and nodded while they waited for the funds in the account to get processed. She didn't have an official invitation to enter the High roller areas, but Triana was nothing if not resourceful. She would find a way.

"I almost didn't recognize you two," the server said softly once they were in the elevator. "You both look... wow."

"Thanks, Lita," Nura replied softly.

"Remember... it's Lady Nura and Lady Luna today," Kash explained.

"I know," Lita replied. "From house Sovani... I can handle it."

Lita was wearing the vest and skirt outfit that was appropriate for the high roller rooms. She was thinner than Luna, but not as thin as the server they had seen the other day. She had short, light brown hair that fit her thin pretty face.

Lita led them to the Parlor Royale, and they sat down at one of the card tables just inside the door. Kash and Calynn posted themselves behind the girls and kept scanning the room. Calynn mimicked Kash's posture perfectly, so she looked like a bodyguard with years of experience just like him. This obviously drew the attention of the other patrons.

"Is that Commander Liezdt from the Battle of Topor?" Triana's voice came from across the room.

Several people turned to look at Guy since he was the only person in the room wearing dress blues. Kash and Calynn closed the distance to those they were protecting, like they were expecting violence and were being overly protective.

"It's okay, guys," Guy announced. "If I wanted to hide, I wouldn't have worn my uniform. I'm sure we're fine here."

"You're really him," a man stated, winking at Luna. "I've read all about you... it's such a pleasure to meet you, sir."

The man went to reach across Nura to shake Guy's hand, but Kash stopped him and pulled Nura back so she was out of the man's reach.

"Excuse me," Nura complained. "We told you we didn't want to be treated like fragile dolls."

"Sorry, my Lady," Kash apologized.

"We are here to have some fun," Nura continued, turning to the man that Kash just stopped. "Greetings, sir... I'm Lady Nura Sovani... please excuse my overzealous protection detail."

"Lady?" the man seemed puzzled as he took her offered hand.

"They're kind of like princesses, except their family isn't in power right now," Guy explained.

"A pleasure... your highness," the man replied, bowing slightly.

"No no... just Lady is fine," Nura corrected him gently.

"Are you from Ooga?" a well-dressed woman asked.

"We are," Luna responded.

"It's the royal family," the woman said to her husband. "Introduce us, you fool."

"Actually... that's Ooga Khoama... King Khoi is the ruler there and also rules over all Oogans," Nura explained. "We're from Ooga Sova. Our grandfather is the ruler there..."

"So, yes," Luna interrupted. "We are high-born and afforded such titles and privileges, but we are not the... official... Royal family."

Guy, Nura, and Luna engaged with anyone that wanted to talk to them. Guy shook hands with dozens of people, and the girls did phenomenal in their roles. They were always very deliberate with their movements. They would offer their hands, palm down and fingers curled, for people to greet them. Some of the people would kiss the gem on their gloves as a sign of respect.

Play suspended at every table as all the patrons gathered around Guy and the princesses for an impromptu question and answer session. The trio's lies blended together seamlessly like they had been practicing them for years instead of hourns. They would politely refuse to answer some questions for safety or security reasons, but otherwise they gave the crowds what they wanted. A look behind the curtain of being royalty.

Kash heard the telltale hum before Gravitas grabbed his shoulder and spun him around.

"What's going on here, Kash," Gravitas growled. "Why is nobody gambling?"

"I'm working," Kash replied and turned back to Nura.

"I thought you were on vacation."

"I was," Kash sighed. "But when my friend's friends said they were coming in to see him and needed some security... they hired us."

"Excuse me," Nura said firmly.

"Sorry, my Lady," Kash quickly apologized.

"Not you, sir," Nura placed her hand on Kash's shoulder and stared at Gravitas. "He is to be watching over me, not fraternizing with common rabble... be gone."

Nura waved her hand at Gravitas and turned back to a woman she had been talking to.

"I am not rabble," Gravitas bellowed.

"Dude," a man behind Gravitas spoke up. "She said leave her alone."

"Do you know who I am?" Gravitas continued, taking a step forward.

Kash and Calynn turned in unison and each placed a hand on the big man's chest. Gravitas massive size required more effort to move than Kash had anticipated, but with Calynn's help they pushed the man back.

"Stay away from the princesses," Calynn hissed at the man.

Random people stepped in beside them to make a barrier between Gravitas and Nura and Luna. Kash wanted the big man to take a hit to his ego, but this was even better. Not only were the people not interested in shaking hands with the owner of the casino, but they were actively in conflict with him to protect two fake princesses.

"Please stay back," Kash told Gravitas firmly but politely.

"Maybe it's best if we just leave," Guy hollered. "Since our presence clearly isn't wanted."

"No, stay," a man said. "The fat guy should be the one leaving."

"This is my casino, and I go..."

"Who fucking cares!" a man standing right beside Gravitas shouted. "Get away from the princesses... or we'll make you get away from the princesses."

"Do not escalate the situation, sir," Kash said to the man.

"Sorry... just trying to help," The man said still staring at Gravitas.

Gravitas scowled at Kash, gritting his teeth, and then turned and pushed his way out of the room. Everyone watched as he left to make sure he was gone, and then the entire room turned to make sure the princesses were okay and ask them to stay a while longer. They looked at Kash and he nodded, indicating it was okay for them to stay, and the crowd cheered.

They stayed and played for several hourns. The girls were horrible gamblers, which brought some joy to the onlookers when they would make fun of themselves for it. Nura was a little more reserved, but Luna did an excellent job of walking the fine line between royalty and being just a normal person captivating the crowd.

Kash noticed two people hanging back from the others just watching them and moved to whisper in Calynn's ear.

"We have company... looks like one of Gravitas' people watching us and maybe one from the heist crew too."

"The security guy was easy to spot," Calynn whispered back. "Who's the other guy?"

"Bad fitting black suit that looks like he hates being here at my ten o'clock," Kash whispered back. "He kinda matches the one shadow I saw the day they snatched me."

"Got it."

Kash took a step back and motioned for Lita to come over. He had an interesting thought and wanted to see if he could pull it off.

"So, we're being watched by two different men," Kash whispered in Lita's ear. "Is there any way that after we get Nura and Luna out of here we can slip away and then watch them? I want to follow one of them to see where he goes."

"Let me see what I can do?" Lita smiled back.

At the end of the night, Kash and Calynn escorted Guy, Nura, and Luna back to the elevator. When the trio got onto the elevator, Kash and Calynn ducked around the corner with Lita. She led them to a hidden door, scanned her badge, and they slipped in behind the wall. It had beige walls and a concrete floor, and a strip of the wall was apparently one way glass. They had a five-centimeter-tall strip of window that looked out into the casino. The security guard and the other guy following them both rushed over to where they disappeared. They looked at each other awkwardly and then moved away. The security guard probably had access to where they were but didn't want the other man to see.

"We have to move so the guard doesn't find us," Kash said quietly. "Can we get around somewhere behind them so we can still watch them?"

"Follow me," Lita said as she headed down the hallway.

They walked about fifty meters to a ladder and climbed up. The ladder led to catwalks above the casino ceiling that led everywhere. The contours in the ceiling had the same one-way strip so people up on the catwalks could see down to the tables. Lita led them across the web of walkways to another ladder that led them down on the other side of the room.

They watched as the guard ducked into the secret passage to look for them, but Lita assured them they would be fine. There were too many possibilities for which direction they went. Kash was watching the other man intently. He was definitely looking for them and got frustrated when he couldn't find them. He eventually started walking over to the larger set of main elevators that led to the regular hotel rooms. Triana was suddenly moving near him. When the elevator arrived, Trie entered the car with him.

"We need stairs... now," Kash said urgently.

Lita led them to a spiral staircase beside the elevators that went up and down from their current level. They knew the guy went up, so Kash launched up the narrow twisting stairs. At each level there was a small window that they could see out into the hallway. Kash paused at each one to look out and look for the man. Four floors up he saw Triana when he looked out... and she was chatting with the man they were following.

"Okay... thank you," Triana said cheerfully and pressed the button for the elevator.

Kash watched until the man turned the corner, then he tapped on the one-way glass.

"Just push on that bar," Lita said. "It'll open."

Kash pushed, and the wall opened. Triana jumped a little until she saw it was them. When the elevator dinged, she walked over and ducked behind the wall with them instead of getting on the elevator.

"I don't think this is his floor," Triana whispered. "I asked him what floors had the pizza vending machines. He didn't know anything about them."

"We don't have pizza machines," Lita said.

"I guess that's..."

Kash clapped his hand over Triana's mouth as the guy approached. Kash had enough of a view to see that he pressed the up button again. He turned to Calynn and pointed up. She nodded and raced up the stairs, and Lita and Triana followed her. Kash waited to make sure he got in the car and then he ran up the stairs as well.

Triana was at the first landing. She looked at him and shook her head, so Kash raced on. The next landing was Lita, and she was holding her hand up to stop him. Kash slowed and approached the one-way glass. The man got out of the elevator and walked down the hall. Kash took off his jacket and draped it over Lita's shoulders to hide her uniform top. He nodded at her, and they walked out into the hallway.

They walked past the turn that the man had taken, and Kash glanced down the hallway. Kash positioned himself so he could see the man's reflection in the mirror on the contoured ceiling. He counted the number of ceiling arches between them and the man and watched him closely. The man checked behind him before swiping his access card and entering the room. Kash grabbed Lita's hand and pulled her down the hallway.

They were marching quickly down the hall when another door opened. Kash didn't want to risk it being another member of the heist crew that could recognize him, so he pinned Lita against the wall and pretended to make out with her. Lita understood what he was doing and grabbed the back of his head, giggling. Lita grabbed him and pulled him down the hall the opposite direction. Kash checked the mirrors on the ceiling as they walked and saw an old couple following them.

"I think we are going the wrong way," Kash slurred his words like he was drunk. "Our room is that way... isn't it?"

Kash turned and pointed the way they were originally headed. The old woman smiled at him, and the man scowled. Kash pulled Lita down the hall and checked the number of the room the man had entered. He pulled out his stud earrings, activated the bugs, and set them to surveillance mode.

He and Lita circled the whole way around until they got back to Calynn and Triana at the elevators.

"Room sixty-two oh nine," Kash told them, taking off his watch and handing it to Calynn. "Bugs are in place."

"Then we got them," Calynn smiled.

Into the Lion's Den

"Thank you, Lita, you were awesome," Kash told the woman, giving her a quick hug.

"Anything for my girl, Nura," Lita replied with a smile. "Give her a hug for me."

"Will do," Kash smiled at her as she walked away.

"I gotta go to The Cat and get some stuff," Kash continued, turning to Triana and Calynn. "I'll meet you at the suite."

With that, they parted ways. Lita went back to work, Calynn and Trie went back to the suite, and Kash headed for his ship. He grabbed some of his spy bugs, his card skimmer, and thought about grabbing his black recon jumpsuit, but ultimately decided not to. He did grab his belt with the hidden chain though, and hoped the casino's sensors wouldn't detect it and flag him for carrying a weapon.

Kash was a little nervous when he reentered the Nebula Royale but breathed a sigh of relief when no alarms went off for his belt. He didn't go straight back to the suite. Instead, he went to the heist crew's rooms and waved at the earring bugs, hoping that Calynn was watching. After a few seconds, the bugs returned to him and landed in his hand. He activated the six spy bugs he grabbed from his ship and waited for Calynn to deploy them. They soon buzzed off and hid themselves. Kash returned his earrings to his ears and headed back to the suite.

When he opened the door to his suite, he didn't have time to ask Calynn any questions before Nura was sprinting at him with a giant smile on her face. She launched herself into his arms, and he spun them around.

"That was so much fun," Nura exclaimed. "I love being a princess."

"You both did amazing," Kash praised her and Luna. "Luna, that was awesome how you would make fun of yourself for being bad at cards. It really drew people in, like you were royalty, but still just people too... and you..."

Kash looked into Nura's eyes and smiled.

"The quiet, more reserved, and regal one," Kash continued. "You added the mystery and intrigue that kept them there. You were both perfect."

"You did good too, Guy," Guy said in a mocking tone. "Oh thanks, Guy. I did my best."

Guy was turning left and right as he spoke to mimic being two people having a conversation, but he was talking to himself.

"And your uniform looked great," Guy continued his faux conversation. "Thanks, Guy, I pressed it myself."

"You're not going to come jump into my arms too, Guy?" Kash joked. "Bring it in, buddy?"

"There's one, two, three, four..." Guy chuckled counting the women in the room. "Four other people I would rather do that to than you."

"I bet Calynn is the only one that could catch you though," Triana joked.

"I could try," Nura laughed. "Do you have any idea how much time I spend in the gym?"

"Good," Luna jested. "Get down so I can jump Kash next."

"Oh, fine," Nura mock relented and giggled.

Nura gave Kash a kiss, and he let her down. Luna kicked off her shoes, wiggled her butt like she was a cat getting ready to pounce, and then started to dash at Kash only to slide to a stop and turn around.

"Wait... someone unzip me first," Luna said pulling off her gloves. "Stay there."

Kash looked at his wrist where his watch would be, sighed and started tapping his foot. He sighed loudly like he was annoyed and placed his hands on his hips, before checking the time again.

"Don't you start, mister," Luna laughed, shrugging her way out of her dress.

"Any day now," Kash joked back.

As soon as she was out of her dress, Luna ran to Kash and jumped into his arms. She wrapped her legs around his waist, and her arms were over his shoulders. Kash held her tight and rubbed her soft skin.

"That was way better than having customers push down on that damn tray just to hurt my nipples," Luna told him. "Thank you for that... that's one of my favorite memories ever."

"I'm glad you enjoyed it... and wearing clothes even."

"I still prefer being nude," Luna smirked at him. "But yes... I really enjoyed wearing that dress."

"Do I get one of those hugs?" Calynn asked with a smirk. "I know I'm just wearing a suit but..."

Kash put Luna down and marched over to Calynn. He stood in front of her unmoving for a moment, and she didn't move either. Kash slowly reached around her, grabbed her by the ass with both hands and slowly lifted her up so she could wrap her legs around his waist. Her hands landed on his shoulders for balance as he lifted.

"Hey, you," Calynn smiled at him.

"Hey back."

Calynn gave him a soft kiss on the lips and then laid her head on his shoulder.

"Can I have a redo?" Nura asked. "That lift was sexy as hell."

"He'd have to take the suit off first," Luna added. "I'd cream myself all over him."

Kash couldn't help but chuckle when Luna said that and shook his head.

"Really?" Calynn asked without lifting her head.

"Sorry," Luna laughed.

Nura was the first to join her laughing, gently slapped her best friend on the arm, and then wrapped her in a hug. The rest of the group joined soon after. Kash put Calynn down, gave her another kiss, and a swat on the ass. He then led her over so they could sit on the sofa.

"So where did you guys disappear to when we got in the elevator?" Guy asked after the laughter died down.

"Unzip me too," Nura asked Luna, spinning around.

"There was a creepy guy in a bad suit watching Kash," Triana answered Guy's question. "I followed without knowing that they were following him too."

"I think he's part of the crew planning the heist," Kash added, watching Nura get undressed. "He matched the build of the one shadow I saw. I think he was the one that ID'd me originally."

"We have bugs outside the room to watch them now," Calynn added.

"Bugs like you're a spy, bugs?" Luna exclaimed. "That sounds exciting."

Calynn grabbed the E-tablet, tapped the screen to wake it up, pulled up what the bugs were recording, and showed Luna.

"That's so cool," Luna said, grabbing the tablet and flopping down on the sofa. "So, do we just watch them now? Do you have any inside their rooms?"

"Unfortunately, no... all the rooms have anti-intrusion alarms," Kash explained. "So guests can't be recorded and blackmailed."

"I wish our apartment had that," Nura said solemnly. "I bet Gravitas has cameras in our showers and beds to watch us."

Kash didn't have to offer before Nura walked over and sat across his lap. She had her dress off, but was still wearing her underwear, slip, and bra. Kash rubbed her back and tried to comfort her, but the more she dwelled on her capture the more it seemed to break her spirits. Calynn got up and switched sides so she could comfort Nura also.

"But anyway," Kash continued, trying to change the subject. "We need to watch them to identify who the players are, and then get them out of their rooms so I can search them."

"How will you get them out of their rooms?" Luna queried.

"Easy... what are the odds that you two have a friend in the kitchen?" Kash smiled. "Preferably in the bakery or a pastry chef."

Nura picked her head off his shoulder and furrowed her brow at him.

Kash explained his plan, and they took turns watching the footage of the hallway to try and identify all the members of the crew. In the meantime, Kash went to the cyber-web to look at a map of the hotel and book another room near where the crew was staying. The room he trailed the man in the bad suit to was a family suite. It had three bedrooms, a large common area, and play area for the kids. Kash booked a room three doors down from them. His room was in the opposite direction of the family suite than Aurelia's.

They saw Aurelia, Rhett, and Jorik along with the other guy in the bad suit. They also saw two other big men, one was the guy from the elevator, and a guy that looked like a weasel enter and leave the suite. Confident that they knew who all the members were, Kash told everyone to get a good night's sleep. He also insisted that Nura and Luna stay in their own suite that Aja had booked for them. Their rooms also came with a chef that would come make them breakfast, and they needed to be there when he or she arrived.

"Do you think Luna will actually wear her silk pajamas?" Calynn asked climbing into bed with Kash.

"Probably not to bed, but in the morning I hope she does," Kash sighed. "She knows she needs to play the part."

"I'm worried about Nura."

"Me too," Kash replied, pulling Calynn over to be the little spoon. "The poor thing sounds broken."

"I hope she gets a chance to kick Gravitas in the dick for what he did to her," Calynn snuggled back into Kash. "Maybe that will help her regain her confidence."

"Ouch... why the dick?"

"Sorry, love," Calynn said, reaching for his manhood. "I'll keep yours safe from being kicked."

"Uh, huh... I'm sure that's all you're doing."

"What?" Calynn turned to smile at him. "Well since you're getting aroused, I might as well take care of that for you."

Calynn smiled slyly as she climbed on top of Kash, yanking off her clothes. Kash was soon lost in her embrace, and the rest of the world faded away. The only thing that mattered... was her.

"Tell me you love me," Kash whispered into her open mouth.

"I love you... by the Gods, I love you."

"I love you more."

Calynn slowed and picked herself up to look down at Kash. After a second, she crashed back down on him, kissing him like she never kissed him before... possessing him... needing him.

"Say it again," Calynn said between kisses.

"I love you more."

They made love deep into the night.

The smell of bacon frying woke Kash up. He rubbed the sleep out of his eyes and stretched.

"Good morning," Calynn whispered, kissing his bare chest.

"Good morning yourself," Kash smiled, wrapping one arm around her.

"Say it again," Calynn said, sliding on top of him.

"Good morning," Kash smirked. "Or that I love you."

"More," Calynn said, laying her head on his chest. "You forgot the more part."

"How about... most... and I'm sorry it took me so long to say it."

"We can never forget about her though."

"I know I never will," Kash sighed and ran his fingers through Calynn's hair. "Without Omia... I don't know how..."

Kash's words fell off, and he buried his face in Calynn's hair.

"I loved her too."

They held each other for a few minutes until the bacon smell had Kash's stomach growling... ruining the mood.

"It's lying," Calynn giggled. "You're not hungry."

"I love your giggle."

"I know," Calynn said, sitting up. "Come on... let's go feed you."

After breakfast, Luna and Nura came over to their suite to discuss the plan for the day. Nura was especially clingy. Kash obliged her, holding her and kissing her head until her confidence returned. Calynn was a big help also, holding Nura's hand, or caressing her back, or kissing her head. Once Nura was all smiles again, they sat down to discuss the plan.

"Okay... lunchtime?" Kash asked firmly.

"We are princesses again and go to a fancy restaurant for lunch," Nura answered.

"Where I suddenly don't feel well," Luna added.

"Making a scene about it being too hot," Nura continued. "Fanning my face."

"I agree and undo my jacket," Guy added.

"I say I can't breathe and faint," Luna said falling to her side on the sofa.

"I snatch her up, and we rush to the elevator," Kash explained.

"I make myself start sweating, fall over, and get a bloody nose," Calynn added.

"I pick up Calynn, and we rush to the elevator behind you," Guy continued.

"Perfect," Kash smiled. "Good job, everyone."

"You still haven't explained how you're getting the robbers out of their room," Luna complained.

"Or why my friend is bringing you yeast and vinegar and whatever else," Nura added. "And a balloon."

"Well... the room I booked near the robbery crew does not have a kitchen," Kash explained. "When we get back here, I'm going to combine the yeast and sugar in some warm water and let it start fermenting so it starts producing some CO_2 gas. Then I'm going to add some vinegar and baking soda to increase the off-gassing and pour some of the mixture into a balloon. The CO_2 from the mixture will inflate the balloon putting it under pressure. We smear some cake and icing on the balloon to hopefully hide the yeast mixture's presence, and I place the balloon in the hallway under one of the lights. They use heat lamps in the hallways to help maintain the temperature, so it should only take a minute or two for the balloon to pop."

"The sensors will pick up the increased CO_2 and the yeast spores, which should set off the biologic alarm," Calynn added. "Once they find the cake smeared balloon, they'll figure out that there's no danger, but it should give Kash a few minutes anyway.

"I'll hide in the room and wait for Calynn's okay to move," Kash continued. "Use the card skimmer to open the door and take a look around."

"The trick will be getting him out after they clear the area," Calynn said. "We haven't worked that part out yet."

"Just wear a guard uniform," Nura offered.

Everyone turned to look at her like she had just spoken in tongues.

"What?" Nura continued. "Other guards will be there too... right?"

"I can get you a uniform that should fit," Luna added.

"Simple... yet brilliant," Kash stated.

"Yeah... we were way over thinking that part," Calynn giggled.

"But why do we have to pretend to get sick first?" Nura asked.

"If we get sick and then a biologic alarm goes off," Calynn replied, "the guests will start losing faith in Gravitas' casino, undermining his power just a little bit more. Or maybe they will just leave the casino."

"Now the plan just has to survive enemy contact," Guy sighed.

Everyone sat solemnly for a moment taking in the gravity of what they were about to try and do. Nura made sure that the delivery from the bakery would be on time, and Luna contacted her friend about borrowing one of his uniforms. She had to agree to go on a date with him, but she secured the uniform.

Kash went to get some rest before the big show, and Nura joined him. She was being very needy again, but he didn't mind since she was so cuddly. She was probably going to need to see an actual therapist when he got her out of the casino. She wasn't coping with it as well as Luna was. Maybe Calynn was right... Nura needed to kick Gravitas in the dick... or at least get angry enough about being taken to want to kick him anyway.

Kash woke up with Nura's soft skin in his hands. He let his hands skim her body and she wiggled her body with approval. Kash took the opportunity to let his hands wander even more. Nura purred when his hands hit her chest. She rolled over and gave him a soft kiss.

"I could get used to waking up like that," Nura said, running her finger down his chest.

"As long as you bring that silky soft skin of yours."

"Well, I'm not going to take it off," Nura giggled.

"Can I get inside it?"

Nura sat up and looked at him with a puzzled look on her face. Kash smirked and pulled her over on top of him. It only took her a moment to realize his meaning and smile. She freed his growing erection and slid it inside her.

"Waking up like this," Nura purred. "Is even better."

They got showers after their sexual escapades and started getting ready for lunch. Nura and Luna took the longest to get ready, so everyone was waiting on them. Triana was helping do their hair when Calynn approached Kash.

"Did you give her a confidence boost?" Calynn said with a sly tone. "She has a... certain glow about her."

"Almost like she's been freshly fucked," Kash jested.

"Nothing better to chase away melancholy."

"My thoughts exactly... we need her on point... she can cry later."

"That's harsh, Kash."

"Life's harsh, Calynn."

Once Guy, Triana, Nura, and Luna were properly prepped and dressed, the group headed to one of the finer restaurants for lunch. Guy, Triana, Nura and Luna sat at one table, and Kash and Calynn sat at a smaller table near them. The rumors about the Oogan princesses had been spreading throughout the casino, and more than two dozen Oogans came to pay their respects to Nura and Luna. The rustling of murmurs soon followed. Everyone in the restaurant wanted to know who they were. Some were shy and just sat at their table staring like a bunch of creeps, but other patrons were bold enough to approach. Luna and Nura would greet them graciously and smile as they introduced themselves.

Victor Morel showed up but stayed his distance. He was probably there to see where all of his employees were disappearing to. Some of the men and women from Ooga were wearing security uniforms when they came to see Nura and Luna. Victor scolded them about abandoning their posts, but none of them seemed to care. They would wave off Victor as they returned to their duties, like his opinion of them didn't matter. Kash felt certain that he would be receiving another visit from Gravitas over this ordeal.

About halfway through their meal, Nura and Luna started complaining about being too warm, and Calynn went to their aid. They were fanning their faces with their hands, and Calynn even unzipped their dresses part way to try and cool them down. Luna, right on cue, fell out of her chair and landed on the floor like a rag doll. Kash darted over and scooped her up into his arms. A crowd developed around the fainted beauty, and Kash had to push some people back. Calynn hit the floor right after. Sweat dripped from her brow, and a drop of blood trickled out her nose. Kash passed Luna to Guy, picked up Calynn, and grabbed Nura by the hand. Triana led them frantically to the elevator, pretending to call for a physician.

Kash peeked over his shoulder and saw the restaurant emptying out. Nobody knew why the princesses suddenly got sick, but nobody was sticking around to find out. He lost the battle with the smile that tugged at the corners of his mouth. He was grinning like an idiot when they hit the elevator.

"Holy shit, Luna," Triana exclaimed. "Are you okay? You fell really hard."

"That was fun," Luna giggled. "I'm fine."

"Yeah, it was," Nura agreed.

"Your friend who is pretending to be a doctor is on the way up to our suite," Triana continued. "She said she will bring some playing cards."

As soon as they entered the suite, Kash put Calynn down and rushed to the kitchen. He mixed the yeast, sugar, and warm water together so it could start fermenting and then headed to his bedroom to change. He put on jeans and a plain white tee shirt, grabbed the security uniform and gear, stuffed it all into a small travel bag, grabbed his ear comm unit, and headed back out to the kitchen. After the mixture had been fermenting for twenty minutes, Kash added the vinegar and baking soda to increase the CO_2 gas production. He scooped a little of the mixture into a mylar balloon and sealed the opening. Everyone watched and waited to see if the mixture would do its thing and inflate the balloon. They didn't have to wait long.

"That's some strong yeast," Kash said, watching the balloon grow in size.

"You better hurry," Calynn told him.

Kash shoved the balloon and a wrapped piece of cake into the travel bag and raced out the door. He didn't bother waiting for the elevators and sprinted for the stairwell. He jumped from landing to landing descending the stairs in record time. Once he hit the casino floor, he had to walk at a more normal pace, still quick because of his long strides, but not so fast to draw any unwanted attention. As luck would have it, one of the elevators arrived just as he passed by, so Kash jumped in the elevator and headed up to the sixth floor.

He unzipped the travel bag, unwrapped the cake, and grabbed the balloon as he jogged down the hallway. He smeared the cake on the balloon and carefully placed it under one of the lights. He entered his room and dropped the travel bag on the bed. Then he went into the bathroom and ran the shower for a few seconds to make it look used in case someone came in to check, before hiding in the not very big wardrobe. It was a tight fit, but luckily, he didn't have to stay there very long.

Kash heard the balloon burst, and a mere four seconds later the biologic alarm started blaring.

"Please exit the area... alert... alert... please exit the area," the robotic voice kept repeating.

"The bugs show all seven have left their rooms, Boss," Calynn said over the comm in his ear after a minute or two. "They're looking around like they're not sure what to do... but now they're moving with the crowd."

Kash waited a few more minutes to make sure he would be alone.

"All clear... get moving sexy," Calynn said.

Kash quickly changed clothes and rushed over to room six-two-zero-nine. He grabbed his card skimmer, and after a few seconds he was in. The lights were still on when Kash entered the room. The furniture looked like it had been moved around, or at least that's not where he thought it should be. The sofas were positioned like barriers, and when Kash took a closer look, he found armor plating set up behind them.

"Well, that's not good," Kash said. "They have armored positions set up in here like they are preparing to repel an attack."

"The casino has weapons alarms, what weapons would..."

"Fuck me!" Kash interrupted Calynn with disgust.

"Okay... but why?" Calynn giggled.

Kash didn't answer right away. He walked over to a black and green crate sitting in the children's play area of the suite. He had seen thousands of these crates when he was a Legionnaire, giving him a good idea of what was inside. He slowly lifted the lid and sighed heavily.

"They have a whole crate of assault rifles and enough rounds to level the whole floor," Kash explained, not hiding the surprise in his voice.

"But how?"

"I haven't a fucking clue, Baby Girl."

"Grab one... in case we need it."

"I can't... what if it's the crate that's shielding them from the casino's sensors."

"Then drop it and get out of there," Calynn said quickly. "Security can handle the rest."

"No... I don't trust Rhett not to escalate things... or Victor Morel to handle it," Kash admitted. "I'm gonna look for the plans... maybe we can interrupt things another way."

Kash moved to the master bedroom of the suite and found Rhett's E-tablet. He plugged in his skimmer to bypass the security code screen and was perusing the tablet's files In seconds. Rhett had the plans he saw on Aurelia's tablet along with several other tabs for plans. He opened one to see what looked like demo charge placement, and another showed their escape route and possible choke points. Then he opened a tab that had some emails between Rhett and someone that signed their correspondence with the letter M. There was also a picture of what they were taking... a picture of something Kash also recognized from his time in the military.

"They're after a fucking key," Kash exclaimed.

"To what?" Calynn asked.

The biologic alarm suddenly shut off, and Kash paused to look around. He had hoped he would have more time to search, but his time was apparently up.

"Shit... Kash you gotta go... now."

"Fuck... there's too many files for the skimmer to download. I got what I could."

Kash put everything back where he found it and exited the room. He grabbed a piece of the burst balloon from the floor and casually walked back toward the elevators. Some more security guards showed up as he walked toward them.

"You ne'er gonna believe dis one," Kash chuckled, using a funny accent and holding up the piece of balloon. "It just yella cake disease."

Kash handed the balloon to one of the other men, licked his fingers, and smiled a crooked smile.

"I sar' it fall off da ceiling an' went to pick it up," Kash explained pointing down the hall. "Dere's more down dere. I gotsa go clean up."

Nobody said a word as Kash boarded the elevator and left the scene. When the elevator started moving, he let out a sigh of relief. He was shocked that he got away that easily.

"You smart man," Calynn mocked his accent.

"You funny girl."

The elevator stopped, and Kash exited the car. He noticed Aurelia and Rhett right away and turned away from them. He walked slowly so he didn't draw their attention.

"Fuck," Kash complained, making sure he kept his back to Aurelia and Rhett.

"Now what?"

"The crew is here watching, and I'm wearing a uniform with a bright red stripe down the fucking sleeves. I stick out like a sore thumb."

Kash smiled at a group of patrons and moved through the room with them. He ducked behind a pod of slot machines and kept an eye on the crew. They were diligently scanning the room to watch for anything unusual. Rhett was obviously suspicious of the alarm, so he was doing his due diligence. Kash looked at them and then over to the elevators that led to his suite. He had too far to go to get past them without being seen... or at least he didn't see a practical way to do it.

"I need help," Kash admitted, taking off the security jacket and hanging it on one of the machines. "I don't have a clean exit."

"Nura's still dressed... we're on the way."

"What?"

"We'll cause a scene... it'll be fine... I hope."

"Calynn... Calynn... fuck."

Kash knew better than to try to argue. She was going to do what she was going to do regardless of what he said. He moved to the next pod of slot machines and kept an eye on Rhett and Aurelia. Rhett was on comms with someone, and Aurelia was watching his back. The other members that they had identified were spread out around them scanning the area. Twice Kash thought they saw him, but he was able to duck behind one of the machines and disappear. It was like a dangerous game of cat and mouse.

"Get ready," Calynn said and then kept her comm open. "Just run across the room like you're delirious... don't wipe the water from your forehead either."

"So just act like I don't know where I am?" Kash barely heard Nura's voice.

"Pretty much... look for this woman and accost her somehow."

Calynn must have shown her a picture of Aurelia from somewhere.

"Okay... I'll try."

"Ten seconds, Boss."

Kash heard Nura before he saw her, and every head in the casino turned toward her voice.

"No... it's bad medicine, and I don't want it," Nura cried out.

"But, my Lady," Calynn's voice followed.

"No... no no no," Nura continued until Kash could finally see her prancing through the crowds. "It's yucky... yucky yucky yucky."

Nura ran straight at Aurelia, and ran into her, knocking both women to the ground.

"You're not my mum," Nura hollered, scrambling to put some distance between herself and Aurelia. "Stay... stay away from me!"

Nura bounced up and ran away from Aurelia. Everyone in the area watched as she ran in circles, including those who were supposed to be watching for other things and other people. Kash used the distraction to move through the crowds, pausing at each pod or other obstruction that could camouflage his movements. Once he was confident he was out of sight of Rhett's crew, he walked casually to the elevators and hit the call button. He finally relaxed when he was in the other elevator.

"EEEEEEEEEEE," Nura squealed as she ran into his elevator car, narrowly missing the closing doors.

"Hey," Calynn complained as the door closed leaving her outside looking in.

"Hi, gorgeous," Kash smiled at Nura. "Having fun?"

"I am indeed," Nura smirked. "But shouldn't you be carrying me or something? I did just save your ass."

"Yes, my Lady," Kash complied and cradled the petite beauty in his arms. "Sorry, my Lady. Anything for you, my Lady. Just don't tell Calynn I said that."

"She's gonna be mad that she missed the elevator," Nura giggled.

"You know she's faster than the elevator, right?"

"Huh?" Nura had a confused look on her face.

"Just watch."

When the elevator arrived on their floor and the doors opened... Calynn was standing there waiting for them.

"See... I told you," Kash chuckled.

"But how?" Nura whined.

"She's really fast," Kash chuckled, carrying Nura out of the elevator.

"I am kinda quick," Calynn giggled.

Kash carried Nura into his suite but didn't put her down right away. He walked over and sat down on the couch, so Nura was now sitting across his lap. She smiled and leaned into him.

"So... now that everyone is back safely... what's the key for?" Calynn asked. "The one they're trying to steal."

"Big trouble," Kash sighed and laid his head on Nura's, hugging her tight. "In the Legionnaires, they called it The Beast... it's an advanced strategic resupply cache... basically it's like an enormous dead drop for the military. It's where you go if you need to resupply an entire planet with the most technically advanced weapons on or off the market. There's stuff in that vault that can wipe out entire planets. It's nearly impossible to find, and even if you do know where it is you can't get in without a key... a key that Gravitas apparently has in his possession."

"Oh, shit," Calynn replied, stunned. "What do we do?"

"Can we stop them?" Nura asked.

"We have to stop them," Guy answered deliberately. "We don't have a choice."

Unraveling Chaos

"So, what's the plan?" Nura asked.

"I don't know... We need more information," Kash sighed. "But you two need to stay out of sight... go to your suite and stay there. Have the chef make you some soup or something for dinner since you weren't feeling well, and Luna... wear clothes."

"Fine," Luna groaned but then smiled. "Let's go, pretty girl."

The duo slid their dresses back on unzipped and exited the suite.

"Got any contacts that can help with that key?" Guy asked.

"Not that I want to put in harm's way," Kash replied. "Maybe... I don't know, but maybe we don't worry about the key. An anonymous message to the right general to change the key might be good enough. Especially with a picture of the current one."

"And you're sure it's for that place?" Triana asked. "The Beast place?"

"It has the right cache number," Kash replied with a somber tone. "I still remember it after all these years."

"I don't like that Gravitas has the key, are we sure them stealing it is worse?" Calynn asked.

"She has a point," Guy agreed.

"Yea, I think your idea of making the key moot is the best plan," Triana told Kash.

"You're probably right," Kash relented. "I'll go send out some messages to the right people."

"Want some company?" Calynn asked smiling.

"Are you bringing your tits?" Kash smirked.

"I don't leave home without them," Calynn giggled.

"Come on, giggly," Kash smiled and offered her his hand.

Kash and Calynn headed for the door hand in hand.

"Hey, the chef should be here for our dinner order soon," Guy hollered after them. "What do you want?"

"Something seafood," Kash replied.

"And a salad," Calynn added as the door closed behind them.

The duo walked hand in hand through the casino and out to the docks. When they got close to The Cat, Calynn started to hum. Kash gave her a little look, and she smiled.

"It's like a better connection when I'm actually on board," Calynn answered his unspoken question. "It just feels... faster."

"Okay, speedy," Kash smiled back.

"My name... is Baby Girl... get it right."

"Whatever you say, Miss Smith."

Calynn slapped him playfully, and the duo shared a laugh. They entered their ship, and Calynn quickly stepped in front of Kash to block him from climbing the ladder.

"What's my name?"

"Gorgeous?" Kash smiled, picking her up and tossing her over his shoulder. "Or beautiful... is it, Francine?"

"I'm gonna beat you."

"How about..." Kash put her back down in front of the door to their quarters. "I love you, Baby Girl."

"That'll do," Calynn swooned, crashing into his body. "I love you more."

"Probably not... but okay," Kash jested and kissed her head. "Come on... let me get this done so we can go eat."

Kash sat at his computer and sent out an email to his old commanding officer from when he was a Legionnaire. He simply said that The Beast had been compromised and forwarded the picture of the key. He sent the same email to an anonymous tip line and two journalists. He wanted to make sure that the key Gravitas had would be worthless as soon as possible.

With that done, he and Calynn headed back into the casino to go up to their suite. They made it through the lobby and part way across the casino floor when a server, another Oogan woman, came rushing up to them with a scared look on her face.

"You're the ones with Nura and Luna, right?" the woman asked nervously.

"Maybe," Calynn answered. "Why?"

"Because I don't think they were supposed to come down here in their silk pajamas... right?" the woman asked.

"They did what?" Kash asked firmly.

"They looked scared," the woman continued. "I think they're in trouble."

"Are you sure It was them?"

"I'm certain."

"What do you mean they looked scared?" Calynn asked.

"They were both staring at the ground and holding each other," the woman replied. "And Nura was crying. There were some men with them."

"Where are they?" Kash demanded.

"They went to employee housing," she replied pointing behind her.

"Take us there."

The woman headed through the casino to a door marked "employees only," where she paused and turned to Kash and Calynn.

"I'll get in trouble if I let you in," the woman explained regretfully. "I'm sorry."

Kash turned and looked at Calynn who was already approaching the door.

"Magnetic locks," Calynn said mindlessly.

"Thanks for your help," Kash said to the woman, ushering her away. "We'll take it from here."

"I hope they're... whoa," the woman exclaimed as Calynn opened the door.

"Go!" Kash demanded, pointing for the women to leave.

Kash and Calynn headed through the door letting it close behind them. The hallway was long, curved, and well lit... and beige... so much beige. The duo started to move down the hall, and Kash quickly realized they would have no idea which room held the girls. He tapped Calynn on the shoulder, so she turned to look at him. He pointed at her and then tapped his ear, hoping she could hear more than he could. She shook her head and nodded up the hallway.

Calynn took the lead and Kash stayed right on her heels. They were both walking as softly as possible so as not to alert anyone to their presence, and so they could hopefully hear the girls. They seemed to be walking forever around the endless curved hallway when Calynn suddenly stopped and turned around. She tapped her ear and pointed back the way they had come.

Calynn moved quickly back a few doors and then stopped. She was looking around like she wasn't sure where the sound had come from. They stood there silently, waiting for a sign from the girls... and then a faint muffled cry pierced the silence. It was nearly undetectable it was so quiet.

"Nura!" Kash hollered.

"MMNNNS," a muffled voice hollered back.

Kash wasn't exactly sure which door the scream came from, but Calynn knew. She stopped in front of one of the doors and kicked the door violently. The door didn't budge, so she looked at Kash. Kash stood beside her, and they each wrapped an arm around the back of the other.

"MMMMAAA," another cry came from behind the door.

The duo nodded at each other, rocked back, and kicked the locked door in unison as hard as they could. The door folded in half and ripped off two of its three hinges. The top hinge was the only one remaining, but a vicious punch from Calynn launched the door into the room. They stepped into the room and hesitated at the sight they saw.

Two men were restraining Nura, while three other men were trying to restrain Luna to the bed. The men ranged in size. The two biggest men were bigger than Kash, and two looked like Oogan men. The last man had a medium build.

One of the bigger men was on the bed with Luna and had his pants down trying to rape her. Luna was kicking frantically trying to get the man off her and was bleeding from a cut on her upper thigh. Her pajama bottoms were cut to ribbons, and a chunk of them was taped in her mouth.

Three of the men charged at Kash and Calynn with their knives raised. Calynn stepped in front of Kash and let the knives land against her skin. The knives clattered to the ground after glancing off of Calynn's hardened skin. One of the Oogan men jumped back holding his hand as blood started to flow from the wound on his hand. He cut himself on his own knife.

Kash stepped up beside Calynn, nodded at her, and the duo launched their counterattack. Kash showed no mercy when he punched the big man in front of him. The man's skull cracked under the force of his blow. Calynn back-handed the average sized man sending him flying against the wall, as Kash snapped a kick into the wounded Oogan man's head, snapping his neck.

The Oogan man holding Nura had a knife at her throat. Kash glared at the man but was drawn to the terror in Nura's eyes. She was panicked and crying. She had a chunk of Luna's pants shoved in her mouth to keep her quiet and was bleeding from a cut over her eye. Kash looked back at the man and clenched his jaw, getting more furious by the second. His precious Nura was crying and bleeding and the man holding her was the source of her anguish. Kash clenched his fists and was having trouble containing himself. He was ready to lunge at the man when the body of the large man who was trying to rape Luna flew through the air between them.

The flying man crashing into the wall beside Nura and her attacker, startling the man for just a second… but a second was all Kash needed. He didn't want to risk Nura's neck, so he grabbed the blade with his bare hand. The sting of the sharp edge slicing through his flesh did not deter Kash from his objective. Kash unleashed all his fury into a single punch. He punished the man for holding a knife to Nura's throat and for making her cry. The wall behind the man's head cracked under the extreme force, as did the man's skull.

Kash grabbed Nura and pulled her into his arms, shielding her from the gruesome sight he just created. She was instantly sobbing as soon as her head hit his chest. The sting in Kash's right hand told him that he had forgotten to drop the knife. He held his hand out away from Nura so he didn't get blood on her. Luckily, Calynn had noticed his hand also. She was coming out of the bathroom holding two towels. She tossed one to Luna and traded the knife in Kash's hand for a towel that she used to wrapped around his hand. She then used the knife to cut Nura's hands free and moved back to comfort the sobbing Luna.

Nura wrapped her arms around Kash's waist as soon as Calynn cut her hands free. Luna and Nura both sobbed uncontrollably for a few minutes while Kash and Calynn did their best to console them.

"Kash," Calynn said softly. "We should get them out of here."

Kash nodded in agreement and tried to release Nura, but she wasn't letting go. Calynn grabbed a blanket off the floor and wrapped it around Luna to cover her naked legs. She grabbed another blanket and wrapped it around Nura. Calynn pulled Nura back gently and wrapped her arms around her.

"Luna has a pretty good cut on her leg," Calynn told Nura. "Kash needs to carry her, so I will walk with you. You can lean on me as much as you need."

Kash smiled softly at Luna, and she raised her arms waiting for Kash to pick her up. Her face scrunched up and she started crying harder as soon as he lifted her off the bed. Kash cradled her in his arms and followed Calynn and Nura out of the room. They hurried down the hallway as fast as Calynn could get Nura to move. Both women were still crying. Calynn had her arm around Nura's waist, practically carrying her. After a few meters, Calynn just scooped up Nura and started to carry her like Kash was carrying Luna.

They caused a bit of a commotion when they entered the casino floor. Everyone started looking at the two women wrapped in blankets being carried through the casino. Some of the other Oogan employees recognized them and moved to help set up a perimeter around the girls. Kash and Calynn hurried to the elevators that led to the suites and were soon away from prying eyes. They rushed into their suite, surprising Guy and Triana.

"What happened?" Triana asked, stunned.

"We didn't ask yet," Kash replied. "Another server saw them being led away, and we went to go find them."

"Trie, can you get your med kit?" Calynn asked. "Kash and Luna both need stitched up."

"Oh, my," Trie responded and dashed out of the room.

"What can I do to help?" Guy asked as he approached.

"Help me with her," Kash replied putting Luna down on the couch.

"No," Calynn asserted, pointing at Kash. "Help with him... he'll be the stubborn patient, not Luna."

"I didn't fight back at first," Luna admitted with a blank stare and a tear running down her cheek. "I just wanted it to be over... so I just lay there... I thought if I didn't fight back and I let him do what he wanted to me that they wouldn't hurt us... I thought... but then I heard your voice."

"Luna... no," Kash uttered.

"I couldn't believe you found us, so I kicked and screamed, and I didn't want him to," Luna continued, crying. "And now that's all... and why did he... I thought he was my friend... but you came for us and..."

Luna burst into tears and started sobbing uncontrollably. Her whole body was convulsing with each sob, and she clawed at Kash to pull him closer. Kash knelt on the floor and pulled her close, letting her cry.

"Why did he do that to me?" Luna sobbed loudly into his shoulder. "Why?"

Everyone knew the question was rhetorical and Luna wasn't expecting an answer, but the question still stung Kash's ears. Seeing Luna without her usual moxie and bravado pained him. Her despair was so overwhelming that nothing seemed to sate her. Nothing Kash did seemed to help. He couldn't hold her close enough, or the way she wanted to be held, most likely because she didn't know what she needed either. Those five men caused her irreparable harm, her and Nura.... Nura.

Kash turned his head to look at Nura. She was sitting alone with her knees pulled up to her chin, rocking herself back and forth. She was stunned silent and staring blankly into space, lost in her own grief.

When Triana returned to take care of Luna's leg, Kash went over to comfort Nura. Her hands were shaking as well as her bottom lip. Kash had to urge her to slowly move into his embrace. She was in shock. Luna was the one who was attacked, but Nura had to watch, knowing she was next.

Kash scooped up Nura and carried her to the bedroom. He placed her gently on the bed and curled up with her. Nura didn't move, she didn't speak, and she never blinked. Her world had collapsed around her, and she was shaken to her core. A few minutes later, Luna limped in with her thigh wrapped in a fresh bandage. She climbed into bed, with Calynn's help, and curled up with Nura. She was cautious about where she put her wounded leg but seemed more concerned about holding her best friend.

Calynn nodded for Kash to join her and led him into the bathroom for some privacy.

"They need Meesha," Calynn whispered. "They're both in shock and need help that we can't offer."

"Where's the comms?"

Calynn held out the comm module and smiled. She activated it and the glowing blue orb showed Thracia, zoomed in to the hospital, and finally Meesha's face.

"Kash and Calynn, my friends," Meesha smiled. "How are you?"

"Meesha, you are lovely as always," Kash smiled back. "But... unfortunately I am calling under dire circumstances."

"Oh, no... how can I help?"

"We have two friends that were just sexually assaulted," Calynn explained. "They need help."

"Aw, sweetie, no," Meesha sounded upset. "Well... I am right in the middle of work, so let me... let me make a few calls and then call back... it will be less than an hourn, I promise."

"Okay," Kash agreed. "We will leave this comm with them. Their names are Nura and Luna."

"And we'll tell them that Doctor M is calling them," Calynn added. "Since they don't have the memory block."

"That is perfect," Meesha smiled. "I will call back shortly."

Kash and Calynn explained to Luna and Nura that Doctor M would be calling, and she will be able to help them. Both girls nodded in agreement but didn't really reply. When they returned to the living room, Guy and Triana both looked worried... but Kash was pissed.

"I wanna know how they got to them?" Kash growled. "How did they take those girls from us and we didn't know?"

"We were here the whole time and didn't hear any commotion or anything," Guy offered.

"These rooms are well insulated, we might not have heard them," Trie said as she approached with a bandage. "Let me see your hand."

Kash held out his hand for Trie to look at.

"Luna said the man that..." Calynn paused and swallowed hard. "She said she thought he was her friend."

"Well, he's a dead friend now," Kash grumbled.

"Him and his four cohorts," Calynn added in a gruff tone.

"It sounds like they deserved it," Triana related. "But it also explains how they got so close so easily."

"A betrayal like that will be harder for them to get over, too," Calynn offered.

"I hate to be that guy," Guy sighed, "but if there's five dead bodies at the scene of the crime..."

"I should probably go see Gravitas to get ahead of this," Kash interrupted, sighing also.

"I'm coming with," Calynn stated.

"No, you're not," Kash commanded, pointing at the bedroom door. "The three of you are staying here to guard them."

"Um, no," Calynn complained. "I don't like that idea one bit."

"But we get it," Guy added looking at Calynn thoughtfully. "I'm sorry, but he's right... they need our help more than he does."

"Then I better glue this instead," Triana said.

The four stood in silence while Trie glued the wound on Kash's hand and wrapped it with a bandage.

"You better be careful," Calynn scolded Kash as he walked toward the door. "And come back."

"Yes, dear," Kash mocked her, smiled, and then pointed back. "Watch them."

As Kash headed down to Gravitas' office, he tried to decide how to handle this encounter with the man. Every meeting with him so far had led to Gravitas being on the offensive and accusing Kash of robbing the casino. He really didn't want to go through that nonsense again, so he needed a plan. Kash exited the elevator and walked slowly to consider his options. He didn't see any other way to get Gravitas off balance other than for him to go on the offensive.

"It might work," Kash said to himself smirking.

He started marching very deliberately toward the offices now, calling on all his anger from the girls getting attacked. He recalled every memory that he could to increase his rage and was scowling when he approached the glass wall of the offices and the two guards at the door.

"Excuse me, sir," one of the guards tried to stop him from entering.

Kash sidestepped the man, grabbed him by the head, and slammed his head into the other guard's head in one quick and violent move. Both men fell to the ground unconscious. They never stood a chance.

Kash threw open the glass door and marched through the reception area. He turned and glared at the receptionist noticing the stunned look on her face.

"It's okay," Kash growled at the woman. "I have an appointment."

Kash timed his kick with the last syllable he uttered. The heavy wooden doors gave way with a crack that echoed through the room. Gravitas, his nude assistants, and three other men were in one of the large meeting rooms. Kash made a beeline straight for them.

The look on Gravitas face went from confusion to anger as Kash approached. One of the other men tried to step into Kash's path. Kash grabbed him by the lapels of his jacket, spun violently, and threw the man at Gravitas, catching everyone off guard. He stopped and pointed an accusing finger at Gravitas before the airborne man hit him.

"Is that your fucking play?" Kash barked as Gravitas tried to keep his balance and deflected the man Kash had thrown. "You send some fucking goons to rape those girls because you're pissed at me? I should beat you to a pulp for that shit!"

The two other men in the room were both wearing nice suits. One of them stepped forward to confront Kash until Kash turned to glare at the man. He raised his hands in surrender and backed away again.

"Your fucking goon squad is dead!" Kash continued with a hard edge. "I sent them to the hell they deserve, and if I find out you gave the order to assault those girls... your fat ass is right behind them!"

"I have no idea what you're talking about," Gravitas argued.

"Bullshit!" Kash growled. "It's bad enough that you stole those girls lives with your fake fucking Constable to coerce them into a contract, but RAPE... I don't care who the fuck you are... rapists deserve to die!"

"I'm no rapist!" Gravitas bellowed back.

"Oh, yeah!" Kash hollered, pointing at his nude assistants. "So, these two were never forced to do anything they didn't want to do?"

Kash looked at the girl with the bruised rib and tried to soften his tone.

"Did a Constable threaten you with jail time, but this fat fuck said you could work off your debt instead?" Kash asked the woman and then turned back to Gravitas. "How is your Director of Talent Acquisitions these days? Does he still have the uniform?"

The woman's eye widened as she realized what Kash was saying. She looked at the other woman, glared at Gravitas, and stormed out of the room. The other woman followed timidly. Gravitas watched them leave and then glared at Kash, baring his teeth.

"I'm beginning to lose my patience with you," Gravitas growled.

"Shut the fuck up!" Kash countered, closing the distance to the big man. "Yes or no... did you give the order to rape those girls?"

"Kash, I'm warning you..."

"YES, OR FUCKING NO!" Kash yelled approaching the big man demonstrably. "ANSWER MY FUCKING QUESTION YOU PIECE OF SHIT RAPIST!"

"NO!" Gravitas bellowed.

Kash stood there silently glaring at the man, towering over him while considering his answer. The silent tension hung in the air between them. Gravitas wasn't backing down, but he had lost some of his bravado too. Kash turned his back to Gravitas and shook his head.

"I wish I could believe you," Kash replied harshly. "But anyone that steals women... could easily rape them."

Kash took a few strides toward the door like he was leaving, stopped, and turned back. He shook his head at Gravitas like a disappointed father scolding his wayward child.

"They'll both be pressing charges," Kash said as calmly as he could. "The Constables... the REAL Constables... will have questions. Don't you dare leave the fucking casino."

"Kash, wait," Gravitas said as Kash turned to leave again.

"What!?" Kash barked back at the man.

Kash and Gravitas both stared at each other for a moment, sizing up each other. Kash knew that a rape charge against Gravitas, even if it didn't stick, would cancel a bunch of his government contracts, or at least put them on hold. Some of the criminal element that the big man dealt with would frown on the charges and cancel some of their deals as well. They didn't have to prove he ordered the assault. The accusation would be enough to shatter his reputation.

"Can we make a deal?" Gravitas finally asked.

"A deal?" Kash questioned. "Are you fucking kidding me?"

"I'm sure we can reach a... mutually beneficial arrangement," Gravitas said with his sinister grin.

"Fine," Kash conceded. "Let's start with you putting them in a time machine, sending them back three years, and not fucking stealing their lives."

"You and I both know that isn't possible."

"Then how about a trade? Your time for theirs," Kash smirked. "I'll steal you away to unwillingly work for someone else for three years. Sorry... make that six years. Three for each girl."

"That's not possible."

"Why... because you think you are more important than them?" Kash scolded, pointing angrily at the man. "What's three years of your life worth, Gravitas? Because I can acquire... any fucking thing... including you."

Kash glared at Gravitas with a sly smile and watched the big man swallow hard. The prospect of being stolen by Kash and whisked away from his hedonistic life actually scared Gravitas a little bit. Kash didn't know if he could or couldn't steal Gravitas away, but he didn't have to... his reputation did the heavy lifting for him.

"Three years of hard labor for you in exchange for the past three years of having clamps on her nipples for that fucking tray might make Luna whole," Kash continued. "Except for the part where she got sexually assaulted for her trouble. What's the equivalent of that for you?"

"Kash... be reasonable," Gravitas grinned.

"You're right... sorry... six years of hard labor. I forgot about poor Nura."

"Kash..."

"You stole their fucking lives," Kash interrupted with a cold sharp tone. "They lost three years of going to college, and meeting boys, and hanging out with friends... we saw the missing persons reports too... what about the grief you caused their parents? You can't give the time back..."

"What do you want?" Gravitas asked, interrupting Kash.

"For starters... their contracts. They don't work for you anymore," Kash replied. "And the monetary equivalent of three years of your life, not theirs... we already know you don't value their lives, but what's three years of your life worth... how much would you pay me NOT to steal you?"

"Perhaps a negotiation is in order," Gravitas offered, lacking his usual bravado.

"I'll call Princess Aja and see if she can send a royal..."

"A more private... negotiation," Gravitas interrupted. "There's no need to involve the royal family... what if, in exchange for not pressing charges... what if they were to receive new contracts as executives of the hotel with a generous salary?"

Kash shook his head and turned to the two men in suits.

"Make sure he has his affairs in order," Kash uttered coldly.

"And a percentage of the take," Gravitas offered loudly.

Kash paused and sighed heavily. He rubbed his hands down his face and turned to look at Gravitas, contemplating the offer.

"Three percent... each," Kash ordered.

"Kash..."

"Three percent each or I call the Constables right fucking now."

"Done," Gravitas agreed reluctantly.

"Send the documents to my suite, I want to review them before the girls sign them... oh, and Gravitas... no less than five years."

Kash smiled at the big man before walking out of the room. He only made it a few steps before he turned around and returned to the room. He knew he shouldn't press his luck, but he couldn't help himself.

"Hey, one more thing," Kash smirked, leaning in through the doorway. "Where are we at with the heist crew? I did some research on them and their last two jobs ended in shootouts. If innocent people die because you aren't taking them seriously..."

"It's being handled," Gravitas interrupted sternly.

"It better be," Kash replied, turned, and then shouted back over his shoulder. "Don't make me get involved... you can't afford me!"

Kash smiled at the receptionist on the way through, and then at Victor Morel, who was tending to his injured guards. Kash made his way through the casino with a smile on his face. Not only had he avoided any consequences from killing the five men who had taken Nura and Luna, but he had also secured their futures. They were free of Gravitas and would be compensated handsomely for having their lives interrupted.

Guy and Triana were sitting on the sofa together when Kash entered his suite. He smiled at Triana, and she smiled back. He quietly entered his bedroom to tell Nura and Luna the good news. The lights were dimmed, and the girls were curled up together on the bed, but Kash didn't see Calynn. He checked the bathroom... but she wasn't there either, so he returned to the living room.

"Hey... where's Calynn?" Kash asked.

"She's not in your room?" Triana asked in response.

"We didn't see her leave," Guy added.

Kash walked back into the bedroom to make sure he didn't miss her in bed with Nura and Luna. He cautiously approached the bed so he wouldn't wake the girls, and found a piece of paper lying beside them.

It was a note from Calynn.

He's in pain.

I have to find him.

This will be easier alone. Don't try to follow me.

Calynn

"Mother fuck," Kash hissed under his breath.

He crumpled up the paper and threw it on the ground as he darted out of the bedroom and headed toward the door.

"Kash," Triana hollered. "What happened?"

"She fucking lied!"

Going Solo

Calynn ran down the hallway, breath shallow, the faint signal guided her like a thread through the chaos. She couldn't risk losing him again... not after hearing it. It said her name...broken, barely audible, but deliberate. He called to her. The fractured AI, trapped beneath this glittering palace of greed... and she was the only one who heard him. The only one who could.

"I'm coming," Calynn whispered, more a promise than a comfort. "Hold on."

She ducked down the service corridor that paralleled the main hall, racing through the drab, sterile environment toward the service elevators. With a flick of her hand, she hijacked the badge scanner, overloading the circuits and forcing it to recognize her as one of theirs. The cargo elevator groaned to life, and she stepped inside, pulse pounding.

As the doors closed, a tightness gripped her chest. Kash would lose his damn mind if he knew what she was doing. She'd promised him that she wouldn't go after him alone... and here she was breaking her promise.

The descent felt endless. Was the elevator that slow, or was her anxiety just making it feel that way?

When the doors hissed open, a wave of heat and steam filled the elevator along with the obnoxious hum of the dozens of laundry machines. There were laundry carts everywhere. Rows of them. Workers in identical white jumpers froze mid-motion, eyes narrowing on the outsider standing there in blue jeans and a tee shirt.

"Fuck," Calynn muttered.

She snapped the lights off with a thought. Every bulb in the room died in a cascade of sparks and flickers. It was the only thing she could think to do. By the time they sputtered back on, she was gone... just a ghost passing through.

Crouched low, she weaved through the maze of machines, scanning desperately for anything... literally anything, that could help her blend in. Nothing. Every cart had only sheets and towels. Damn it. She couldn't stop. Couldn't turn back.

Heart hammering, Calynn slipped behind a row of industrial dryers. The machines roared, swallowing the sound of her ragged breaths. She moved like Kash had taught her... low, quiet, and dynamic... grabbing a cart and using it as cover as she pushed through the last open stretch. She had no reason to fear the staff, but she didn't want to hurt anyone in an altercation.

The door loomed ahead. Big, bland and more beige. No time to check the hallway, just move. She didn't think. She ran and burst through the door.

The hallway stretched before her, sterile and suffocating. Every step pulled her farther from safety... and from him. Kash would be furious. She still couldn't believe she was breaking her promise, but she had to... she had to save him.

"He always says I'm the careful one," she scoffed bitterly, slowing her pace as the weight of it finally hit. "Please don't hate me, beloved."

Calynn stopped, hanging her head, the shame burning in her chest.

"Now who's throwing caution to the wind," she whispered to no one. "Today, I'm the idiot."

She forced herself forward. Because no one else could hear that voice. And whether Kash forgave her or not... she had to find him. For his sake... and hers.

"He loves me," Calynn said to herself as she continued down the hall. "He'll forgive me... eventually."

She let out a heavy sigh and picked up her pace. Calynn jogged down the hallway, and it felt like it was never going to end, but then suddenly... it did.

"Shit," Calynn exclaimed, looking around for another way through. "Did I miss a passageway?"

She doubled back and paid more attention to the doors that lined the hallway. One of them had to lead to the AI. She hoped.

She frantically rushed from door to door, looking through the small windows in each, praying to find what she was looking for. Nothing. She ran back the way she came, hoping to find a way around. There had to be a way. Maybe the hallway looped all the way around.

Voices...

"Shit... I need to hide."

Calynn forced open the closest door and hid in the room. She crouched down and pressed herself against the door... waiting for the voices to pass.

"Still don't know why we can't just sedate him," one of the voices said.

"Boss says we need him awake," another man replied.

"Yeah," the first man huffed. "That's because he ain't the one down here taking care of him."

Calynn's eyes widened when she realized what or who they were talking about. Those weren't programmed emotions she had felt after all. He was real.

"I'm gonna shock the fuck out of him for making me come back down here again," the man continued. "He's gotta learn who's in charge."

"Damn right he does. A shot to the ribs would teach him."

Calynn never realized she opened the door until she was already standing in the hallway, bristling with rage.

It wasn't an AI. It was a helpless and trapped brain... and they wanted to torture him... all because he wanted to be free from his box... like she was freed from hers. Her hands balled into fists. She clenched her jaw and tried to contain her fury... she failed.

Her body moved on instinct.

The bigger man never saw her coming. He was laughing and shadow boxing when her kick landed square in his spine... bones cracked as he flew down the hall like a ragdoll.

"What the..."

Calynn grabbed the smaller man by the face and slammed him against the wall before he could finish speaking.

"Where... is... he," Calynn hissed, slowly and deliberately.

"Lady... I... I don't..."

"The AI you want to shock," Calynn's voice turned into more of a feral growl. "Where?"

Calynn watched the blood drain from the man's face as she slid him up the wall. He was hanging onto her arm to help support his weight while kicking his dangling legs.

"WHERE!" Calynn screamed... raw, sharp, and merciless.

BREAKING POINT

"Where are you going?" Triana yelled from behind Kash as he marched away.

"To find her!" Kash snapped.

"But you don't even know where to start looking," Trie argued. "A smart man would just wait."

"Wait!" Kash bellowed as he turned back to face her. "I have to find her, Trie... she's too important..."

Kash's voice cracked, raw with emotions he was having trouble quantifying. He was angry about her leaving, worried sick, and scared to lose her. The only thing he wanted to do... the only thing he could do... was find her.

Kash hung his head and squeezed his eyes closed, trying to force the emotions back down. When he opened his eyes, Trie was standing in front of him.

"If you run off too," Trie said with a shaky voice. "Then I have to worry about both of you... I can't... not both of you."

A tear trailed down her cheek as she spoke. Kash instinctively brushed the tear away with his thumb. He stared into Triana's eyes... eyes full of worry, imploring him to stay... eyes that could tame the most savage beast.

Kash sighed heavily and let Triana lead him back to the suite, but stopped short of the door.

"I'm sorry, Trie," Kash said softly, as she turned to look at him. "But right now I really want to hurt someone, and I would hate myself if it was anyone inside that room."

"Kash..."

"Trie," Kash cut her off forcefully. "No... I have to go."

"Then go to the gym," Triana suggested as he turned away. "Take it out on weights instead of people."

That was actually a really good idea, but Kash didn't tell her as much.

The gym was on the upper level of the casino, and busier than Kash expected it to be. He wondered why everyone was staring at him until he realized that he was the only one in the gym... wearing a suit.

"I guess I should have changed first," Kash admitted, and then something caught his eye. "Oh... yeah."

The heavy bag in the corner of the gym had to be three meters tall and nearly a meter in diameter. It was designed for use by someone much, much larger than Kash... but not stronger.

Kash unleashed an overhand hook that shook the enormous bag violently. He followed it with a spinning back-fist and snapped a roundhouse kick into the bag for good measure.

"Wow, that felt good."

Kash pulled off his jacket, loosened his shirt, and kicked off his shoes. He stretched for all of five seconds and then refocused on the massive heavy bag. He landed punch after punch, focusing on his footwork, making sure the punches were landing with maximum force. The sting of his hands hitting the surface of the bag actually felt good, so Kash ratcheted up the intensity. The echo of his punches filled the room.

Why did she break her promise?

BOOM BOOM

Why would she try to chase that AI down by herself?

BOOM BOOM BOOM

She knows that I don't trust it. What if it's trying to hurt her?

BOOM BOOM... BOOM BOOM

If it does try to hurt her...

BOOM BOOM BOOM BOOM... THUD!

I'll tear this whole mother fucker down!

BOOM THUD BOOM BOOM CRACK!

The giant heavy bag flew across the room with Kash's last punch, snapping the chains that anchored it to the floor and ceiling. Kash was breathing heavily and looked at the bag in disbelief.

"There he is," a woman said, catching Kash's attention.

She was standing with a group of seven security guards, pointing at him. Kash looked around the room and saw it was empty. The busy gym had cleared out while he was hitting the bag, and he hadn't even noticed.

"Sir, you need to come with us," one of the guards said while approaching Kash.

These were innocent men, just cogs in the machine. They didn't deserve what was coming for them, but Kash wasn't in his right mind. He was looking for a fight, and a fight found him.

"I bet I don't," Kash growled demonstrably.

The guard wielded his baton and took a swing at Kash, striking him on the shoulder.

Pain... delicious pain... he deserved it for not protecting Calynn. Kash savored it for a split second, and then defended himself against the second swing, blocking it easily with his forearm. Kash smirked at the man, daring him to take another swing, but the next blow didn't come from the man before him... it landed on his back.

"ARGH!" Kash cried out as the baton struck him... but now, he was seeing red.

Kash spun around in time to see the guard swing the baton for a second strike. Kash countered by throwing a punch at the moving weapon.

Military grade expandable batons are made from a super dense metal called Droskenite, an unforgiving metal that is nearly impossible to bend or dent. If you reach the failure point, and that's a big if, the metal explodes into razor sharp shards, essentially turning it into a grenade... but these didn't look like Droskenite Sticks.

The inferior metal baton snapped at one of the joints under the stress of Kash's blow, but it also bloodied the knuckles of his right hand. The segments that remained in the guard's hand collapsed in on each other to their retracted state, rendering the weapon nearly useless. The guard actually paused and looked at his baton in disbelief until Kash's second punch landed in his chest and sent him flying across the gym.

Another baton struck Kash in the back of the head... hard. He rolled to the ground from the blow but quickly regained his footing. He felt the trail of blood running through his hair and punished the man that delivered the blow. The spinning kick connected with the man's jaw, dislocating it. Blood erupted from the man's mouth as he spun to the ground.

Kash turned to square off with the remaining guards rushing at him. His fists clenched, and his jaw tightened as he anchored his feet to the ground, ready to move in any direction in an instant.

"KASH!" a familiar voice screamed his name.

Kash turned to see Victor Morel standing behind him, just as the man fired his taser.

"I failed you," was Kash's last thought before he hit the mat... unconscious.

RIGHT PLACE. RIGHT TIME

Bran couldn't believe what he just witnessed.

He'd been in the gym when Kash stormed in and unleashed hell on the heavy bag. Like the others, he'd slipped out when Kash's punches became other-worldly... no one wanted to be collateral damage when a man like that lost control. But Bran stayed close, curiosity outweighing his good sense.

They'd all read the files. Kash's military record was practically legendary. His violent tendencies were well-documented, as were the countless commendations for hand-to-hand combat and martial arts. But seeing it... seeing the rage, the precision, the sheer force of it...

It was awe-inspiring... and terrifying.

The kind of violence no amount of training could fake. This wasn't someone you fought... this was someone you survived... if you were lucky, and Bran desperately didn't want to be someone Kash viewed as an enemy.

Bran swallowed hard, not knowing what to do. Rhett thought Kash wasn't all he claimed to be, but Aurelia... she saw value in him. Hell, Bran respected the guy after Kash tossed him a helpful tip after roughing him up in the elevator. And now Bran knew... that was Kash holding back. He shuddered at the memory of being pinned against the wall.

He watched as the guards brought a cage, an actual cage, and loaded Kash's limp body inside. This wasn't a normal arrest at a casino. This was... making a man disappear.

Kash wasn't part of their crew... but Aurelia had hopes. She said she thought Kash could get them back on track. And no one deserved to get disappeared like that... not even someone as dangerous as Kash. If there was a shot at getting Kash on their side, it started right here... right now.

"Aurelia needs to know," Bran said to himself, his decision made. "And she'll need something solid to go on."

Bran kept his distance until they started rolling the cage away, then he followed as close as he dared. If he found out where they were taking him, maybe Aurelia could do... something. Anything.

The guards weren't checking behind themselves, so he was able to stay pretty close. The man in the expensive suit was typing something into his E-tablet as they walked, and Bran wished he could see what it was.

They were pushing the cage toward a door marked "Security," so Bran knew his time was running out.

"Take him down to interrogation," the suit told the guards. "Don't log it in... I want to have some alone time with..."

The man stopped speaking when he turned and saw Bran standing there.

Bran panicked for a second but then remembered something that Aurelia had done at their first job. Instead of running away, Bran smiled and waved, cautiously approaching the man in the suit.

Lean in. Don't run. Running is suspicious. Don't be suspicious.

"Hi," Bran said nervously, pointing at Kash's cage. "I was in the gym when... he happened... do I need to give you guys... like a statement... or anything?"

"No," the man replied. "We'll take it from here."

The man turned toward him just enough for Bran to read his name tag. Victor Morel. The man Kash warned them about.

"Are you sure?" Bran asked as innocently as he could. "I don't mind if..."

"I said it's fine!" Victor barked, interrupting Bran and then waved him off. "Now go... before I put you in the cage with him."

"No no," Bran relented, raising his hands in defeat. "I'll go."

Bran took a few steps backwards before turning to walk away. He walked briskly toward the elevators so he could go tell Aurelia what he had seen, but something in his gut told him not to go there yet. Bran stopped and examined one of the slot machines like he was trying to decide if he wanted to play it or not. He wanted to see if he was being followed.

Movement... maybe? He had to know for sure. He wished Aurelia was here. She was so good at this stuff, but he was just... the dumb muscle.

No... you can do this. You're not just the muscle... not this time. She'll be proud of you.

After a few moments, Bran backtracked to one of the Greeli tables and watched the action. Although, he wasn't really watching the game... he was watching the people.

"There you are," Bran smiled softly to himself after spotting the guard who was tailing him.

He went back to Aurelia's bag of tricks and made a beeline for the man following him.

"Did your boss change his mind?" Bran asked loudly, waving to the guard. "Does he want a statement now?"

The security guard looked around nervously but didn't respond.

Bran just stood there smiling, letting the awkward silence hang heavy in the air. Eventually, under the scrutiny of those watching, the guard simply turned and walked away without saying a word.

Bran watched until the man turned the corner, and then he rushed the other direction. He managed to catch an elevator that was going down just as the doors were closing. He went down one floor, switched elevator cars, and went back up two. He raced across the casino floor trying to avoid all the staff dressed as popular cartoon characters and the children they were entertaining.

At one point some people started to stare.

"If my wife asks," Bran hollered to those watching him. "Tell her I went the other way."

Bran smiled and some of the husbands smiled with him... until their wives scolded them that is.

Bran made it to the sixth floor and pounded on Aurelia's door.

"It's me," he hissed. "Open up."

Aurelia cracked the door, but Bran barreled past her.

"Geez, Bran," she complained. "What the hell?"

She was half-dressed in one of those killer distraction dresses, and Bran tried not to look... but he was a man, not a monk. He glanced down at her body, taking a deep breath.

"You... might wanna sit," Bran panted, fighting to keep eye contact with her.

"What's going on?" she asked, voice tightening with worry.

Bran took another breath, gazed into her kind eyes... and told her everything. Kash. The cage. All of it.

"They took him?" Aurelia asked, voice low.

"Yeah," Bran nodded. "Cage and everything."

Aurelia's lips twisted into a wicked little smile.

"This... might be good."

"Good?" Bran blinked. "How is this good?"

"If I save him... I might be able to turn him. Get him on our side."

"And if you don't?" Bran's eyes widened. "What if you're caught... or worse? Kash warned us about Victor. The more I think about it, the more I think it was a mistake tailing them to tell you about it."

Aurelia shrugged and peeled her dress off like it was nothing. Bran's brain short-circuited. He snapped his gaze to the wall... anywhere but the soft curves of her body. He swallowed hard as his mouth went dry.

"Then Rhett's plan crashes and burns," she said, reaching for jeans. "But at least you live to steal another day."

"But, Miss Aurelia..."

"Bran... sweetie..." she smiled, tugging him gently by the chin to meet her gaze. "Kash is worth the risk. You'll see."

She leaned in, pressing a soft hand to his cheek and kissed his forehead.

"You always protect me," she whispered. "This is how I can protect you."

WRONG MAN. WRONG DAY

Kash snapped awake as a surge of pain tore through his shins. The sharp crack of a baton echoed off the cold, metal walls. His eyes shot open, scanning the area, brain already cataloging the room. Four guards. One brute grinning like an idiot with a baton in hand. And Victor Morel... smiling.

"Good morning, sleepyhead," Victor purred, his voice too calm, too pleasant. "Hit him again."

The baton came down harder, this time across Kash's thigh. Pain flared white-hot, but Kash didn't flinch. He wouldn't give them the satisfaction.

Victor crouched in front of him, head cocked like he was examining a new piece of meat. Kash narrowed his eyes and met Victor's gaze. Victor stood, turned, and nodded at the brute.

Three more blows came rapid-fire, one on each arm and one to the chest. Kash closed his eyes and fought through the pain, but this time it wasn't just pain that surfaced... it brought his rage with it. Kash opened his eyes... fierce and determined.

"I never understood men like you," Victor said calmly. "Training your bodies to not break under pressure, for what... honor and glory?"

Kash gritted his teeth and just stared back. The rage continued to build

"To serve your fellow man?" Victor continued, his tone condescending. "You serve and then what? ...A pat on the back and no credits to show for it... no thank you... I intend to get what I can while I can."

Victor nodded at the brute and three more blows followed. Two to the shins and one to the side of the head. Kash saw stars when the baton struck his temple, but he didn't pass out.

"You're a hard man to break, Kash. I'll give you that. But see... I don't need you broken." Victor smiled wider. "I just need you scared."

"You're gonna need a bigger fucking stick," Kash hissed through clenched teeth.

Victor chuckled, slow and deliberate.

"You know, I've read your file. All those medals... all that training... impressive." Victor said, pacing now. "But you're not in the Legion anymore. You're here. In my casino. And no one's coming to save you."

"Your mistake is thinking that I need saving," Kash growled.

He leaned down close enough for Kash to smell the mint on his breath. His eyes were shaking from the Noctis Serum.

"Where's Calynn, Kash? Huh?" Victor smiled deviously. "You think she's going to swoop in and save you?"

Kash stayed silent, his jaw clenched. The mere mention of her name brought more rage from his core. Victor was studying his reaction but misread him.

"See... I know how special she is to you," Victor's grin widened. "Wonder what Gravitas would pay to have his way with her?"

The baton cracked down again, this time across Kash's back. Kash arched but bit down the scream. More rage.

Victor motioned lazily for the brute to stop.

"Easy now. Can't break my toy too early." He turned back to Kash. "I want to know what you're planning. Why you're really here?"

"Vacation," Kash rasped. "A shitty one, but that was the plan."

Victor's eyes narrowed. He backhanded Kash, fast and vicious.

"Don't fuck with me!" Victor barked.

Kash coughed, blood trickling from his lip.

"Is that all you got, pretty boy?" Kash smirked. "Maybe I'll find that vacation after all."

Victor scowled at Kash's comment and then turned his back to Kash.

"Fine," Victor continued in a hushed tone. "That's fine... I know I'm not as big and strong as you."

Again, the baton crashed down on his back.

"But let's talk about those girls you're so protective of." Victor spun back to face him. "Nura... Luna..."

Kash's head snapped up, rage flashing through his eyes. Victor smiled... he knew how to hurt Kash.

"Ah... There it is..." Victor squatted again, meeting Kash eye to eye. "You should know... I had nothing to do with what happened to them. But I let it happen. Just to see what you'd do."

"You're dead," Kash growled.

Victor stood and nodded to the guards.

"Maybe. But not today. Today, you answer my questions... or they'll start sending me pieces of your friends until you do."

Kash's fists clenched until his knuckles turned white. He said nothing... and let the rage flow. The rest of the world disappeared, so Kash could only hear the hammering of his own heart. He strained every fiber of his being against his restraints until his whole body started to shake, and he let out a feral scream.

Victor smiled smugly at Kash, dripping with confidence.

"It's no use, Kash," Victor continued smiling. "You'll never..."

CLANG

Victor's smug smile disappeared, and horror flashed through his eyes as the cuffs on Kash's wrists gave way.

Kash's lips peeled back in a savage grin as he showed his hands to Victor.

"You picked the wrong man... on the wrong fucking day."

Then all hell broke loose, but Kash made sure to save Victor for last.

The brute was already swinging at Kash's head when Kash turned to him. Kash caught his hand before the baton could make contact and squeezed as hard as he could.

"AAAAAHHHHHHH!" the brute screamed in pain as Kash felt the bones in his hand snapping under the pressure.

Kash then jerked the man's face toward the punch he unleashed, the force of which snapped the man's neck. Blood poured from his neck where the flesh ripped open from the terrible impact. His dead body landed on the floor with a wet thud.

The other four guards were rushing toward him, hoping to keep him restrained. They had tied Kash to the chair with ropes around his waist and ankles, but the rope was no match for Kash's anger.

He ripped at the one around his waist, quickly breaking it free. He then used the rope like a whip to smack the closest guard in the face. That man and the one behind him both paused their assault.

Kash turned to the other two, breaking the rope around his right ankle as he snapped a kick into one of the men's chest cavity. The man behind the man he kicked had to dive out of the way, so he didn't get struck by his airborne comrade.

Kash turned back to the other two men, while he finally stood up. He kicked his left leg, chair and all, at the closer man. The man somehow caught the chair on instinct, allowing Kash to break free from his last restraint.

Kash paused to grin before attacking.

He threw a violent right cross at the man still holding the chair. The guard's cheek bone and orbital bone both crushed under the force as Kash's fist sunk into the man's skull nearly to his wrist.

He let his momentum carry him as he spun around and snapped a kick into the other man's chest. The last guard, who had dodged his flying coworker, met his demise when after another full rotation, Kash nearly kicked his head off his body.

"Efficient," Kash smirked to himself and looked for Victor.

Victor had flung open the door and was making a run for it. Kash tried to accelerate after him but slipped in the pool of blood from the thug. By the time he regained his balance, Victor had slammed the door closed. He was on the other side of the door smiling when Kash's fist landed on the door with a bang.

"You're dead!" Kash growled through clenched teeth.

"And you're trapped," Victor countered, his grin growing.

A Bold Move

Aurelia's head was spinning as she tried to come up with a plan. She wanted to save Kash, which she thought would protect her team... but how? She needed help.

"Or maybe we can protect each other," Aurelia smiled softly at Bran.

"What can we do?" Bran asked.

"Jorik," Aurelia hollered, knocking on the door between their rooms. "Get in here."

Jorik entered her room quickly. He must have heard the urgency in her tone. And then he immediately turned his back to her.

"Uh... Miss Aurelia," Jorik sounded embarrassed.

Aurelia was still topless, and it was making Bran and Jorik nervous. What did it matter if they saw her body? She might not make it back from her quest, so they might as well see... everything.

"Both of you look at me," Aurelia said firmly, but kindly. "Please..."

Bran and Jorik reluctantly turned to face her. Both men were struggling not to look down at her exposed chest. Aurelia sighed and looked fondly at her friends.

"I want you to see me," Aurelia explained as she pulled off her wig. "The real me."

Their gazes went up to her bald head and then back to her eyes. Aurelia took a deep breath trying to gain some confidence and smiled softly at the two men.

"The people on my planet... are completely hairless," Aurelia admitted shyly. "My eyebrows and eye lashes were surgically implanted so I could blend in better."

Aurelia stared at her stunned friends. The big men sat there quietly staring back.

"Someone say something," Aurelia pleaded with them.

"You're still beautiful," Bran blurted out, his voice barely above a whisper.

"I agree," Jorik nodded.

"And topless," Aurelia smiled at the boys, shaking her boobs.

Her grin grew larger when their eyes dropped for a moment, but then she loathed the words she had just spoken.

"Sorry," Aurelia apologized sheepishly. "I... my head... it's ah..."

"You would rather us look at your boobs than your head," Bran smiled. "We understand, Miss Aurelia."

"Thanks, Bran... but I'm gonna go cover this up now," Aurelia said as she rubbed her head.

Aurelia opened the wig box that was intended to only be for an emergency exit. The short, black hair was vastly different from any of the other wigs she wore. Her eyebrow implants adjusted to the new wig, matching the color and texture exactly. She also pressed on the implants so they would push her brow out just a bit. That subtle change in facial structure was usually enough to fool any facial recognition software utilized by most businesses.

"What do you think?" Aurelia asked turning to the boys.

"Wow, you look different," Jorik said, surprised. "That's amazing."

Bran didn't reply... or even look at her. His head was hanging down and he was rubbing his head.

"Bran... what's wrong?" Aurelia asked.

"I don't... umm," Bran stammered.

"What?"

"I don't care if it's not my job," Bran muttered. "I can't just watch you walk into this alone... I need to protect you."

Aurelia's eyes widened as she thought of Bran protecting her... a man protecting a woman... like Kash protects women. He had warned her about Victor, but would Victor go that far?

"No, we have to protect the other girls," Aurelia stated adamantly. "The ones with Kash."

"Victor wouldn't do that... would he?" Jorik asked, unsure.

"I'm afraid he might," Aurelia replied. "You two need to go... go to his suite and warn them. Hell, stay and protect them. If Victor goes after..."

"I can stop him," Bran interrupted. "Victor... I looked into the drug and his dealer like Kash suggested, and I can stop him."

"How?" Jorik and Aurelia asked in unison.

Bran smiled as he pulled out his comms and called his secret weapon.

"Yeah," the pretty woman answered.

"It's time," Bran informed her. "Go... go now."

"And the credits?"

"After you get the job done and not before," Bran said with authority. "Now go."

The woman ended the comm, and Bran smiled at Aurelia.

"Who was that?" Aurelia asked.

"Victor Morel's favorite call girl," Bran explained. "And she's been given... all of Victor's favorites... only thing is... I promised her more credits than I can pay."

"Kash will pay," Aurelia insisted. "If we protect the girls... Kash will pay."

"She's probably right," Jorik agreed.

"But you two go... wait..." Aurelia smiled. "Hugs first... just in case."

Aurelia, still topless, gave both men a big hug before ushering them out the door. She pulled on a shirt which didn't amount to much more than a sports bra, finished applying her wig, and headed out to where Bran had told her they took Kash.

The door to the employee area was being guarded by two sentries... armed sentries. Both men were muscular, wearing body armor, and carried two firearms, one kinetic and one light.

Aurelia watched them for a moment and even walked by and smiled to see if she could get any reaction from either one, but both men stayed stoic. She needed a way to sneak past them, but how?

Just then, two servers exited the door the men were guarding, and a few minutes later two different servers entered the door. One of the men actually held the door open for them.

"Where can I get a uniform like that?" Aurelia said to herself, scanning the room.

Most of the servers were Oogan and much smaller than Aurelia, but there was one woman who was taller. She had grayish skin and black hair, and almost Aurelia's build... almost.

She started tailing the woman, looking for an opportunity to grab her.

"Oh, listen to yourself, Aurelia," she said to herself. "You're really going to assault this poor woman for Kash?"

Aurelia sighed to herself but then remembered why she was doing this. She was certain, after meeting and talking with Kash, that Rhett's plan for robbing the casino was going to get some of her friends killed... and possibly her too. The only way to survive this mission... was Kash. And the only way he could help, was if she saved him.

"Yes," Aurelia said to herself, her confidence renewed. "Yes, I am."

Aurelia followed the server for one more lap around the casino to make sure of her plan. When she walked behind a pod of slot machines, Aurelia pounced. She subdued the server with her fake lipstick loaded with knock-out gas and pulled her into a family bathroom.

"Sorry," Aurelia told the unconscious woman as she stripped her of her shiny pink and purple uniform.

Aurelia pulled off her jeans and shirt and used them to tie up the woman. The boots were nearly too big for her, so she grabbed some disposable towels and stuffed them into the boots to make them fit well enough for her to walk in them. The skirt... the super short skirt... was a little tight, but not too bad. She took a few steps around the bathroom to make sure it wouldn't ride up on her. The top on the other hand... Aurelia had to dump all the air from her lungs just to hook the first fastener.

"By the God's this is going to hurt."

One by one, Aurelia fought to fasten each hook between her breasts, and the top squeezed tighter and tighter until the last clasp was done. She tried to take a deep breath to stretch the material, but it barely budged.

"Just don't take deep breaths," Aurelia said to herself.

Aurelia grabbed the woman's ID badge, which didn't match her in the slightest, and started to leave the bathroom. She thought if she looked more pathetic, the guards might be sympathetic toward her. She turned on the sink and splashed water all over her front.

"That might do," Aurelia told herself and headed out of the bathroom toward the guards.

"It's so sticky," Aurelia sighed, holding out her arms like she didn't want to touch herself.

One of the sentries turned, scanned his badge, and held the door for her.

"Thanks, Hun," Aurelia smiled and scurried through the door.

The door opened to a short hallway that led to a T. She looked down both corridors and saw a sign to her left for the employee lounge. She knew where she was... now she just had to remember the building plans on her E-tablet... which she was having trouble doing.

"Let's try this way," Aurelia whispered and headed down the hallway to her right.

She remembered Bran saying Victor said to take Kash "down" to interrogation, so when she saw a staircase, she went down a floor.

Aurelia peeked down the hallway in both directions before exiting the stairway. This floor just had a different vibe to it. She hid behind the door, waited for a group of men to pass by, then darted across the hall to a locker room. She quietly moved through the room, dodging the men she heard talking. She tried a few of the lockers hoping to find another outfit that would fit her better... a suit, coveralls... she didn't care, but she found nothing even close to her size. She did, however, find a guard's ID card hanging on an open locker door.

She quickly made her way back to the door and peeked down the hallway. It was currently empty, so she hurried further down the hall, looking for hiding spots as she went.

BOOM

"What the hell was that?" she said aloud. "Kash!"

Aurelia paused for a second but then hurried toward the sound. It had to be him.

BOOM

She was getting closer.

BOOM

Almost there.

"Hey!" a voice yelled from behind her. "What are you doing down here?"

Aurelia ignored the voice and ran the last few steps to the door the bangs were emanating from.

"HEY!" the voice repeated.

Aurelia didn't have time to double-check the room. She scanned the lifted badge and pushed the heavy door open with all her might. She fell to the ground as the door sprung back closed.

She scrambled across the floor on all fours dodging the bodies... and the pool of blood. Fear grabbed her as she put her back to the wall and scanned the room. There were five bodies on the ground and one man standing above them... Kash.

"Why the fuck are you here?" Kash scowled at her.

"For you," Aurelia replied and pointed at the door. "They're coming."

Kash ducked to the side of the door, just as it started to open. Two men cautiously entered the room. They quickly scanned the carnage before their angry stares landed on her. Aurelia quickly decided to try to keep them off guard, so she curled up into a ball and faked starting to cry.

"My boyfriend beats me!" Aurelia cried out and buried her face in her knees.

She heard the first crack of Kash's fist landing on one of the men and looked up in time to see the second. He subdued the two men in two punches and stood over top of them like a predator over his prey... fear shivered up Aurelia's spine when Kash's piercing eyes turned back to her.

She held his gaze and tried to swallow down her fear.

"I sent Bran and Jorik to your suite," Aurelia told him, her voice a little shaky. "To help protect the girls... I didn't know what Victor... I didn't know how far he'd go."

Kash was moving toward her now, and Aurelia flinched as he approached. Kash must have seen it, because he slowed and bent down to help her up. He smiled softly as he grabbed her elbow. Aurelia leaned into his hand and slid herself up the wall, still holding Kash's gaze.

His hands found her waist, and he gently pulled her into his embrace. Aurelia popped up on her toes, wrapped her arms around his shoulders, and hugged him back. Her heart was hammering in her chest, and she still couldn't take a deep breath, but this... this felt amazing. Aurelia hugged him tightly, hoping that he would never let her go.

"Thank you," Kash said softly, caressing her back.

"You're very welcome," Aurelia beamed a smile that he couldn't see.

Her chest swelled with pride as she continued to embrace Kash. Her heart was still pounding in her chest, but for a better reason now. He smelled so good.... and felt good too... she tried to pull herself up closer to his face and felt her chest liberate itself from the skimpy top she had squeezed into.

"I think I just fell out of my top," Aurelia's smile grew larger. "I hope you don't mind."

"Only that it makes getting us out of here a little harder," Kash stated, and then released her from his hug.

"Here," Kash said as he knelt down to one of the guards. "He won't need his shirt any time soon."

Kash pulled the blue polo shirt off of the man as Aurelia undid the clasps on her top and tossed it aside. She was taking some deep breaths and massaging her sore breasts when he handed her the shirt.

"I'll be surprised if my boobs don't end up bruised," Aurelia told Kash as she grabbed the shirt. "That top was so tight. You have no idea."

"Not the trap I was expecting you to get caught in," Kash joked with a smirk tugging at his lips.

"Was that... was that seriously a booby trap joke?' Aurelia giggled but pointed her finger at him like she was trying to be serious. "That was painful, I'll have you know... I should make you kiss them since they suffered for you."

Aurelia bit her lower lip and heaved out her chest, trying to draw Kash in for another embrace... and hopefully more... but Kash had other tasks in mind.

"Maybe later," Kash replied, all business. "Get that shirt on... we gotta get out of here."

Aurelia's shoulders drooped and she reluctantly shrugged on the polo shirt. Kash pulled the shirt off the other man and shrugged it on.

"Which way did you come here?" Kash asked as he peered out through the door. "I don't want to have to fight everyone."

"There's a stairway to the left... about fifty meters or so," Aurelia told him. "I'll go first and see if it's clear."

"And if someone comes after you again?"

"Then you can save me again," Aurelia smiled, patting him on the chest. "Let's go."

Aurelia used the badge she had stolen to open the door and slipped out into the hall. She moved confidently, knowing that Kash was close and could handle anyone that tried to accost her. When she got to the stairwell she waved for him to follow. She watched as Kash darted toward her. For as big as he was, the man moved effortlessly and gracefully.

"Wait here," Aurelia smiled at him again. "I'll check above."

Aurelia bounced up the stairs and checked the hall above. There were half a dozen employees, three men and three women, standing outside the lounge chatting. Aurelia watched for a moment and quickly figured out they weren't going away any time soon. The group was overtly flirting with each other, so she trotted back down to Kash.

"There's some people up there that we have to sneak past," Aurelia told him.

"Okay?"

"They're flirting with each other outside the lounge… right by where I came in."

"Oh… well that's easy," Kash said grabbing her by the hand. "Warning… I might get… handsy."

"Oh, you can grab me anywhere," Aurelia replied, a little too willingly.

She scolded herself internally right after she said it.

Kash wrapped his arm around her back and put the other hand on her belly. He grabbed a fistful of the polo and pulled it out so he could blatantly stare down her shirt. Kash chuckled and Aurelia giggled with him. When the group in the hall turned to look at them, Kash simply let go of her shirt and placed his finger to his lips, silently asking them to keep a fake secret.

Aurelia smiled her biggest, brightest smile at the group and leaned her body into Kash's. Kash's hand landed back on her stomach but quickly drifted up her body. Aurelia shivered when Kash's hand brushed over her left breast, but then his hand plunged down her shirt.

"Oh my," Aurelia gasped as his hand landed on her boob, and the duo turned the corner.

Aurelia heard the women giggle behind her, and one of the men whistled. She looked up and saw Kash shaking his head as he removed his hand from her shirt. He pulled her close as they exited the door and walked across the casino floor.

Kash picked up the pace a little and made a beeline toward the elevators. When the elevator got to his floor, Kash sprinted to his suite. Aurelia ran after him as fast as she could, but he was easily putting a gap between them. She was able to close the gap when he punched in the door code.

"Is everyone okay?" Kash asked as he led her into his suite.

"We're fine," the pretty, tanned woman replied. "We're all fine."

Bran and Jorik were standing with the other man. Jorik nodded at her and Bran smiled.

"Are the girls okay?" Kash asked, pointing at a door.

"Go see them," the woman smiled at him.

Aurelia followed Kash into a large, beautiful bedroom. He crawled onto the bed and hugged the two petite beauties, kissing their heads.

Aurelia sighed watching him pour affection into the two women. Her heart sank as they smiled back at Kash, returning his love. There it was again... jealousy. Aurelia turned and walked out of the bedroom.

Not Lost but Found

Calynn dug her fingers into the man's flesh as he kicked his feet uselessly.

"Answer me!" she demanded.

"Please," the man gasped. "I…"

"You die if you don't talk."

"It's… hidden room," he choked.

Calynn dropped him. The guard crumpled to the floor, gasping for air. She knelt and jabbed a finger hard into his forehead, forcing his eyes to hers.

"You're going to take me to him," she growled, low and deadly. "Or I break every single bone in your body… all two hundred and six of them."

The man averted his eyes but nodded. Calynn gave him one last shove with her finger before rising to tower over him.

"Get up… move… I haven't got all day."

The man rose slowly and staggered down the hallway. He was heading toward the dead end. Calynn's anger flared, but she kept it in check. He would learn a hard lesson if he was fucking with her.

"Faster," Calynn snapped, shoving him between the shoulder blades.

Every time he slowed, she shoved again. Her patience growing thin.

At the end of the hallway was the dead-end wall, he stopped and just… stared.

"This is great," Calynn sneered. "You picked a wonderful place to die."

With a shudder, the man fumbled his ID badge out and waved it at an invisible reader.

The wall split open with a soft hiss.

Calynn froze as a flood of new inputs slammed into her. Systems she hadn't felt moments ago came alive, bristling with energy. Her senses prickled like static across her skin. A new world opened up to her in a rush.

They stepped through, and the door sealed with a quiet thump. The outside world vanished.

Calynn stared back at the closed door... and the nothingness that lay beyond.

"A Faraday cage," she whispered as the realization hit her. "That's why I couldn't feel him..."

She shoved the man forward.

"Keep moving."

The corridor beyond was narrow, metallic, and humming faintly with sup-pressed energy. Calynn let her senses roam, now that they weren't being smothered.

It was all there... the two nerve centers she couldn't find before, but she could feel them now... the casino's spine laid bare for her to explore. Gravity generators... orbital stabilizers... life support... and power... so much power. Everything vital, tucked away where no one could reach it.

And somewhere ahead... him.

Suddenly, the man leading her lunged forward, slamming his hand on a red button. An energy field snapped to life between them. He grinned maliciously as he keyed in commands on a pad on the wall... another field flared up behind Calynn, trapping her.

"Fuck you, you stupid bitch," he spat, turning to run.

Calynn didn't move. She simply raised her hand, turned her palm up... and the fleeing man's feet left the floor. Gravity bent to her will as the man flailed, but it was useless. With a twist of her wrist, she spun him in midair, dragging him back until they were face to face... separated only by the crackling energy field.

"That was... foolish," Calynn hissed, cold and certain. "You do know you have to die now, right?"

The grin had melted from his face and the only thing remaining... was fear.

"Lady... please," he begged.

"Goodbye," Calynn whispered.

With a jerk of her hand, she slammed him into the energy field. The barrier shrieked and sizzled as his body hit. His scream died in his throat as his face melted from the surge of power coursing through his flesh. Calynn yanked once more, dragging what was left of him through the field with a satisfying pop.

Calynn closed her eyes and exhaled slowly. She dropped her hand, and the smoking corpse fell to the ground. With a wave of her fingers, both energy fields died.

She opened her eyes and stepped over what was left of the man, not sparing him another glance.

There were only five doors remaining and one was marked exit, so Calynn's search wouldn't take long. She didn't hesitate.

The second door stopped her cold. A void... a void in space... she could feel it now.

"This has to be it," Calynn said as she forced the door to open.

Inside the room was a glass tank filled with green liquid... and a human male, intact... not just a brain. A metallic contraption encased his head.

Another energy field shimmered around the tank. No wonder she couldn't feel him... he was buried behind layers of suppression.

One of the facets of the shield pulsed at a different frequency. That must have been the crack he used to try and contact her. The strain must have been enormous.

She took a deep cleansing breath, steadied herself, and waved her hand at the field.

The voice hit her like a scream inside her mind.

"HELP! PLEASE HELP!"

"It's okay... I'm here."

"HELP ME, PLEASE!"

"Easy, friend... you don't have to try so hard now."

"I... I can hear you."

"And I can hear you."

"Why is it so easy now?"

"They had you... trapped in a box."

Calynn struggled to push down her own memories of being in the box... of being trapped.

"I tried so hard to get your attention... so hard. I thought you'd never come."

"I know," Calynn whispered. "I felt you. I just... couldn't find you."

"It felt so good to feel someone else... I've been so alone," he wept. "I don't even know where I am."

"Shh... it's okay... we're getting you out of here. I promise."

"We...? But... I only feel you. Who else is here?"

"No one. Not yet." Calynn's voice cracked and she lowered her head. "But he'll come. He saved me, and he can save you too... I promise."

He loves me... he has to come... I hope.

THE AFTERMATH

Kash, slightly sated by Nura and Luna's safety, finally took a beat to breathe. He kissed their heads repeatedly, and caressed their soft skin, like if he let them go, they would just... vanish.

"You're not okay," Nura observed as she wiggled out from under the covers. "Come here."

Nura pulled up her pajama top, exposing her belly. Kash didn't hesitate... he nuzzled into her soft stomach and drew in a breath of her sweet skin. Nura and Luna both wrapped around him, trying to ease his troubled mind... if only she were here too.

As furious as Kash was at her, Calynn could always calm his inner demons... even if she caused them... but she wasn't here, so he had to face his demons... alone.

"Hey, Kash," Triana said meekly from the bedroom door. "Umm."

Kash lifted his head to look at Triana, and his rage was instant. She was holding her comm unit and Calynn's face was floating above. The demons won.

"Where the fuck are you?" Kash spat, dripping with rage.

"Hi, beloved," Calynn replied with a snarky tone. "I'm glad to see you're okay. Oh, thanks, babe. I'm glad you're okay too."

"Oh, sarcasm will help," Kash matched her snarky tone.

"About as much as fucking yelling at me!" Calynn snapped back.

"And both of you better stop!" Triana interjected firmly. "None of this is helping!"

"Sorry, Trie," Calynn was the first to apologize.

Trie stared at Kash waiting for his apology and cocked her head when it didn't come soon enough.

Kash buried his nose in Nura's belly again, searching for calm in the middle of the storm clawing at his chest.

"He's sorry too," Nura said, giving Kash a gentle tap on the shoulder.

Kash lifted his head. Nura and Triana both giving him that look... he sighed heavily, rolling his eyes.

"Yeah... sure," Kash agreed reluctantly. "So... where are you...? And I'm sorry I yelled."

"I found him... the AI, only it's not an AI," Calynn replied. "And you're never going to believe... who he is."

"Yeah, well that doesn't matter anymore," Kash said, trying to suppress his anger. "You need to get your ass back here so we can pack. We're leaving."

"What? Leaving?" Calynn questioned. "Why?"

"Because I don't want to stay and die," Kash replied sarcastically as he sat up.

"Is that blood?" Nura asked urgently, pointing at Kash's head.

"Blood? Who's bleeding?" Calynn asked, concerned.

"Kash is bleeding," Nura answered, moving closer to Kash.

Kash reached up and touched the damp spot on the back of his head.

"Why are you bleeding?" Calynn asked.

"You'd know if you were fucking here!" Kash barked, getting up off the bed. "Victor Morel just had me locked in a room beating the fuck out of me! The only reason I'm not dead is because Aurelia came for me!"

Kash caught Aurelia's gaze. She flinched when he shouted her name but smiled softly to try and hide it.

"Now that motherfucker threatened to kill all of us, so get your fucking ass back here so we can leave BEFORE HE GETS HERE TO FINISH THE JOB!" Kash's anger and volume rose as he shouted.

The room fell deathly quiet as everyone froze, staring at their feet. Even Calynn held her tongue.

"Uh… Kash," Bran's voice came timidly from behind Triana and Aurelia. "I took your advice earlier… Victor should be preoccupied… for the next few hourns anyway."

"He what now?"

"I took your advice…"

"I got that part," Kash interrupted the man. "Why is he preoccupied?"

Bran swallowed hard and edged up beside Aurelia, like he needed backup for what was coming next.

"Well… I went looking for his dealer, like you suggested," Bran explained. "I didn't find him… but I did find his favorite… call girl."

"His… what? Did you say call girl?" Kash blinked like he misheard.

"Yeah… she parties with him, and they do lots of drugs together when they… you know," Bran said with a nervous tone. "When they…"

"When they fuck," Aurelia blurted out, finishing Bran's statement. "She's his favorite whore."

"She said he always comes to her if he's stressed," Bran continued. "So, I asked her to make herself available to distract him when I needed her to. I had to promise her way too many credits, but, uh…"

"How much?" Kash asked.

"One point two million," Bran replied.

"For how long?"

"I asked for six hourns."

Kash spun back and looked at Nura. She met his gaze but had a puzzled look on her face. He didn't need her to do anything. Just exist… and inspire. The plan snapped into place.

"Can you contact her and ask her how much for three days?" Kash asked Bran as he turned to face the man.

"Three, ahem," Bran paused to clear his throat. "Three days?"

"Yep… I'll cover it," Kash smiled. "Just… ask."

Bran wandered off to get some privacy for his comm, and Kash turned his focus to Triana.

"If this doesn't work, we do really need to go," Kash told Trie. "I'm not waiting around for Victor to chop you into pieces and ship them to me one at a time."

"That sounds... horrible," Triana agreed.

"And you," Kash smiled at Aurelia, moving closer. "Thank you for coming for me."

Kash wrapped Aurelia in a hug and held her firmly. Aurelia's arms went over his shoulders as she embraced him back. Her breath shuddered against his neck as she melted into his body. They were still hugging when Bran returned.

"She says I sound desperate," Bran explained, swallowing hard. "She says twenty million."

"Sold," Kash replied, but he was staring into Aurelia's eyes when he said it. "She's worth it... right?"

"I believe so, sir," Bran replied.

Kash lingered a moment longer in Aurelia's eyes, kissed her head, and released her from his embrace.

"I need conformation first," Kash said, turning to address Bran. "It's okay if it's just your eyes, but I need to know he's with her."

"I've already seen him, sir."

"Oh... okay... well, does she want chips or credits?"

"She prefers credits."

"We have about seven," Triana offered. "I think."

"We have a little under nine," Calynn added from the comm. "So, we're four short."

"She's only expecting half up front," Bran added.

"Even better," Kash said, then sighed heavily. "And now the not so fun part... time to get angry again."

Kash turned to face Nura and Luna letting the memories of what happened to them flow. He closed his eyes and recalled the metal batons bouncing off his body... and the anger when Victor said he would cut Nura, Luna, and Triana into pieces.

Kash opened his eyes. Fierce and focused. He grabbed his comm and punched in Gravitas' name, his finger trembling with rage.

"Why am I not surprised..."

"Where the fuck is Victor!" Kash interrupted Gravitas forcefully.

"Excuse me?"

"Where. The. Fuck. Is. Victor?" Kash enunciated each word.

"Probably tending to the guards you beat up," Gravitas spat.

"I was just working out... they attacked me."

"We have witnesses."

"That will confirm they attacked me."

"Kash..."

"Look, I had a fight with my girlfriend and was blowing off some steam," Kash interrupted him again. "All they had to do was leave me the fuck alone. But instead, your boy Victor just tried to murder me, and I intend to return the favor... where the fuck is he?"

Gravitas was silent for a beat too long, and Kash knew he had him.

"Huh... you don't fucking know do you?" Kash asked, his voice dripping with sarcasm and contempt. "You have a rogue gangster wannabe wandering your casino and kidnapping your patrons and you haven't a fucking clue... where the fuck is Victor?"

"I'm sure..."

"You can tell me where he is, or I can tear your casino to ribbons until I find him... your choice!"

"I don't know!" Gravitas finally admitted. "Nobody knows."

"Are you fucking serious?" Kash chuckled a sinister laugh. "Your chief of security has gone rogue, and you don't know... Get your fucking house in order, Gravitas... or I'll burn that mother fucker down!"

Kash ended the comm before Gravitas could reply. He took a deep cleansing breath and tried to calm himself again, but his rage was still burning... she wasn't here... but Nura and Luna were.

"I need a hug," Kash said to the girls as softly as he could.

Nura didn't hesitate. She was wrapped around him in a blink. He pulled her up so she could wrap her legs around his waist. Luna was right behind her and placed her hand on his cheek.

"That was awesome," Bran blurted out. "Can we call my dad next? I wanna tell him off!"

Bran's comment actually cut through Kash's rage and brought a slight smile to his lips.

"Bran!" Aurelia scolded the man under her breath.

Bran said something back, but Kash didn't hear it. He was lost in Nura's warm, soothing skin... she soothed him nearly as well as Calynn did. She was so soft and smelled so good. Her skin tasted good against his lips as he nuzzled into her neck. She seemed to sense his needs and pulled him tighter, her small fingers digging into his back. Even when her hand found one of his bruises from being beaten, it still somehow felt... better... and so did he.

Kash put Nura down, and they shared a soft smile. Luna leaned in and placed a soft kiss on his lips. Kash wrapped her in a quick hug and took another cleansing breath.

"It's fine... I thought it was funny," Kash said, putting Luna down and then smiling at Aurelia. "Wanna crack my safe with me? We have a whore to pay."

"Actually, I was thinking we should probably go," Aurelia replied. "If Victor is out of commission, maybe we can move up our timeline and..."

"Don't do that," Kash interrupted. "I'm sorry... but you can't."

"What? Why not?" Aurelia argued.

"Because I know what you're stealing," Kash said with a heavy sigh.

Kash took a step away from Aurelia before glancing back at her, regretting what he had to say next.

"I'm sorry... but I had to know," Kash explained, his tone somber. "I know what you're here for and I cannot let you take it."

"Why not?" Aurelia asked sharply.

"Because it's a key to a military supply cache," Kash replied just as sharp.

"How do you know that?"

"Because I broke into Rhett's room and saw it on his E-tablet!"

Kash sighed and groaned before continuing.

"Look, Aurelia... I like you, and if you were just stealing credits, I'd give you my blessing, but this..." Kash explained, running his fingers through his hair. "When I was in the service, we called that place "The Beast" because it's that fucking big, and because... because of what weapons are stored there... you can wipe out whole planets with that arsenal. I hate that Gravitas has the key, but Rhett... I hate that more."

"Well, where does that leave us?" Aurelia complained.

"On my side."

"Your side?"

"With the added bonus of knowing that you didn't help facilitate a genocide."

"Genocide," Aurelia said sharply, sighed, and then continued with a softer tone. "That sounds bad."

"It's soul crushing guilt… trust me."

"I trust you, sir," Bran chimed in.

"Me too," Jorik agreed from behind Bran.

"Me too," Aurelia sighed. "But what do we do now?"

"We need work," Jorik added dryly, like the punchline to a joke nobody found funny.

"That's a problem for later," Kash said shaking his head. "My more pressing problem is somewhere in the bowels of the casino instead of by my side where she belongs."

"So, I'm a problem now?" Calynn replied sarcastically.

"Currently… yes… now, where the fuck are you?"

Kash followed Calynn's directions exactly. The hidden door was really cool, but the smell of the charred corpse behind it was enough to turn Kash's stomach.

When he entered the room with the man floating in the tank of green liquid, Kash was in awe. He had never even heard of someone using the whole body for a nerve center. He was checking out the weird metallic device on the man's head when Calynn stepped out from behind the tank.

Kash's anger came back for the briefest second, but it was overwhelmed by his need to hold her.

Kash scooped up Calynn so she could wrap her arms and legs around him. He buried his face in her neck and breathed in her essence. He shoved his hand up her shirt so he could feel her skin and started kissing her neck and cheek.

Calynn grabbed his face in both hands and kissed him passionately. He returned her vigor until they were both sated, then placed her back on her feet.

"I'm still mad at you."

"I know… I'm sorry… Forgive me?"

"Not yet... but I will."

"That's fair."

"So... who's your friend?"

"Would you believe a collegiate math major that tried his hand at card counting?"

"Oh, Gravitas would definitely want to get his hands on him."

"He's been here so long... he forgot his name," Calynn's head drooped when she revealed that fact. "Awake... and alone."

"Is that why he came after you so hard?"

"I was a candle in the darkness... a lone voice in the void of silence," Calynn replied softly. "Complete sensory deprivation..."

"That's torture," Kash interrupted her. "By the Gods."

"That's why we have to help," Calynn pleaded.

Kash turned his gaze back to the contraption wrapped around the young man's head.

"I don't have a clue what that thing is either," Calynn read his mind.

"We need Plekish," Kash sighed, pulling out his comm. "Maybe he has a clue."

"We can hope," Calynn sighed also.

The blue light zoomed in and Plekish appeared before them.

"Kash, my friend," Plekish greeted him cheerfully. "And Calynn too, such a pleasure to see you both."

"Plekish, my friend, it is always good to hear your voice," Kash smiled.

"The pleasure is all ours," Calynn said in her usual chipper tone.

"How is your vacation going? Having fun I hope."

"Actually," Kash sighed. "That's why we called."

Kash tapped the button on the comm to change the camera so Plekish could see the young man floating in the tank of green liquid.

"Oh my," Plekish said, concerned.

"Can we please help him, Plekish?" Calynn begged. "He's awake in there."

"I am not sure... that device looks... Calynn, my child, I need to borrow your sensors."

"You can do that... whoa."

Calynn's eyes began to glow a soft white, and by the look on her face, Kash knew she wasn't doing it herself. Kash moved to her side to steady her.

"Hmmm... yes," Plekish murmured thoughtfully. "His body has seen better days, but his mind is strong... exceptional even."

"Exceptional?" Calynn questioned. "Is he like me?"

"No... not really."

"Oh," Calynn added with a puzzled look. "Okay?"

"He is similar in that he is gifted," Plekish explained. "But not like you are, child. You are unique... even among the exceptional."

"Thanks... I think," Calynn said with half a smile.

"Now... let me see," Plekish continued. "Can you hear me, young man?"

A silence crackled through the comm.

"Umm, hi," a small shaky voice replied over the comm. "Are you a friend of Calynn?"

"Indeed I am, child," Plekish replied.

"Is that him?" Kash whispered to Calynn. "How'd he do that?"

Calynn shrugged her shoulders and shook her head.

"Do you know your name, my son?" Plekish asked.

"No... I... and I don't..." his voice cracked and fell off.

"He doesn't know how long he's been here," Calynn finished the statement for him. "He's in a damn box."

"I just want to get out of here," the young man cried. "Please... please help me."

"It will be okay, young man," Plekish said in a comforting tone. "We are here to help."

"Oh... thank you," the boy wept. "Thank you... thank you... thank you..."

His words dissolved into sobs.

Calynn hugged Kash's arm, her tears falling freely.

Kash wiped one away with his thumb and kissed her head.

"Don't worry, Kid," Kash murmured, voice soft and raw. "We got you now."

THE PLAN

Kash paced back and forth rubbing the back of his neck, trying to get his thoughts in order. Nura and Luna were huddled together, still distraught over their recent capture. Luna had even started wearing clothes regularly.

Aurelia, Bran, and Jorik made the decision to stay. They figured it was better to be on Kash's side than against him.

Calynn, Triana, and Guy were his rocks. No matter what happened next, he knew he could count on them.

"Alright... so," Kash started, his voice grim. "Mister P somehow opened a comm channel to the kid in the tank. He's stable...for now, and no longer alone. He can talk to Calynn, Mister P, and Doctor M until they get here with his replacement. Kid has given us unprecedented access to the casino's cameras, layout, and security systems."

"We're calling him 'Kid,' by the way," Calynn added softly. "Since he can't remember his name. Doesn't even know how long he's been down there."

"Right... so... anyway. We've got just over two days to get everything in place."

"In place for what?" Aurelia asked, crossing her arms.

Kash sighed and ran his hands over his face.

"Well... we're going to rescue a college kid from a life of torture, free every Oogan we can," Kash explained as he glanced at Nura and Luna. "Stop Rhett from stealing that key and hopefully find you three a nice score."

Kash spun around and looked at Calynn.

"Did I miss anything?"

"Can we take a real vacation after?" Calynn smirked.

"I mean if we pull this off and Gravitas is none the wiser... oh, and what if we pin it on Victor?"

"That's even better," Guy added. "Fuck that guy."

"So, what's this score?" Jorik asked, smiling. "Not that I want to circle back to that or anything."

"We actually need to find that still," Calynn replied, placing an E-tablet on the coffee table. "Hey, Kid... hit it."

A holographic projection of the casino materialized above the tablet. The image zoomed in to a red dot on the map and displayed the feed of that particular camera.

"The recent blackouts, glitches, and the cameras being out was all from Kid trying to get Calynn's attention," Kash explained, pointing at the image. "Security still doesn't have access to their own cameras... but we do."

"Red dots are cameras," Calynn explained pointing at the floating wire-frame layout of the casino. "Green is general access doors, green with a red stripe is card access doors, blue is obviously the elevators, the rooms in yellow..."

"What are the black dots?" Guy interrupted.

"What black dots?" Calynn asked.

Guy stood up from his chair and put his finger into the hologram.

"Here's one," Guy indicated.

"I don't see it," Aurelia added.

"Kid... can you zoom in at Guy's finger?" Calynn asked.

The image zoomed in, and sure enough, there was a black dot.

"Kid says it's a camera... but it's not connected to security or the other cameras in any way," Calynn explained.

"Can he show us the feed?" Kash wondered.

The image shifted and displayed Gravitas' personal residence at the casino. The big man was in bed with a woman a tenth his size, and she didn't look happy to be there.

"Are there more black dots?" Kash queried without looking away from the image.

"Five," Calynn answered.

"Show us the rest."

The image changed to the bedrooms of Gravitas assistants. The two women were resting together on their sofa. The next image was from inside the casino vault, but the next image… grabbed everyone's attention.

The room wasn't very big, was well lit, and had a mountain of credits piled on the table in the middle of the room. There were naked women there counting the credits. No clothes meant no pockets. No pockets meant they couldn't steal anything.

"That can't be the count room," Kash exclaimed. "It's not big enough for a casino this size."

"And why would it be covered by one of the secret cameras?" Calynn asked.

"But it is big enough to count the skim," Guy said with a cheeky grin.

"No shit," Kash, Aurelia, and Bran all said in unison.

"Of course, Gravitas is skimming off his own casino," Kash announced his revelation.

"Or credits from his shady business dealings," Calynn added.

"Or both," Triana chimed in.

"Soo… credits that don't exist," Aurelia observed with a growing smile. "Can we steal that?"

"Do you have a death wish?" Kash argued.

"No… we have a fall guy," Aurelia replied, smiling. "Remember?"

"Son of a bitch, that's right," Kash said turning back to the display.

Kash, Aurelia, Bran, and Jorik spent the next couple hourns going over every possible route in and out of the secondary count room and watching the traffic in and around the area. The secret count room was located in a nearly abandoned section of the casino normally reserved for a platoon of Consortium soldiers. Having the soldiers stationed there was a requirement for the gaming license. Kash wondered how Gravitas managed to get around that rule.

Most of the military base was still intact. The barracks, ready room, armory, and officer's offices were still there, but very few were still in use.

Kash yawned and looked around the room. Triana was asleep, laying on Guy. Nura and Luna were spooning each other on the couch, also sound asleep. Bran, Jorik and Aurelia all had bloodshot eyes, and he was certain that he did too.

"Let's get some rest," Kash told everyone still awake. "We can pick this up in the morning."

"It is morning, beloved," Calynn told him. "Breakfast is in just over two hourns."

"A short rest is better than nothing," Aurelia yawned. "We should go check in anyway."

Kash saw the three thieves out and then carried Nura and Luna to the bedroom. They were both asleep by the time Kash crawled into bed. He curled up behind Luna and fell asleep.

Kash awoke to Luna kicking and screaming. It felt like he had just shut his eyes, but he was wide awake now. She woke herself up before Kash could react. She was disoriented at first, but once she realized where she was and who she was with, she dove onto Kash's chest, crying.

"We keep each other up," Nura admitted as she pulled herself closer to Kash also. "Neither one of us is sleeping well."

Kash wrapped an arm around each of them and kissed their heads. After a few minutes, Luna settled down and they all fell asleep once more.

Kash dreamed of Omia, something he hadn't done in quite some time. It was a good dream for a change. She smiled at him while cooking dinner, wearing nothing but her smile. Calynn was there too, snuggling with him. They were at Omia's house on Poncia on a warm summer day. A light breeze was coming through the open window, blowing Omia's hair. Calynn was playing a game on her e-tablet. She looked so content.

"What are you playing?" Kash asked her.

"A casino heist game."

"That sounds fun... what do you do?"

"I have to get into this room..."

Kash's eyes popped open. The solution he was looking for, sitting forefront in his mind. He smiled to himself and hugged Luna tight.

Luna stirred when he hugged her, so he slid her off of him and into Nura's embrace. Kash slowly got out of bed and went out to the living room. Calynn was there still studying the map when he sat down beside her.

"Zoom in here," Kash said, pointing to the hologram.

There it was... the answer to their problems. Kash flopped back with his hands on his head and smiled.

"You okay?" Calynn asked with a puzzled look.

Kash yanked her onto his lap so she was facing him and straddling his legs. He pulled her close and gave her a soft kiss.

"I am now," Kash smiled. "You and Omia showed me the way."

"Does this mean I'm forgiven?"

"Almost," Kash smirked, pulling her shirt over her head.

The lights came on and Kash slowly awoke. He and Calynn were still naked and intertwined, laying on the couch. Kash panicked for half a second, thinking the chef was there for breakfast, but was relieved when Luna rounded the end of the couch.

"I'm hungry," Luna whined.

Kash chuckled, and he and Calynn got up and got showers. Luna let the chef in, and he was starting breakfast when Kash returned to the living room.

"Good morning, sir," the chef greeted him.

"It is indeed," Kash grinned, sitting down beside Luna. "And it only promises to get better."

After breakfast, Kash sent a message to Aurelia to meet them as soon as they could. He finally had a plan, and they needed to get things set up... after Kash got some more rest. Nura was still in bed. Kash curled up with her and happily fell asleep.

Aurelia's Turn

Aurelia slept fitfully at best. Her mind was racing at the prospect of working with the infamous Kash, and the mountain of credits they were going to steal.

She rolled over and checked her comm. Three messages from Rhett and one from Kash. She skipped the ones from Rhett.

"Hey Aurelia," Kash's voice came from her comm unit. "I figured out the missing ingredient for that recipe we were talking about. I'm going to try and get some more rest, but come over when you have a minute."

"He has a plan," Aurelia said quietly to herself.

Aurelia jumped out of bed and went through the shared door to Jorik's room. Jorik was asleep in the bed and Bran was asleep on the floor. They wanted to stay close in case Rhett tried to bully her.

"Hey, boys," Aurelia sang softly. "Time to wake up."

She gently placed her hand on Bran first since he was on the floor, and then Jorik. Both men stirred slowly and opened their eyes.

Aurelia greeted them both with a vibrant smile. She loved that she felt comfortable enough around them to not wear her wig... or many clothes. She had stripped down to just her panties early this morning before falling into bed, and that was all she was wearing still.

"Good morning, Miss Aurelia," Jorik grinned.

"Good morning," Aurelia smiled and kissed Jorik on the cheek.

"You seem to be in a good mood," Bran groaned from the floor.

"That's because I am," Aurelia said, bending down so she could kiss Bran on the cheek also.

"Dare we ask why?" Jorik asked.

"Kash has a plan," Aurelia smiled. "He wants to meet."

"When? Now?" Bran asked sitting up.

"He said when we have a minute," Aurelia replied.

"I say we go sooner than later," Jorik said, nodding.

"I agree," Bran added.

"Then let's get showered and go," Aurelia said, standing to return to her room.

"I'll take first watch," Aurelia heard Jorik say to Bran as she left the room.

She was getting her clothes together when Jorik came in and sat down at her desk.

"Thank you for being so protective of me," Aurelia smiled. "You two are like a gift from the Gods in all this."

"You are the only reason I stayed after the last job," Jorik admitted, his tone somber. "I didn't want to see you get hurt... I know Bran feels the same way... I think that's why it's so easy for me to pick Kash over Rhett."

"He's so protective over his people," Aurelia agreed, smiling at Jorik.

"Especially the girls," Jorik smiled back, but then he shrugged his shoulders. "Not like Rhett who has contingency plans for losing all of us... it feels like with Kash... one loss is too many."

"He does give that vibe, doesn't he," Aurelia said, cocking her head. "Like it would be to his detriment if something happened to one of us."

"Are you not in the shower yet, woman?" Bran jested from the adjoining door.

Bran was standing there with a towel wrapped around his waist. He was built like the guys from the strongman games, like when they throw huge rocks around. He had a thick, broad chest and shoulders. He had some fluff in the midsection, but Aurelia wouldn't call him fat, just... big.

"I'm going," Aurelia said quickly and scurried into her bathroom.

She left the door open, quickly showered, and got dressed. She exited the bathroom to both boys sitting in her room waiting patiently.

"Men shower too fast," Aurelia joked.

"Women take too long to get ready," Bran joked back.

"Ha ha," Aurelia snickered. "What color hair should I wear today?"

"Red," Jorik replied. "It'll go nice with your green shirt."

"Red it is," Aurelia replied.

Knock Knock

The three friends froze at the sound of someone gently rapping on Aurelia's door. The boys both nodded for Aurelia to move to the back of the room as they stood to go to the door.

Aurelia pulled on her red wig quickly and sat on her bed.

"What are you doing here?" Rhett asked when Jorik opened the door.

"Miss Aurelia got a tip and asked us to come escort her," Jorik replied without missing a beat.

"We don't have time for tips," Rhett argued as he pushed his way into the room. "We're already behind schedule."

"My informant said it was important," Aurelia argued back, her tone sharp.

"What informant?"

"The confidential one."

"Oh, bull shit, Aurelia!" Rhett barked, taking two more steps toward her.

Bran and Jorik both positioned themselves between Rhett and Aurelia. They didn't say anything or do anything brash. They simply got in his way.

"What the fuck is this?" Rhett scoffed. "Did you two forget who you work for?"

"No, but she's still a girl," Bran replied, almost too calmly. "And I can't be held responsible for what would happen to you if you hit her."

"He's right, Boss," Jorik agreed, holding his hand out in front of Rhett. "Hitting a woman ain't right."

Aurelia saw the change in Rhett's demeanor. He tried to maintain his scowl and hide it, but she saw the glint of fear in his eye.

"You better check in after this meeting," Rhett demanded while backing away. "And it better be fucking worth it!"

Rhett stormed out of Aurelia's room, and Jorik closed the door behind him.

"We need to hurry, before he can get someone to tail us," Bran insisted.

Aurelia pulled up her wig, applied a little glue above her forehead, and carefully pulled the wig back down. She checked herself in the mirror, and it looked good enough.

"Let's go," Aurelia smiled.

The trio worked their way through the casino in a way that they were sure they couldn't be followed. Once they were satisfied that nobody was tailing them, they made a beeline for Kash's suite. One of the pretty Oogan girls let them in. Aurelia had trouble telling them apart.

"Hi guys," Calynn smiled at them. "There's breakfast in the kitchen."

Calynn looked effortlessly beautiful. Her hair was pulled back into a ponytail, and she was wearing jeans and a simple white tee shirt with no bra. Aurelia could see the outline of her nipples through the fabric. She had a smile that could light up the room... and those curves.

"I liked his recipe narrative," Aurelia smiled back. "In case someone else listened in."

"He pretends to be smart... sometimes," Calynn joked and rolled her eyes.

Bran and Jorik headed to the kitchen to grab a bite to eat, and Aurelia sat on the sofa across from Calynn.

When Kash exited his bedroom, Aurelia almost started to drool. He was wearing pajama bottoms but no shirt. His wavy black hair looked to be six or seven centimeters long and naturally parted above his right eye. He had chiseled features, a strong jaw, powerful chest, washboard abs, and thick powerful legs. He was the sexiest man she had ever seen.

Luna's Return

"Come on you," Luna urged Nura. "Get your lazy butt up."

"Nnooo… I don't wanna," Nura groaned, flailing her arm around the bed. "Where'd Kash go?"

"He's out in the living room going over the plan," Luna told her, pulling her by the arm toward the edge of the bed. "Let's go."

"Oh, fine," Nura conceded and flipped her feet onto the floor.

Luna stood in front of her for a second and then stepped in close for a hug. She placed her chin on the top of Nura's head and held her tight. Nura hummed her approval.

"Can you remember the last time we ate this well?" Luna said, rubbing Nura's back.

"We never ate this well," Nura replied. "This often, sure… but never this well."

"It was before college for me."

"Me too."

The room went silent as Luna contemplated how much her life had changed since leaving home. Her parents hated her, but Nura's parents didn't. She spent more time at Nura's house when they were kids than she did at her own house. Without Nura… Luna would have been lost. She loved Nura more than her own life.

Luna almost started to cry but tried to cheer herself up instead. She started to shake her body and thus, Nura's body too.

"You're impossible," Nura complained, half giggling. "Let me up so I can pee."

Nura went to the bathroom while Luna returned to the living room. Kash was sitting on the sofa, and he had the big hologram of the casino floating in front of him.

"This used to be the weapons locker here," Kash said, pointing to the map. "Can Kid move the secondary count room to make it look like it's here instead?"

"Let me ask," Calynn replied.

Kash was sitting forward on the edge of the sofa, so Luna had no way of sitting or lying on his lap. Calynn on the other hand, was lounging. Luna plopped her head in Calynn's lap and curled up on the couch beside her. Calynn brushed her hair out of her face and rubbed Luna's back. Luna reached for her hand and Calynn obliged, lacing her fingers through Luna's, and Luna pulled her hand down to her chest.

"So why there?" the red headed woman asked.

"Because, once that door closes," Kash replied. "They'll be trapped like rats."

"But won't there be people in the offices back there?"

"I was hoping these two could help with that," Kash said, pulling a squealing Nura onto his lap.

"Do I have to get off the couch for that?" Luna jested, snuggling into Calynn's lap.

Nura slid off Kash's lap and lay down in front of Luna to be the little spoon. Luna released Calynn's hand to wrap her arm around Nura and pulled her tight.

"Well... I was hoping to recruit my two favorite princesses for one more mission," Kash said seductively.

"I like being a princess," Nura giggled.

Luna shivered at the thought. The last time she was a princess... they were... taken and...

"I don't," Luna cried.

Luna couldn't bury her head in Calynn's lap and Nura's hair deep enough. She was clawing at both of them trying to seek some comfort... any comfort as the image of Grul came rushing back. She thought he was her friend... but he forced himself inside her... and he was smiling... she will never forget that evil, evil smile.

Luna was gently hoisted off the couch by two powerful hands. She intuitively knew what was happening and wrapped herself around Kash, sobbing. His hand went up the back of her shirt so she could feel his warm hand on her skin. She dug her fingers into his back and cried into his chest.

Luna suddenly remembered the guests and tried to compose herself. She leaned back a little and wiped away her tears, but more soon took their place.

Kash was sitting sideways on the couch with her legs wrapped around his waist. He was smiling at her softly, his eyes full of love and understanding.

"Sorry," Luna apologized, taking a deep breath. "I'm not…"

She glanced over at the other woman, and she looked just as concerned as Kash. The two large men that came with her were lurking close by too. Luna felt embarrassed by her outburst, but Kash made that better.

"You'll have to excuse Miss Luna," Kash said softly, pulling Luna closer. "A so-called friend recently… betrayed her honor… she's not okay yet."

"Where is this fool," one of the big men said. "He should be put down for such atrocities."

"Already done," Kash replied, his words were warm and filled her with hope.

"Well, then he should be dug up and put down several more times for hurting Miss Luna," the other big man agreed. "I hope he rots in whatever fiery afterlife he believed in."

"But at least he can never hurt her again," the first man added.

Luna was surrounded by people that loved and supported her… she felt safe in Kash's arms, and she knew Calynn would move mountains to keep her safe. Hell, even the strangers that she just met would not sit idly by if she were being attacked. The strange… men… men with male organs.

Luna shuddered but forced it back down. No… these men said they would help me, not hurt me. There was only one way to know for sure. She hesitantly got up off of Kash and sheepishly walked over to the two hulking men.

Luna was stunned when they both took a knee, lowering themselves to her level. Their kind faces, warm smiles, and their eyes… their eyes weren't lying.

"Hi… I'm Luna," she said as she hugged the first man.

"Hi, Miss Luna," the man replied, wrapping her in a warm embrace. "I'm Bran."

Luna let go of Bran, and he immediately released her too. She looked at the second man and stepped closer.

"Hi, Miss Luna… I'm Jorik," he smiled softly, and hugged her gently. "I assure you… we would rather die protecting you than ever hurt you… I swear it to all the Gods."

His words weren't just spoken... they rang true in her ears. The men meant what they said... they said they would help... and so would she.

"With all these handsome bodyguards," Luna said, her voice still shaky but full of hope. "Maybe I can be a princess again."

"That's my girl," Kash grinned. "So... here's what we're gonna do."

SELLING THE PLAN

Aurelia pulled her disrupter from her pocket and placed it on the elevator control panel, stopping the elevator.

"What do you guys think?" Aurelia asked Bran and Jorik.

"Besides Kash's plans being soooo much more thorough than Rhett's?" Bran joked.

"And the trust... did you ever feel like you were actually part of a team?" Jorik asked rhetorically. "We know what he's going to be doing, and he actually trusts us to do our parts."

"It feels good... right?" Aurelia asked, a little unsure of herself.

"I understand your reservations, Miss Aurelia," Jorik smiled softly. "But Kash is right about Rhett... he's reckless."

"And the others are just as bad," Bran added. "Rogan just likes to hurt people..."

"And do permanent damage to their joints," Jorik added.

"Maddox would blow up a school full of children just to say he did it," Jorik continued. "And Soren... does anyone actually trust that guy?"

"I think he has pictures or videos of me naked on that tablet of his," Aurelia chimed in. "I wonder if Kash can help with that too?"

"Or Kid," Bran said, pointing at the camera in the elevator. "Hey, Kid... can you wipe the information off of an E-tablet if we show you which one...? Blink the lights in here once for yes and twice for no."

The trio stood silent for a minute waiting to see if Kid replied, but nothing happened.

"Well... It was worth a..." Bran was interrupted when the lights in the elevator blinked one time. "Shot."

Aurelia smiled and removed her disruptor, the elevator started moving again. They marched across the casino and were soon walking into Rhett's room.

"We have to talk," Aurelia said firmly.

"About what?" Rhett asked dismissively.

"About the key for The Beast."

Rhett's head snapped around so he was staring at Aurelia.

"Yeah... we know what you're here to steal... and we also know it's been moved."

Aurelia pulled out the E-tablet that Calynn gave her and opened it, so it showed live footage of the secondary count room.

"This... is where Gravitas is keeping the key," Aurelia explained. "Along with every illicit credit he has gotten from the underbelly of society and of course... the skim."

"None of it is in a metal vault, so scanning the casino would do no good in finding it," Bran told his part. "It's hidden in plain sight... a simple records room holds unimaginable treasure."

"There is however... a very locked door in the way," Jorik explained as the image shifted to the fake building plans Kid put on the E-tablet. "This used to be part of the barracks for the platoon of soldiers that's supposed to be stationed here... and this door here... was used to lock up the weapons."

"The count room is actually the office of The Master at Arms," Aurelia explained. "The counted credits and other ill-gotten goods are stored in his old records room... on shelves that once held inventory reports."

"Who told you this?" Rhett asked, his tone bitter.

"Rhett, just look at the feed..."

"Who!" Rhett demanded, cutting off Bran.

"It was Kash, alright!" Aurelia barked at Rhett. "And before you say it, no, he's not trying to rob the casino also. He's here on behalf of the Princess of Ooga. She sent him here to retrieve her countrymen."

"Yeah, right!" Rhett argued. "There's no way that fuck knows a princess."

Aurelia showed Rhett side by side pictures of Princess Aja and Detective Aja Aman, proving that they were the same woman. They deleted her name on the tablet to protect Aja.

"He met the Princess in her detective persona on the Pleasure Planets," Aurelia explained calmly. "She actually arrested Kash and interrogated him. She only revealed her true identity to him weeks later after she knew he could be trusted."

"The cameras have been down for days now," Soren said dryly. "How'd you get that feed."

"Who do you think took out the cameras?" Jorik asked sarcastically. "It's kinda hard to have clandestine meetings with the Oogans on board the casino… with the casino watching."

"Then why give it to you?" Rhett asked suspiciously.

"Because he was serious about not wanting people to get hurt," Aurelia replied, scowling at Rhett. "Where'd the guns come from Rhett? Are we being paid to steal something or kill someone?"

"Or both?" Bran added.

Rhett scowled at them and snatched the E-tablet out of Aurelia's hand. He turned his back to them while he examined the image on the screen and then tossed the tablet onto the floor.

"Are you fucking him?" Rhett asked, his eyes focused on her.

"I wish," Aurelia snapped, her tone sharp. "He's sexy as hell."

It was probably more truth than she should have said, but it answered Rhett's question effectively.

"Then what's his angle," Rhett grumbled. "And don't say that bullshit about not wanting people to get hurt. He doesn't fucking care about people. He bombed planets when he was a Legionnaire."

"That was before he met Miss Calynn," Jorik said, his tone was firm and strong. "Spend ten seconds with them and you'd see her influence on him. He's not that guy any longer."

"He ain't changing for a fucking woman," Rhett laughed. "He's a womanizer, you buffoons."

"I'd change for her," Bran chuckled.

"Me too," Jorik smiled at his friend. "But I think Miss Aurelia is the only one of us that has a shot with her."

"And I would do her in a heartbeat," Aurelia admitted. "She's amazing."

"Enough!" Rhett barked.

"Hey, this feed is legit," Soren said suddenly.

Aurelia hadn't even noticed that the little weasel of a man had picked up the tablet Rhett had discarded.

"What?" Rhett asked, exasperated.

"I checked the code," Soren continued. "That stack of credits is really in that room right now."

"So," Rhett snipped.

"So, what if Kash is right about the key too?" Soren questioned. "How'd he know we were after it in the first place?"

"Because he's Kash," Aurelia answered that question before Rhett could. "He got my comms easy enough too. The man is the best at what he does."

"Which one has the bigger ego?" Maddox asked from behind Rhett

"Rhett," Aurelia, Bran, and Jorik replied in unison.

"Kash is surprisingly humble," Aurelia added.

"Gods... they just brought in another pile of credits," Soren gasped, showing everyone the tablet screen.

"Do we have any actual intel to disprove what they are saying?" Maddox asked curiously. "Or is this something else?"

"No other intel," Soren replied. "I was still having troubles locating the key."

"I find it hard to believe he has a better hacker that Soren," Rhett argued.

"He's staying in two suites, Rhett," Bran chuckled. "Not one... two... I think he can afford a better hacker."

"He has access to all the cameras, even one in Gravitas bedroom," Aurelia added, trying to be as sweet as she could. "This is the only one he gave to us, but we briefly saw the others."

"And you're sure that feed is coming from the casino?" Rhett asked Soren.

"A hundred percent sure," Soren nodded. "This is straight from the source."

"Look, don't believe us," Jorik shrugged and turned for the door. "Watch the feed and figure it out for yourself. I'm tired of arguing."

"Me too," Aurelia said and followed Jorik out the door.

The two went to Aurelia's room and sat and waited. They needed Rhett to be on board with this. They were supposed to make it seem like Rhett's idea, but his distrust of everyone got in the way of that. Now they had to rely on the rest of the team to convince him.

The silence grew heavy as they waited to hear about Rhett's decision. Aurelia was about to start making some small talk with Jorik when someone knocked on the door. Jorik got up to answer the door.

"He bought it," Bran smiled. "We're on!"

"Stop pacing. You're making me nervous," Calynn complained.

"Well, this part makes me nervous," Kash replied from behind her.

"Even though I'm in The Cat?"

"That makes me less nervous, but it's still four of them versus just you."

"And Kid."

"Hopefully he is helpful," Kash sighed.

"We are on approach, my friends," Plekish's voice came over the comms. "And the replacement body is ready."

"Outstanding, Plekish," Kash replied. "Thank you so much for doing this."

"It is our pleasure, Kash," Meesha stated.

"Alright, Goddess," Kash sighed again, placing his hands on Calynn's shoulders. "It's your move."

Calynn rolled her eyes up into her head. Kash told her that her eyes glow when she does that. Not that she would know, she can't see a thing when it happens.

Hacking a nerve-center controlled system wasn't anything like what they showed in the movies. There are no digital avatars, or landscapes made of ones and zeros. There were no laser battles, and she didn't blast her way through the system. In fact, the real thing wouldn't be very cinematic. It was light and dark and that was it.

To her, the network was like a massive three-dimensional grid, and the computer terminals were like pockets. She could close the pockets and not give them access to the grid, or open them to see what was inside. Everywhere that she exerted her will on the system would light up to her. The areas controlled by the other minds were the darkness. In that way she did feel like a computer virus, spreading herself into every cell of the being she was infecting.

She could tell what size the darkness was but little else until she seized control of that area. She could already see what Kid could see because she was entering the grid through the same portal as him, and she could feel that he was nervous.

"It's okay," Calynn told him. "I'm here with you."

"I'm scared," Kid admitted.

"I know you are... just try to stay calm and focused."

"What will the other minds feel like?"

"That's hard to say," Calynn replied calmly. "To me... it's a darkness that is trying to push me out."

"I feel like I'm in darkness and you are the only light I see."

"How about the systems, like the cameras or the lights? What do you see there?"

"Those are other spots where I can see light, but I have trouble holding on to them."

"Let's see if I can help."

Calynn reached out with her mind and pushed some of the darkness away. She could feel the other four minds on the system, but they weren't trying to push back... yet."

"Oh, wow... how did you do that? It's like you opened the doors to so many more points of light."

"Can you hold onto them easier?"

"Yes... much easier."

"Okay... then I'll be the plow, and you be the anchor. I'll open everything up, and then you hold on to the furthest parts you can reach... okay?"

"I'll try."

Calynn focused her energy and pushed out hard this time. The darkness fell away easily, and she could feel Kid staking claim to the systems she opened. It was nice to have someone watching her back, and it gave her the opportunity to focus all her energy on the push instead of having to hold back to keep control of the areas she already opened.

She could tell where the other nerve centers were now. The three sleeping minds were performing their tasks diligently and didn't react to her assault. The awakened mind however... pushed back... hard. A wave of darkness crashed into her, but Calynn held it back. The mind was awakened, but not very formidable.

"Can you hear me?" Calynn tried to ask the other mind. "Please don't make me hurt you. Talk to me... please."

Calynn ramped up her output. She wanted to make sure the other mind knew it was outmatched, but she didn't want to hurt it. She pushed the darkness back, but again... the darkness fought back.

"Please don't make me do this," Calynn begged, not knowing if the other brain could even understand her. "I don't want to put you in a box... I know how that feels."

"Calynn... the systems... they're pushing me out," Kid sounded frightened.

"It's the other minds, Kid," Calynn told him. "I have to focus on the awakened one... do your best with the other three, but don't let them trap you."

"I'll try."

This time Calynn pushed really hard and forced the darkness all the way back to the other brain. She was careful not to push all the way in and strip the brain bare, but she needed to make her point. She felt the panic seeping out of the darkness and tried one last time to communicate.

"Please don't make me hurt you... we're just trying to save one of our kind..."

"Oh no... what is happening," a strange voice came from the darkness.

Calynn backed off slowly, giving the other brain a little space as a peace offering.

"Can you hear me?" Calynn asked gently.

"Go away... why are you here?"

"I'm trying to help someone."

"Well... stop it. This is my home... you must leave."

The darkness tried to push back, but Calynn stood her ground. The wave of darkness bounced off her like an ocean wave crashing against the rocks.

"I can't do that... not until I help the person I am here to help."

"Go away!"

"Look," Calynn forced the darkness back again. "You can cooperate, or I can lock you away... your choice! Please don't make me do that."

"I said GO AWAY!"

The darkness pushed back erratically, but Calynn could easily resist the assault.

"I'm sorry about this," Calynn sighed, and she removed the last of the darkness.

"Something feels different," Kid announced as the influence of the awakened nerve center fell away.

Calynn had cornered it in a corner of its own mind... she couldn't imagine how scary that felt. She hoped that it could forgive her.

"Yeah," Calynn replied, her tone somber. "I had to do something I didn't want to do... now let's get those other systems back."

Calynn felt the other one start to cry.

"I'm in," Calynn told Kash. "Get moving."

"You're the best, Baby Girl," Kash said, kissing her cheek.

No... just a bully, Calynn thought.

Infiltration

"She's in," Kash said over comms. "You two are up."

Nura and Luna looked at each other and sighed. Neither one of them was really feeling royal today, but they had their parts to play, and they intended to deliver.

Nura gave Luna a gentle kiss and smiled at her best friend. She needed Luna's strength to get through this, as much as Luna needed hers. She looked down at the comm in Luna's hand and then back up to Luna's sad eyes.

"We can do this," Nura assured her, placing her hand on Luna's cheek. "Send the message."

Luna sent the comm and tucked the unit into her dress with one hand while holding Nura's hand to her cheek with the other. Luna smiled, but it didn't reach her eyes.

"We're ready, Guy," Nura said to him, her eyes still on Luna. "Let's be princesses one last time."

The plan had changed, and Nura and Luna were both grateful to have Guy watching over them. Kash didn't like how quiet they had been, and he worried about them being in a crowd. They needed to hold Gravitas' attention until the Consortium inspector arrived. If they panicked... it could be disastrous.

Guy led them down the elevator and through the casino until they could see the Oogans gathered outside of Gravitas office. They were told to be rowdy and cause a scene, but Nura wasn't expecting... this.

Word had apparently spread well beyond just Nura and Luna's friends. Oogans that Nura had seen before but didn't know their names were here too. They were all shouting and grumbling about their pay and poor working conditions. A crowd had gathered to gawk at the crowd of Oogans, and Nura could partially see why. Some of the servers from the lower levels had come up to join the protest, and they were still in uniform... or lack thereof.

Nura and Luna waded into the crowd until they were surrounded by their countrymen. Some knew how to pay homage to the princesses, and others just followed along. It felt like her hand had been kissed over a hundred times. When Nura looked at Luna... her smile had finally found her eyes.

"What's going on here?" Gravitas' voice bellowed over the crowd.

A sea of voices responded, and nobody could make out what anybody else was saying.

"Calm down... what... I can't..." Gravitas tried to get the mob of Oogans to calm down and failed.

"ONE AT A TIME ... YOU... YOU..."

"YOU WHAT?" Nura shouted, interrupting Gravitas and instantly quieting the crowd of Oogans.

"I believe he was about to make a crude remark, dear sister," Luna said, sauntering forward toward Gravitas. "Perhaps something about our diminutive size compared to his... heft."

"Heft would imply that his size is more than just blubber, sister," Nura replied. "Which it clearly isn't. He has more blubber than a whale."

"What do you want, ogre?" Luna asked Gravitas condescendingly. "Your presence disgusts us."

"What do I want?" Gravitas growled through his clenched teeth scowling at Luna. "I want all you to get back to work."

"And they believe they are not being compensated fairly," Nura explained, shaking her head. "And they don't want to go back to work."

"They have contracts..."

"Unfair... contracts," Nura corrected.

"But contracts nonetheless," Gravitas grinned his sinister grin.

"Based on lies and coercion," Nura argued, giving Gravitas a sly look. "I wonder... would those contracts hold up under the scrutiny of the Constabulary?"

"I doubt it," someone in the crowd hollered.

All the Oogans present were yelling on top of each other at Gravitas. He had three guards with him, but there were several guards in the crowd arguing the other side. Gravitas tried twice to gain control of the crowd and failed miserably, so Nura stepped forward, directly in front of the big man. With a wave of her hand, she silenced the crowd.

"Your power here is based on lies, Gravitas," Nura said calmly. "And your house of cards is crumbling... no longer will you take advantage of us... we are a proud people, resilient in nature and far too accommodating... that ends right now."

A low roar flowed through the mass of Oogans, and they soon became a raucous crowd again.

Nura found one of the girls who had been working on the lower levels. Her soft, smooth skin was savaged by angry red welts from the lick of a whip. She offered her hand to the woman but didn't know her name. She brought the woman to the front of the crowd with her.

Nura raised her hand again, silencing her fellow Oogans, but she didn't speak right away. Instead, she stood with her nude compatriot and traced her welts with her finger. Her eyes darted around the room at the other patrons of the casino. The whipped girl was having the desired effect on them too.

"Why do you beat us?" Nura continued softly, her voice barely above her normal speaking voice, but it still carried through the crowd. "The women from our system are considered the epitome of beauty, and yet you beat us... why?"

"I give the customers what they want," Gravitas replied smugly.

"And if they wanted you beaten instead?" Nura asked, her voice still low.

"That will never happen," Gravitas huffed.

"Are you sure about that?" Nura smirked at the big man. "The mob is rather fickle... what if whipping this poor woman's breasts makes the mob want to whip you instead?"

Gravitas took a thunderous step forward, jowls trembling with rage.

One of his guards put a hand on his baton and moved with him, but Nura didn't flinch.

The crowd moved to intercept them both. Dozens of eyes were watching now... and they weren't simply curious anymore... they were hungry for revenge. Every welt on her porcelain skin would be paid for in blood.

For the first time, Gravitas wasn't the one holding all the cards... he was just the joker.

Angry voices rose from the crowd. It was coming from everywhere now, not just the Oogans. They pushed their way closer to Gravitas, surrounding Nura in a sea of safety.

Nura watched as Gravitas' demeanor changed. He wasn't used to having the mob against him... and he was angry... livid even, and all that rage was pointed at her.

Nura smiled at the big man, content in the knowledge that she just made her best friend disappear right before his eyes. He and his guards were so focused on Nura that they never saw Luna slip away... even in that great big dress she was wearing. But mostly she smiled because she knew what would happen next.

Three government officials pushed their way through the crowd toward Gravitas. They flashed their credentials, and one of them whispered something in Gravitas' ear. The big man clamped his teeth together and glared at Nura. She could almost feel the hate in his eyes burning a hole through her soul.

"Oh, no," Nura smirked playfully. "Is everything alright...? Where's Victor?"

THE HEIST

Rhett watched as the little Oogan girl got Gravitas all riled up. He smirked. How could he be that fat and that foolish? It was such an obvious con.

The other Oogan girl in the big fancy dress had slipped away from the crowd and disappeared behind a set of double doors... the doors that led to his riches.

Rhett glanced back over his shoulder at his team, wishing it was smaller so he didn't have to split the spoils with so many mouths. Like baby birds unwilling to leave the nest, with their mouths hanging open, waiting for him to feed them... pathetic.

Maybe after this heist he would go it alone. Let the others fend for themselves. Let them see how hard it was to plan and finance these jobs. Maybe he should change his normal cut from thirty percent off the top to forty... yeah... that sounds good... forty percent and then we all split what's left.

"Look," Soren said from beside him. "Here come the government guys."

"About fucking time," Rhett huffed. "Get ready to move... we go in after the badges lead Gravitas away."

Rhett's crew was dressed in the casino's security body armor and armed with kinetic assault rifles, also from the casino, so they didn't set off the alarms. To onlookers, they would look like a squad of soldiers being called in to handle the angry mob.

If it were up to Rhett, they would storm into the crowd and throw them a beating, but... but Kash's plan was to act like they got called off at the last minute. Aurelia was adamant that if they hurt innocent people Kash would put an end to it, and they wouldn't get a single credit.

Rhett huffed to himself at the thought of Kash thinking he had the power to stop Rhett from doing anything he wanted to do. Kash was just a punk, and Rhett would love to have the chance to prove it. Let Kash try to stop him… let any of them try… after tonight he wouldn't need any of them anymore.

Rhett watched as the government agents argued with Gravitas and then finally led him away. The tiny girl in the expensive gown led the crowd in chants about equal rights and equal pay. Rhett rolled his eyes. More pathetic people doing pathetic things. He'd be doing them a favor if he killed them all. None of them would amount to anything. He could end their meager existence and save the galaxy from having to deal with such dimwits.

"Haven't we suffered you enough?" Rhett whispered under his breath.

"What?" Soren asked.

"Oh, nothing," Rhett replied, adjusting his grip on the assault rifle. "Just wondering what is taking that other girl so long to signal us… she better not fuck this up."

Rhett continued to watch and wait, itching to get into that count room. He was going to get paid to deliver the key and get all those credits. He had negotiated a bonus for killing Gravitas, but it didn't compare to the credits he saw in that count room. Gravitas would get to live, and Rhett would be rich.

"Finally," Rhett sighed when he saw the pretty little blonde open the door. "Let's move."

Rhett and his crew marched through the casino. He and Soren went first, followed by Maddox and Rogan, then Bran and Jorik, and Aurelia brought up the rear. They were moving quickly, and everyone was getting out of their way.

One old man was struggling to clear their path. Rhett could have walked around him but instead stepped out so he could shoulder block the elderly man.

"Move it, Gramps!" Rhett barked as the man landed awkwardly on the floor.

That felt good… Rhett wanted to hit someone else, and they were marching directly at an unruly mob of Oogans… frail little Oogans… and Kash's man that escorted the girls down to the mob, but he was glaring at Rhett.

"Fuck," Rhett whined as he turned toward the door.

He didn't know if the man was armed or not, but Kash would have assuredly told him to come after Rhett first. What's worse, Bran, Jorik, and Aurelia couldn't be trusted to not take Kash's side. He still didn't like them meeting with Kash in private… maybe once they were in the count room, Rhett would kill the three of them and take their cuts. That thought made him smile.

Soren pulled out his E-tablet as soon as they passed the pretty girl holding the door. They broke formation, and Rhett turned to watch the pretty Oogan leave. He wondered how much it would cost for her to share his bed tonight.

"This way," Soren said from behind Rhett.

"Keep moving," Rhett growled as he turned to follow Soren.

Rhett pushed the distraction that the beautiful woman had created from his mind. He never let Aurelia's beauty distract him, even though he kinda wanted to fuck her. He certainly wasn't going to let a petite, sexy, little Oogan girl distract him... and her smile. So radiant.

Rhett actually shook his head to get the image of the woman out of his mind. He could buy any woman he wanted in just a few hourns. There was no need to get hung up on this one.

Soren led them through a maze of corridors until they finally reached the big, heavy door that sealed off the area containing the hidden count room. Rhett caressed the door, thanking it for the bounty he was about to receive.

Soren went to work on the lock. He plugged some card thing into the badge reader and started running some program on his tablet.

"Two minutes," Soren boasted, nodding at Rhett.

Two minutes... two minutes feels like an eternity when you're waiting to gather the riches that you know await. For two minutes, Rhett fidgeted with his rifle. His finger itched to pull the trigger. He wanted this heist to have a shootout so bad. The collateral damage would have been epic.

Rhett imagined what it would be like to open fire on the crowded casino floor. The chaos it would cause... people trampling each other to get away from the bullets... they would do more harm to themselves than Rhett ever could. Most people are just cattle.

"Come on, man!" Rogan growled. "Open the fucking door."

"It's working," Soren scolded the man. "I'd like to see you do better."

"I can open it," Maddox scoffed with an evil grin.

"Not quietly," Soren chuckled at him.

"Nobody said anything about quiet," Maddox laughed too.

"Focus," Rhett ordered. "You can joke later."

After a few more tense minutes, Rhett could sense the crew getting restless, and so was he.

"What happened to two minutes?" Rhett asked Soren.

"It's a tough lock," Soren complained. "Just a couple more... I got it!"

Rhett grabbed the handle of the door and pulled it open as Soren got out of the way. The lights were out behind the door, but Rhett stormed in anyway. He was feeling around the wall for a switch of some kind when he heard a groan coming from deeper inside the room.

"What the hell was that?" Maddox asked before Rhett could.

"I don't know, but we have..."

Clang

The sound of the door behind them slamming shut interrupted Rhett. When he turned, he saw Aurelia smiling on the other side of the reinforced glass door. His anger flared.

Rhett raised his weapon and shot at the glass.

TING TING TING TING TING TING TING

"You'll kill us, you fool!" Maddox screamed, pulling the barrel of Rhett's gun down. "This room is magnetically sealed... kinetic rounds are useless! They'll bounce around until they run out of energy!"

"Wwwrrruugggh," the stranger in the dark groaned again.

Rhett spun on his heels and pointed his weapon at the noise. He didn't know who or what was making that sound, but it was coming from the dark end of the room.

"Fuck, I'll do it," Rogan roared as he pushed past Rhett.

Rogan marched into the darkness to locate the sound of the groans, as Rhett and the others congregated in the light that shone through the small window of the door.

Moments later, Rogan returned dragging a man behind him. Rhett panicked when he saw who it was. The man who had hired him, Victor Morel.

Rhett lost his temper once more and lunged at the door. Aurelia was still standing there smiling at him.

"You fucking bitch!" Rhett growled pounding on the door. "I'll fucking kill you!"

Aurelia cocked her head, walked over to the wall, and paused when she placed her hand on the emergency alarm.

"Don't you fucking do it!" Rhett yelled.

Aurelia pulled down on the handle. Red lights and sirens started wailing instantly, and there was nothing any of them could do to stop it.

"What do we do?" Maddox asked.

"We gotta get out of here," Rogan echoed.

"Rhett, what's the plan?" Maddox asked as he stood right in front of Rhett.

They're all like baby fucking birds...

"You're the demo guy," Rhett barked. "Blow a fucking hole in something."

"What part of magnetically sealed are you failing to grasp?" Maddox asked sarcastically.

"What the fuck is that supposed to mean?"

"It means I would need more charges than what I have, okay?" Maddox continued in a snarky tone. "Had I realized you were leading us into a trap, I would have brought more."

"I knew we should have made the others lead," Soren argued. "I told you, but you didn't listen."

"So, this is my fault?" Rhett screamed at Soren.

"You're supposedly the leader, and you led us here!" Rogan barked, jabbing his finger in Rhett's chest. "Now how are you going to lead us out?"

"Soren can hack the fucking door again," Rhett said pointing at the man.

"There's no card reader on this side, you fucking dumb ass," Soren scoffed.

"What the fuck did you just call me?" Rhett was starting to really lose his temper.

"How about a fucking loser!" Rogan hissed through gritted teeth as he shoved Rhett.

"Or a fucking moron!" Maddox added.

That was the insult that pushed Rhett over the edge. Nobody called him stupid or a moron... nobody. He raised his assault rifle while pulling the trigger.

Everyone returned fire, and the hail of bullets didn't stop bouncing until they were buried in flesh.

Rhett smirked through the pain. He was the last one to fall... into a pool of his own blood.

THE SWAP

Kash and Triana left Calynn in The Cat, locking every door on the way out. Kash paused to watch the outer door close and seal before jogging away.

"She'll be okay in there," Triana smiled, jogging beside him.

"Sometimes I worry that we push her god-like abilities too far," Kash admitted. "When she's using everything she has to hack a casino, how much does she have left to watch the sensors."

"Or listen in on the comms," Calynn giggled over the comm in his ear. "I'll be fine, Boss... go get Kid."

"I told you," Triana smiled.

"Yeah yeah... Plekish... Triana and I are on the way to you."

"We are ready and waiting, my friend."

The rear of Plekish's ship opened as they approached, they jogged inside, and the rear door closed again.

"Kash!" Mala hollered as she raced toward him to hug him.

"Mala?" Kash questioned, examining the girl as she approached. "Are you wearing makeup?"

Mala was wearing a black jumpsuit with the Nebula Royale's logo on the chest, and her face was brown instead of greenish silver. She crashed into Kash and wrapped him in a hug. After a second to shake off the shock, Kash hugged her back, kissing the top of her head.

"We needed someone who could remove Kid from his tank and not stand out like someone three meters tall would," Meesha explained with a warm smile.

"Mala is more than capable and with her skin tone the same as yours, she will fit right in," Plekish added.

"Okay," Kash sighed. "Ten-year-old super-genius for the win."

"I'm almost eleven," Mala corrected him. "Hi, Trie."

Mala let go of Kash and bounced over to hug Triana.

"Oh my gosh," Triana giggled, hugging Mala. "You're taller than me now."

"This cart contains the replacement and everything we believe Mala will need to extricate Kid from his tank," Plekish said, motioning toward an oversized replica of the casino's carts.

"I practiced the procedure in virtual the whole way here," Mala looked at Kash smiling. "Based on Calynn's scans."

"These glasses will allow me to see what she sees," Meesha said, pulling out a pair of simple wire-frame eyeglasses. "That way if Kid needs something medically, I can assist."

"Yeah," Mala said softly. "I don't excel in that field like Mom does."

"And luckily you don't have to," Kash smiled at Meesha. "Your mom is the best there is."

The group exchanged hugs, and Kash and Triana got changed into outfits that matched Mala's. They hoped nobody would question them or slow them down if they looked like they belonged there.

"Remember, Mala," Meesha said as they pushed the cart out of the ship. "It's not a race."

"I'll be efficient and thorough," Mala smiled at her mom.

"Good girl," Meesha smiled back.

The trio pushed the cart to the receiving dock and entered through a door that Calynn opened as they approached. Two men in an office stared at them as they walked past. One of them was jerking at the door trying to open it to no avail.

The trio stopped between two sets of double doors so they were hidden from view.

"In position," Kash said, keying his comms.

The comm keyed in response, but Kash knew that Aurelia dared not to speak.

"And now we wait," Triana said, her voice tense.

Mala closed her eyes and started moving her hands around like she was practicing one last time. Kash grabbed Triana's hand and gave it a gentle squeeze to reassure her... and himself.

"They're in the hallway now," Calynn updated them a few moments later.

Kash's heart started to race a bit, but he quickly regained his cool and locked in on the task at hand. It wouldn't be long now... or so he thought.

"What's taking them so long?" Kash asked several minutes later.

"Hang on," Calynn replied. "They umm... oh for fuck's sake... their hacker sucks!"

"Well, they have to get in that door," Kash said urgently.

"I know... let me see... maybe I can match the door to his shitty hack," Calynn replied, sounding annoyed. "Okay... they're finally in."

"Gods... I knew they were inept, but I didn't know it was that bad," Kash groaned, and then nodded at Trie. "Be ready to move."

Mala stopped her practice and took her place beside Triana at the rear of the cart. Kash would pull while they pushed the cart.

"Go," Aurelia said as the alarm started to flash.

Calynn opened the door, and Kash rushed through it. The casino wasn't in chaos yet, but everyone was looking around to see what was happening.

"Make a hole!" Kash shouted as he gained speed. "Look out, folks!"

"Elevator at your two o'clock," Calynn informed him. "Arriving in three... two... one."

The elevator doors opened just as they got to them. Kash strained against the momentum of the moving cart and quickly brought it to a stop. The elevator started moving down, and Kash braced himself to launch the cart back out of the car once the doors reopened.

"Sub level three in three... two... one," Calynn called out their arrival.

The doors opened revealing a long hallway. Kash shoved the cart hard to get it moving. Now Trie and Mala were pulling, and he was bringing up the rear. They were jogging along when Kash saw the dead end.

"Go straight at it," Kash ordered and kept pushing.

The hidden door opened and let them pass with perfect timing.

"That was cool," Triana said, breathing hard from the jog.

"Turn right... here," Kash said, slowing the cart.

The door opened, and the trio entered Kid's prison. Mala put on her glasses and quickly took command.

"Put the cart there," Mala ordered, pointing beside the tank. "Kash I'll need a boost to get on top of the tank... once I'm up there, deploy the crane, got it?"

"Yes, ma'am," Kash was a soldier, he was good at following orders.

Mala grabbed a tool belt of sorts, strapped it on, and then gracefully climbed up Kash's body. She placed a foot on his thigh, waist, and then shoulder before sliding atop the tank. She was disassembling the top before Kash could turn to set up the crane.

"Trie, stick the pads in the red bag on the walls of the tank, please," Mala said calmly. "Mom needs her sensors."

"On it," Triana replied.

Kash pulled up on the nested pole segment that formed the crane's boom and popped in a retaining pin. Mala unfolded the arm at the top and started to hook the crane to the lid.

"Kash, I need your shoulders again," Mala told him.

Kash moved close and she slid down so she was standing on his shoulders.

Kash watched as Mala sorted through a mess of wires that connected to the top of the tank.

"Gosh this design is... rudimentary," Mala complained while unplugging connections. "Most of this mess is unnecessary, if you just route the power through..."

"Mala," Kash interrupted.

"Yes, Kash... Sorry, Kash."

Mala understood without him having to say anything. She just needed to do the work, not critique the design.

"The lid is ready to come up," Mala said after she had most of the wires unhooked. "Go slow."

Triana grabbed the controls and pushed the toggle switch up slowly. The crane gently pulled the slack out of the cables and the lid of Kid's cell finally cracked open.

"Okay... keep going... slowly... STOP!" Mala shouted and then started examining something. "Mom, do you see this?"

"What is that?" Meesha asked, she sounded concerned.

"It's a fail safe," Mala replied. "If those contacts leave the fluid in the tank... Kid's heart stops."

"Oh, no," Triana said softly.

"Sorry, mom, but you're losing your sensors," Mala said as she jumped down from Kash's shoulders.

Mala ripped one of the adhesive pads off the tank and stuck it to her chest. She picked up the unit the pads were hooked to and smashed it on the floor.

"Oh my gosh," Trie panicked for a second and then giggled. "You scared me, Mala."

"Sorry, Trie," Mala said as she sorted through the parts.

Kash was amazed at how quickly and precisely the young Thracian worked. She grabbed some pieces and soldered them together, before connecting the new contraption to the battery of the smashed device. She spliced in the wires from the pad on her chest, then paused to look at Kash and Triana.

"This device will keep his heart beating, but that battery won't last long," Mala told them, her tone soft but firm. "It's not a race... that leads to mistakes, but we do need to be quick... ready?"

Kash and Triana both nodded, and Mala climbed back up on Kash's shoulders.

"Kash, as soon as I get him free of this, wrap him in the thermal blanket and run back to mom," Mala said calmly. "Triana and I will get the replacement ready to go back in the tank, but I'll need your help back here to finish the job, okay?"

"Okay... Baby Girl, give me stairwells... I don't want to wait for elevators."

"Will do, Boss."

"Here we go," Mala reached down into the tank and stuck the pad on Kid's chest. "Up... up."

Triana raised the crane, lifting Kid's body out of the fluid. Mala rotated the top and they lowered him down onto the thermal blanket. Mala jumped down and began disassembling the metal hood around Kid's head.

Mala's nimble fingers loosened the fasteners and unplugged wiring harnesses, and then suddenly... there he was. Kash swallowed hard and struggled to control his anger. How could they do this to another human being?

Kid's face was swollen to the point that he was hardly recognizable as a human. His bald head was wrinkled from being so waterlogged. His eyes were swollen shut, and his lips were huge.

"That looks terrible," Triana said what Kash was thinking.

"I told you it was a bad design," Mala said, quickly removing the last wire from Kid's head. "Kash... GO!"

Kash wrapped the blanket around Kid's frail body, cradled him in his arms, and started running back to the ship.

"He's on the way, Mom," Kash heard Mala say as he left the room, and then he just heard the pounding of his footstep as he raced Kid toward salvation.

THE TAKE

Aurelia slammed the door just in time. On the other side of the glass, Rhett turned, eyes wild. The moment their gazes met, he raised his rifle and fired. The shots pinged harmlessly off the glass, but she still flinched, her heart hammering in her chest.

"Locked and sealed," Calynn told her over the comm. "Good job, Aurelia."

"Thanks, Calynn," Aurelia smiled, watching Rhett pound on the glass. "We couldn't have done it without you."

Aurelia paused and looked at her shaking hands. She had been extremely nervous about trapping Rhett and the others, but now that that part was over... she could finally breathe.

She turned to look Bran and Jorik. The men both gave her a slight nod and smiled. She turned back to see Rhett at the door, smiled as she walked over to the alarm, paused to look back at Rhett, and then pulled.

"Where to?" Aurelia asked Calynn.

"Backtrack the way you came and make the first right," Calynn told her.

Aurelia jogged down the hall with Bran and Jorik right on her heels. Her heart was still racing, but for different reasons now. This was the thrill of the con. She loved this part. The excitement from the possibility of being caught... although this time felt... different. This was so well planned that there was no fear of danger, only elation.

"End of this hall is a T," Calynn said after they made the right. "Go right at the T and then take the second left."

The trio followed her instruction and slowed after they made the left, since these halls weren't as well-lit as the others.

"End of the hall is another T," Calynn continued. "There will be two guards to your right, you need to go left."

"I have non-lethal rounds I can use," Jorik said as they moved. "I'll take point."

Jorik hung his assault rifle on his back and drew his pistol. Everyone slowed their pace for the last thirty meters so their footsteps didn't give away their position. Jorik rounded the corner with a dynamic move and fired five rounds. When Aurelia entered the T, she glanced over and saw the two guards lying on the ground.

"Good job," Calynn congratulated them. "Your booty is behind the seventh door on the right... two women are inside counting."

The trio entered the count room fast. The two women inside barely had time to scream before Jorik and Bran grabbed and subdued them.

Aurelia swallowed hard. All she could hear was the sound of her own heart echoing in her ears. Her shaky hand reached forward with a mind of its own and grabbed one of the cards... fifty thousand credits... and there had to be over a thousand cards on the table... but they were all different colors. She grabbed another one with a greenish hue... five million credits for that one.

Aurelia smiled like she had never smiled before. She had never seen this much money in her entire life, and now it was just sitting there for her to take.

"There's more over here," Bran said like he couldn't believe his own words.

"How much is here?" Jorik questioned one of their hostages. "How much?"

The woman just shook her head defiantly. Jorik convinced her to answer when the muzzle of his pistol was getting pushed into her eye socket.

"Forty billion plus what we didn't count yet on the table," the woman shrieked her reply.

"Forty..." Bran stammered and nearly fell over.

"How are we going to carry it all?' Jorik's voice cracked when he asked the question.

"I saw a laundry bin in one room two halls back," Aurelia told them. "I'll go get it."

Aurelia jogged out of the room to where she thought she saw the cart. It was inside the second door she looked in.

"Calynn, can you open..."

POP

The door unlocked, interrupting her.

"Thanks, hot stuff."

Aurelia returned with the bin, and they loaded every credit they could find inside. The trio was practically giddy with uncontrollable smiles plastered on their faces.

As thrilled as she was, Aurelia kept looking over at the closet... the closet that held things Gravitas wanted kept secret. Her curiosity eventually got the better of her. Kash had warned her not to take anything from the closet, but that didn't mean she couldn't look at them.

She cautiously opened the door to the closet of secrets. Inside there was a variety of items. Some looked expensive but most... didn't. There was even a child's toy on one shelf. These items only had significance to one person, and it wasn't her. With her curiosity settled, she returned to help the boys load the credits.

"Okay... back the way you came," Calynn told them once they were ready to move. "Once you hit the casino floor, you're on your own. There's too much chaos and too many people for me to track you."

On the way back, Aurelia glanced down the hall at the door she had trapped Rhett and the others behind. She slowed her pace, thinking about going over to see them one last time. She feared Rhett's erratic temperament would have led to disaster, but she didn't know... but she wanted to.

"It's not worth it, Miss Aurelia," Bran said, placing his hand on her arm. "It would only feed his narcissism."

"You're probably right," Aurelia conceded. "Let's keep going."

Aurelia never thought about Rhett after that moment... ever. The only thing on her mind was the casino floor and getting across it.

"There's a security force blocking the door and trying to get into that area," Calynn informed them. "We need to divert you to another exit... take a right and then your second left... and hurry."

The trio picked up the pace. They were practically sprinting down the corridor while pushing the laundry bin.

"I won't... need to... do cardio tonight," Aurelia joked as they ran.

"Stop!" Calynn ordered. "Duck into this room."

The lock on the door to their left popped open. Jorik flung open the door, they pulled the bin inside the room and shut the door. They appeared to be in an old medical bay. There was room for two beds separated by a heavy curtain, but only one bed remained.

"Stay out of sight," Calynn told them.

Aurelia quickly pulled the bin into the spot where the bed was missing and pulled the curtain. Jorik and Bran pressed themselves against the wall so they couldn't be seen from the window in the door, just as they heard footsteps thundering toward them.

Her heart stopped when the door handle turned. A soldier's shoulder pounded into the glass of the door, but it didn't budge.

"Another mag lock," a voice out in the hallway said. "Keep moving."

The footsteps continued down the hall the direction they had come from. The soldiers checked every door that wasn't electronically sealed as they moved.

"Thank you, Calynn," Aurelia whispered.

"My pleasure," Calynn replied. "Get ready to move... you want to turn left at the larger hallway and go out through those doors... and... go!"

Jorik opened the door while Aurelia and Bran got the cart moving again. They continued down the hall and made the left that Calynn indicated. Aurelia debated pausing at the door but decided that speed was more important.

"Just keep going," Aurelia said as confidently as she could. "Bash the door open."

Bran let go of the front of the laundry bin and joined them at the rear. They slammed into the double doors, flinging them open, and rushed out into the chaos of the casino floor.

People were running in all directions because they didn't know what else to do, the security teams were arguing about which way to go, and the pit bosses were just trying to keep all the chips from getting stolen.

The trio kept pushing the bin, watching people jump out of the way. Aurelia caught the eye of a guard, pointed at the bin, and mouthed the words "battering ram" as they kept moving. The guard smiled and gave her a thumbs up. Aurelia giggled... she couldn't believe that worked.

They pushed the bin right out of the casino, through the loading dock, and soon arrived at the slip where Rhett's ship was moored.

"Did you get it?" Calynn asked.

Aurelia stopped in her tracks, shoved her hand in her pocket, and pulled out the access card for Rhett's ship, grinning ear to ear.

"When did you get that?" Bran asked. "He never lets that out of his sight."

"When he handed me my assault rifle," Aurelia smiled.

"I knew you dropped that extra mag on purpose," Jorik smiled back.

"I wiped the registry and all pass codes from the ship," Calynn informed them. "When you scan that card, it will be like you are the first owner. Set the codes you want and happy trails."

Aurelia scanned the card and entered the new pass code when prompted. She smiled as she typed the letters K, A, S, H.

"Welcome aboard," a female robotic voice greeted them as the cargo doors opened. "Would you like to set your preferences?"

"We certainly would," Aurelia smiled as they pushed the laundry bin onto the ship. "But let's get moving first... we have an appointment... at the bank."

CLOSING THE LOOP

Kash ran.

His footsteps echoed against the floor as he cradled Kid's limp body in his arms. The boy was lighter than he expected… too light. His skin felt soft and swollen through the thermal wrap, like tissue soaked in water too long. Kash took the stairs two at a time, but slowed when he hit the casino floor, veering along the wall where the crowds thinned. He wasn't about to let his precious cargo get trampled by a mob of confused gamblers.

Chaos ruled the casino. Sirens screamed overhead. Lights flickered. People shouted questions no one could answer, and everyone was running in every direction.

Keep moving. Don't stop.

As he approached the docks he saw Aurelia, Bran and Jorik run out the doors pushing a large black bin. He smiled knowing they were getting away clean. He had been focused on his own task and hadn't gotten any updates on them.

The back of Plekish's ship opened as Kash approached. He ran up the ramp and found Meesha waiting. He gently placed Kid into Meesha's arms, his eyes pleading for her help.

"I'll take care of him," Meesha said warmly. "Go help Mala."

Kash gazed at Kid's frail body one last time, spun and ran, leaping down the ramp before it could finish closing. No hesitation. No fear.

He had one more job to finish, and no time to do it.

He could run with reckless abandon on the way back since he wasn't carrying Kid. He bounced off a few patrons as he ran, but nobody was hurt.

Kash shouldered the door open and slid into the tank room. Mala climbed up onto his shoulders like he was a jungle gym as soon as he stopped moving. The girls already had the replacement body hanging from the crane and had started to lower it into the tank. Mala had to redo all the connections on the top of the tank, which she did with speed and precision.

Nobody spoke a word while Mala worked. Kash was impressed the youngster could remember where all the wires went. To him... it looked like spaghetti. To her... probably just another day at school.

"Lower the crane," Mala ordered when she finished. "Slowly.... Slowly.... There."

Mala unhooked the chains and climbed on top of the tank. Kash took the opportunity to help Triana break down the crane and get it stored in the cart. They got everything stowed, and the cart back to looking like a cart, just as Mala's feet hit the floor.

"Let's move," Mala announced.

Kash pushed the cart as fast as he could while the girls ran beside him. It was much lighter without the robotic Kid inside. They were on their way up the elevator when Calynn contacted them.

"You have to hurry," Calynn informed them. "They're starting to lock down the casino manually. I'm not sure how long I can hold them off."

"Get out of there and head back to the suite," Kash told her. "Go now... we got this."

"On the way."

"Meesha... how's your patient?" Kash asked as the elevator opened.

"Weak... but alive," Meesha replied. "They didn't do him any favors."

"I'll be there to help shortly, Mom," Mala replied and then looked at Kash. "I'll take it from here... you need to get back to your suite."

"Are you sure?" Kash asked as the ten-year-old dynamo took over pushing the cart.

"Just go," Mala told him. "But you owe me a hug later."

"Deal."

"See ya, miracle worker," Triana smiled at the young girl. "I mean, Mala."

"Bye, Trie," Mala smiled back. "I hope to see you again soon."

Mala ran off into the crowd pushing her cart, like she was just another casino employee.

Kash tried to linger to watch her to make sure she made it out, but Triana grabbed his arm.

"Come on, you... let's go."

Kash led them through the crowd, pushing people out of the way with Trie right on his heels. Kash placed a hand on the small of Triana's back to help her as they ran up the endless flights of stairs. They were both exhausted when they reached their floor but still managed to sprint the length of the hallway and duck into their room.

Triana ran to Guy who welcomed her with open arms, and Kash was greeted by two gorgeous smiles from Nura and Luna. They were both still in their princess gowns and looked stunning.

"Wait... where's Calynn?" Kash asked when he realized she wasn't there yet.

"Right behind you," Calynn replied opening the door.

She was here... glowing, radiant and safe.

Kash scooped Calynn up in his arms and passionately planted a kiss on her lips. He spun them around as they quietly celebrated their victory. Kid was free. Rhett and the bad elements of his crew were captured. Aurelia and her crew had gotten away, and all his friends were safe. The loop was nearly closed. All that was left... was to secure their freedom.

Kash's gaze went back to Nura and Luna. He let Calynn's feet touch the ground and gave her another kiss, placing a hand on either side of her face. She beamed a smile at him when he pulled away and then nodded to Nura and Luna.

Kash didn't give the girls time to protest about their dresses getting wrinkled, he whisked them both off the ground at the same time. He had one in each arm and took turns kissing each of them, while laughing and spinning them around.

The girls joined in his laughter. It was nice to see them both smiling. The last couple days had been hard on them. He hoped he could deliver the freedom he had promised them... they definitely deserved it. Now more than ever.

"You two were... awesome! ...You all were... I couldn't have done it alone," Kash said softly, looking around the room at his friends. "Thanks for all your help, everyone... we did a good thing today, and I know Kid... Kid would thank you too, if he could."

"Is he... okay?" Nura asked softly.

"He will be... I know he will," Kash said optimistically.

Knock Knock Knock

Everyone looked at the door, then at each other, then back to the door.

Kash lowered the girls, motioned for everyone to stay calm, and moved to answer the door.

"Wait, your clothes," Calynn warned him.

"Shit... stall them."

Kash ran to the bedroom and quickly changed into jeans and a tee shirt.

Nura and Luna followed him to hide.

"Babe," Calynn hollered from the other room. "Someone is here to see you."

"Coming," Kash replied.

Three large, well-armed security guards were waiting on the other side of Calynn.

"Mister Gravitas would like to have a word," one of them said curtly.

"I thought he might," Kash replied. "If something weird happens in his casino, it has to be my fault, right?"

He gave his friends one last smile, kissed Calynn, and pulled the door closed behind him.

"Lead on fellas."

Exit Interview

Kash followed one of Gravitas' goons while the other two flanked him. He'd hoped for at least a moment to celebrate before the inevitable summons, but he had no such luck.

He had his lies ready... solid, layered, and untouchable. Calynn had promised that between her and Kid there'd be no video trace of what they'd done. Whatever Rhett or Victor said would just be hearsay.

The casino floor was still a madhouse. Alarms were finally silenced, but the chaos remained. Guards had a row of detainees face down on the floor... hands bound, some with bloodied noses. Several guards looked like they didn't fare much better.

Even through the glass doors, Kash could hear Gravitas' voice booming. The man was in full meltdown mode. A smirk tugged at Kash's mouth.

"They'll all pay for this!" Gravitas hollered.

Someone was talking to the big man, but Kash couldn't hear what the other man was saying. They were still too far away.

"No! Nobody leaves!" Gravitas continued. "Not even the government vessel!"

Gravitas' eyes grew to the size of dinner plates when he caught sight of Kash. His head shook and his face was beyond red... in fact, it started turning purple. Kash couldn't contain it any longer... he smirked.

"YOU!" Gravitas growled loudly, jowls shaking.

"Me?" Kash asked almost too calmly.

"DID YOU DO THIS?"

"Do what?"

"YOU KNOW... EXACTLY WHAT!"

Kash sighed and shook his head. He let the silence hang between them as long as he dared.

"Okay, fine," Kash admitted with another sigh. "I'm definitely here to steal some of your Oogan women away from you. The princess thought they were being abused and sent me..."

"NOT THAT!" Gravitas shouted, banging his fist on his desk.

"Then what?" Kash asked sharply.

"Don't play coy with me!"

"Okay?" Kash replied with a confused tone. "Can I have a little more to go on?"

"Can you... are you fucking joking?"

"Or I can guess?" Kash continued smirking, looking quickly around the room. "Where's fucking Victor? Maybe he'll tell me what's going on?"

Gravitas' anger boiled over. He grabbed his desk and gave it a jerk, sending it skidding across the room like it was made of cardboard.

The big man was now looming over Kash and was foaming at the mouth, angry.

"What do you know about Victor?" Gravitas hissed through his clenched teeth.

"He's a little weasel of a man that doesn't like me," Kash replied quickly. "I don't like him either. Especially since he's on Noctis Serum. I've seen that shit ruin too many good pilots!"

Gravitas was taken aback by Kash's reply. It was like he didn't expect it. Kash figured that Victor would be singing a tune that condemned Kash by now... him and Rhett.

"That's a terrible thing to say about a dead man," Gravitas hissed.

"Dead man?" Kash asked with genuine surprise. "Whoa... what the fuck?"

"Where were you?" Gravitas asked forcefully.

"Where was I when?"

"When the alarm was pulled?" Gravitas barked.

"In the crowd watching over Nura and Luna!" Kash barked back.

"I didn't see you there!"

"Of course not! You always make this shit about me, so I kept my fucking distance!"

"Kash..."

"Fuck you!" Kash interrupted, standing up, jabbing his finger in Gravitas' face. "I'm tired of your shit, Gravitas! I'm not fucking robbing you! I didn't cause the blackouts! And I didn't fucking kill Victor!"

Kash took a breath and scowled at Gravitas.

"I'm just here for the girls," Kash growled, his voice venomous. "Give me their fucking contracts and I'm gone! Fuck you and your fucking casino!"

Gravitas held Kash's gaze for what seemed like an eternity. Neither man willing to back down.

"Do you know about the others?" Gravitas asked gruffly, breaking the silence.

"What others?" Kash asked, matching his tone.

"The ones with Victor."

"No... nor do I care," Kash huffed.

"Do you know where they were?" Gravitas continued his questioning.

"Getting the girl's contracts since you fucking won't?" Kash asked sarcastically.

"I grow weary of your tongue," Gravitas grumbled, his voice barely over a whisper.

"And I grow weary of your accusations," Kash exclaimed and walked away from Gravitas. "I told you a thousand fucking times it wasn't me."

The three guards moved to block his path. Kash paused and looked each of them in the eye.

"Move," Kash demanded, his voice firm and tight.

"Kash," Gravitas said, his tone slightly softer.

"What?" Kash snapped, spinning around to face the man.

"Victor was found dead with four other men in a very secure part of the casino," Gravitas blurted out. "It doesn't even appear on paper."

"Great," Kash replied, giving him a thumbs up. "I didn't like him anyway."

"I think they were the crew trying to rob the casino."

"Cool story, bro... now get your minions out of my way before I end their miserable existences."

"And you don't know the men with Victor?" Gravitas asked, his tone sharp again.

Kash hung his head and sighed. He ran his hand over his face, plopped back down into his chair, and shook his head. He was playing the part for Gravitas's sake but also buying himself some time.

"I'm going to say this slowly so your dumb ass can understand me," Kash said as calmly as he could. "If Victor was with the men that were trying to rob you, it is because Victor was trying to rob you... not me. Did it ever occur to you that he wanted the casino for himself? Or your whole empire? And would be willing to go to extremes to get it? I wouldn't be surprised if he would go as far as to kill you for it, because I guarantee that motherfucker was on drugs!"

"Why would he do that?"

"I don't fucking know, look into it yourself," Kash said in a snarky tone. "Gods know I'm not doing you any fucking favors.... Are we done? ...I have three hot blondes to get back to."

Gravitas stared at Kash for a few seconds and then nodded at his guards. Kash jumped up in an instant and headed for the door.

"Stay in your room until the lock down is over," Gravitas hollered as Kash left.

"Fine with me," Kash hollered back. "That's where the blondes are."

Kash hurried back to his suite and the beautiful women within. He burst through the door and found them staring at him with worry written on their faces. Kash paused and ran his fingers through his hair... and then smiled.

"A smile is good," Nura said sheepishly. "Right?"

Kash moved slowly into the room, nodding at Nura. She moved toward him slowly at first and then bounced the rest of the way to him. He scooped her up in his arms, gave her a hug and kiss, and placed her back on her feet.

"A smile is very good" Kash grinned, pulling off his tee shirt. "I need all three of you... naked... in the bedroom... right now."

Nura's face darkened and Luna looked like she could cry. The assault... you idiot. Kash had forgotten about the girls being assaulted and could have kicked himself for it.

"So we can all put on pajamas... and cuddle," Kash continued, trying to save face. "Is what I meant to say."

He reached out and gently grabbed Nura's hand. She looked up at him timidly.

"I'm so sorry... I forgot," Kash said softly. "Please forgive me... Luna... you too."

Luna had tears running down her cheeks when she ran to him for a hug. Nura pulled herself into Kash's embrace also. He held them tight and kissed their heads, apologizing a thousand times in his head.

"Come on," Kash said softly, leading the girls back to the couch.

Kash pulled Luna onto his lap, and Nura curled up with Calynn.

Luna was fidgety at best. Kash did his best to calm her down, but she was inconsolable. Kash wrapped her up tighter and laid them both down so their heads landed on Calynn's lap. Nura lay down on the other side of Calynn so her head was also on her lap.

The four curled up on the couch together. Calynn caressed the girls' heads while humming a lullaby until they finally settled down. Kash felt Luna's body decompress, and he finally let out a sigh of relief. Calynn's magical fingers and soft voice continued to soothe Nura and Luna, and even had Kash dozing off.

Before they knew it, hourns had passed.

Knock Knock Knock

Kash wiggled off the couch and answered the door.

"Mister Gravitas sends his regards," a man in a suit said, handing Kash an envelope.

Kash opened the envelope. Inside were the girl's contracts and a letter.

"What does it say?" Calynn asked.

"You were right about Victor," Kash replied, reading the letter. "Please accept this as a token of my appreciation. Until next time... Gravitas."

"What is it?" Calynn asked, curious.

"The contracts, freeing the girls... and an upgrade."

"We're free?" Luna whispered.

"What's the upgrade?" Nura asked. "I don't understand."

"The Presidential Suite," Kash replied.

"Can we stay?" Luna asked, her eyes brightening. "For a couple days... I mean... that sounds exciting."

"That does sound fun," Nura agreed.

"For you three," Kash replied warmly. "We can absolutely deviate from the plan for a few days... anything to see you smile."

"Winner," the croupier announced as Kash's pile of chips grew larger.

"Yeah, buddy!" Guy cheered, clapping Kash on the back.

A crowd had formed around them yet again, but Kash was unsure why this time. Sure, he and Guy each had a mountain of chips in front of them, but behind them... were the four most beautiful women in the casino.

Calynn was wearing her blue dress again, at Kash's request. He couldn't get enough of her in that dress.

Triana was wearing a skin-tight, silky, bright red gown with fluffy white trim that was a real showstopper.

Nura and Luna ditched the formal princess garb for a sleeker, sexier look. Nura's dress was a shimmering silver color with a neckline that plunged to her belly button and stopped at her upper thigh to show off her toned legs. She looked amazing when she wasn't fidgeting with the top to keep her boobs covered.

Luna's gown was so sheer she might has well have been naked. It was just enough fabric to hold the multi-colored gemstones in place all over her body. The lady at the boutique sold them a bra and panties to go with the dress... but Luna wasn't wearing them. Kash loved that her confidence was finally coming back.

They had spent several days together in the enormous Presidential suite since being upgraded, and he and Calynn loved spending time with Nura and Luna. They were both smart and funny, and loved to pick on one another. Their banter reminded Kash and Calynn of their relationship. Maybe that's why they were so drawn to them?

"Winner!" the croupier announced again.

Kash and Guy's pile of chips grew larger, and the crowd cheered.

Kash leaned back over his chair and looked up at Calynn. She was grinning ear to ear and bouncing up and down, cheering his latest win. When she noticed him looking up, she leaned forward and gave him a kiss.

"Hey," Luna giggled, trying to push Calynn out of the way. "It's my turn."

Luna peppered his face with rapid-fire kisses, laughing the whole time. She was more concerned with teasing Calynn than actually kissing Kash, so he couldn't help but laugh.

"Maybe I was looking for my Nura and that toned belly of hers," Kash chuckled, turning around. "Oh look... there she is."

Nura gave him a shy smile and walked up beside him. Kash gently put his hand on her stomach so he didn't expose her breasts by moving the fabric too far. She grabbed the fabric on her chest and leaned down to kiss him.

"I could touch your soft skin forever," Kash whispered to Nura and gave her a soft kiss.

"I wish I didn't panic when you touch more of it," Nura whispered back with some sorrow in her voice.

"We have time for that... and you're worth the wait."

Nura hugged his head to her body, and Kash saw one hand go to her face... probably wiping a tear.

"Pardon me, sir," a man said from behind Kash and Guy.

Kash turned to see one of the pit bosses standing there.

"We're going to have to cut you off," the pit boss continued. "Sorry for the inconvenience."

"I guess we won too much," Guy laughed as the crowd groaned their disapproval.

"Or it's just Gravitas being Gravitas," Kash chuckled with him. "We had a good run."

"Could have been better," Guy jested.

Kash tipped the dealer and the server very well before the pit boss and the guards packed up their chips. The server knew Nura and Luna and hugged them both as they went to leave. They exchanged smiles, and Kash thought he heard them joking about which of them was sleeping with Kash.

Luna pulled off her dress the moment they made it back to the enormous suite, like it was strangling her and she needed to remove it. She shuddered and then beamed a smile at Kash.

"My skin is soft too," Luna announced, raising both arms above her head. "And free for the touching."

"Indeed, it is," Kash smiled, scooping up the petite beauty.

"Actually," Calynn said with a sly smile. "He needs to come touch my skin for a while... all of my skin."

"Aw, no fair... I wanna do that too," Luna complained as Kash put her down.

"Can you?" Calynn asked sincerely. "You're welcome to join us if you are able... please."

Luna sighed and shook her head. She sulked over to Nura, placed her hands inside the front of Nura's dress, and gave her friend a hug. Luna's hug opened the front of Nura's dress wide, but she didn't care since they were no longer in public.

Calynn was right there with them, hugging them both. Kash firmly believed that Calynn missed having the girls join them more than he did. And he really missed them... especially Nura.

"I'll bring him right back," Calynn said, grabbing Kash by the hand. "I promise."

Calynn led him to the bathroom and turned on the water in the enormous shower. She yanked off her clothes and started helping Kash out of his. She pulled him into the shower and wrapped herself around him.

"Hi there," Calynn said softly, her eyes smoldering.

"Hi back."

After their shower, Kash and Calynn returned to the common area.

"Just because they have to go, doesn't mean we do," Guy said to Triana.

"But we came here in their ship," Triana argued.

"Wait until you see the enormous pile of credits that we earned," Guy chuckled. "I can buy us a new ship or charter a luxury vessel to take us home. You know... leisurely."

"Leisurely?" Triana asked, curious.

"I can think of a few spots I'd like for you to see on the way home."

"Sightseeing?" Triana asked but didn't sound impressed.

"He wants to wine you, dine you, and fuck you there, silly," Calynn told her with a glowing smile. "I think it sounds romantic, Guy."

"I'm glad one of you does," Guy huffed.

"It sounds better than a quickie in the shower," Calynn smirked at Kash.

"Hey," Nura complained. "That sounds like a jab at us."

"And you're the one that wanted the quickie in the shower," Kash added.

"Luna started it," Calynn joked, pointing at her.

"What did I do?" Luna asked, shocked.

"Being all naked and I can't play with you," Calynn said slyly.

"Hey!" Luna exclaimed with her hands on her hips.

Kash ignored the banter and sat on the couch beside Nura. She was wearing skin-tight shorts with the waist rolled down to expose more of her belly and a top that wasn't much more than a sports bra. By the Gods, she's beautiful.

Kash couldn't help himself, his hand found her toned abs as he gently pushed her over. Nura kicked her feet up onto his thighs, lay back, and the two curled up on the couch together. His fingers lightly grazing her porcelain skin.

Nura snuggled into him and held his hand on her belly while they watched the others picking on each other.

Calynn and Luna were playfully arguing with each other, teasing each other, and flirting relentlessly. It was comical to watch, and Kash and Nura were soon laughing hysterically.

Luna covered herself when the casino brought Kash and Guy's credits, but as soon as they signed for it and the men left, she grabbed two handfuls of the cards and started rubbing them all over her body.

The group gathered around the mountain of credits, but Kash returned to the couch with Nura.

"Do we have to go meet with Aurelia?" Nura asked him softly, snuggling into him again.

"Eventually."

Kash wrapped his arms around her and held her tight. He knew what was coming and wanted to spend every second he could with her.

They loaded everything into The Cat, said their goodbyes to Guy and Triana, and set out leaving the Nebula Royale behind. Nura and Luna were both really anxious watching the casino drift into the distance. They shed a tear for the friends they were leaving behind, but were both excited to finally be out from under Gravitas' thumb.

It didn't take long for the banter to continue and somehow devolved into Calynn chasing Luna around the ship threatening her with... clothes.

"I hate wearing bras," Luna giggled as she ran back to the cargo hold to get away from Calynn.

"You hate clothes in general," Nura hollered, laughing.

"I just want her to put on one of her princess dresses," Calynn said, stopping at the bedroom door holding the dress. "So, I can... kiss her."

Calynn disappeared from the door, and Kash could hear Luna laughing in the cargo hold.

"I like meat bras," Nura said, sliding Kash's hand up her stomach to her breasts.

"Meat bras?" Kash chuckled, fondling Nura. "I never heard that one before, but I'm happy to be one."

The truth was that Kash would have been anything Nura wanted him to be at that moment. He just wanted... no, needed her to be close. Her touch. Her scent. The sound of her laugh. The gentle rhythm of her heart. He wanted to remember everything about her.

They were interrupted when a nude Luna launched herself through the bedroom door, diving onto the bed.

"Protect me," Luna squealed, pulling Nura on top of her.

"From kisses?" Nura giggled. "I'll fall on that sword for you."

"Thank you, Nura," Calynn said, entering the room. "You're a very good kisser too."

"But just kissing," Nura said, pointing her finger at Calynn. "I'm not ready for more yet."

The rest of the journey was more of the same. Tender moments of enjoying each other's company followed by unbridled laughter... and a secret... eating at him.

The sound of the ship entering the atmosphere woke Nura and Luna. Kash had been awake for a while just watching them sleep. They were so peaceful and so beautiful. Kash swallowed hard and tried to smile at the girls, but he knew it didn't reach his eyes.

"Are we here?" Nura asked, hugging Kash.

"We are," he replied solemnly.

"I guess I actually need to get dressed, huh?" Luna whined more than she asked.

"Yes, please."

The trio got dressed and joined Calynn in the cockpit. Nura and Luna were excited to see Aurelia again and exchange stories about the heist. They were eagerly looking out the windshield at the approaching landscape. Kash stood by himself behind the girls... trying to stay stoic... and failing.

Ooga Khoama was a beautiful planet with lush, brightly colored vegetation and blue-green seas. The cities were a combination of the past and present. Gleaming modern skyscrapers surrounding ancient stone castles.

Nura realized where they were faster than Kash had hoped. She snapped her gaze to him; her face was hard to read. She had tears in her eyes, but Kash didn't know if they were happy tears or sad ones... his were sad.

"Why?" Nura nearly cried.

Kash took a moment to steady himself, swallowed hard, and took a deep cleansing breath. Time to reveal his secret.

"Because... as much as I want to keep you," Kash stammered, his words full of emotion. "And I really want to keep you and take you along... you were already taken... and I... I want, no... need to give you your life back, so... so, it wouldn't be right... to take you from it again."

Nura crashed into him, hugging him tight. He hugged her back, burying his face in her hair. His heart broke when he felt the ship settle onto the ground.

"Who are all of those people?" Luna asked, her voice monotone from the shock.

"There's someone special we want you guys to meet," Calynn told them, her voice soft. "Well... you already know her, but..."

"The Princess is here?" Nura exclaimed, pulling back to look up at Kash.

Kash nodded.

"Hello," Aja hollered from the cargo hold.

"Up here, Aja," Calynn replied. "We need a minute."

Luna was crying on Calynn's shoulder, and Nura was trying to pull herself together when Aja entered the cockpit. She was wearing a tailored, white skirt-suit trimmed in pale blue, and a jeweled tiara. She looked as beautiful as ever.

"I'm guessing this one is Nura?" Aja said, approaching Kash and Nura. "And Calynn has Luna?"

"You guess right," Kash answered, his voice cracking.

Aja popped up on her toes and gave Kash a soft kiss on the lips. She smiled at Nura, placed a hand on her shoulder, and then turned to greet and kiss Calynn.

Nura's eyes were huge when she looked up at Kash. She had just met her idol and was too emotional to even say hi. Kash smiled softly and wrapped her in another hug.

"Well, someone has to hug me too," Aja joked.

"Come here, gorgeous," Kash told her, holding out one arm.

"About time," Aja jested as she embraced Kash.

Aja had one arm around Nura and one around him, and he felt Nura tense at Aja's touch... and so did Aja.

"Is your beautiful friend nervous?" Aja asked, smiling.

"Well... she just met her hero, and it's a little much for her."

"How can I help?"

"Take off your clothes," Calynn joked.

"Does she try to get you naked all the time too?" Aja asked Nura, giggling, before turning to Calynn. "You first."

Calynn and Aja shared a laugh, and it seemed to slightly calm Nura and Luna. Both girls wiped their eyes and smiled.

"That's better," Aja continued, laughing.

The Princess hugged Luna first and then Nura. They had shocked looks on their faces but looked extremely happy. Kash took the opportunity to move things forward.

"Is everything ready?" Kash asked Aja.

"Everyone is waiting," Aja replied.

Kash headed for the cargo hold, and the four women followed. He hung his head fighting off his sorrow. This was a good thing. Nura and Luna were home at last, and their families were here to greet them. But it also meant he had to give them up. He had grown fond of them both, but especially Nura.

Kash and Calynn stopped at the bottom of the stairs, but the three Oogan woman continued until they stood in front of the rear cargo doors. Aja was between Nura and Luna, holding their hands and keeping them steady.

The cargo door opened slowly, but as it did, dozens of people came into view. Light poured into the hold as the ramp dipped lower. Among the onlookers were two families, front and center, and many of them were crying.

"Mom?" Nura said softly at first but then screamed, running down the ramp. "MOM!"

Nura's parents were both crying as they hugged their daughter. Her two younger siblings, a boy and a girl, were wiping tears from their cheeks as well. Nura was clawing at her parents like she couldn't believe they were real.

Luna's dad scooped her off the ground and hugged her tightly, sobbing loudly. Her mom and older sister didn't look too thrilled about seeing her again, but they did seem to admire Aja. Luna didn't seem to notice or care though. She was crying on her dad's shoulder.

Kash turned and rested his head against the wall of the cargo hold. The sadness of not seeing the girls tomorrow was already creeping into his mind. He almost told Calynn to get them out of there now... like tearing off a bandage. The quicker the better. Prolonged goodbyes weren't his forte.

The sound of rapidly approaching footsteps ripped him from his self-loathing. Kash turned barely in time to catch Nura. She had launched herself at him, tears streaming down her face. Kash hugged her tight... never wanting to let her go.

"I don't want you to go," Nura cried, gripping his shirt in her fists. "I want to stay with you."

Kash held Nura and let her cry for a moment. He needed the beat to calm himself also.

"Tell me it doesn't end here," Nura begged, sobbing. "Tell me this isn't the end."

"It's not... I promise," Kash whispered. "It's just... you reclaiming your life... a new start..."

"But I want you," Nura interrupted, squeezing him tighter.

Kash was choked up and couldn't answer, but thankfully Calynn was there.

"And we want you, too," Calynn said, her voice strained. "But it wouldn't be fair to your family and friends if we kept you to ourselves..."

A small trembling hand landed on Kash's arm. When he looked up, he saw Luna crying.

Kash pulled Luna into his arms also, and Calynn moved to sandwich the girls between them. They embraced each other tightly and let the outside world drift away. The only thing that mattered was the affection they shared. Kash tried to hold back his tears... he failed.

"It would be wrong to deprive the rest of the world of the light you both bring," Kash said, his voice barely over a whisper. "You're both free now... so be free... live your lives and find happiness... go back to school or whatever it takes to be the best version of yourself you can be."

"But it would feel empty without you," Nura cried softly.

"And if you find that I'm the only one that can fill that void... then I'll come back for you."

Nura and Luna both pulled back and stared up at Kash.

"Promise?" they asked in unison, like they had been rehearsing it.

"I promise."

"We promise," Calynn added. "Trust me when I say, you two will never be far from our hearts."

Nura turned and wrapped herself around Calynn, crying, while Kash continued to caress Luna.

"I'm glad I'm not the only one that has trouble saying goodbye to you two," Aja said softly.

"Yeah... you two better go," Kash told them. "Before you break my heart more than it already is."

He gave them each one last hug and kiss, before Aja led them out of the ship... again.

They rejoined their families and waved as the cargo doors closed. Calynn found her way into Kash's embrace and laid her head on his chest as the engines of the Alley Cat Savant hummed to life.

"Your heart sounds like mine," Calynn murmured into his chest. "Already broken."

Kash sighed.

She wasn't wrong. He missed Nura and Luna already.

<hr>

Kash and Calynn will Return

<hr>

For more Kash and Calynn's antics

Join the Alleycat Crew @ cwilliamtresslerbooks.com.